THE GOD OF TOMORROW

A QUANTUM MURDER MYSTERY

ROBERT ARTWOHL

FarView Press

CONTENT WARNING

This book contains mature themes including sexual content, violence and killing, child illness, and child sexual abuse. Reader discretion is advised.

TABLE OF CONTENTS

God does not play dice with the Universe.

— ALBERT EINSTEIN

*Consciousness is not just interaction of neurotransmitters
in the brain it also some quantum cosmic component.*

— AMIT RAY

QUANTUM NOIR: where sardonicism and hope are in superposition.

AUTHOR'S NOTE

The God of Tomorrow is a work of fiction. The names, characters, and incidents are either the product of the author's imagination or are used fictitiously. Any resemblance to actual persons, living or dead, is entirely coincidental.

Many of the locations in this novel, however, actually exist.

1

DRACULE

Standing in the shadows of a building alcove, Grayson Lange slid his coat sleeve up his wrist to look at his watch.

Two minutes until midnight.

Time for the meeting arranged through a veil of lies.

He looked up and down 4th Avenue. After seeing no one approaching, he moved quickly to cross the empty street, side-stepping treacherous ice patches. Earlier in the day, warm Chinook winds from the Pacific had blown through Turnagain Arm, melting Anchorage's snow only to leave it to refreeze in the cold night.

He passed the front of the Church of the Holy Redeemer. Its drab, unimaginative, and uninspiring boxy facade was uplit by spotlights. He turned down a dark alley. He stopped at a side entrance. He took a deep breath, then thumped on the door with the side of his fist. Almost immediately, a bolt slid, a latch turned, and the door cracked open. A craggy-faced man twice his age peered out.

"Mister, er, Smith, yes?" The croakiness of the voice grated on Grayson's skull. He wanted to reach out and throttle the man's neck. But that would be too easy. And too kind.

He simply answered, "Yes." A lie, of course. "And you're Father Dracule?"

"Yes." Another lie.

The priest smiled, exposing gray teeth, then opened the door wider. He wore the traditional garb—black pants and a long-sleeved black collarino shirt with a white square at his throat.

"Come in."

The nave was weakly illuminated by dim electric sconces attached to columns. Empty wooden pews with worn varnish stretched out before them.

"You brought the money?" asked Dracule.

"Right here," Grayson said. He reached into his coat and pulled out an envelope. Dracule took it and raised the unsealed flap.

"This is most generous of you. His eyes widened as he flipped through the bills with his thumb. "May I ask what you do for a living?"

"I'm a surgeon."

"Ah. So, it's Doctor Smith."

"Yes."

The old man looked up at him briefly, then closed the envelope and slid it into his right front pants pocket. His lips formed an expression somewhere between a smile and a grimace.

"This will help children, so thank you. And don't worry—as you requested, your donation will remain anonymous. Would you like to remove your coat and gloves before we start?"

"No, I'll leave them on."

Grayson followed the priest as he led him through the nave toward the confessional booth. He noted the old man's kyphosis. Perhaps his back was bent by the years of bearing the unrelenting sin of humanity, including his own. The doctor imagined how the spine would appear on X-ray—osteoporotic and spurred. It would be easy to snap it in two.

AS FATHER DRACULE led Grayson toward the confessional, he noticed that the familiar scent of the aging oak pews seemed to carry notes of decay. He hesitated and turned to look at the surgeon.

"Do you smell that?"

"Smell what?"

Dracule sniffed. The odor was gone. "Oh, nothing, I guess."

As they spoke, Dracule took in the appearance of the man who was calling himself Dr. Smith. It was almost with a sense of pride that Dracule noted he was handsome, tall, and lean. Longish black hair protruded from beneath a toque. His blue-gray eyes remained inscrutable above a straight, resolute mouth, and a beard covered his face. A cashmere mock turtleneck rose up his neck to the jawline. The outfit was completed with woolen slacks and a knee-length down coat. A priest and a healer, both dressed in black. He tried to convince himself that his encounter with this man would turn out fine. But as he turned back toward the confessional, it seemed to loom.

"I could take your confession here; the cathedral is empty. No one will come in at this hour. It would just us."

"No, Father. I want the whole bit. In the confessional."

The surgeon's face seemed calm, at peace. And yet, Dracule couldn't shake the feeling of menace. The priest concealed a shiver with a shrug. He would have to trust the God who had forgiven his past sins.

"Very well. This way."

The confessional sat to the left of the altar—a central compartment flanked by two kneelers, each fronted with elaborately carved panels depicting biblical scenes of forgiveness.

"As you can see, we have two kneelers. You may choose whichever one you want."

"I'll take the one from Luke 7," Grayson said as he headed toward the one on the left. Its screen depicted a woman washing Jesus' feet.

"Jesus forgave the woman who led a sinful life," Dracule said. There was almost a pleading tone to the comment.

Grayson said nothing and went behind the screen.

Dracule entered the central compartment and closed the door behind him, and turn the latch to lock the door. After sitting down, he rubbed the bulge of the cash-filled envelope in his pants pocket and smiled. Five thousand. Somehow, the realness of the cash made him calmer. Three to the church, two for him as baksheesh—a win-win situation. Worth this little battle with paranoia. He slid the small side panel open to face his confessant and made the sign of the cross, perhaps not as perfunctorily as he normally would.

"May the Lord be in your heart to make a good confession. Proceed."

"What is the unforgivable sin, Father?" Grayson said.

Foreboding layered itself over Dracule's unease. He sat up straight and drew on his years as a priest to force authority into his voice.

"You know, my boy, confessions don't start this way. The sacrament of penance is to ask forgiveness for your sins. After my blessing, you tell me how long it has been since your last confession, and we go from there."

"Yes, I know. Be blunt, be brief, and be gone."

Dracule chuckled with slight relief. A bit of humor—perhaps this wouldn't be so bad. "Because of your generous gift, I will indulge you. As Matthew said, anyone who rejects the Holy Spirit's convicting influence and does not repent will not be forgiven."

"I'm talking about in the real world."

"Is faith not of the real world?"

"For some."

"What about you, my boy? Is faith part of your world?"

"No. It was taken from me long ago."

Dracule nodded solemnly. "So then, what is the unforgivable sin in the real world?"

"Stealing the innocence of a child is the unforgivable sin, and since you quoted Matthew, allow me to do the same. If anyone causes one of these little ones who believe in me to sin, it would be better for him to have a large millstone around his neck and to be drowned in the depths of the sea."

He mentioned children. Dracule's throat constricted. The fore-boding was giving way to panic. Control yourself. We'll have a reckoning, and it will be over. I'll show contrition. After all, is this not why I'm here?

"Yes, Grayson, I suppose I should have drowned years ago."

"So, you know it's me."

"Yes. I've known since your first email."

"And you came to this contrived meeting anyway?"

Dracule's voice took on a pleading tone. "Yes. I want to know—are you going to turn me in?"

"You came to see if I was going to turn you in."

"No, son. I came—I returned to Alaska because I needed to face you before I died."

"You've been here for months."

"It's not easy to ask for forgiveness, Grayson."

"There is no forgiveness for killing your family."

"All sins shall be forgiven the sons of men, Grayson." Dracule was pleading now. "Let's talk like- like father and son."

"I'm not your son."

"Man to man, then."

"You're not a man, John Gower."

"I am no longer John Gower. He died years ago. I buried him and have served God since."

"No, John Gower will die tonight."

"What do you—" Dracule grimaced and brought his hand up to his nose. "What–what is that smell?"

"Sulfur," said Grayson. "'Upon the wicked He will rain coals; Fire and brimstone and a burning wind.' Only you can smell it."

With his other hand, he reached for the latch on the door. It jiggled, but wouldn't open. He worked the handle more forcefully—still nothing. With both hands, Dracule pushed on the door, then rammed his shoulder against it. It wouldn't budge.

"Grayson, what have you done to this door?" He banged his fists on the confessional wall, the thumps echoing through the cathedral.

"Help me! Somebody, help me!"

"No one will hear you at this hour."

A force slammed Dracule back. He was suddenly superpositioned in two worlds, each as real to him as the other. In the first world, he struggled against invisible restraints, his back pressed against the dark confessional wall. In the other, his mind was constructing an unbearable nightmare. He saw himself falling down a spiraling, endless vortex.

In both realities, terror bored through his chest, contorting his face into a rigid mask of horror. He gasped, realizing he was trapped in his own damnation.

"Oh, Holy God. Please save me."

In his mind's eye, a massive, grotesque hand ripped through the vortex and seized him. He felt the leathery skin as he was pulled out of the vortex into an infinite black space.

Was this salvation? Had the Lord answered his prayer? Perhaps this was purgatory, where he would be purified of his sins. After all, had he not accepted Christ?

"I accept my purgatory, O Lord!" he cried, his voice echoing within the confessional and out into the nave but falling short of the ears of God.

Then he saw the Beast—immense, twisted horns crowning its head. Crimson eyes glared at him. Jagged teeth bristled from its maw as it exhaled a hot, sulfurous breath.

In the confessional, Dracule's stomach turned. He vomited onto his chest, his eyes widening with terror. Still, he pleaded. "Have you come to save me?"

The Beast did not answer, but grasped his torso, and with a twisting motion, tore him in two.

The priest screamed in unimaginable pain. His body arched; he kicked his left leg through the lower panel of the confessional door, splintering the wood. At the same time, his bowels emptied—he felt the wetness soak him, smelled the acrid stench. The final, humiliating reminder of his moral rot.

In the darkness, he watched his blood and entrails trailing behind. A diaphanous, opalescent form detached itself from his ruined body, fighting to swim upward, away from the Beast and toward any possible mercy. But the Beast dropped the body and seized the fleeing soul.

As they plunged toward an immense canyon, he first heard the hissing, then saw a seething, fiery molten river. Even from above the precipice, the heat was unbearable. The Beast cocked its arm and flung him toward the river of fire.

As he sat in the confessional, Dracule watched his soul streak toward the river—white to blue to red. Hot wind seared his face; he imagined the flesh burning away. As he raised his hands to keep his flesh from sloughing off, he saw tissue dripping from his fingers, exposing charred bone. His soul struck the molten torrent, submerged, then resurfaced on fire. As it was consumed by flames, the current swept him over a fall into another abyss. His scream echoed and faded as he fell from view.

In the confessional, Dracule's eyes bulged. His face turned purple. He took one last gasp, then collapsed onto the bench. The dual realities collapsed into the singularity of infinite blackness.

Grayson stepped out from behind the kneeler panel and walked around to the front of the confessional. *Have you come to save me he said.* Grayson's lips curled into a silent sneer. John Gower's sense of entitlement did not save him from his own hell.

He shifted his gaze to Dracule's motionless leg protruding through the splintered confessional door. That kick might raise the suspicion of a decent homicide detective. They might note the flimsy latch and wonder how an old man kicked a hole through one-inch oak without someone holding it closed. Otherwise, he regarded the leg with the same clinical detachment he'd show after nicking a liver during a tough gallbladder removal—an unfortunate but minor complication.

As he retraced his steps out of the church, he looked up and noticed a small surveillance camera with a blinking red light. No matter—he was confident in his disguise.

After leaving the church, Grayson walked six blocks to Valley of the Moon Park, named so by a planner enamored of Jack London's novel. It was part of the Anchorage trail system. Grayson ducked into a stand of trees a few yards off the trail and retrieved a backpack, skis, poles, and skate ski boots. He slipped off his coat and slacks, revealing ski pants and a jacket underneath, and stuffed them into the backpack. He took off the ankle boots and threw them behind some bushes. He had paid cash for them at the Goodwill store on Dimond months ago, never touching them with his bare hands or feet, and worn two layers of new socks tonight to avoid the transfer of DNA. He put on the ski boots.

He clicked his ski boots into his bindings. Seeing no one, he pushed onto the trail to head home. He skied skate-style, with smooth, efficient strokes. The cold stung his face, and his lungs filled with purifying air. His route took him southeast, following Chester Creek until he reached Goose Lake, where he turned south through University Lake Park and then back west on the Campbell Creek trail. An hour later, he arrived at his late-'70s home on Campbell Lake, a seaplane base serving the private homes skirting it.

In the garage, Grayson placed his skis and boots on the wall rack and shelf with his others, slid off his ski pants, and hung them on a hook beside the ski rack. Underneath, he wore a base layer. He stepped into his house slippers and grabbed his backpack.

Grayson passed through the kitchen and living room into the bedroom, where he picked up his phone from the nightstand. No missed calls or messages. Excellent—no one would claim they hadn't been able to reach him. A colleague was covering for him for the week, making it unlikely someone from the hospital would have tried to contact him.

Standing at the sink in the master bath, he pulled off the glued-on beard, the mirror revealing the scar that ran at an angle from just in front of his right ear down over his jawline and neck. He removed his turtleneck and T-shirt, exposing another scar, this one vertical, along the midline of his muscular abdomen. The scars Dracule had given him in childhood. The man in the mirror was a man who, against all odds, survived his childhood to become Grayson Lange, M.D.

The beard went into the backpack, and the backpack went under the sink. He showered off the night and went to bed.

His last thought before drifting off to sleep was, *It's better that he died knowing it was me.*

2

MORNING RITUAL

The electronic arpeggio of Eddie Vaugner's phone pulled him from a world where he still walked on two legs, where Anne's blue eyes looked into his, and where a medical sword of Damocles did not hang over his son. He reached over and turned off the alarm—6 a.m.

In the world he woke up to, it was Sunday, and he had the weekend duty. He swung his right leg over the side of the bed, sat up, and switched on the lamp. The sun wouldn't be up for another few hours. His crutches and below-the-knee prosthesis leaned against the wall next to the bed. Grabbing the crutches, he headed into the bathroom.

Eddie turned on the shower to let the water warm up, dropped his shorts, and crutched over to what he now called the ironic urinal to relieve himself. Just before the accident, they had remodeled the bathroom. Anne had insisted on the stand-up urinal for him. No more missing with the first shot, dribbles on the floor, pissing on the toilet seat, or even worse, forgetting to lower it when finished, leaving her to tumble through the porcelain rim when she sat down.

Now it was just him, standing on one leg, but fuck it if he would piss sitting down.

After emptying his bladder, he crutched into the shower. They had designed the shower stall to be roomy, with two shower heads and separate controls so they could shower together. Sitting on the teak stool to wash himself, he looked over to Anne's side of the shower.

He imagined her leaning forward, bracing herself with her hands —he loved her hands—flat against the wall. Water ran down her back. Eddie was getting hard. He took himself in his hand and started stroking. He leaned back and closed his eyes. He was standing behind her. She was wet, and he slid in easily. He reached around to caress her breasts and thrust into her as deeply as he could. She coaxed him. Her voice echoed in his mind: *I love you*. It didn't take him long to ejaculate onto the shower floor. He felt both his feet—the one still there and the phantom one—flexing as he came.

Eddie washed off and shaved using the mirror suction-cupped to the glass door. His face looked back at him. Even though he still had a couple of years until forty, his dark brown hair was graying at the sides. He saw a hint of bags under his eyes, but he had just gotten out of bed. The frown lines were getting craggier, but his jawline was still good, with no sag. Not too bad. But who was looking for someone like him? One leg, a dead wife, and a post-leukemic kid on the spectrum?

After showering, drying off, and crutching back into the bedroom, he pulled a fresh pair of briefs and a T-shirt from the dresser. From the closet, he selected a pair of gray slacks. Once he had them on, he began the morning ritual of putting on his leg.

He pulled the left leg of his pants up over his thigh. Everything he needed was stored in the nightstand drawer next to his bed. It started with the gel liner—a long, tapered, silicone rubber tube with a rounded end. He turned it inside out, placed the cupped end against the end of his stump, and rolled it over the knee to the thigh, massaging out any air between the liner and his skin. As Kyle, his prosthetics tech, kept harping, "Chafing is the enemy of the amputee."

Eddie grabbed one of several folded nylon stump socks from the nightstand's top drawer, put it over the liner, and smoothed it down. He grabbed his prosthesis—carbon fiber socket with a LimbLogic vacuum pump and an ElanC microprocessor foot—and set it in front of him. Eddie wasn't a six-million-dollar man, but he did have a two-hundred-thousand-dollar leg. It came with a five-thousand-dollar deductible, which fundraising colleagues at the APD had covered.

After shoving his stump into the socket, he rolled a silicone sleeve over the upper edge and up his thigh to help maintain the vacuum. Picking up his phone, he stood, scrolled to his LimbLogic app, and pushed a button. A reassuring tug of negative pressure pulled the tissues of his leg out to the socket wall to secure his stump in place. The prosthesis now felt like part of him. Finally, he slipped on his lightweight half-boots, which had good gripping soles for the icy conditions of mid-winter Anchorage. He slid the pants leg down over it and took a few steps.

Good to go.

Eddie completed the outfit with a white shirt and red tie. Opening the jewelry box, he passed over his abandoned gold crucifix for simple silver cufflinks. Shoulder holster, then his Smith & Wesson and badge from the lockbox. Blue blazer, wallet in the front pocket. Eddie had never been a big believer in Alaska casual at work.

From the bedroom, Eddie headed out into the upstairs hallway. Thanks to the mechanics of his prosthesis, his gait had only a slight limp that most people didn't notice. As he did every morning, he stopped at Daniel's bedroom and quietly opened the door.

There was Albert Einstein, looking out at him from that famous poster on the wall, proclaiming, "Two things are infinite: the universe and human stupidity. And I'm not sure about the universe." Daniel had once informed Eddie he knew the quote was apocryphal, but he still liked it. Vaugner understood what he meant by apocryphal after looking the word up.

Next to Einstein hung the poster of Joni Mitchell, another genius of the twentieth century, bearing the lyric, I've looked at life from both sides now. Gertie, Eddie's mother, had gifted it to Daniel when she moved in with them. Joni, her face framed by bangs and straight, long hair, gazed up to her left with an expression of consternation—maybe distracted by jet bomber death planes riding shotgun in the sky, or maybe, like Eddie, seeing nothing at all. Daniel liked the poster because Mitchell reminded him of his mother. He'd said he liked to imagine himself and Eddie on one side, with his mom on the other.

On another wall, a Fortnite Battle Royale poster displayed a riot of colorful character skins. Fortnite was Daniel's favorite game.

Eddie's eyes moved to the photos, following his familiar morning ritual. On the desk by the iMac, a picture taken three years ago— Daniel in a hospital bed, bald and pale in his gown, yet mustering a smile and raising a V for victory. Eddie stood on one side, Dr. Benjamin Blake on the other.

On the nightstand sat another photo, an earlier one: Daniel with a full head of hair, sitting in Anne's lap out in the backyard. Both squinted and smiled at the camera, Anne's straight blond hair and toothy grin glinting in the low evening sunlight of Anchorage. That was the last photograph Eddie ever took of her. Anne had never known a son with leukemia.

Finally, Eddie looked at Daniel's bed. A shock of brown hair stuck out beyond the covers. The crucifix over the headboard had slipped, tilting to the left where one of the nails had worked free. Eddie kept meaning to fix it.

He gently closed the door, then headed downstairs to the kitchen. His mother, still tall even in her seventies, was dressed for Mass. An apron protected her Sunday going-to-church clothes as she scrambled eggs in a cast-iron skillet, tilting her head to keep her long, graying hair out of the way. After the car accident that took Anne's life, Gertie sold the house she'd lived in for thirty years. They used part of the proceeds to build her a cozy one-bedroom apartment above the garage and put the rest in a college fund for Daniel.

"Good morning, son."

"Morning, Mom."

"You're going into work?"

"Yeah, got some paperwork to catch up on."

"Well, you look nice."

There was a slightly accusatory tone in Gertie's voice, as if she wanted to complete her compliment with "good enough to go to Mass." Or maybe he was projecting.

Eddie poured some coffee and sat down at the counter.

His cell phone went off, and he pulled it from his jacket.

It was Charles "Chik" Uttaq, an Alaskan native, born and raised near Bethel, a small coastal community on the Kuskokwim River in Southwest Alaska. Twenty-four years on the force and one of its sharpest detectives.

"Hey, Chik, what's up?" Eddie splashed some cream into his coffee.

"I'm at Holy Redeemer. They found a priest dead in his confessional," Chik said.

"You're shitting me." The Holy Redeemer used to be Eddie's church.

"Eddie, language," his mom called from the stove.

"Do you know which one?" Eddie asked.

"Father Dracule. Know him?"

Eddie thought for a second, but he didn't. "No. See you in fifteen." He hung up. "Wow."

From the oven, Gertie took out a warm plate holding two pieces of buttered wheat toast and scooped on some scrambled eggs.

"What is it, dear?"

"You won't be going to Mass today."

"Why not?"

"You know a Father Dracule?"

She put the plate in front of him.

"The old guy. He's a retired priest living out his last days in Anchorage," she said. "He showed up last summer, attends Mass, and lives in the clergy house." As if she'd just remembered her son was a homicide detective, she asked, "Has he been murdered?"

"Found dead in the confessional this morning."

"Oh, dear."

"Chik says he probably died sometime during the night."

"What would he be doing in a confessional then?" she asked as he started to scarf down his eggs and toast. "Slow down. You don't want to go to a murder scene with indigestion."

"Who said it was murder?"

"Okay, an unattended death scene, as you say."

The Church of the Holy Redeemer used to be his church. Three years ago, when Daniel came down with leukemia—a year after the car accident—Eddie had stopped going. Fuck it. Years of faithful attendance had not afforded him or those he loved any grace. Gertie kept going every Sunday, but had given up trying to persuade her son to return to the flock. She still took Daniel as often as he was willing to go. Eddie had lost his faith, but he avoided disparaging hers, especially in front of Daniel.

Finishing up, he stood from the counter. "Thanks for breakfast, Mom. I'm off to see about a dead priest."

Gertie came over and gave him a peck on the cheek.

"At least it's not another dead drug dealer in Mountain View."

"Yeah, there's that."

Lots of drug dealers get whacked. Priests, who push a different opiate, not so much.

3

CONFESSIONAL

Eddie arrived at the Church of the Holy Redeemer at 7:15 a.m., two hours before the Anchorage winter sunrise. His boots crunched on salt crystals scattered over the icy sidewalk as he approached the stairway to the lighted entrance.

A few congregants, averaging around seventy years old, huddled nearby, trying to figure out what to do with their morning. They exhaled clouds of vapor, asking questions but getting no answers.

Eddie carefully walked up the icy stairs to the entrance, passed a sign that read "Services canceled today," and ducked under the tape. At the door, he signed in with the patrolman acting as the gatekeeper to the crime scene.

Once inside the church, Eddie headed down the center aisle. Father Joseph, the pastor, sat at the edge of a pew a few rows from the front. Two patrol officers were securing the area around the confessional. Chik sat in the front pew, jotting down some notes. He had responded to the scene to help protect it, but he was coming off his shift. This would be Eddie's case.

The door of the center compartment confessional was open wide, and Eddie could see a leg protruding from inside the confessional's central compartment. He noted the jagged hole in the bottom door panel.

Father Joseph stood up to greet him.

"Hello, Edward," he said. Was there a hint of scolding in Father Joseph's voice? Eddie hadn't attended Mass for two years.

"Hi, Father. Who's the victim?" Gertie had already told him it was Father Dracule, but he liked to ask open questions to avoid coaching answers.

"Father Dracule. As I told Detective Uttaq, I found him when I entered the cathedral at six-thirty to prepare for the seven-thirty Mass. His leg was sticking out through that hole in the confessional door. I went over and called out to him and got no response, so I lifted his foot to get the door open."

"You lifted his leg to get the door open. Did you move or touch the body in any other way? Try to resuscitate him?"

"I touched his forehead to check his temperature and his neck to check for a pulse. He felt cold, and there was no pulse."

"Did you perform CPR?"

"Father Dracule's body was cold, and I could see postmortem lividity in his hands. As a priest, I have given the last rites to many dead bodies. He was clearly long dead. I saw no reason to give him CPR."

Eddie did a time-of-death estimate in his head. Discovered by Father Joseph at six-thirty. Postmortem lividity, the purplish-red discoloration caused by blood pooling, can become visible about two hours after death. Rigor mortis could set in as early as four to six hours. So, the victim had been dead since around midnight to 2:30 a.m.

"What is his full name?"

"Dracule Vincent. No middle name I'm aware of."

"Gertie told me he lives in the clergy house?"

"Yes. We have a few efficiency apartments for retired clergy."

"He wasn't a priest here, though."

"No, but not many who retire here want to stay in Alaska, so it's not unusual for us to have a vacancy or two."

"Where did he come from?"

"He recently retired from St. Anthony's Catholic Church in Fargo."

"How long has he been here?"

"Oh, about five months. Came up this past summer."

"Do you know why he would be in the confessional in the middle of the night?"

"No idea whatsoever."

"Can you wait here, Father?"

"Of course, but let me ask, how's Daniel?" To Eddie, this question was perfunctory, meant to show concern. Gertie had taken Daniel to church just last Sunday, so the priest should have already known.

"Good. Still in remission."

"Wonderful news, Edward. Our prayers have been answered."

Yeah, sure. God let my son's bone marrow go berserk in the first place. So, fuck you and your fuck-all prayers.

Eddie nodded and managed a thin smile. "Thank you, Father."

As he walked over to the confessional, Eddie pulled a pair of nitrile gloves from his jacket pocket and slipped them on.

Chik closed his notebook and stood up, turning toward Eddie. He was a stocky man in his mid-fifties, about five-foot-eight, with slightly bowed legs, almond-shaped dark eyes, and a broad nose. His graying black hair was cut close.

"Hi, Eddie."

"Hey, Chik. What do we have here?"

As Eddie took in the scene, Chik looked down at his notes and gave him a summary.

"911 received a call from Father Joseph claiming he had discovered a dead person in the confessional. Despite the description given by the priest, medics arrived at zero-six-five-five, confirming Father Dracule was dead, with rigor mortis setting in. They left him where he was to preserve a potential crime scene and called the cops."

Eddie passed in front of the altar and looked up at Jesus, pinned to a cross, unable to intervene as one of his henchmen died under his unblinking gaze. He suppressed a Pavlovian urge to perform the sign of the cross.

He noted how the wood fragments still attached to the open confessional door jutted outward, indicating a kick from inside. An old man dressed in black pants and a long-sleeved black shirt with a clerical collar sat motionless, slumped to his right. He had seen a lot of dead bodies—shot, beaten, poisoned, drowned, strangled, stabbed—even one decapitation—and in various stages of decomposition. But he had never seen one with a face twisted in terror like this. Dried vomit covered the front of his shirt, and a stench indicated the priest had lost control of his bowels.

"Whew," said Eddie, waving a hand in front of his nose. "And nice face."

"I guess you could say something scared him shitless," Chik deadpanned.

Eddie smiled and continued his observations. No contusions on the face or hands. The fingernails were clean, without evidence of clawing. The clothes were undisturbed, without visible tears. No blood in or around the booth.

The jagged hole in the confessional door was the only sign of physical violence.

"Our working theory is some sort of seizure," said Chik.

Eddie stepped back and pulled out his camera. He took some photos. The hands with dependent rubor. The hole in the confessional door. That face.

The side of the confessional looked intact. There were no marks or discarded items, and the mesh screen showed no damage. He took out his camera and snapped a few pictures from various angles, then moved back to the front of the confessional and inspected the door latch.

"This latch seems flimsy," Chik said. "How does an old man kick a hole through the door instead of breaking the latch and having it fly open?"

"Like the straw going through a brick in a hurricane? If the foot is going fast enough," Eddie conjectured.

Chik looked skeptical. "His days of fast kicks were behind him, don't you think?"

"Somebody was holding it closed, and he was trying to kick his way out?"

"Now you're thinking like a homicide detective. Still, he's an old man and this is one-inch oak."

Eddie chuckled. When he first came to homicide, Chik was his mentor. Ten years later, the man still enjoyed playing the role.

He snapped some more photos. "Has the medical examiner been called?"

"On her way."

"Her?"

"Yeah. From what I understand, the new assistant ME is a gal."

"Really, Chik? A gal?"

"Quite a looker, from what I hear."

"You're up on all the latest lingo."

"That's me, Daddy-O. Anyway, a confession in the middle of the night? Not normal, is it?"

"No, but we don't know if this Father Dracule was actually hearing a confession. Maybe he was reliving his glory days, soaking up the sinner vibes."

The sharp click of heels on the marble floor echoed through the cathedral, interrupting their speculation. Eddie looked up.

Holy shit.

A woman approached, dressed in a smart black suit and simple white blouse beneath a sable fur coat. Her long, deep red hair framed a pale face and intense green eyes. She wore sensible heels, if any heels could be sensible in the Anchorage winter. She carried a satchel as she strode down the aisle toward the crime scene, two attendants following with a stretcher.

As she neared, Eddie noticed a small silver crucifix dangling from her neck. Jesus hung from the cross, head bent over as if unable or unwilling to avert his eyes from the cleavage just below his feet. Eddie briefly wondered if she, like Gertie, had been thwarted in attending a church service.

She stopped at the front row of the nave, took off her coat, and draped it over the backrest of a pew. She approached the altar carrying her satchel and made the sign of the cross with her free hand.

"Who's in charge here?" she asked.

Eddie stood up. "Me. Detective Eddie Vaugner, homicide."

She extended a silky white hand. Eddie shook it with a warm, firm grip. "Pleased to meet you. I'm Rebecca Raven, the new assistant medical examiner. May I approach the body?"

"Sure, we've been waiting for you."

Raven set her bag on the floor, reached into it, and pulled out shoe covers, a paper gown, and a bouffant cap. She donned them efficiently, then backed up to Eddie.

"Would you mind tying me up?"

"Sure." Eddie tied her gown and offered no wisecracks, even though she had perfectly set him up for a few. Maybe his post-amputation state made him less flirty. He did, however, note the smooth white skin of the back of her neck, crossed by the gold chain and a few wisps of red hair and a small mole on her nape just to the left of the midline. Anne had a mole on her neck. But was it on the right or the left? Some details had started to fade.

"Thank you," she said.

She took out a pair of surgical gloves and snapped them on. Eddie followed her over to the confessional. Chik hovered nearby as she looked in.

"What a face. Has the body been moved?"

"The confessional door was closed with the right leg sticking out of the hole you see there when Father Joseph discovered the body. He lifted the leg to open the door, but otherwise no."

"'Kay."

She opened her case, took out a digital camera, and photographed from various angles and distances. She put the camera back, then pulled out an infrared thermometer leaned into the booth and inserted it into Dracule's ear.

"He defecated. With that face and the kick through the door, could have been a fight-or-flight response." She removed the thermometer and stood back up. "Ninety degrees. Given the ambient temperature, I would say he died around midnight."

She took off her gloves. "Can we remove the body?"

"Sure," Eddie said, "it's all yours."

Raven motioned to her attendants. "Okay, boys, load him up."

Eddie was impressed by her proficiency and professionalism. There were no wasted moves, no unnecessary comments.

Dracule's body was in a fixed sitting position. That and the vomit and excrement made the attendants struggle to get it out of the confessional. They pulled it forward out of the confessional, then hoisted it onto the stretcher on its side, taking care not to soil themselves.

A white envelope stuck out from Dracule's right front pants pocket. Eddie raised his camera and took a shot of it.

"One second, Doc."

Eddie pulled the envelope from the pocket, holding by one corner. It was a standard white business envelope.

On the front, a printed label read *For the HR Children's Fund.*

He held the envelope by the edges, avoiding touching its surface, and laid it down on top of the priest's thigh. "The flap's not sealed, and the glue is dry and unsmeared."

No one had licked the envelope, so there would be no DNA to find there. Eddie used a pen to lift the flap. Inside was a wad of hundred-dollar bills about half an inch thick.

"I'd guess about five grand."

"A large amount of cash on a dead person," said Chik.

Raven nodded. "Hardly ever a good thing."

"Maybe whoever gave him the money knew he would be found dead," Chik said.

Eddie looked over at the hole in the confessional door. "Broken door. Money in the pocket."

"Ploy to get him into the confessional?"

Eddie shrugged and waved Father Joseph over to show him the cash-stuffed envelope. "Do you know anything about this, Father?"

"No, not a thing."

"We'll have to take this and process it for evidence."

"Evidence, Edward? Are you saying this is a crime scene?"

"I can't say this *isn't* a crime scene."

Chik called out to the patrolmen. "Do any of you have an evidence bag in your vehicle?"

One officer responded affirmatively and trotted out to get one.

"Can you hold on a second, Doctor?" Eddie asked.

"Sure."

He called the desk sergeant on speakerphone.

"Sweeney."

"Hey Jim, this is Eddie. I need a CSI team at an unattended death scene."

"It's Sunday; you're talking overtime."

"I got a dead priest with five thousand in cash on him."

"Any sign of foul play?"

"There's a busted confessional door."

"On the body."

"Would a face frozen in terror count?"

There was a pause as the desk sergeant did a mental cost-benefit analysis.

"Has the scene been preserved?"

"Mostly. The ME moved the body before we found the cash on him; otherwise, it's pristine. There won't be much. Prints, trace evidence, a broken confessional door, and wood fragments."

"Okay. They're on the way."

"I'll let the medical examiner take the body since it's already been moved. I got some pictures beforehand, though."

Raven smiled at him and mouthed, *Thank you.*

"It's your scene, Eddie," Sweeney said, then hung up.

Raven reached into her purse and pulled out a business card. Eddie looked at it: "Rebecca J. Raven, M.D., Assistant Medical Examiner." On it was the familiar address of the medical examiner's office, the office number, and her cell phone number.

Eddie looked down at her left hand. No wedding ring. It could mean she was single. Or not. *Oh, Jesus, why are you even going there?*

He reached into his coat pocket and took out his own card.

"Do you want to be called for the autopsy?"

"Always. When?"

She pulled out her smartphone and tapped on it a few times. "How about Tuesday, around 9 a.m.?"

"My son has a doctor's appointment at eleven on Tuesday."

She looked down at her phone and scrolled. "Okay, can you make it 7 a.m.?"

"I'll be there."

They all watched Raven remove her cap, gown, and shoe covers. She looked around for a place to put them.

"Just put them on the pew; we'll take care of them," Eddie said as he removed his own gloves and added them to the pile.

"Thank you."

She put on her coat and headed up the back of the cathedral toward the exit, following the two attendants trundling Dracule's body. As Eddie watched Raven walk up the aisle, a blinking red light above the mezzanine distracted him. It was a surveillance camera, pointing toward the altar. Unlike Jesus up on the wall, it may have seen something.

The patrolman returned with the evidence bag, and Chik dropped the envelope and the note into the bag.

"Father Joseph is that surveillance camera operative?" asked Eddie.

"Yes. We put it in several years ago when we were having problems with thieves."

Another problem Jesus can't solve.

4

RECTORY

Chik took his leave. He had a morning golf foursome at Full Swing, an indoor golf facility. Father Joseph led Vaugner to the clergy house through a covered walkway. At the front entrance, Father Joseph punched in 316 to unlock the rectory door.

"Pretty obvious code, Father," Eddie said, recalling John 3:16. *For God so loved the world, that he gave his only begotten Son, that whosoever believeth in him should not perish, but have everlasting life.*

"Not to people who would break into a rectory."

Eddie smirked to himself. *Yeah, sure. Lots of recidivists in prison lead Bible groups.*

They went up a flight of stairs to Father Dracule's apartment. Same code.

Once inside, Eddie slipped on his second pair of nitrile gloves of the morning. Dracule's apartment consisted of one room and a bathroom. To one side, a kitchenette alcove held a two-burner range, microwave oven, toaster oven, sink, coffeemaker, and small refrigerator-freezer. A twin bed, a nightstand, and a dresser were positioned against the opposite wall. A Bible lay on the nightstand, with a mobile phone resting on it. In the center stood a round bistro table with two dining chairs and a cushioned chair with an ottoman. A stand-up reading light and a writing desk completed the furniture. A mobile phone, a laptop, and a wallet lay on the desk.

Adjustable shelving along one wall—six shelves high and eight feet wide—bulged with hardbound and paperback books. The collection included *Don Quixote*, *Moby Dick*, *The Sound and the Fury*, *Great Expectations*, *Middlemarch*, *The Grapes of Wrath*, and many more. No photographs.

Eddie gingerly opened the laptop with one finger.

The screen lit up with a blue background and white text:

SECURITY NOTICE! Authentication required to prevent data wipe! Attempts remaining: 3

Below was a password field.

Eddie immediately closed the laptop.

"Anything wrong?" Father Joseph asked.

"Dead man's switch - I'll let the lab handle this."

He picked up the phone on the nightstand and swiped it. Same blue screen, same warning.

"Matching security on both devices."

Father Joseph raised an eyebrow. "How does a seventy-year-old priest even know about such things?"

"That's the question, isn't it?" Eddie said. "Someone was very serious about privacy." He started a mental checklist of why someone would have a wipe protocol: porn, criminal activity, espionage, corporate secrets, novel in progress.

He picked up the wallet by the edges and carefully opened it. Inside were a North Dakota driver's license with Father Dracule's photo, $60 in cash, a Key Bank debit card, a Visa credit card, and a Title Wave Books loyalty card.

Eddie carefully removed the license, photographed both sides, replaced it, and placed the wallet next to the phone.

"Did you know of any friends or family?" Eddie asked.

"Not that I'm aware of. Father Dracule kept pretty much to himself. When he first arrived, I had him over for dinner once. He was pleasant, but he seemed uncomfortable with my company. I waited for him to return the invitation, but one never came."

"What did you talk about?"

"Small talk. For instance, about a book he was reading. It was *Lord of the World* by Robert Hugh Benson. We talked about the *Grantchester* series on PBS, what he liked and didn't like about the Pope and the state of the church."

"What was his general demeanor?"

"He was friendly but not particularly engaging."

"Did he talk much about himself?"

"No, not in conversation, no."

"The way you said, 'in conversation'—what about in confession?"

Father Joseph blinked at Eddie.

"Edward, you know the seal of confession is an inviolate duty of Catholic priests. Without exception. Even after the confessor is dead. Praise be to St. John of Nepomuk."

Vaugner shrugged.

"You know who he is, of course."

"It's been a long time since Sunday school. But it's okay."

"John refused to reveal the confessions of the Queen of Bohemia and was thrown into a river and drowned. For this, he became noted as a protector saint against calumny and floods. He is also thought to be the first martyr of the seal of the confessional. And others have followed."

"Okay, Father. I get it."

"I will tell you this, Eddie. I don't believe I heard anything that would have a bearing on this man's death or why he would have those wipe programs."

"Fair enough. Do you have any knowledge of Father Dracule's daily routine?"

"Somewhat. He volunteered in the office for the Children's Fund for about three hours each morning, Monday through Friday, and had a part-time job at Title Wave Books on Northern Lights, from noon to five a few days a week. It would vary. Usually walked each way, unless it was inclement; then he would Uber. It's about a forty-five-minute walk each way. I figure it was his way of exercising."

As they talked, Eddie started to open and close the dresser drawers. He just looked inside, touching none of the contents.

"Not much here. Underwear, socks, black pants, and jeans."

The room had a small closet, and the door was ajar. Eddie opened it, using a penknife as a lever. Some shirts, a jacket, and a black parka with a fur-lined hood. A few pairs of shoes and some snow boots on the floor.

Above the desk hung a framed print many Catholics would have recognized, the *Alba Madonna* by Raphael. It depicted a full-frontal naked baby Jesus sitting on the right thigh of Mary, who nestled him in her arm. Jesus clung to a cross with his right hand, and to their right sat John the Baptist. They were all gazing at the cross with stern expressions, as if they knew what was coming. In this context, the painting gave Eddie the creeps. *Slow down*, he told himself. *You have no idea who or what this man was.*

There was a small bathroom equipped with a sink, toilet, and shower stall. A toothbrush holder held a single toothbrush with worn bristles. Eddie used his pen again to open the medicine cabinet over the sink. A tube of toothpaste, a can of shaving cream, a razor, a bottle of aspirin, and some Rolaids. A small vial of medicine—*testosterone cypionate*—and half a dozen syringes. There was no prescription label, so Eddie assumed the priest had purchased it online. He took out his camera and snapped a picture of it.

They finished the search, going through cabinets, drawers, pockets, and even lifting the mattress. Nothing of interest. Eddie thought of leafing through the books but decided that a man with a wipe program would not leave things to be discovered between the pages of the classics.

"Okay, Father, I'm done here. Do you have a personnel file on Father Dracule?"

"Yes, but..."

"I'll need it. If you like, I can get a court order."

Father Joseph sighed. "No, that won't be necessary."

Eddie walked back to the cathedral, where the CSI team was finishing up.

"I need one of you to go back to the rectory with Father Joseph," he told the lead CSI tech. "There's a laptop, a phone, and a wallet in the main room, and a vial of testosterone and some syringes in the bathroom medicine cabinet that need to be collected. Apartment 2B."

The tech nodded. "On it."

Whatever secrets this man held, the lab would have to find them.

5

FLIGHT

By 6:30 the next morning, Grayson had completed his workout—thirty minutes on the treadmill and thirty minutes on the double-stack weight system.

He went to the kitchen, ground some Kaladi Brothers Red Goat beans, and made a pot. As the coffee brewed, he fried two strips of bacon, scrambled three eggs, and toasted two slices of bread. He sat down to eat, opened his laptop, and navigated to the *New York Times* Sunday crossword. He scarfed down his breakfast, completed the puzzle, and then logged in to his Self-Education and Surgical Assessment account. He answered the Continuing Medical Education questions for the section on trauma and recorded the credits into his CME tracker.

He put in a call to Jennifer, who lived in Seattle, also a physician, an infectious disease specialist. She had the weekend call for her group.

"Hey, hon."

"How was your night?"

"Couldn't sleep. Skied the trail to 4th Avenue and back."

Jennifer gave out a short laugh. "Maybe you're nervous about your Falls trip."

"Yeah, maybe. How's call going?"

"Oh, you know, same shit, different day. Bugs and drugs."

"I thought I'd call you before I headed north."

"You mean in case you die?" she teased. "Shit, another call's coming in. Gotta go. Don't get yourself killed, okay?"

"That's the idea."

"Love you."

"Love you too."

After hanging up, Grayson logged on to his ForeFlight account and filed a VFR flight plan to his cabin on Question Lake, ninety miles northeast of Anchorage. Not all small plane pilots filed VFRs, but Grayson always did. The program informed him he would have clear skies, low winds, and unlimited visibility.

After a quick shower, he dressed in ski pants, a flannel shirt, a down vest, a shearling jacket, and boots. He grabbed the backpack from underneath the sink, his book from the nightstand, and his cell phone, and headed out the back door to the lake and his Cessna four-seater Skylane, moored in its slip, on skis for the winter.

After taxiing out to the middle of the lake, Grayson throttled up the Turbo Skylane's 235-horsepower Lycoming TIO engine, the skis lifting off from the frozen lake surface at sixty-five knots. Turning to heading 270, he kept his altitude at one thousand feet ASL to stay below Ted Stevens's Class C airspace. The Garmin G1000 NXi avionics flight deck displayed his course clearly as he monitored his rate of climb.

Leveling off, he tuned in to Anchorage Approach. "Skylane 4-5-2 Charlie Alpha, VFR to Talkeetna, one soul on board, maintaining one thousand."

"Skylane 452CA, squawk 0241, proceed on course."

He dialed in the transponder code to 0241 so his plane could communicate with ground radar and banked north over downtown Anchorage. His flight path took him directly over the Church of the Holy Redeemer. Several police vehicles and two white CSI vans clustered around the entrance. The kick through the door, of course. Oh well, you couldn't anticipate everything, but he had confidence in his precautions.

From downtown Anchorage, he followed the Knik Arm of Cook Inlet, the Skylane's skis gleaming against the snow-covered terrain below.

As he headed 360, he looked out at the great white north spread out in front of him. Denali stood wide and majestic just off the left.

The world is a better place today.

The G1000's moving map showed his progress as he entered the Matanuska Valley, following the meandering Susitna River at 120 knots groundspeed. Checking the OAT gauge, which showed minus 15 degrees Celsius, he made a slight mixture adjustment before turning northeast toward Question Lake, maintaining 2,500 feet MSL to clear the rising terrain. The half-mile-long lake lay just outside Talkeetna, the small town known as the Gateway to Denali.

Forty minutes after he lifted off from Lake Campbell, he was over Question Lake. Four lakefront properties had plane slips, all vacant. His was the Swiss chalet-style bungalow perched atop a gentle rise from the lake's edge.

He entered the landing pattern at 800 feet AGL, performing his pre-landing checks: mixture rich, carb heat on, and fuel selector on the full tank. Making his first pass downwind at ninety knots, he scanned for snow drifts or debris that could snag his skis. Clear.

Banking into the base leg, he dropped his speed to eighty and began his descent. As the plane's skis hit the surface of the frozen lake, he kept his speed up and deliberately ski-dragged to test ice conditions. The Skylane's engine growled as it fought the resistance. After about 75 yards, he climbed back to pattern altitude and inspected his ski tracks. Any gray coloring would indicate overflow—water seeping up through cracks in the ice. The tracks showed pristine white against the snow. Solid ice. It was safe to land.

"452CA, turning final for Question Lake," he announced on the CTAF frequency, though he knew he was the only aircraft for miles.

This time, he committed to the landing, keeping his approach speed at sixty-five knots into the wind and the flaps at thirty degrees. The skis kissed the snow, and the Skylane settled onto the frozen surface with a gentle shush. He held back pressure on the yoke, allowing the increased drag and the friction of the skis to slow the plane while he maintained directional control with the rudder.

After slowing to a safe speed, Grayson taxied to his slip. He completed his shutdown checklist: avionics off, mixture to idle cutoff, master switch off. He tied down the Skylane with arctic ropes, installed the control locks, and grabbed his backpack from behind the pilot's seat.

In his cabin, he started a large blaze in the fireplace with a gas fire starter. The hardwood crackled, and the fire warmed the great room. He unzipped his backpack, removed the beard, and threw it into the hearth. It burst into flames and burned to ashes. It was probably overkill, but the coat and pants followed.

Grayson walked over to his fishing hut near the middle of the lake. Once inside, he turned on a propane heater and removed the catch cover lid. Using an ice auger attached to an electric drill, he bored a hole in the ice and inserted a hole sleeve through the open catch cover to prevent a draft from coming up. After baiting a hook, he dropped his line through the fishing hole into the water and secured the rod in a rod holder. He settled into a lawn chair, opened his book—*The Physician's Path*—and began reading:

Any fool can bring death to man, for destruction requires little skill. But to preserve life, to nurture health from the grasp of illness—therein lies our sacred calling. It demands vigilance, wisdom, and humility before the mysteries of nature's design.

A FEW HOURS LATER, as the sun started dipping beneath the pines. As the early-afternoon sky filled with orange, pink, magenta, and dark blue, Grayson emerged from the fishing hut and headed over to his cabin with his backpack and two blue-purple graylings, a fish best prepared and eaten freshly caught.

In the kitchen, he filleted the fish using a gutless technique and sautéed them in a beurre blanc sauce.

After dinner, he cleaned up and rewarded himself with two fingers of John Walker & Sons King George V blended Scotch in a Glencairn glass. The Scotch was a gift from a grateful patient Grayson had saved from dying of a ruptured abdominal aortic aneurysm. He brought the glass up to his nose and inhaled, taking in the smoky aroma and fruity notes. Then he took a sip and savored the smooth peatiness, well-balanced with caramel and vanilla, with a smoky caramel finish. He settled into his Scandinavian-style lounger for a night of reading.

6

AN INCOMPLETE PAST

Back at homicide, Eddie sat at his desk and flipped through Father Dracule's file from the Redeemer. A recent four-by-six-inch photo showed an expressionless elderly man with a crew cut, hollow cheeks, and deep-set eyes.

"Hey, Chik, can you run a photo for me?"

"Sure."

Eddie pulled the photo from underneath the clip and handed it to Chik.

A short autobiography on a letterhead spelled out Dracule Vincent's life in a few short lines:

Born in 1953 in Minot, North Dakota.

Graduated from Bishop Dworschak Senior High School in 1971.

Worked various jobs in labor and construction from 1971 to 1998. Self-educated through avid reading.

Attended St. Mary's College, Winona, Minnesota, from 1998 to 2000. Awarded credit for "life experience" and strong score on ACT (32).

Attended St. John's Seminary, Collegeville, Minnesota, from 2000 to 2004.

Served as a priest at St. Anthony's Catholic Church in Fargo from 2004 to 2025. Retired from active ministry in March, 2025.

Transcripts showed Dracule was a slightly above-average student. Three letters were in the file: one from Dracule to Father Joseph, expressing a desire to fulfill a "lifelong dream of spending his final days near the primitive wilderness of the Last Frontier." Another from Bishop Thomas Sullivan of the Fargo Diocese, endorsing Father Dracule's move to Alaska, attesting to his "over two decades of devoted service." And finally, a photocopy of the letter from Father Joseph granting Father Dracule an apartment in the rectory.

A celebret dated April 2025, signed by Bishop Sullivan, confirmed Father Dracule's status as a priest in good standing with faculties to perform sacraments.

The vague gap was not unusual for someone who'd basically lived life as a laborer.

Started seminary school in his forties? Not unheard of. Eddie had a few colleagues who had decided to attend law school at that age.

Chik came back.

"Nothing in the system with that photo."

Eddie dialed the number for the Diocese of Fargo listed on Bishop Sullivan's letterhead. After two rings, a pleasant female voice answered.

"Diocese of Fargo, how may I help you?"

"This is Detective Eddie Vaugner with the Anchorage Police Department. I'm investigating a death and need to verify some information about a priest who served in your diocese."

"One moment, please."

After a pause, a male voice came on the line. "This is Father Moran, chancellor of the diocese. Can I help you?"

"This is Detective Edward Vaugner with the Anchorage Police Department. I'm looking into the background of Father Dracule Vincent, who apparently served at St. Anthony's in your diocese from 2004 until earlier this year."

"Are you in your office now?"

"Yes."

"Detective Edward Vaugner, I'll pull up his records and call you back. How do you spell your last name?"

"Would you like my cell number?"

"No, I'll go through your switchboard. To confirm your identity, I've pulled up the APD homepage. Give me five minutes."

"Very good, sir."

After spelling his last name and hanging up, Eddie called the main switchboard and told them he was expecting a call and to put it right through to his desk.

Five minutes later, his phone rang.

"Yes, Detective, we do have a record of Father Dracule Vincent. He was ordained here in 2004 after completing seminary at St. John's in Minnesota. He served at St. Anthony's until his retirement this past spring."

Eddie sat up straighter. "So he was a legitimate priest in good standing?"

"Yes, of course. He served for over twenty years, and we issued a celebret when he moved to Alaska. He was well-regarded in the parish —quiet, dedicated, kept to himself, but always reliable."

This was interesting. The priesthood part of Dracule's life checked out.

"Did he ever mention any connection to Alaska before deciding to retire there, or that he knew anybody here?"

"Not that I'm aware of. His decision to move to Alaska came as something of a surprise. He seemed settled here. Is he okay?"

"He's deceased."

"Oh, dear. May I ask why this is a police matter?"

"Mostly routine. It was an unwitnessed death. No sign of injury or assault. Just a routine matter, really."

"I'm very sorry to hear that. I'll contact you if we find anything noteworthy in his file."

After thanking Father Moran and hanging up, Eddie called St. John's Seminary in Minnesota. He had to navigate several administrative channels before he reached the registrar's office, which confirmed that he had been a student from 2000 to 2004 and had been recommended for ordination.

"Do you have any information about his background before seminary?"

"I can tell you he had a bachelor's degree in Literature and Religion from St. Mary's College dated 1999."

He called St. Mary's Registrar's office and inquired once again. They told him that due to FERPA, they weren't allowed to share information on students.

"But you might try *Yearbooks.com*. You might get lucky."

Eddie spent another fifteen minutes signing up for a free thirty-day trial on the website. He was able to navigate to the yearbook of Dracule's graduating class and found his name under the list of those "Not pictured." He canceled his free trial. He'd mark that down as tentative confirmation.

After that, he continued working backward. Bishop Dworschak Senior High School had indeed existed in Minot in the 1970s but had closed in 1979.

Chik came over, holding the photo.

"Nothing from before 1996."

"Nothing?"

"No matches in the FBI's FACE database before that time. There was nothing in North Dakota state records for that name prior to his driver's license application in 1996. It's like Dracule Vincent didn't exist before then."

Eddie pursed his lips and formed a steeple with his hands as he stared down at Dracule's folder.

"So I've got a legitimately ordained Catholic priest who came out of thin air in the mid-1990s."

"It was a lot easier to create a new identity back then than it is today," Chik said, pointing at Dracule's file. "You could pay someone a grand, and they'd have a whole new identity for you, including a legitimate Social Security number. No biometrics, minimal cross-checking between databases. Most records weren't digitized."

"Why would someone create a new identity, then use it to be a priest?"

"*Mal pasado, mi amigo.*"

Eddie smiled at Uttaq's Spanish, and googled "Dracule Vincent." An AI overview said, "likely refers to Vincent Price's connection to the Dracula story..." which made him laugh. There was a Karl Vincent, Vampire Hunter, and a Dracule Milhawk, apparently an anime pirate. But no Dracule Vincent.

He leaned back in his chair and ran through the things that didn't add up. A late-night visit to a confessional that ended in death and a hole kicked through its door. Wipe protocols on his electronics. Five thousand in cash. An unlabeled vial of testosterone. A recent move to Alaska. A bad past could explain a lot of it. A bad past that caught up with him?

7

CRUCIBLE

After a restful sleep and a light breakfast, Grayson headed out into the gray Alaskan early morning. His Ford F-150 carried a snowmachine on a sled deck. The 125-mile drive north would get him to the Natnooklik Twin Falls recreational area just after the 9:42 sunrise.

The falls were located near the southern end of Denali National Park. Known colloquially as the Natty Twins, they were a pair of waterfalls whose source was the receding Natnooklik glacier.

The meltwater from the glacier filled a small tarn. From there, it spilled into two parallel 110-foot vertical couloirs separated by a narrow rocky ridge. After crashing to the bottom, the water percolated another fifty feet through a rockfall into Lake Natnooklik, a small lake with a surface area of just under three acres.

All this froze over in the winter and attracted ice climbers from all over.

He maneuvered his snowmachine off his truck, then pulled on soft-shell pants and a jacket over his wool base layers and snapped on his helmet. He sped across the lake, with equipment stashed in bins.

After reaching the rockfall, he strapped on his harness—already pre-loaded with gear—and lashed two 140-foot belaying ropes to it. He stowed his technical crampons in his backpack and slipped his two

Petzl Nomics ice tools through the axe loops. He trekked up the rock-fall to the base of the icefalls. There, he strapped on the crampons, adjusted them for precise front-pointing, and gripped his axes.

He chose the right icefall. The lower section started with a WI3+ pillar—relatively straightforward but requiring careful tool placement. Grayson moved with the rhythm born from years of technical climbing. Place. Test. Kick. Kick. Weight test. Move up. The ice was cold and brittle—at minus 20, every stick had to be perfect, or you risked dinner-plating the surface.

At forty feet up, the route steepened to a sustained WI4, a nearly vertical section. The ice here was marble-hard and dinner-plating badly. Each placement of his Nomics required multiple strikes to get a good bite, sending shards of ice cascading down the face. His calves burned from prolonged front-pointing, but he maintained the discipline of keeping his heels level and hips close to the ice.

ABOUT THREE HUNDRED yards to the west, two uniformed Park Rangers clad in olive-drab anoraks with the National Park Service's sequoia and bison logo on their upper left sleeves were riding their snowmachines on a vast snow plain.

Rick Westfield, a Denali Park Ranger for twelve years, was showing newbie Sam Dyson the ropes. The low Alaskan winter sun cast long shadows despite it being just past two-thirty. He stopped the snowmachine and pointed toward Natnooklik Falls.

"Look at that," Westfield said. They raised their binoculars to get a closer look at the lone climber about forty feet from the top.

"Solo climbing with an avalanche risk of four?" Dyson said. "Who's the lunatic?"

Westfield pulled out his phone, bit down on a fingertip of his glove as he pulled it off. With his ungloved hand, he tapped the screen. "Today's permits," he said through clenched teeth. "A Dr. Grayson Lange. Summited Denali in '22." He tapped his phone a few more times. "Surgeon in Anchorage. Five-star Google reviews."

"You'd think cutting people open for a living would be thrills enough."

"Apparently not," replied Westfield as he continued tapping, "he also summited Everest ten years ago."

"A real peak-bagger, eh?"

"I don't know." Westfield lifted his binoculars again. "His technique looks pretty solid."

LESS THAN THIRTY feet from the top, Grayson was breathing heavily, hammering his carbon fiber ice axes, one after the other, into the ice sheet, testing the purchase, then jamming the toe of each crampon, one after the other, into the ice. Pick. Pick. Test. Kick. Kick. Test. Lift. Six inches at a time. Keep the feet wide apart, hips close to the ice, and heels level. Don't pick or kick too hard. Just enough to hold the ice and not break off a chunk. And ignore the burning hands and calf muscles.

Whumpf!

It was the distinctive sound of a slab releasing, followed by the deep-throated roar of moving snow. The vibration was transmitted through Grayson's tools, causing them to buzz in his hands. The rumbling grew louder and closer.

Avalanche!

"Uh-oh."

THE RANGERS WATCHED as the large slab of snow hurtled down the mountainside, over the tarn, and approached the two couloirs, emitting a loud, low rumbling noise.

"Fucking Christ, he is so fucked," Westfield said.

The rangers looked through their binoculars. A white mountain of snow rumbled across the lake toward the edge of the falls. They saw Grayson scrambling like a desperate crab to get to the ridge.

"Come on, man," Dyson said.

. . .

GRAYSON LOOKED AROUND FOR AN ESCAPE. There—a rock horn a few feet up between the couloirs poking out from the verglas. If he could get there, it might provide enough protection, but he only had seconds. He furiously worked his ice axes and crampons to maneuver himself to the ice's edge. One chance. He swung his left Nomic and felt it bite into a thin seam underneath the craggy horn.

The tool torqued perfectly into the crack. He hoisted himself onto the ridge underneath the outcropping.

Another loud crack sounded over the rumbling. The vibrations from the avalanche had caused the icefall to break free, sending it in a rapid and jolting descent down the couloir. Then, from above, tons of ice and snow came crashing toward him in a sudden boom and flash of white. He gripped the axe tightly.

Please hold.

THE RANGERS WATCHED, awestruck, as snow exploded over the edge of the falls and plummeted downward, a screaming, angry white curtain concealing everything, including Grayson.

"Jesus, hold on," Westfield said.

GRAYSON HUDDLED under the outcropping as it deflected the crushing mass of snow and ice over him, just enough to keep him from being dragged down and crushed on the rockfall below.

The sound was deafening.

The rush of wind caused by the avalanche almost sucked the air out of his lungs.

Despite his predicament, he laughed to himself. If hell ever froze over, this would be it.

It seemed like an eternity, but after a few seconds, silence replaced the roar.

The view cleared, and Grayson could again see the dark blue sky of the impending Alaskan winter night.

"Whooooh!"

. . .

THE SCREAM of exhilaration echoed over the lake to the rangers. Westfield lowered his binoculars. "Incredible."

"Better lucky than smart," Dyson said.

"I guess he'll need a ride, now that his machine is buried," Westfield said. "Let's go." They started their machines and headed down the slope from the ridge to the lake.

TO GRAYSON'S RIGHT, the dispatched ice fall left a wall of ice-covered rocks coated with thin ice. This would be impossible to climb, but the left fall had held. Grayson sidled over to it. He slammed an ice pick into it, then eased onto it.

The fall held. He picked his way up to the top.

With one hand, he dug out a space in the deep snowpack left by the avalanche, then stood for a few moments, catching his breath and taking in his victory.

He surveyed the landscape below him. It was 3 p.m., and the sun was dropping behind the peaks of the Alaska Range.

Tons of fallen snow had driven over the rock falls and buried his snowmachine. He heard the sounds of other snowmachines and spotted a pair of rangers heading his way. He waved to them. One of them waved back.

Grayson prepared for the rappel down the icefall. He placed two Black Diamond Turbo Express screws, a foot apart and angled for strength, then clipped a locking carabiner to each one. He tied his two 140-foot ropes together and threaded the joined midpoint through both carabiners, the strands hanging evenly. He gave the setup a hard tug—solid. He tossed the doubled ropes over the falls, rigged his rappel device to both strands, and started down.

Reaching the bottom, Grayson pulled his rope down, coiled it over his shoulder, and crunched over the snow down the rockfall to the lake's surface. He waved at the park rangers approaching him. It was barely light out now, and their headlights cast beams in front of them.

Westfield shouted, "Hey, Doc! Bend over, and I'll pull that lucky horseshoe out of your ass!"

He looked back toward the heap of snow burying his snowmachine, unzipped his pocket, and took out his cell phone. He then pulled up the GPS coordinates and saved them to his notes.

"An avalanche risk of four! What were you thinking?" Dyson asked.

"A crucible," Lange said.

"Like something you drink from?"

"No," said Westfield. "Like a trial, or a test, right?"

"Yeah." Grayson pointed west. "My truck's over on the McKenzie Road parking lot. Can I get a ride from one of you guys?"

"Hop on!" Westfield said.

Grayson swung his leg over the backseat behind Westfield.

"What about your machine?"

"I'll call Talkeetna Plow and Wrecking. They'll dig it out and return it to my cabin."

The two snowmachines started up. As they roared off, Grayson looked back at the single ice fall and the pile of ice and snow left by the avalanche. He had submitted himself to the test. Once again, the universe had tipped the scales in his favor.

Later, back at his cabin, Jennifer called and asked how it went. He answered, "Perfect!"

8

THE CASTRATO

After the accident, Anne was brought to this room at the Medical Examiner's Office. Eddie almost requested a transfer out of homicide so he wouldn't have to stand here and imagine Anne lying on one of the tables. But she would have called him a wimp, so he pushed through those feelings. Even now, four years after her death, the images still lurked.

Three stainless steel tables, numbered 1, 2, and 3, were arranged side by side. Raven and Karl, the autopsy technician, stood gowned and masked astride table 3, the farthest from the door. Dracule's naked body lay face-up between them.

"Hey, Detective," Karl said.

"Hi, Karl. Hey, Dr. Raven."

"Good morning," she said. "We've completed X-rays, the CT scan, and the external exam, along with fingerprints and photographs. So far, we have a Caucasian male, height five feet nine inches, weight 165 pounds, with hyperkyphosis, abnormal forward curvature of the spine, most likely from degenerative disease. No fresh wounds, bullets, or other metallic fragments. Nothing on the CT scan indicates a cause of death."

She was more efficient than her predecessor.

"The clothing was soiled with stool and urine—no surprise there—but no blood stains and nothing torn," Raven continued. "We'll biohazard process them and get them over to you. But on the body itself, we have interesting findings."

Raven lifted Dracule's penis with her gloved hand. She pointed to a scar running down the middle of a flat, wrinkled patch of skin. "Finding number one."

"Is that trying to be a scrotum?" Eddie asked.

"Yes, but it's hard to be one without testicles. He's castrated. You can see a scar in the midline of the scrotum. It's not very anatomical, so this may have been a self-castration or done by an amateur."

"Yeesh. Why would someone do that to himself?" It was rhetorical, really. Nothing about human behavior surprised Eddie.

"At one time, human castration was done to prevent the maturing effects of testosterone, like deepening of the voice, hence the castrato sopranos of old Italian opera. These days, it's psychotics or extreme neurotics trying to suppress sexual thoughts and impulses. And based on the body's appearance, this castration was done long after puberty."

Looking at Raven's eyes over her mask, Eddie felt an unwelcome stirring of his own. *Jesus, Vaugner.* He forced his eyes back to the body on the table. *Not the time. Not the place.*

"What about cancer, like Lance Armstrong."

"No. Orchiectomy—surgical removal of the testicles—is done through inguinal incisions in the groin area, never through the scrotum. Also, bilateral testicular cancer is rare."

"We found a vial of testosterone in his medicine cabinet," Eddie said.

"Testosterone is prescribed for the effects of decreased muscle mass and strength, reduced bone density, low energy, deteriorating mood and cognition, and, of course, decreased sex drive. Which explains finding number two."

Eddie thought of the Alba Madonna in Dracule's apartment with the full-frontal naked Jesus infant.

"Okay, Karl, on his side," Raven said.

As they rolled Dracule over, Eddie wondered if a national database on sex offenders who had undergone castration existed. It would narrow the field.

"Finding number two." Raven tapped a small mark on the upper outer aspect of Dracule's left buttocks. "This appears to be a recent injection. The testosterone, I presume. Was it testosterone cypionate, by any chance?"

"Yes, actually."

"So around one injection every two to four weeks, depending on the testosterone levels."

Next, Raven outlined the exaggerated curve of the upper back. "Finding number three—as mentioned before—marked kyphosis. The loss of testosterone leads to bone demineralization, weakening the vertebrae and resulting in overcurvature of the back. It's common in men castrated in adulthood. Testosterone replacement right after castration would have prevented this, so in this individual, replacement would have started long after the castration."

Maybe the priest had had enough sexual repression for one life.

Using a ruler, Raven indicated two scars on the left side of his midback, just below the shoulder blade. Each scar was about one and a half inches long.

"Finding number four. Notice these scars. While I couldn't testify with certainty in court, these are possibly healed stab wounds. See how they're oriented? Oriented diagonally downward from right to left. Surgical incisions would be vertical or oriented along relaxed skin tension lines, not in the directions these scars run."

She took the ruler and held it in her left fist. "Turn around, Karl." Karl turned, and Raven made overhand stabbing motions toward his back, resting the ruler on it. The end of the ruler tilted downward from right to left, matching the angle of Father Dracule's scars.

"See? The blade has the same orientation as the forearm. Assuming the victim was standing, and the assailant came up from behind, these probably were made by a left-handed person. And given the position, by a short person."

"Makes sense," Eddie said.

"But these scars are years old, so non-contributory as to the cause of death. There are no signs of acute trauma. No contusions, lacerations, or other signs of foul play."

They rolled the body back over.

"So. Quite the story before we open him up. Okay, Karl."

Karl took a scalpel and made a Y-shaped incision, starting from each shoulder to where they joined at the center of the chest at the upper aspect of the breastbone and continued down as a single line through the center of the chest and the abdomen to the pubic bone. Because of pooling from sitting upright dead in the confessional, no blood oozed from the incision. After peeling the skin back to expose the rib cage, Karl took a cutting instrument resembling stainless steel pruning shears and snipped the ribs at each side of the corpse. This allowed him to remove the front part of the rib cage off the chest, almost like lifting the hood of a car, to expose the heart and lungs. He opened the abdominal wall through a midline incision. All of Father Dracule's organs were on display.

In a quick, choreographed sequence, Karl eviscerated the corpse, organ by organ, placing them on the back table for Raven. Raven set each organ on a scale, noted the weight, set it down on a cutting board, and made several sections in quick strokes with a sharp knife.

"Liver, 2,350 grams." Slice. "Normal without evidence of cirrhosis or fatty infiltration."

"Heart, 326 grams." Slice. "Valves, normal, no evidence of coronary artery disease or myopathy."

"Right lung, 720 grams." Slice. "Carbonaceous deposits, compatible with the decedent's smoking history. No evidence of pulmonary embolism or tumor."

And so on.

After the evisceration, they rolled the body back over. Raven excised a two-inch square of skin around a recent injection mark and some subcutaneous fat and muscle tissue deeper down.

"We'll send this out to confirm testosterone injections."

Karl finished the last part of the autopsy, which was to remove the brain. He made a sweeping incision of the scalp from just behind one ear, over the top of the head, and over to the other ear, then pulled the two edges of the scalp away from each other, one toward the front and one toward the back, exposing the skull. Using an oscillating saw, Karl made a circumferential cut around the top half of the skull and pulled it off. Using scissors, he reached down into the depths of the skull cavity, cut away all the connections to the brain, lifted it out, and put it in a bucket filled with formaldehyde.

"We'll let it harden up in formaldehyde for about two weeks," Raven said. She stepped away from the table and peeled off her surgical gown, gloves, and mask. She was wearing green scrubs with a V-neck top.

"Nice autopsy, Dr. Raven."

"Please, call me Becca. The brain should be ready for sectioning in about two weeks. I should have the blood and tissue tox screens back and microscopic studies done in about a week. But for now, no obvious cause of death."

And there was Jesus again, hanging from the chain, pinned to his cross, still downblousing Raven's cleavage as intently as Eddie was trying not to do. When you're the Son of Man, Eddie thought, you get away with a lot. *If the Savior of Mankind takes a peek into a nice V-neck, who am I to judge?*

"I'll keep you posted."

"Yes, I'll look forward to that."

What the fuck Eddie. Could you have said anything more idiotic?

9

TENUOUS REMISSION

After the autopsy, Eddie picked up Daniel at Romig Middle School for his checkup with Dr. Benjamin Blake, Daniel's pediatric oncologist. Daniel was enrolled in the Gifted Program. Eddie and Anne had picked up on Daniel's brightness when he began speaking in complete sentences at eighteen months.

"What should we do about this intelligence of his?" Anne had asked at one point.

"Find out who the father is."

"Oh, shut up, Mr. 3.9 GPA. Not only did he get your smarts, but he also got your curiosity, which is even better, if you ask me."

As a baby, Daniel was unusually attentive and wide-eyed. He was reading by three. Often, they woke up at night to the sound of giggling, only to find him in his room entertaining himself by taking apart a puzzle and putting it together again or buried in a book. They gave up telling him to go back to sleep. He never seemed to need much, and he never seemed to be tired.

As he grew older, his distant yet endearing aspect became more manifest in his behavior. He seemed unable to connect to people or filter his comments. He tended to be pedantic. His speech, while not "clinically flat," as one psychologist put it, had less "tonal variety" than most boys his age. He wasn't exactly clumsy, but he didn't enjoy team sports.

When he was six, they'd signed him up for soccer. In Daniel's first game, after minutes on the field, he just started focusing on the grass and ignoring the game. A ball kicked toward him went unnoticed and out of bounds. Other kids yelled at him. The coach took him out of the game. Smiling, Daniel ran over to his parents, holding two four-leaf clovers. Oblivious to the ejection and the criticism, he held the clovers up and told his parents not to be shocked that he'd found two. "A survey of five million clovers determined the frequency of four-leaf clovers was closer to five-thousand-to-one, twice as frequent as the ten-thousand-to-one most people believed," he informed them.

What six-year-old talks like that? That was Daniel's first and last soccer game or any other team sport. He did enjoy individual activities, like bicycle riding and cross-country skiing.

On the way over to Dr. Blake's office, Daniel asked his father, "Hey, Dad, can we visit Mom after the doctor's appointment?"

"Sure."

"I'd like to get her pink carnations. I read they symbolize 'I'll never forget you.'"

"You bet."

AFTER THEY'D SIGNED in at the Pediatric Oncology Center, a nurse led them back to an exam room and instructed Daniel to remove his clothes and put on a patient gown.

Daniel sat on the exam table, playing Fortnite on his phone, while Eddie sat in a chair, flipping through a magazine. They didn't converse, perhaps avoiding the subject, though the question filled Eddie's mind. *Is the leukemia back?*

Dr. Blake came in, holding Daniel's chart. Blake was a short, stocky man with graying temples and a receding hairline. He often joked that he'd chosen pediatrics so he could be taller than his patients.

"Hey guys," the doctor said. His voice was soft and calm.

"Hey, Dr. Blake," Daniel replied.

"How are things going, Daniel?"

"Good. No fevers, sweats, bruising, unusual bleeding, weight loss, or change in appetite."

Blake chuckled. "Excellent, Daniel."

"My energy and strength are good. Dad and I skied the Powerline Trail from the Glen Alps trailhead up to Prospect Heights last Saturday. Ten miles. And this weekend, we're doing Tony Knowles."

"Wow." The doctor raised his eyebrows.

Daniel was thirty-seven months removed from completing treatment for acute lymphoblastic leukemia, or ALL. Through Blake's discussions, Daniel's dissertations on the subject, and his own reading, Eddie had a decent knowledge of Daniel's disease. Lymphoblasts were precursor cells in the bone marrow, giving rise to lymphocytes, the cells responsible for a large part of the human immune system. ALL was when the lymphoblasts overproliferated and took over the bone marrow, crowding out the other blood-forming cells. They also spilled into the bloodstream and went to the lymph nodes, liver, spleen, brain, spinal cord, and testicles.

Acute lymphoblastic leukemia had a cure rate of over 85 percent in children. Unfortunately, Daniel was twice unlucky. His leukemia cells carried the Philadelphia chromosome and had the KZF1 gene deletions. The KZF1 acted as a tumor suppressor in normal cells. Both factors combined made his prognosis poor. His best five-year survival rate was around 50 percent, but many pediatric oncologists thought that figure was too optimistic.

Daniel had failed standard chemotherapy and required a bone marrow transplant, which he'd gotten from his father. The donor's bone marrow needed to be as compatible with the recipient's bone marrow as possible. Because Daniel was Eddie's son, he would automatically be 50 percent compatible. But it had turned out even better —Daniel and Eddie matched 100 percent. Only if Eddie and Anne had the same HLA genes could that happen, about a million-to-one random chance. The HLA genes directed the production of HLA anti-gens, molecules found on cell surfaces, greatly influencing the compatibility of tissue and organ donations.

Daniel saw the HLA match as his mom's intervention from heaven, while Eddie saw it as a random but lucky jumble of genes. Providential or not, Eddie took comfort that Anne, even in death, was still looking out for their boy.

When Daniel was discharged from the hospital, he was still immunologically frail and at risk for infection. No one except Gertie and Eddie was allowed into the house for eight months. He couldn't go to school, crowded restaurants, or movies. No group activities were permitted. He could have friends over, but not in the house. He could visit with them in the yard, but they had to stay at least six feet apart so he wouldn't catch their bugs. Winter in Alaska was not conducive to outdoor visits involving more than a quick hello. These social restrictions had been an emotional burden for many kids, but isolation posed no difficulty for Daniel. He was content on his own.

Through Daniel's illness, Eddie took as much paid leave as possible but remained on active duty to maintain medical insurance and salary.

So today, over three years after his remission, Eddie understood the subtext of Daniel's tale of skiing: *Look at me, Dr. Blake. I skied the Powerline trail. I'm a specimen of health and fitness, so there is no way you can find I have relapsed.* But Eddie knew it wasn't up to Dr. Blake. Sure, there is personal grit, but much of what you get in this world is defined by your life colliding with random events, no more and no less. Like a drunk driver or a cell gone wild.

What really irked Eddie was the platitude, "It's in God's hands." As far as he was concerned, the only thing in God's hand was a pair of dice. *Ha! Why do you think they call it paradise?* God tossed them and then turned away before they stopped tumbling. He couldn't have cared less if they came up boxcars or snake-eyes.

While Eddie engaged in this reverie, Blake turned to the physical exam. He palpated Daniel's neck and the area above the collarbones, looking for pathological lymph nodes. With a penlight and tongue depressor, he checked Daniel's mouth and throat, having Daniel say, "Ah." Daniel smiled at his father. The doctor took out his stethoscope, listened to Daniel's heart and lungs, and asked Daniel to lie down. He palpated his abdomen and both groin areas, again checking for an enlarged spleen and abnormal lymph nodes. Finally, he palpated the testicles, a common place where leukemia could relapse.

"Everything looks good, Daniel," Blake said.

"Yep, I feel good." Daniel gave his father a thumbs-up. Eddie returned the gesture, along with a reassuring smile.

"We'll get some blood tests, and I'll call you with the results."

"Ugh," Daniel said.

The doctor left, and they waited a few minutes before a nurse came in and drew his blood.

"I vant to suck your blood!" Daniel said in his best Bela Lugosi. The nurse smiled and took two red tops and one blue top. Daniel showed little reaction to the pain of the needle.

After the blood draw, father and son left the hospital and stopped by a flower shop to buy a dozen pink carnations.

THE ANCHORAGE MEMORIAL PARK CEMETERY was a twenty-two-acre tract in downtown Anchorage. In an act of petty corruption, Eddie parked in a spot reserved for "Official Vehicles Only."

They got out and walked to Anne's grave. Daniel placed the bouquet into the vase next to the headstone. "Hi, Mom. I hope every-thing is okay. Not that it shouldn't be. I mean, it's heaven. My appoint-ment with Dr. Blake went okay. I'm still feeling good. It's been three years since my bone marrow transplant, as you know, so thanks. School's going well. That's about it. Oh yeah, I love you."

Daniel stood back and made the sign of the cross. Eddie stepped forward and put his hand on the tombstone, patting it twice.

"If it comes down to it, Dad, you'll bury me next to Mom, right?"

Eddie felt his gut heave.

"It will not come down to that, Daniel; you've beat this thing."

"Yes, but you will, right?"

"Of course, son, but it won't happen. You'll be burying me some-day, but not for a long time. Now, can we get off this subject?"

"Okay, fine."

"Hungry?"

"Yes. Can we go to North Star?"

10

THE GOD OF TOMORROW

No tables were available at the North Star diner, so the hostess offered Eddie and Daniel two seats at the end of the counter. A wall-mounted television blared the local news. The well-coiffed anchor Frank Balmer appeared on screen. An over-the-shoulder graphic showed two atoms with their electron clouds connected by a luminous stream. "And we're back talking with Dr. Jocelyn Meyers, a professor of physics at the University of Alaska Anchorage." The screen cut to a double box with Balmer on the left and a woman sitting at a desk in what appeared to be an academic office.

A server working the counter dropped off menus. "Welcome to the North Star. I'll be right back."

"Dr. Meyers, what is quantum entanglement?" Balmer asked on the screen.

"Imagine a pair of dice, but each die is in a different room. When you roll one of them, the other instantly rolls to a matching number or, maybe, the number on the opposite side of the die. That's quantum entanglement—photons, electrons, and even atoms and small molecules that are linked in ways that defy our everyday understanding of space and time."

"Interesting theory, Doctor, but has this ever been demonstrated?"

"Oh, yes. In 2023, a team at MIT demonstrated this quantum entanglement between photons separated by three hundred kilometers through fiber-optic cables while maintaining a remarkable 95 percent fidelity in their quantum states."

"Okay, I'll pretend I understand what you just said. But why should our viewers care about this?" Balmer asked.

"Because it fundamentally changes our understanding of reality. These quantum connections suggest our universe isn't made of separate parts but is deeply interconnected at its most basic level. We're discovering the universe is both stranger and more unified than we ever imagined. Some people, like Christian theologian John Polkinghorne, view it as evidence of how God works."

The server came back over. "You gentlemen ready to order?"

Without taking his eyes off the screen, Daniel said, "I'll have a cheeseburger with fries and a vanilla milkshake."

"And I'll have the tuna salad, no bread, and a Coke Zero," Eddie added.

The anchor broke in. "But are there any practical benefits to this?"

"Absolutely. We're already using quantum entanglement to develop ultrasecure communication systems that can't be hacked. It's also the key to quantum computers, which could solve problems our current computers can't handle—like discovering new medicines or optimizing supply chains. Major tech companies are investing billions in this technology because they see its enormous potential."

"I tell you, Doctor, I'm having a hard time wrapping my head around this."

"Spooky action," Daniel said. "Here it comes."

Dr. Meyers chuckled. "Don't feel bad. Everyone has a hard time with quantum entanglement. Even Einstein refused to accept it when the concept first came out. He derided the theory as 'spooky action at a distance.'"

"We'll have to leave it there. Thank you very much, Dr. Meyers, for this interesting discussion."

"My pleasure."

"Rachelle?"

The TV switched to a two-shot with the anchor named Rachelle Peaks sitting next to Balmer.

"We now shift our focus to church versus state," Rachelle said.

The screen cut to a double-box with Rachelle in one box and a distinguished-looking man, fiftyish, outside the cathedral situated on a large campus. The silver threading of his dark hair lent him the gravitas of wisdom, while his impeccable suit provided an air of prosperity.

"With us is Reverend Revus Roche, the pastor of the America Salvation Church. The Anchorage megachurch is fighting a federal lawsuit to revoke its tax-exempt status for advocating for political candidates who want to change our Constitution. But before we get to that, Reverend, did you hear Dr. Meyers say quantum entanglement might explain how God works?"

"I did. Fascinating stuff, as God continues to reveal Himself."

"So, you're buying it?"

Roche laughed. "You know, guys, this quantum stuff is like the Septuagint—it's all Greek to me!"

"And there you have it," Rachelle said. "We'll be right back to talk with Reverend Roche about his fight with the Feds."

As the program went to a car commercial, Eddie noticed a booth had opened up. He asked their server if they could move, and she quickly transferred them over.

Once they were situated in the booth, Eddie smiled at Daniel. "How did you know that professor was going to bring up spooky action?"

"Because everyone who's explaining quantum entanglement uses that Einstein quote to make people feel better about not getting it. It's like what Richard Feynman said about quantum mechanics: 'If you think you understand quantum mechanics, you don't understand quantum mechanics.'"

"Thanks, kid. Now I don't feel so stupid about being so dumb."

"Of course, if you think you don't understand, you don't understand it either."

The server brought over the milkshake and Coke Zero. "Here you go, fellas. The food will be out in a sec."

"You know what's interesting about all this from the religious standpoint?" Daniel asked.

"No?"

"How God has evolved. Primitive man started with animism, spirits in everything, even rocks. Then came multiple gods, like the Greeks and Romans. Now, most religions have just one god." The boy paused, stirring his milkshake. "I wonder what the God of tomorrow will be like when we finally understand how everything works?"

"Maybe by then, we won't need a god." Eddie instantly regretted his words, but Daniel continued unfazed.

"Or maybe it won't be human-like. Maybe it'll be something more —like a force or a connection. You know how they say God is within us, and we're all connected? Maybe that's true. Maybe that guy— Pokemon Horn?—is right."

Daniel took a sip of his milkshake and then pulled out his phone and tapped it. "It's Polkinghorne, John Polkinghorne, an English physicist and theologian. He wrote a book called *The Quantum Physics and Theology: An Unexpected Kinship.*"

Daniel put his phone down. After taking another big sip of his milkshake, he winced and pressed his palm against his forehead. "Brain freeze!" He laughed with mock pain for a moment. "I just thought of something."

"What's that?" asked Eddie, somewhat surprised that Daniel didn't go on to describe the physiology of brain freeze.

"You know what the Big Bang is, right?"

"Think so. First, there was nothing, and then the entire universe exploded out of the Big Bang, and now everyone keeps moving farther and farther apart."

"Yes. There is a term for what was before the Big Bang—a singularity. At one time, everything, all matter, energy, space, and time, was concentrated into a point—singularity. Maybe God was in there, too. And the explosion came, and God, being infinite, just expanded along with everything else, so now He's everywhere, in everything. Just like the animists believed. That's why God is a lot like quantum mechanics. Spooky action at a distance that no one really understands."

Eddie smiled at Daniel. Most of his teachers and counselors agreed Daniel was intellectually gifted, but they debated the rest. Apparently, there could be a fine line between a precocious nerd and autism spectrum disorder. His intense focus on whatever caught his curiosity and tendency to lecture anyone who'd listen about his latest discoveries, his difficulty with eye contact and social cues—these might be autism spectrum disorder or just the awkwardness of a bright kid smarter than most of his peers.

The developmental psychologist had suggested testing for genius-level IQ, but Eddie and Anne declined. Still, some of the thoughts coming from the kid's brain... *Holy smokes.*

If Daniel were older, Eddie might have challenged him. Why does God stand by while millions die? *If there were a just and loving God, I'd be out of a job.* Or makes absurd, petty demands while sending mixed messages? Why expect the God of tomorrow to be different? But perhaps this was what Daniel meant—the God of tomorrow was not a petty moralist but a force of nature. But then, Daniel would be talking about a quantum God, not a personal one.

As if reading his mind, Daniel asked, "Are you mad at God for what happened to Mom and me getting sick?"

Eddie wondered if Daniel realized he held two competing concepts of what God was at the same time.

"I used to be."

"What about now that I'm better? Wait. I know what you're going to say. He shouldn't have let me get sick in the first place."

"I'm just glad you're better now, son."

"I heard you and Grandma arguing about church. You said God hasn't done much for our family, and you couldn't care less if He existed or not."

"You heard that?"

"Yeah. I found a term for you—apatheist. Someone who doesn't care if God exists or not."

"Apathetic to the existence of God."

"Exactly."

"Well, maybe that's what I am. But you don't have to be."

. . .

AS THEY STARTED HOME, Daniel kept his head down in his phone.

After a few minutes, he said, "Did you know that brain freeze happens when extreme cold in the mouth or throat causes a rapid constriction followed by dilation of blood vessels? This irritates the nerves that supply sensation to the face and head. It's actually called sphenopalatine ganglioneuralgia?"

"I was just about to say that," Eddie said, suppressing a smile.

"Ha ha."

Daniel started muttering to himself: "Need to rotate to zone... got some decent mats..."

Eddie recognized the interjections—Fortnite.

Eddie remembered the psychologist telling him video games were a godsend in managing children on the spectrum. They served as sensory regulators and coping mechanisms for these kids, who tended to be overloaded and overwhelmed by their environments.

"I had a dream about Mom last night," Daniel said without looking up.

"I dream about her sometimes, too."

"You might think this is crazy, but she told me not to worry; she's sending someone to look out for me."

"I don't think it's crazy at all, Daniel."

The rest of the way home, he played his game. "YT_SweatGod with a default skin? Yeah, right... probably doesn't even have channel... nice piece control..."

11

DEVIL DOC

Later that week, Eddie was at his desk when his cell went off. It was Chik.

"I'm in the ER at Prov," Chik said.

"What's up?" Eddie said. "I didn't get any calls."

"No, I'm here for me. I'm sick."

"What's wrong?"

"I might have botulism."

"Jesus, Chik, botulism?"

"Yeah. Yesterday, I ate some pickled seal fat. An hour later, I got sick. Stomach pain and puking."

"Okay, I'm coming over."

When he arrived at the hospital, the ER triage nurse sent Eddie back to the acute care area, and a nurse pointed him toward the back. "He's back there, cubicle eleven."

On his way to Chik's cubicle, he passed by Trauma Bay 1, where four years ago, the EMTs had dropped him off after the car accident. Anne had never made it this far.

Chik sat on an ER gurney in a hospital gown. A small, thin, elderly Inuit man with jet-black hair and alert eyes the color of coal sat in a chair beside him. When the old man looked up at Eddie, he smiled, and his face crinkled into a thousand creases.

"Hey, Eddie. This is my father-in-law, Inuksuk."

"Hello, sir," Eddie said, extending his hand. Inuksuk smiled and shook it.

"He's from Copenhagen. Speaks Inuit, Greenlandic, and Danish, but no English."

"Visiting?"

"I'll give you the short version," Chik said. "As you know, Christina's mother died last year, and he's been living by himself, so Christina invited him here to stay with us for a while. He's on a B-2 visa, so he's got six months. We're empty nesters, so he's using one of the kids' rooms."

"Have you seen a doctor yet?"

"Not yet."

"And where's Christina now?"

"She's at her own doctor's appointment. Has a touch of arthritis and had an appointment with a rheumatologist. It took her eight months to get in, so I told her not to cancel."

A doctor entered the cubicle—a hospital lanyard identified him as Jason Defner, MD. He had a muscular build and close-cropped hair. His blue scrubs fitted his frame tightly, with biceps straining at the sleeves. Eddie figured he could have chosen a top one size larger but went for a tight-fitting scrub to emphasize his physique. A gold crucifix hung from his neck, shining against his skin.

Two tattoos, one on each forearm, caught Eddie's attention. The right one was a modified American flag, with a cross replacing the field of stars. Eddie recognized it as the symbol of America Salvation Church rallies, that radical megachurch gaining momentum in their push to make Christianity the official religion of the United States. He took an immediate dislike to the man.

The one on the left marked him as a Navy medic who'd deployed with the Marine Corps in a combat operation: the Marine Corps Eagle, Globe, and Anchor merged with the twin-serpent caduceus of military medicine. "SEMPER FI" arched above the design, with "DEVIL DOC" inscribed below.

Eddie noted the irony: a religious zealot embracing the "Devil Doc" nickname. But zealots weren't exactly known for their self-awareness.

"Mr. Uttaq?"

"That's me. I'm the one wearing the gown."

Not a smile or acknowledgment of the attempt at humor. "I'm Dr. Defner." He looked at Inuksuk and Eddie. "Would you two mind stepping out?"

"It's okay. This is my father-in-law, and this is my partner, Detective Vaugner. We're with the Anchorage Police Department. Homicide. I'd like them to stay."

Defner hesitated a second, then said, "Fine."

"Devil Doc, huh? I served with some good ones in Third Battalion, Fifth Marines. Put in five years as an MP myself during Desert Shield and Desert Storm. We were part of the push into Kuwait back in '91. Saw action securing routes and processing EPWs."

"Landstuhl," Defner said dismissively. He seemed annoyed. "So why don't you tell me what brings you to the ER today?" Eddie watched the interaction, noting how Defner seemed to look past Chik rather than at him. He was keeping to his basic script without trying to feign actual concern, being dismissive of a Native Alaskan—and one who had served in harm's way.

While Eddie was getting angry, Chik seemed to shrug it off.

"Okay. Yesterday, after eating some pickled seal fat, I came down with abdominal pain and started puking."

"Where did the pickled seal fat come from?"

"My father-in-law, here, brought it from Greenland. I'm worried it might be botulism."

"Pickled fish from Greenland? Is that even legal? Did anyone else eat it and get sick?"

Eddie wanted to tell the doctor a seal wasn't a fish, but he let it go.

"No. Not yet."

"Are you having any vision problems? Like seeing double?"

"No."

"Weakness?"

"No."

"Any problems swallowing, or does your tongue feel thick?"

"No."

"It's not botulism. Let me have a look at your belly."

Defner reached down and pulled up Chik's gown. There were four circular marks on his abdomen.

"What are these?" the doctor asked as he started to push on Chik's abdomen.

Inuksuk gave him a collegial smile.

"My father-in-law is an angakkuq, a shaman. He treated me yesterday."

Defner pressed on the right lower quadrant of the abdomen. Chik winced.

"Treat you?" Defner looked over at Inuksuk and shook his head. "With this bullshit?" He muttered to himself, "Shame on the shaman," as if they weren't worth the effort of addressing his insult at them directly.

He pressed down on the right lower quadrant again, and Chik winced, "Jesus, Doc, how many times do you have to do that?"

"It's almost certainly appendicitis. You should have come in yesterday; you'll be lucky if you haven't ruptured."

Inuksuk tapped Chik on the shoulder. They had a brief Inuit exchange, ending with the older man nodding and letting out a slight chuckle.

"What did he say?" Defner asked.

Chik translated, "He said he knew the food was good, and it was appendicitis, and I should have come in yesterday when he told me to."

Defner's face flashed red, but he suppressed a reaction. "I'll get the surgeon on call to see you."

The doctor exited the cubicle.

"What a fucking asshole," Chik said.

Eddie chuckled. "We're becoming like an old married couple. I came up with the same word for him, but I gotta hand it to you. You nailed it with 'fucking.'"

"If my father-in-law could have understood what he said, I would have punched his lights out."

"Sure. He's six-four, an ex-Marine with biceps bigger than your thighs."

"Yeah, well, the bigger they come, you know."

While they were waiting for the surgeon to arrive, Eddie received a call from Raven. He stepped out of the cubicle and answered.

"Hi, Detective Vaugner, this is Dr. Raven."

"Please, call me Eddie."

"Sure, if you call me Becca."

"Okay, Becca, what's up?"

"I looked at Dracule's brain and did some microscope work. There are a few areas where the cells look funny, probably the mitochondria. I'm sending some samples out to some mitochondrial experts to have a look. It'll take a few weeks."

A man in scrubs and a long white coat approached Chik's cubicle. He was in his thirties, fit, and slightly taller than Eddie. A scar traced from his right ear down his neck, vanishing beneath his scrubs. Despite the scar, he remained handsome. This must have been the day for doctors with distinguishing marks.

"Okay, thanks, Becca."

Eddie hung up and went back into the cubicle.

"Hi, folks, I'm Dr. Lange, the surgeon on call."

"Chik Uttaq," Chik said, then gestured to the others. "My father-in-law, Inuksuk—he doesn't speak English—and Detective Vaugner. We're both homicide detectives."

Lange smiled warmly at each of them. "Pleased to meet you all." To Inuksuk, Lange said, "*Qanuippit*," which meant "how are you" in Inuit.

Inuksuk beamed back and nodded enthusiastically. "*Quanuinn-gittunga!*"

"Rumor has it you have appendicitis, Detective Uttaq."

"That's what your colleague, Sergeant Shithole, thinks," Chik said.

Lange chuckled. "Ah, the charming Dr. Defner. Hates the sin and the sinner."

He reviewed Chik's story, medical history (none), and past operations (none). Eddie appreciated the surgeon's bedside manner. He spoke plainly, used normal conversational tones, smiled frequently, and cracked a few jokes to put everyone at ease.

Eddie looked over at Inuksuk. The Inuit elder seemed quite taken by the doctor. His gaze remained fixed on Grayson, his dark eyes wide as if he were seeing someone or something familiar. His lips curved in a slight smile.

"You mind if I poke on your belly a few times?"

"Why not? It seems to be the thing to do."

Chik pulled up his gown, exposing Inuksuk's circular marks. Inuksuk smiled at Grayson, raised his hand, and nodded.

"*Angakkuq?*" Grayson asked.

Inuksuk smiled and nodded his head. Grayson smiled back.

Grayson pushed on Chik's abdomen, avoiding the area of the right lower quadrant until last. When he pressed this area, Chik jumped. Grayson pulled down Chik's gown to cover his torso.

"Yes, I think Sergeant Shithole's right. You do have acute appendicitis."

"So now what?" Chik asked.

"You have two options. I'm about 95 percent sure of the diagnosis. We could increase the probability of a correct diagnosis to a hundred by doing a CT scan. Or we could go to the OR now, remove your appendix, and save time, money, and radiation."

Inuksuk said something to Chik. Chik said something back, and the older man nodded.

"My father-in-law asks what do you recommend."

"I recommend going right to the OR."

They had another exchange.

"He says I should follow your recommendations."

Inuksuk tapped Chik on the shoulder, spoke to him more authoritatively, and gestured toward Grayson.

"Because you have been given a gift not found in many healers."

Inuksuk looked up at Grayson, nodded, and smiled.

"*Qujannamilk*," Grayson said. It meant "thank you," and was one of the few Inuit words Eddie knew. "To the OR then."

The surgeon gave Inuksuk a thumbs-up and gave Chik a brief description of the operation. It would be done laparoscopically through three small half-inch incisions. He outlined the risks, including infection, finding a normal appendix, and the need to convert to a regular open appendectomy. If the appendix was normal, he would take it out to prevent any future abdominal pain being confused for appendicitis. If everything went well and the appendix wasn't ruptured, Chik could go home a few hours after the operation.

"Any questions?"

"No sir," Chik said.

Grayson picked up the phone on the cubicle wall and dialed an extension. As he spoke, Eddie compared the two doctors. The ER doctor had been brusque, condescending, and dismissive, while the surgeon moved with an unhurried, calm, and caring attitude. Chik had lucked out in getting him as his surgeon.

"Hey Lynn, it's Grayson Lange. I have a lap appy in the ER. When can we go?... Yeah, he's ready now." Grayson winked at Chik. "Great." He hung up.

"We got a room. A nurse will bring in a consent for you to sign, and someone from the OR will come for you."

Grayson held out his hand to shake Chik's hand. "I'll take good care of you, Mr. Uttaq." He smiled at Inuksuk and shook his hand, then Eddie's.

After the surgeon left, Inuksuk said something to Chik and Eddie in Inuit. Eddie looked over to Chik, who rolled his eyes. "He asked if we could feel the word—what's the word—uh, magic, or power, maybe magical healing power, I guess. Not sure how to translate it. It's a shaman thing."

Eddie shrugged and smiled. He felt a warm, dry hand and a firm handshake but no magic. However, the doctor seemed to be someone you could trust your life to.

12

TIME GLITCH

Chik's appendectomy was uneventful, and, as Dr. Lange had promised, he went home a few hours after the operation and was back at work in a week.

Three weeks after Dracule's death, Eddie and Chik stood in the audiovisual lab of technician Stanley Grimes, in front of multiple monitors. Stanley had the recovered video surveillance from the Church of the Redeemer cued up. One monitor displayed a schematic of the cathedral. Superimposed on the image was a translucent yellow fan-shaped area extending from the cathedral's entrance to the apse.

"This yellow represents the viewing angle of the surveillance camera," Stanley said. "Everything within the yellow sweep, you see on camera; everything outside, you don't. The cathedral is oriented north-south. A side door to the west opens into the western aisle. The door and the aisle are under a balcony, so they aren't visible to the camera. The confessional, as you can see, is to the east. It appears to be a central box with a door flanked by two kneelers. You can see the door and the kneeler on the right—as you face the confessional—but the left kneeler is just outside the surveillance camera's view. Any questions?"

"Let's see what Father Dracule's last moments were like," Eddie said.

"Strange," Stanley said, clicking the play symbol on the screen. A grainy picture of the apse, the large crucifix, and the confessional appeared.

"Not exactly a high-tech system," Chik said.

"No, it's an old TVL 480i VHS system. The tape runs for twenty-four hours and then rewinds and records over itself. So not only is the image intrinsically of low definition, but the multiple re-recordings also degrade the image." Stanley pointed out details on the screen. "This is the apse and the crucifix of Jesus."

Aren't all crucifixes of Jesus? Eddie thought.

Seconds ticked by on the on-screen clock, the only indication of time passing in the video.

"Ah. Here we go." Stanley hit pause and pointed to a smudge on the right side of the screen. "This is a shadow of an individual cast by the sconces on the north wall of the cathedral on the pews."

He pushed play.

"Now we see the shadow moving up the right side. This is the priest. The shadow stops near the side door on the right side of the cathedral. Again, we can't see the person or the door, just the shadow extending from underneath the balcony."

For a few minutes, there was no movement, as if Dracule was waiting. A swath of light swept from underneath the balcony and remained there for a few minutes.

"That's the west door of the cathedral opening, letting in light from the street. The door will close, and we now see the light disappear. Notice the time stamp: just after midnight."

Stanley pointed to two dark smudges emerging from beneath the balcony. "Now we see two shadows projected across the pews. Another person has entered the cathedral through the west door. The shadows remain in the same place for a few minutes."

"Having a parley," Chik said.

"I guess this is when the money was handed over," Eddie noted.

The two figures appeared on screen, walking in front of the altar toward the confessionals. The video was too grainy and dark to make out facial features, but one man appeared to have a beard.

"Here are the two subjects. Father Dracule is in front, and another individual, four to six inches taller, follows. I call him Bearded Man."

"Got it," Eddie said.

"Notice Bearded Man's dressed in dark clothes to make himself less visible at night and wearing gloves to avoid leaving prints or DNA behind," Stanley said.

"Can you enhance these images?" Eddie asked.

"Unfortunately, not to any meaningful degree. We're stuck with a low-resolution analog signal on tape."

"Okay, go on," Eddie said.

"So, we have the two figures walking across the screen, Dracule and Bearded Man. They stop in front of the apse. Father Dracule turns back to look at Bearded Man, and the two have a short exchange. Dracule enters the confessional, and Bearded Man goes off-screen left, presumably to take a position in the left kneeler. But here's where it gets strange."

"You keep saying that," Eddie said.

"Yeah, just watch." The screen abruptly filled with gray and black lines, jumpy and jagged.

Stanley counted out ten seconds, using the "one-thousand-one, two-thousand-two" technique. When he got to ten, the interference resolved, and an image reappeared.

"Now we see the priest's foot protruding through the confessional door. It doesn't move, indicating he's dead or unconscious at this point. Okay, here comes Bearded Man back on-screen. He pauses a second, steps over the leg, walks back across the apse, and goes off-screen.

"You can see his shadow now and then, the light coming in from the west indicating the west door opening and the unsub exiting the cathedral at this point." Stanley hit the stop button. "That's it."

"Some sort of interference. The Bearded Man didn't stop to help or check on Dracule," Eddie said. "And the priest wasn't found until the morning, so obviously, no calls to 9-1-1."

"He knew the priest was beyond help," Chik said.

"Hey, guys," Stanley interrupted. "That detective shit is interesting and all, but here's the weird part."

Eddie and Chik glanced at each other. "Uh okay," Eddie said.

"So you watched me count out ten seconds, right?"

"Yeah," Chik said.

"That's exactly what the time stamp shows." He rewound the tape.

"See? Here it is at 00:05:12." Stanley fast-forwarded through the static and stopped when the image reappeared.

"Now, it's 00:05:22. Ten seconds. The control track was perfect before and after. No flutter, no tracking issues. The system was working exactly as it should."

"Bearded Man walks off the screen behind the kneeler panel, static. Ten seconds later, he walks back, and the priest has kicked a hole in the door and died," Chik said.

"That's a lot to happen in ten seconds, and Bearded Man doesn't even seem surprised or check on the man," Eddie said.

"Bingo! Winner, winner, chicken dinner!"

"Maybe while they were off to the side, Bearded Man slipped him something," Chik said.

"Could be, but the tox screen came back negative."

"How does that happen in ten seconds?" Stanley asked. "It could be some sort of electronic glitch, but it's like the room went relativistic."

Eddie thought of Daniel's fascination with quantum physics. "Relativity doesn't happen to people or rooms, does it?"

"No, not in any universe I've been to lately."

13

A CALL FROM REBECCA

The Vaugner family celebrated a quiet holiday season. Gertie trimmed the tree with her treasured old-world German wooden ornaments alongside modern decorations. Beneath it, she arranged the nativity scene her grandmother had carried from Bavaria decades ago. The LED outdoor lights, now installed by a landscaping company since Eddie's amputation, went up on December 11 and came down on January 2.

ON CHRISTMAS EVE, Eddie, for the sake of family harmony, accompanied Gertie and Daniel to midnight mass. He spent most the service staring at the repaired confessional thing about time glitches and the weirdness of relativity.

Gertie roasted a goose and served it with potato dumplings and red cabbage. For dessert, she made *Donauwelle*, or Danube Wave Cake, a classic German chocolate cake with a marbled vanilla-chocolate base in a distinctive wavy pattern giving it its name, a layer of sour cherries, buttercream filling, and dark chocolate topping. Daniel ate around the cherries.

· · ·

NEW YEAR'S Eve brought them together for popcorn, hot chocolate, and a movie.

ON THE FIRST Saturday of January, Eddie and Daniel got ready to go cross-country skiing. The days were starting to get longer. Just a few minutes each day for now, but the lengthening would accelerate.

"How's it going, Dad?"

"Almost done."

Daniel lingered in the garage doorway, watching his father make the final adjustments to his prosthesis. The specialized Ossur Re-Flex Shock "skiing foot" clicked into place, ready for the day's adventure, skiing the Tony Knowles Coastal Trail, an eleven-mile multiuse paved trail running along the Cook Inlet on the northeast coast of Anchorage. In the winter, it served as a cross-country ski and fat tire trail; in the summer, it was a jogging, skating, and biking trail. Today, they were doing the entire eleven miles from downtown to Kincaid Park.

"Good to go, Daniel. Go get Gertie."

Eddie finished loading the gear. They took off in two SUVs. Gertie followed them to Kincaid Park, where the trail ended. Eddie parked his car in the chalet's parking lot. Then, he and Daniel hopped into Gertie's car, and she dropped them off downtown at Second Avenue and H Street, where the trail began.

They skied skate-style. The start was flat and easy, and cold air nipped at their faces. It was a clear day. The sun didn't get high during the Anchorage winter, so even though they started shortly before noon, the trail was dappled by long shadows of needled spruce and bare birch trees. About halfway to the trail's end at Kincaid Park, they chugged up a steep hill to Point Woronzof, a bluff just beyond North-South runway 15/33 of the Ted Stevens International Airport. It marked the beginning of the Knik Arm of the Cook Inlet.

They stopped to rest and to take in the view. Across the Cook Inlet and 160 miles to the north, snow-covered Denali, the tallest mountain in North America, dominated the Alaska range. Thirty miles to the northwest, snow-covered Mt. Susitna, otherwise known as Sleeping Lady, lay in a grand white repose. Eddie's gaze drifted to the rocky shoreline just below, where victims of a double homicide had been discovered two years ago.

They continued skating south in a silent single file toward Kincaid Park, starting up one last nine percent grade, thigh-burning rise. As they climbed, Eddie's phone went off.

"Daniel! Hold on a sec, phone!"

The boy didn't slow down. "I'll meet you at the top, Dad!"

Eddie watched Daniel ski up the hill in a pubescent declaration of independence as he touched his earpiece.

"Vaugner."

"Hi, Eddie. This is Becca Raven. I have something interesting about Father Dracule."

"You're working on Saturday?"

"Yep. We're heading out of town this evening for two weeks, so I'm trying to catch up on a few things before I go."

He chided himself for being disappointed at the term "we're."

"Going outside to get warm?" When people left the state, Alaskans called it "going outside."

"Yes, actually. Mayo Clinic, the one in Phoenix. A forensics conference, then some R and R."

"What do you have on the priest?"

"Do you know what a mitochondrion is?"

"A doohickey inside a cell. Something about energy." Eddie knew a little bit about mitochondria. "Just last year, before you started here, we used mtDNA from the mother to identify a badly decomposed body of a missing hiker."

"Good. Do you work on Saturdays? If you can come by my office, I'll explain everything in person, with pictures."

"I'm out at Kincaid, just finishing skiing Tony Knowles with my son. I'll bring him along, if that's okay. He loves this sort of stuff. Being a doctor is on his list of career choices."

"Absolutely. Looking forward to meeting him."

"Can be there in about fifteen, twenty minutes?"

"Perfect. The place is closed, so call me when you get out front, and I'll come down and let you in."

"Roger."

Eddie tapped his earpiece to hang up and skated the hill to the park.

"Over here, Dad!"

Daniel was sitting on a bench by the Chalet with his skis stuck in the snow, holding his water bottle.

Eddie skied to Daniel, unclipped his skis, and sat beside him.

"Who was on the phone?"

"The assistant medical examiner. She wants to show me something. About some mitochondria. You want to come?"

"Sure! Sounds cool."

"You know what those are, I guess."

"Duh, Dad."

"Good. You can explain on the way over."

"Sure."

IN THE CAR, Eddie called Gertie using the speakerphone, telling her they were going to the medical examiner's office and would get home a little later than planned. "Fine," Gertie said, "but don't let Daniel see anything too gross or upsetting."

"Grandma, I love blood and guts!" countered Daniel.

"Oh, you," she said.

Eddie hung up. "Okay, Daniel," he said, "give me the mitochondria-for-dummies talk."

"Okay. As you probably know, we're made up of cells."

"Yes, I know that much."

"Well, about 3.8 billion years ago, when cells first formed, everything inside of them was mixed together. The DNA and all the other stuff. Today, bacteria are still made that way. But in the animal and plant world, the DNA is in a separate compartment called the nucleus. We need nuclei to help protect the DNA from getting mutated by the chemicals and stuff produced inside more complicated cells."

"Interesting," Eddie said.

"Organisms with a nucleus to separate the DNA from the rest of the cell are called eukaryotes, and their cells are called eukaryotic cells, okay?"

"Got it."

"So eukaryotic cells, whether brain cells, muscle cells, cells that line our intestines, or whatever, have two main components: the nucleus, where the DNA is, and the cytoplasm, which makes up the rest of the cell. It's the cytoplasm where all the stuff that the cell does is carried out. The cytoplasm of the brain cell is different from the cytoplasm of the stomach or muscle cell. The muscle cell's cytoplasm is so special there is a special name for it—sarcoplasm. Got it?"

"I'm still with you." Eddie knew when he asked Daniel to explain something, he would not get a terse answer.

"Good. Inside the cytoplasm of each cell, there is a structure responsible for providing energy that the cell needs to work. That structure is the mitochondrion."

"Okay."

"You know our cells need oxygen, right? And without oxygen, they die?

"Uh, yeah, I know that much."

"Well, mitochondria need oxygen to make the energy. If they're deprived of oxygen, the mitochondria can't produce energy, and our cells stop working. When you investigate a death by strangulation, that's what happened to the victim. No oxygen for their mitochondria."

Like Fergus Jones, Eddie recalled, a local hoodlum found tied up, smothered from a plastic bag around his head. "Okay, I think I got it. At least the basics."

"You know the coolest thing about mitochondria?"

"No, son. What's the coolest thing about mitochondria?"

"They think mitochondria were once separate bacteria and over millions of years evolved to be incorporated into our cells. In fact, mitochondria have their own DNA."

"I did know about the mitochondrial DNA. They call it mtDNA. Forensic scientists use mtDNA sometimes."

"Oh, you know to call it mtDNA."

"Yes, but you just gave me a clearer picture of what mtDNA is, so thank you."

"Hey, you're welcome."

Daniel's eyes darted back and forth, and his lips pursed. He was in his visualization mode.

"What is it, Daniel?"

"You believe in evolution, right?"

"I have no problem believing we came from an ape. And frankly, I wonder if we're much of an improvement."

"Dad. Evolution doesn't mean we came from apes. Humans and apes evolved from a common ancestor about thirteen million years ago."

"I see."

They drove for a few minutes in silence.

"You know how a lot of religious people don't believe in evolution?"

"Yep."

"That's just crazy. You know how I think of evolution?"

"How?"

"I think evolution is a sign of God's patience. And when you're God and live for eternity, the billions of years it took for the universe to form and for us to evolve could seem like six days."

Eddie had noticed that since the leukemia, Daniel seemed more drawn to questions about God and meaning. Maybe facing death at eight years old did that to a person, even one who beat it. At least for now.

Mitochondrion

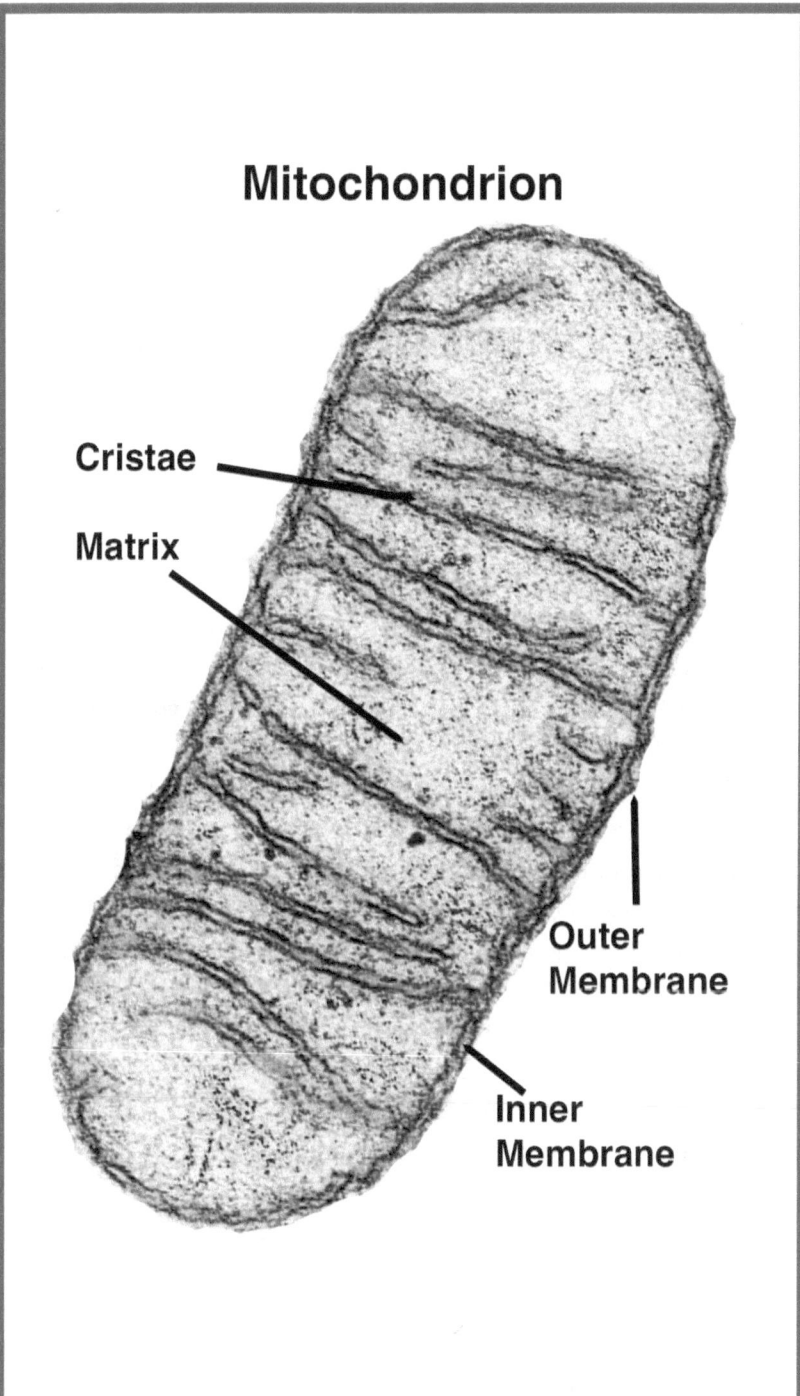

Cristae

Matrix

Outer
Membrane

Inner
Membrane

14

MYSTERIOUS MITOCHONDRIA

Becca met Eddie and Daniel at the main entrance to let them in.

"Dr. Raven, this is my son, Daniel."

"Daniel," she said, holding out her hand. "When your father said you were interested in medicine—"

"You thought I'd be older," interjected Daniel. "We get that a lot."

Daniel met her handshake. "Nice to meet you, Dr. Raven."

She led them to her office on the third floor, which was furnished with light blond Scandinavian-style furniture.

"Let me pull some stuff together, and we'll go to the conference room."

A wall was filled with a bookcase-credenza combo containing photographs, degrees, and certificates. Eddie walked over to one picture, a photo of a younger Rebecca Raven in a graduation cap and gown standing next to a tall, uniformed police officer.

"Who's the cop?" Eddie asked.

"That's my father, Robert Raven. He was Chief of Police in Baltimore, now retired."

"You and your father have alliterative names," Daniel said. Becca smiled at Eddie as if to say, *He knows alliterative?* Eddie shrugged back as if to reply, *That's Daniel.*

"Why yes, the whole family does. It was my mom's idea. Her name is Rose, and my brothers are Richard and Russell."

"Makes monogramming easier," Eddie said.

"Or more confusing," Daniel countered.

Degrees lined the wall: Johns Hopkins for undergrad and medical school, pathology training at Mass General, then a forensic fellowship with the NYC Medical Examiner.

An engraved brass plaque on the wall behind her desk caught his attention. It read *Hic locus est ubi mors gaudet succurrere vitae.*

"Latin?" Eddie asked.

"'This is the place where death delights in helping life.'"

"What you learn from doing autopsies can help the living," Daniel said.

"That's right."

"I can think of a few homicides that benefited the living," cracked Eddie. "Off the record, of course."

"That's a bit noir," Becca laughed, "but true. Let's go into the conference room and talk mitochondria."

She unplugged the power cord and Ethernet cable from a laptop computer on her cluttered desk and led them out of her office to a small conference room a few doors down.

"Have a seat, guys." Becca opened her laptop and pushed a button. It chimed, signaling it was booting up.

"Daniel, your father says you have an interest in medicine."

"Yes, although recently, I've gotten interested in physics. So, I'm trying to decide between medicine or physics."

"Oh, interesting. Why?" she asked.

"'Cause physics is so cool. And it's the basis of everything."

Becca chuckled. "Reminds me of one of my professors in medical school. He was a physics major and even had a PhD in quantum mechanics before going to med school. He was the opposite of you. First, he was into physics, and then into medicine. In one of his classes, he told us almost exactly what you said."

"Really?" Daniel's chest filled with pride.

"Really. He said everything is physics. Anatomy is physics in proper arrangement, physiology is just physics in action, and disease is just physics in trouble."

"Good one," Daniel said.

Becca walked to the wall near the end of the table and pulled down a projection screen.

"You know, Daniel, you don't necessarily need to choose between the two," she said. "Some of the biggest advances in medicine came from physics. Take the MRI, for example—that whole technology exists because physicists figured out how to use magnetic fields to manipulate hydrogen atoms. Now, we use it every day in medicine."

"Yeah, that's true."

"PET scans? That's quantum mechanics in action. Positron emission—basically using antimatter to help us see inside bodies."

"Yep, so cool," Daniel said.

"So, medicine and physics are not mutually exclusive. In fact, many physics-based MD-PhD programs are popping up around the country."

"Something to think about, eh, Daniel?" Eddie said.

"Yeah, actually."

"You know, Daniel, I sort of chose a blended career."

"Really? What two careers?"

"My dad was an old-school, tough guy type. Started as a regular cop, then became a detective like your dad, and then rose to become chief. When I was young, I wanted to be a detective like him. He, uh—let's say he wasn't thrilled with the idea. Thought police work wasn't for girls. Too dangerous."

"That's old-fashioned," Daniel said with his characteristic directness.

"Yeah, Dad was old-school Baltimore Italian."

"Raven?" Daniel queried. "That doesn't sound very Italian."

"My father's family came from Ravenna, in Northern Italy."

"That explains your red hair and green eyes. Northern Italians look different than Southern Italians because of Celtic and Germanic influence."

"Yes, you're right. But Dad came around with time. His assistant chief was a woman. By then, I had finished medical school and become a forensic pathologist. So, in a way, I've wound up in law enforcement helping catch bad guys."

Back at her computer, Becca clicked through a few folder icons until what Eddie assumed was a cell appeared on the screen. "Here we go. Interesting case."

"Great," Eddie said. "More interesting usually means more paperwork."

"Daniel, would you mind running the slideshow?"

His eyes lit up, and he smiled at Eddie. "Sure!"

Eddie smiled back. He appreciated the way Becca took the time to chat with Daniel and gave him a task to make him an active part of the meeting—maternal instincts.

Becca winked at Eddie. She slid the laptop in front of Daniel.

"Good. If I say next, can you hit the right arrow, and if I say back, hit the left arrow?"

"Okay." Daniel smiled at his father.

Becca took a retractable pointer from her lab coat pocket, slid it open, and approached the screen. The cell variegated her fine form.

"Okay, this is a microphotograph taken from a neuron in a human brain. The two arrows point to synaptic release points, where the neurotransmitter is released into a receiving neuron, and these dark round structures inside the oval that look like crinkled potatoes are mitochondria. The synapse is where communication between neurons occurs. This is a very energy-intensive process, so it's no surprise the synaptic terminals of neurons are packed with mitochondria."

The following image appeared to be an extreme enlargement of the mitochondrion. It had the basic shape of a bean. Threadlike structures extended at roughly right angles from the sides toward the center at regular intervals. Dark, granular-looking objects were scattered throughout.

"These threadlike structures running across the mitochondrion are called cristae and are actually a continuous inner membrane folded on itself many times. This is where a sequence of chemical reactions, known as oxidative phosphorylation, occurs. And what is the result of oxidative phosphorylation, Daniel?"

Daniel smiled, pleased to be asked a question. "ATP—adenosine triphosphate."

Becca nodded enthusiastically. "Wow, excellent, Daniel."

Daniel gave himself a fist pump.

Her cell phone went off.

"Dr. Raven... Oh hi, Jim... I thought we were meeting at the restaurant... Okay, I'll be right down." She hung up. "My friend is downstairs. I'll be right back."

Becca left the room, and in a few minutes, she was back with a tall, well-groomed man who looked like he just stepped out of an Eddie Bauer catalog—jeans, a flannel shirt, a down vest, and a corduroy jacket.

"Guys, this is my friend, Jim Brockman."

The man grinned with a lopsided, dominant sort of smile and his eyes were flat and empty. To Eddie, the guy might as well have had a neon sign on his forehead—sociopath. He glanced at Becca, who was smiling at Brockman. *I guess Becca's pathological expertise is limited to dead people, but then again, sociopaths can be real charmers, at least for a while.*

"They have kids coming to autopsies now?"

"It's not an autopsy, sir," Daniel said, not looking up from the laptop. "We're discussing mitochondria."

An awkward silence hung in the air.

Brockman walked over and gave Becca a peck on the cheek, then shot Eddie a look to make sure everyone knew who the alpha male in the room was.

"If you could just give us a few minutes, Jim. Maybe you can wait in my office?"

"Fine."

Brockman walked out of the room with exaggerated casualness. They could hear him whistling down the hallway. Even his whistle had a hostile edge to it, as if he were claiming territory.

"Okay, where were we?" Becca asked, trying to hide her discomfort. It didn't escape Eddie.

"ATP," Daniel said.

A door closed loudly down the hall. Not quite a slam, but definitely a statement. Becca seemed to suppress a flinch.

"ATP. I'm with you."

"Next."

Daniel left-clicked. The following image looked like an empty bag with the inner membrane scattered into bits and pieces. "Wow," he said, "looks like a bomb went off in it."

"Yes, near complete inner membrane disintegration. Shutting down ATP production and causing cell death. This is from Father Dracule's brain."

"You're telling me he died of mitochondrial—what, disintegration?" Eddie asked.

"We call it dissolution, but yes."

"What causes this?"

"That's the thing. I've never seen this before. But it gets even more interesting. This mitochondrial dissolution was found in discrete areas of the brain: in the limbic system, where fear is generated; in the visual cortex, where images are processed; in the auditory cortex, where sound waves are interpreted; in the olfactory bulb, where smell is processed; and in the brainstem, where vital functions like heartbeat and breathing are controlled. Perception, emotions, and vital functions —all affected."

"What does that mean, exactly?" asked Eddie.

"With rapid disruption of the mitochondria in a cell, the first thing to happen is a massive release of ATP. This release would cause a temporary upsurge in activity in these areas of the brain."

"That doesn't sound good," said Daniel.

"Yeah, no, you're probably right. Olfactory, auditory, and visual hallucinations. And a surge in the limbic system could produce extreme fear."

"That could explain the look on his face," said Eddie.

"Yes. Then in the brainstem, this would lead to erratic cardiac activity, swings in blood pressure and... you know."

"You can say death, Dr. Raven," said Daniel. "My mom died. So basically he was getting jump-scared like some twisted horror map or brain hack where all your senses are getting griefed at once."

"Huh," said Becca quizzically.

"Fortnite stuff," Eddie said. "One of those MMOs"

"It's not an MMO, Dad. It's a battle royale game."

"Well whatever it is, if I wanted to cause someone a miserable and frightening, uh, experience without leaving an obvious source, I couldn't come up with a better way of doing it," said Becca.

"And you don't know what caused this. Some sort of poison?"

"His toxicology screen was negative."

"You know, there was static on the tape at the time this was happening. Some sort of radiation?"

"Interesting, but if it were radiation, I would expect we'd see more widespread damage, not in discrete areas."

"So now what?" Eddie asked.

"I've had some mitochondrial experts look at the case. They're also stumped."

"How are you calling this?"

"Right now, I'd have to say natural, but unexplained causes."

"There was an unsub at the scene."

Becca shrugged. "Unsub or not, I couldn't tell you how anyone or anything could have done this. One of the experts wondered if these were random artifacts occurring during the preparation of the specimens."

She walked over to the laptop and closed the top. The projector went dark.

"That was interesting," Daniel said.

"Thanks for coming on a Saturday. Wish I had something more definitive."

Becca picked up her laptop.

"Oh yes, his testosterone level came back normal. For a thirty-year-old, that is, so he was definitely taking testosterone injections."

Outside in the hallway, Becca looked up toward her office.

"Everything okay?" Eddie asked.

"What do you mean?"

He let it go. "Nothing. Have a nice trip."

IN THE CAR, on their way home, Daniel asked, "Hey, Dad, can we do Moose's Tooth for dinner?"

Moose's Tooth Pizza, ranked as one of the best pizzerias in the United States, was a local pizza and brew house named after a rocky peak of the Alaska Range resembling a moose's molar. A throng constantly waited for tables at the entrance, even when it was below freezing outside, evoking the classic Yogi Berra quote: "That place is so crowded, no one goes there anymore."

"If Grandma hasn't started anything," Eddie said. "Call her first, but let's do takeout; I don't want to wait an hour for a table."

After calling Gertie and confirming she had yet to start dinner and would also like some pizza, Daniel used Eddie's phone to order and pay for two mediums: an All-American and a Thai Chicken.

"How much tip, Dad?"

"Fifteen percent."

Daniel volunteered to run in and pick up the pizza when they pulled into the Moose's Tooth. Eddie's text message alert went off. It was from Becca.

This just came in.

There was a PDF file attached. Eddie opened it.

THE CRIMINAL JUSTICE *Information Services (CJIS) Division of the Federal Bureau of Investigation has completed the following fingerprint submission:*

Subject Name: Dracule, Vincent, NMI

SSN: not provided.

Eddie scrolled down to the results.

Result: A search of the fingerprints provided by this individual revealed no matching fingerprints in the NGI database.

He read it through twice. No prints. No record. Vincent Dracule did not forensically exist before his death.

Can a man really ghost himself in this day and age?

15

ASSASSINATION

In their suite at the Hotel Captain Cook, Dana Peplow adjusted her light wool blazer. The weather forecast had predicted scattered snow showers later—typical of mid-January in Anchorage—but the morning was sunny.

Before leaving the room, Dana quickly studied herself in the full-length mirror, trying to ignore how her reflection had changed over the decades. The woman staring back at her retained her delicate wrists and ankles, but her torso and neck had grown increasingly rotund over the years. It was the stress, she told herself. And the punishing schedule. She touched the string of pearls Jack had given her on their thirtieth anniversary, drawing comfort from their familiar smoothness.

"You look great, dear," Jack said, coming up behind her. He put a hand on her shoulder and pecked her on the cheek. His reflection smiled at hers, his silver hair catching the morning light streaming through the windows. Despite her gains, he had kept in shape, and his light hazel eyes were just as bright and warm as they'd been on the day they first met.

"Oh, stop," Dana replied, but she reached up and squeezed his hand.

. . .

ON THEIR WAY down the elevator, Dana's phone chimed. She pulled it out of the pocket of her wool and mohair coat. "It's Junior."

She opened her phone, and a smile beamed from her face. "He wrote, 'Wish Dad luck on his lecture today.'"

"Tell him thank you," Jack said.

They got off the elevator and walked through the lobby. As they approached the main entrance of the hotel on Fourth Street, a smiling young doorman in a red greatcoat greeted them.

"Peplows?" he asked.

"That's us," Jack said, pausing to zip his down coat.

"Your car is here."

The doorman led the way through the revolving door into the driveway. Their car was a black GMC Denali. A man in a chauffeur's cap stood outside the driver's door and greeted the Peplows with a smile and a wave.

A young man wearing a hoodie approached them. He held a book in his hand. The front of the hoodie displayed a church steeple and Capitol dome separated by a wall, with the slogan "Keep This Wall!" on the chest.

Something about him made Dana uneasy.

His face seemed fixed into an eager fan's smile. His eyes briefly flicked toward the black 1995 Chevy Van across from the hotel's entrance on the corner of Fourth Avenue and I Street. It had a clear view of the entrance. It had a missing rear panel window, but Dana couldn't make out any details inside the van. "Mr. Peplow, your work has really challenged my thinking. Would you sign this?"

"Of course." Peplow smiled, oblivious. "And your name is?"

"Thomas, sir."

Dana kept glancing back and forth between Thomas and the van.

"Where are you from? I detect a slight accent."

"Born in Moscow, but came to America when I was six."

Dana heard the first shot as a crack that echoed off the downtown buildings as her husband's head exploded violently.

She felt warm droplets splatter across her face.

She startled and stumbled backward.

She didn't hear the second shot, but in the seconds it took for her to realize what had happened, she felt a punch between her ribs, then a searing pain.

Oh my god, they're killing us!

She fell to the ground, and everything went dark.

THOMAS SAW the woman get hit by the second shot as she pivoted to break her fall.

She collapsed to the ground.

Thomas snatched up the blood-spattered book, and then walked quickly toward Fourth Avenue, where the van would circle around to pick him up. He turned once more to see chaos erupting behind him.

The doorman was now crouched behind a concrete planter, frantically tapping on his phone.

Tourists scattered, their shouts a distant background noise to Thomas's focused mind.

The Peplow woman lay on the ground, eyes closed, gasping for air. The second shot had not yet killed her.

The driver of the Suburban yelled out, "Fuck this shit!" and scurried into his car before speeding away.

The Chevy van had rounded the block and was heading east on 4th Avenue. It stopped just long enough for Thomas to jump in through the side door.

"Excellent shooting!" Thomas said in Russian to the man in the back, dressed entirely in black, cradling a custom 6.5 Grendel sniper rifle with a scope and suppressor.

The shooter frowned. "I'm not sure about the woman," he replied, also in Russian. "She fell just as I fired the second shot."

Thomas waved away his concern. "The man was the critical target. We were paid for two shots. No guarantees."

16

SAVING A LIFE

"Status One Trauma is here!" blared over the local ER intercom.

Jason Defner, hearing the alert, came out of a cubicle to see two emergency medical technicians crash through the doors leading from the ambulance bay into the ER, wheeling an obese woman. She appeared to be in shock, and her white blouse was stained with blood. Her overcoat had been cut away, and an IV had been started in the hollow of her right elbow—the side opposite the gunshot wound in her left chest.

A nurse leaped out from behind the nurses' station and ran alongside the gurney. "Trauma Bay One, guys," she said.

The EMT at the head of the gurney ventilated the patient with an Ambu bag. The EMT at the foot of the stretcher called out, "Gunshot wound, left chest, systolic pressure 90, no breath sounds on the left side. We have a 14-gauge IV in the left antecubital fossa running lactated Ringer's."

Two other physicians and nurses joined him.

"Okay, people, you know the drill!" Defner shouted. "A-B-C. Airway, breathing, circulation. Ransom, get her intubated; let's get a femoral line in her, run lactated Ringer's, call for six units of uncross-matched blood, and get the surgeon on call down here."

This was Defner's métier. Action. Blood and guts. His jaw set in the same rigid line he'd worn since his Navy days as he hustled toward Trauma Bay One. He knew the protocols, and he was ready to strut his stuff.

"Dr. Lange has been called," a clerk called out.

Defner bristled at the name but kept focused as the trauma bay buzzed with the organized chaos of saving a life. The paramedic continued with his brief rundown. "She was getting into a limousine at the Hotel Captain Cook when shots were fired. One fatality at the scene."

Ransom intubated her, and a nurse cut away the rest of her clothes.

Defner listened to the lungs and heard no breathing sounds on the left side, an indication of a collapsed lung, bleeding into the chest cavity, or both. He would need to insert a tube through the chest to re-expand the lung or evacuate the blood.

"Absent breath sounds on the left side. Hemothorax. Get me a chest tube tray and a 36 French chest tube."

Another physician started a large-bore triple-lumen IV catheter in her right femoral vein, and fluids were hung and run wide open. A nurse inserted a Foley catheter into her bladder. Another nurse placed heart monitor leads on the upper aspect of both sides of her chest near the shoulders. "Sinus rhythm."

A nurse palpated the left femoral artery. "She's got a femoral pulse." Defner knew a palpable femoral pulse meant her blood pressure was at least seventy.

"Start the level one infuser," he ordered.

An aide rolled a chest tube tray next to the patient. A nurse opened it by peeling back the blue cover. Defner snapped on gloves, smeared iodine solution on the patient's left chest, and draped it off.

A nurse was taking blood pressure. She put two fingers of one hand on the woman's brachial artery pulse point and, with the other hand, inflated the blood pressure cuff, then let the air out until she could feel the pulse. "Pressure is eighty palp."

Defner called out, "Let's go, guys. Get some blood into her. Massive transfusion protocol!"

A nurse picked up a red phone with a direct line to the blood bank. "I need four units of uncrossed O-negative blood per trauma massive transfusion protocol."

Defner made a two-inch incision into the left side of her chest, then grabbed a large clamp off the chest tube tray. He inserted it into her chest cavity and spread the clamp open. Blood poured out from the wound. He grabbed the chest tube, placed it through the incision, and tried to put it through the woman's massive chest. Despite numerous attempts, he couldn't slide the tube into her chest.

The nurse taking the blood pressure yelled out, "Sixty palp!" Her voice was edged with panic. They were losing the patient.

The muscles in Defner's tattooed forearms tensed with each failed attempt to insert the chest tube. His face was becoming increasingly flushed, and he was growing angry with the patient.

"Come on, lady, lose some weight, will ya?"

He heard a voice behind him. "Hey, Defner, let me in there."

Defner continued his struggle to slide the tube in. "I got this, Lange."

The nurse who was palpating the femoral pulse cried out, "I lost her pulse!"

Another one called out, "She's flatlined!"

Defner felt a hand grab the back of his scrub suit and pull him back from the patient. Despite his size, Lange jerked him back like he was a child.

GRAYSON STEPPED UP, reached for the scalpel on the chest tube tray, and made a large gash on the left side of the patient's chest down to the ribs in one quick motion.

He heard Defner hiss, "Damn you, Lange."

Grayson ignored him and moved fast. With scissors, he cut through the muscles between the ribs to enter the chest cavity. Blood accumulating in the chest cavity from the torn vessels now poured out onto the side of the stretcher and the floor. He placed a rib spreader and ratcheted the rib cage open. He reached his right hand through the opening and into the chest cavity.

"It's the hilum—lacerated the pulmonary artery. And the lung is mush."

Grayson took a large clamp from the tray, inserted it into the chest, and, by feel, clamped the hilum, the structure through which the major blood vessels and bronchial tubes leave the mediastinum and enter the chest cavity.

An anesthesiologist showed up and took over ventilating the patient.

"I've got the hilum clamped," Grayson said. "You're ventilating only one lung."

"Got it, Grayson," the anesthesiologist said.

"Keep running fluid; give her an amp of epinephrine."

Grayson put flat hands on the front and back of Dana Peplow's heart and started compressing the heart at a rate of about 100 beats a minute. The anesthesiologist cracked open a preloaded syringe of epinephrine and pushed it through an IV.

As he was performing cardiac massage, Grayson reflected on how lucky she was. For a bullet to go through the left hilum and not hit the heart, causing instant death, was a one-in-a-million occurrence.

After a minute, the heart monitor started to beep. Grayson felt Dana's heart begin to beat. Weakly and slowly at first, but soon more vigorously and rapidly.

"Good," Grayson said. "I'm getting cardiac activity."

A nurse called out, "I got a femoral pulse!"

"Pressure 70 palp!" another called.

Satisfied with the heart action, Grayson took his hands out of her chest. The handle of the hilar clamp bounced up and down with each heartbeat.

"Keep the fluid going, and get some fresh blood up here."

Grayson snapped off his gloves, went to the phone, and dialed the operating room's front desk.

"Hi Sally, this is Grayson Lange. We're coming over now for the GSW."

The OR was on full alert and was expecting the call.

"Gunshot wound left chest. I'll need a thoracotomy tray for a pneumonectomy. Thanks."

Grayson hung up. "Okay, let's get her to the OR." The team packed the stretcher, grabbed IV poles, covered the patient, and headed for the OR.

He walked behind the gurney. Defner caught up to him, fists clenched at his sides, and got in his face. "This isn't over, Lange."

Still walking, Grayson turned and smirked back at the doctor like he was talking to a petulant child. "Fucking Christ, Defner, get over yourself."

DEFNER WATCHED Lange leave the ER with the patient, further enraged by the man's blasphemy.

You fucking son of a bitch, Defner thought to himself. *The one who blasphemes against the Holy Spirit will not be forgiven.*

Humiliation, resentment, and anger churned his guts. Being manhandled in front of the ER staff was bad enough, but even worse, Lange had been right. The chest tube would have taken too long and might not have worked at all. Lange had read the situation instantly and acted decisively, while Defner had been a slave to protocol, wasting precious seconds.

Lange became the hero, and Defner had been demoted to a meddling obstructionist to be pushed aside.

He stood there, fuming—he was an ex-Navy combat medic, a Devil Doc attached to the Marines no less, easily pushed aside by this surgeon whose lights he could punch out.

No, this is definitely not over.

IN THE OPERATING ROOM, the patient was placed right-side down. The left side of her chest was prepped and draped as Grayson tied on a surgical mask, quickly scrubbed, and donned a sterile gown and gloves.

As he extended the incision made in the ER around the entire side of the chest using a scalpel and electrocautery, the anesthesiologist asked, "Any music requests?"

"How about some Journey, 'Don't Stop Believin'?" Lange said.

"You got it."

The piano intro filled the room, setting a hopeful and energetic feeling, and then Steve Perry's voice singing about a small-town girl joined in.

"Great sound," Grayson said as he operated. "What system are you using?"

"KEF LSX IIs powered wireless speakers playing through my iPhone."

"I love you guys. It's like you did fellowships at the Columbia School of Broadcasting."

As the music played, Grayson operated coolly and efficiently. He knew he could save this patient's life. He had been here before—not only as a surgeon but years ago as a child, and had the scars to prove it. Just as he had been saved from the brink of death, he would save her.

It would be up to him to set the mood. There would be no emotional outbursts, no wasted movements. They would bask in his confidence, his kindness, and, most importantly, his surgical skill and clinical judgment. They would all know they were on a winning team. This would sharpen their own skills and enhance their performances. He would lead by example.

Once the incision was complete, he opened the chest cavity further with a rib spreader and inspected the damage. Dana Peplow had suffered a Grade V pulmonary injury—hilar vessel disruption. In addition, the lung was severely bruised from the shock wave of the high-velocity round. The only option was damage control—remove the entire lung and get the patient off the table. Grayson dissected connective tissue away from the hilum, took a TA-55 stapler, and positioned it just behind the clamp he had placed in the ER. He took a scalpel and cut through the hilum between the clamp and the staple line. and positioned it just behind the clamp he had placed in the ER. He took a scalpel and cut through the hilum between the clamp and the staple line. And with that, by the time Neal Schon broke into his wailing guitar solo, the lung was free. Grayson lifted it out of Dana Peplow's chest and put it in a stainless-steel basin.

"How's she doing?"

"Holding her own. BP 90, peak airway pressure 35, and PaO2 of 90. Making urine."

"Not too shabby. We're closing. Any information on this patient?"

The circulating nurse said, "The patient's name is Dana Peplow, visiting from Maryland. Her husband was killed at the scene. I have some phone numbers."

"Wheel in the Sky" queued up.

I hope the patient holds on a little longer, thought Grayson.

"You need a chest tube, Doc?" the scrub tech asked.

"No chest tube in a total pneumonectomy."

It took him an hour to save Dana Peplow's life skin to skin.

After Grayson applied the last skin staple to the chest incision, he asked the anesthesiologist, "What's her core temperature?"

"Thirty-five degrees," the anesthesiologist answered, using the Centigrade scale.

"Let's get some warm blankets on her and move her upstairs." The patient was at a higher risk of bleeding or death if her temperature dropped below 34 degrees centigrade.

Grayson snapped off his gloves and took off his surgical gown. "Thanks, everyone. Good job."

The anesthesiologist, OR nurse, and several aides transferred the patient from the OR table onto her ICU bed and headed up to the ICU.

The crew was buoyant.

They had all been a part of saving a life. In so many cases like these, the patient wound up dead, and the monitor and ventilator got turned off, leaving only somber murmurs around an expired patient covered with a sheet, awaiting a pickup by the medical examiner's office.

But tonight, Grayson Lange had gotten his patient through the operation. She still had other battles ahead of her—recovery in the ICU and adapting to life with one lung.

But tonight, they got one back.

Tonight the ventilator was still on. Dana Peplow's chest rose and fell with each life-sustaining breath, and the monitor beeped steadily.

The circulating nurse hung up the phone and announced the victory in simple terms. "She'll be going to bed seven, Doc."

17

A BLACK EYE

Eddie pulled up to the police barricade on Fourth Avenue, where cruisers blocked access to the Hotel Captain Cook. The oblique spring sun harshly illuminated every detail of the crime scene. He parked next to the driveway, where Chik waited with six patrolmen who were securing the perimeter. The CSI team was setting up their equipment.

Jack Peplow's body lay sprawled across the boundary between sidewalk and driveway, covered with a tarp. Eddie lifted up one corner and saw the destruction of his skull. It told Eddie everything he needed to know about the shooter's skill and intent.

"This was an assassination, Eddie," Chik said.

"Looks to be," he replied, studying the scene. The hotel towers blocked much of the view; the only line of sight was from the corner of 4th Avenue and I Street.

Eddie waved a patrolman over. "Hendricks, take Hopkins and start surveying for all surveillance videos within a four-block radius."

"On it," Hendricks said.

Chik let out a sigh. "Reminds me of JFK's head in that Zapruder film."

"Any witnesses?" Eddie asked.

"The doorman was standing right next to the victim when he was shot," a patrolman said. "He's in the lobby, just inside the double doors."

Eddie and Chik walked into the lobby. The doorman was easy to spot; he hadn't succeeded in wiping all the blood off his face, neck, and ears. His scarlet double-breasted overcoat couldn't quite conceal the blood spatter. Two men in suits stood next to him, along with a patrolman, talking to him and taking notes.

"Hi, Detectives," the patrolman said as Eddie approached. He folded his notepad and put it in his shirt pocket. "This is Fredrico. He was standing next to the vic when the shooting went down."

Before Eddie could ask Fredrico anything, one of the suits spoke. "Detective, I'm Willard Loonis, the general manager, and this is Rob Worsten, head of security."

They shook hands with Eddie and Chik. Fredrico was Hispanic-looking, thin, his hair cut short. He looked shaken. Ex-military, Eddie guessed.

"Hi, Fredrico, I'm Detective Vaugner. This is my partner, Detective Uttaq. How are you holding up?"

Fredrico looked up at him. "I did two tours in Iraq. This is as bad as anything I saw there, man."

No accent. American-born.

"Can you describe what happened, as best you can?"

"Sure. The guest and his wife came out the door. I greeted them and confirmed that they were Mr. and Mrs. Peplow. Just as I opened the back door to the Denali, a kid came up, handed Dr. Peplow a book, and asked for his autograph. Dr. Peplow took out a pen from his coat pocket, and as he was signing the book, I heard a loud crack, and his head exploded at the same time. I was instantly splattered with blood and tissue. I ducked—it was pure reflex. Then I heard another crack and a muffled thunk. I guess that's when the bullet hit the Mrs. I have no clue where the shots came from."

Hearing the head burst and the shot at the same time. Suppressed rifle, firing supersonic rounds, Eddie thought. Means Fredrico only heard the bullet's shock wave and the impact, not the muzzle blast. No way anyone could tell where the shot came from.

"Then what?"

"I hit the ground, called 911, and asked for the police and an ambulance. Dr. Peplow was dead, but the wife was breathing, and there was some blood staining on her left chest. I took out my handkerchief and tried to apply pressure. The ambulance came in about seven minutes, scooped her up, and took her to the hospital. They were going to take her to Prov."

"The kid who wanted the autograph—what did he look like? What was he wearing?"

"He was a little shorter than me, so I figure about five eight or nine. He was wearing a Mariners baseball cap and aviator-style sunglasses. He had on a white hoodie with a drawing of a brick wall. On one side of the wall was a cross, and on the other side was the Congress building, I think, and just below the drawing was the phrase, 'Keep them separated,' with an exclamation mark. Or something like that."

"Did you see what happened to him, where he went after the victims were hit?"

"I think he picked up the book and ran up the driveway."

"He didn't stop to help?" Chik asked.

"No, I'm sure the only thing he was thinking about was getting the fuck out of there. Same thing with the limo driver."

"Do you think you could recognize him if you saw him again?"

"I'm not sure, you know, with the hat and shades. Jesus, this has triggered a flashback."

"I'm sorry." Eddie pulled out his card and handed it to him. "Detective Uttaq will take you to headquarters and get a full statement from you."

"Can I go home first and take a shower?"

"We'd prefer to get everything down while it's still fresh." Eddie knew that witnesses' brains began to alter memories almost immediately after traumatic events. Every passing hour increased the risk of memory contamination, whether from internal processing or external influences like news reports or conversations with others.

Eddie signaled Loonis over. "Yes, Detective?" "Mr. Loonis, do you have another coat Fredrico can wear? We'll keep this one for evidence." "I believe so. If not, we have a few coats in lost and found we could lend him."

"Fredrico, if you could go over there and hand it to one of the CSI people, that would be great." "Let's get you a new coat and head down to headquarters," Chik said.

As they walked away, Eddie heard Chik tell the doorman, "Iraq, huh? I served in Desert Storm—know what you mean about seeing some shit, brother…"

Eddie turned to the head of security. "Mr. Worsten, I'd like you to secure the hotel surveillance video twenty-four hours before and twelve hours after this incident."

"No problem."

"Mr. Loonis, what can you tell me about the Peplows?"

"Jack and Dana Peplow, from Bethesda, Maryland. The University is paying for their rooms. I believe he was giving a talk. Other than that, I couldn't say."

Back outside, Eddie noted the CSI team was in full investigation mode. They were taking pictures of the body, measuring, photographing and swabbing the blood spatter. Some were assessing angles, others searching for bullet fragments.

The medical examiner's van pulled up next to the crime scene. Two attendants exited, opened the rear doors, and pulled out a stretcher. Right behind them, Rebecca Raven pulled up in her BMW SUV.

This time, she was dressed in a more casual Alaskan mode: ankle boots, khaki slacks, a flannel shirt, a down vest, and a Canada Goose long parka. She walked over to the van and pulled out a shoe covers. She came right up to Eddie. "Hi, Eddie."

"Hi, Becca."

As she slipped on the shoe covers, he noticed a bruise under her left eye and blood staining the white of it. He gestured toward it.

"What happened to your eye?"

"Took a spill coming down Flattop, slipped on some loose dirt." Eddie had hiked the popular 1,350-foot peak in East Anchorage many times, but not since his amputation.

He looked at her face. No accompanying abrasions on the nose or cheek, as one would expect from a fall on a rocky mountain trail. Someone had hit her, and he was pretty sure he knew who.

She smiled weakly, glanced at Eddie, then quickly looked away, her face stiffening. He could tell she knew he saw through her bullshit.

"Are you still seeing Brockman?"

Becca frowned. "Eddie. Not here, not now."

Eddie felt his face redden as she walked over to Peplow's body to get a closer look at the head. "Lot of energy transfer, judging from the destruction." She stood up, walked over to the two medical examiner attendants, and exchanged a few words.

Mayor Rotig and Howard Dell, the police chief, showed up.

"Who is leading this investigation?" the mayor asked.

Eddie, who had been once again studying Becca's injuries, turned and said, "I am."

"Mayor, this is Detective Eddie Vaugner, one of our top cops," Dell said.

"Well, what do we know so far?" Rotig asked.

"It was a well-executed crime," he said, "using a high-powered rifle. Other than that, not much."

The mayor's eyes widened. "Can we get the FBI involved?"

"I'd like to keep primary jurisdiction local if we can, at least in these early stages."

"Why?"

"Because right now, speed is critical. Once they're formally brought in, everything slows down. Right now, we need to move fast."

"He's got a point," the chief said. "We'll coordinate with the FBI as needed on specific aspects—money trails, interstate connections, their behavioral analysis resources. But let's not turn this into a federal case unless we have to."

"As long as we're not missing anything," Rotig said. "This is already a black eye on the city. I don't want headlines about us refusing federal help."

"We're not refusing help," Eddie said. "We're being strategic about how we use it."

Dell called over to Becca, who was heading toward the van. "Dr. Raven, when will you post this?"

"Nine tomorrow morning."

"You can't do it tonight?"

"My technician isn't available. And trust me, you want this done by the book." She threw the shoe covers into the van.

"We'll be there," the mayor said. "I'm announcing a presser for tomorrow at eleven. So, will you be able to give me the preliminary findings by then?"

"I can give them to you right now. The victim got his brains blown out. I'll have better language tomorrow, but I don't think the facts will be much different."

Rotig smiled. "Fair enough."

Rotig turned to walk back to his car. Chief Dell accompanied him.

"Chief, I want an update every week and on any significant developments. I am considering setting up a task force, but for now, I'll see how you guys fare in your investigation."

"See you tomorrow, then?" Becca said, avoiding eye contact with Eddie.

"Of course."

She walked back to her car. To Eddie, she seemed more guarded, as if a barrier had been thrown up.

Had he blown things with Becca? Not that there was anything to blow.

18

THE OLD STOMPING GROUNDS

At the Providence Alaska Medical Center, Eddie punched the intercom at the ICU door.

"Can I help you?" a woman's voice asked.

"Yes. I'm Detective Vaugner, with APD homicide. I'm here to see about Dana Peplow."

The door buzzed. Eddie pulled it open and walked in.

He held up his badge for a plump clerk sitting at the desk.

"Yes, Mr. Vaugner. I remember you," she said.

This was his first time in the ICU since the car accident, when he had been a patient for three days.

"She's in Seven, just around the corner. Just came up from the OR."

Eddie thanked her.

"You look great! How is everything?" she asked.

"I'm good."

"How's that little boy of yours? He's doing okay, I hope."

Not sure if she was referring to the loss of his mother or the bout with leukemia, Eddie answered, "Yes, he's doing fine. Thanks for asking."

He walked through the unit with mixed emotions. He was grateful for the care he'd gotten, but Anne had never had the chance to struggle for her life. No ICU vigil for her, no chance for goodbye. From the accident scene to the ME's office. Do not pass Go. He still hadn't read the forensics report.

The beds, each in a separate cubicle, lined the periphery of the ICU. The steady beeping of monitors and hiss of respirators made a cacophony of life hanging in the balance, held above the precipice by technology.

Nurses adjusted IVs and tapped at computer terminals.

Eddie passed Cubicle 3, his old bed. Besides the leg injury, he'd suffered five fractured ribs and a pulmonary contusion, enough to need an epidural catheter and constant monitoring for respiratory failure. He didn't recognize any of the nurses. Of course, it had been five years, and he'd been doped up on narcotics. Most of his ICU stay was a broken-up dream.

Dana Peplow's cubicle was brightly lit, and several nurses were scurrying around. A respiratory therapist was setting up a ventilator. A doctor near the head of the bed—probably an anesthesiologist—called out an order while squeezing the Ambu bag connected to her endotracheal tube.

"Let's start with a tidal volume of, let's see, five milliliters per kilogram, so let's make it four hundred, rate of twelve, PEEP of five, with pressure control."

"Got it," the respiratory therapist said, punching in some parameters on the ventilator.

A nurse looked over at him.

"Can I help you?"

"I'm Detective Vaugner, APD homicide. How's Dana Peplow doing?"

The nurse's eyes lit up. "Oh my god. Detective Vaugner. I'm Rita! You were my patient for two days! I didn't recognize you. You look great!"

She glanced down to his right leg and looked back up.

"Thanks," Eddie said. "I don't remember much from those days. I was in la-la land for most of it."

"Not many patients do, which is a merciful thing." She gestured toward her patient. "I can tell you that Mrs. Peplow is stable at the moment. Dr. Lange, her surgeon, should be up here soon."

Eddie stood by and watched the team settle the patient. The heart monitor showed a steady heartbeat, and the blood pressure monitor read 110/70 mmHg. Eventually, he might have a witness.

"And here comes Dr. Lange, now."

Passing Eddie, Lange came into the cubicle and stood at the foot of the bed. He held a scrap of paper in his hand.

"How's she doing?"

Eddie studied the vertical scar starting at the doctor's right cheek, running down the right side of his neck, and into the V of his scrub suit. It appeared to be a scar from a blade attack. Most knife wounds were on the left side of the body, since most people were right-handed. So, a left-handed assailant?

"Stable vital signs," the anesthesiologist responded. "She's oxygenating well, good lung compliance. A little cold, though—34.2."

Eddie noticed the number 2316 tattooed on the underside of Lange's left forearm in a simple sans-serif type. He wondered what it meant and could only come up with John 3:16.

"Sounds good. Let's send an ABG, CBC, basic metabolic panel, and full coags. And she's cold as hell, so get a Bair Hugger on her and get her warmed up."

"Last I checked," Rita joked, "hell's not very cold."

Lange smiled. "You got me there. And a portable chest X-ray."

Eddie noted the banter was easy, good-natured. Clearly, Lange was respected and had earned the confidence of those who cared for his patients.

Rita began unfolding what appeared to be a large paper and plastic blanket. She placed it over Dana Peplow and connected a four-inch-diameter hose to it. Next to the bed, she flipped a switch on a unit that reminded Eddie of a little R2-D2. It started a gentle hum, and air rushed into the blanket, inflating it and giving it the appearance of an air mattress.

Lange turned to Eddie. "You were the detective in the ER—with Mr. Uttaq and the Shaman."

"That's me. Detective Vaugner."

The doctor gestured toward the bed. "Here's what I presume you want to know. What appears to be a high-velocity bullet entered the chest and blew out the left hilum, which contains the main blood vessels and bronchi leading to the lung. Not fixable, so I had to remove the lung. It's a minor miracle her heart or aorta wasn't hit. Assuming no complications, I expect her to be on the ventilator for at least a day or two, in the ICU for about four days. Seven to ten days in the hospital, then either go home or to a rehab center, depending on how she's doing. Well, not home to Maryland, she won't be able to fly for four to six weeks. She'll be up to talking to you in about a week."

"Did she say anything when she came in?"

"No, she was unconscious and in shock when she arrived, and she flatlined in the ER. I had to crack her chest and give her internal cardiac massage to get her back."

"Do you know if there are any family members around?"

"No, the Peplows are visiting from Bethesda, Maryland." Lange handed Eddie the scrap of paper he was holding. "I filled them in on Mrs. Peplow's condition. This is the number of the oldest son, Jack Peplow Jr., who will be the point person for the family. He wanted you to call them as soon as possible. It's past midnight in Bethesda, but they're probably not getting much sleep anyway."

"Strong work, Doctor." Maybe Inuksuk was right about Lange having a gift, Eddie thought.

"Thanks, but I'm just doing what I was trained to do."

19

THE SUSPECT

Eddie found a family counseling room just off the ICU. He took out his work phone and dialed the Peplows' phone number.

A man answered, "Hello?"

"Is this Jack Peplow, Jr.?"

"Yes, who is this?"

"Mr. Peplow, this is Detective Edward Vaugner; I'm with Anchorage Homicide."

"Yes, Detective, thank you for calling. I'm here with my sister, Helen, and my wife, Susan. Would you mind if I put you on speaker-phone so they can participate?"

"Absolutely. And this call is being recorded."

"Hi, Detective, this is Susan," a woman with a husky voice said.

"And this is Helen, Jack's sister."

"First, my condolences about Mr. Peplow," Eddie said. "I can assure you we'll do everything we can to catch his killer or killers. I've just been in the ICU. Mrs. Peplow seems to be holding her own."

"Yes, we just talked with Dr. Lange," Helen said.

"Can you tell me anything to help me in this case?"

"Yes," Jack Jr. said. "Revus Roche and the America Salvation Church. They did this."

Eddie took out his notepad. "Why do you suspect Revus Roche?"

"Are you familiar with the Gage Society?"

He shook his head out of habit even as he spoke into the phone. "No."

"It's an organization founded by my father supporting the separation of church and state. He was up there to lecture on this matter and was also going to consult with the U.S. attorney's office on possible litigation against Roche's church."

"Plus, have you been to his church?" Susan said. "I've seen videos. It's like a camp with disgruntled creepos prowling around with assault rifles."

Jack Jr. took back over. "Revus' security operation is more like a paramilitary force. No doubt they have snipers capable of carrying out an assassination like this."

"And who else in Anchorage would want my father dead?" Helen asked.

"Had your father ever interacted with Roche? Exchanged emails? Or made any public statements against him or the America Salvation Church?"

"He received an invitation to debate Pastor Roche at the America Salvation Church on what the Constitution really says about the separation of church and state while he was in Anchorage, but he declined. He decided long ago that the radical clergy were not interested in honest debates; they just wanted to present him as a threat to 'freedom of religion' to drive donations to their churches. I'm sure Dad would have had an aide send a polite letter saying he had other commitments."

Eddie wrote this down in his notebook. Roche and the America Salvation Church were obvious suspects. But the obvious ones often ended up being the ones railroaded into wrongful convictions. He had to keep an open mind.

"Do you know if he had received any death threats?"

"Dad had been receiving death threats since founding the Gage Society," Jack said. "I'm sure they have them on file somewhere."

"All from fine Christian folk like those who follow Roche," Helen added.

"Any threats from the America Salvation Church or any of its members you know of?"

"I'm not aware of any," Jack said. "Not that they would telegraph their intent."

"Anything else anyone wants to tell me?"

"Yes," Jack said. "Helen and I have a flight to Anchorage tomorrow. And let me repeat myself: Revus Roche. He's my dad's killer, Detective. I know it."

20

THE ANGRY DOCTOR

Defner spent the rest of his shift seething. After being pulled away from his patient by Lange and humiliated in public, it was all he could do not to snap at the stupid welfare mothers bringing in their kids because of a cold, the idiot who came to have back pain he had been suffering with for eight years get checked out, and the other "victims" of stupid Godless living.

His shift was finally over, and the route from the ER to the locker room took him past the operating rooms. He approached the clerk sitting at the front desk.

"How did the gunshot wound Lange operated on do?" he asked.

"She went up to the ICU about two hours ago."

Fuck. Lange had saved the patient.

He went to the changing room and opened his locker door. Taped to the inside was a full-page ad for the America Salvation Church, featuring a photograph of the façade of the church and a studio portrait of Reverend Roche. Below that, a Devil Docs Corpsman bumper sticker. He'd placed them there to remind himself that the military had made him a man and the Church had saved his soul.

Setting his phone and wallet on the shelf, he took off his scrub suit and threw it in a hamper. He got a view of himself in a wall mirror.

Thirty-eight years old, still cut and buffed with a thirty-four-inch waist, eighteen-inch biceps, a six-pack, and well-defined pecs. He loved his tattoos.

After four years as a Navy Hospital Corpsman, serving as a Devil Doc with the Marines, Defner had made it through medical school and a residency in emergency medicine despite a cocaine and oxycodone habit he'd picked up after separation.

It had started with the cocaine. He supposed he missed the "high" of serving at Landstuhl Regional Medical Center, treating the combat wounded. He moved on to oxy to take the edge off when coming down from coke.

After landing an ER job in Anchorage, he became involved in the America Salvation Church movement when a colleague recommended the Clean for Christ drug rehab program. After getting off oxy and hearing Revus Roche speak about the battle to save America from the atheistic liberal traitors, he was all in. As the saying went, he used to be hooked on oxy; now he was hooked on Jesus.

He approached his red Corvette 3LT, with the Z51 performance package, parked in a slot marked "ER Physicians Only." He'd chosen red because it represented the blood of Christ. His vanity plates read JC4USA.

Defner curled his tall frame into it and started it up, loving the throaty sound of the 6.2-liter engine. He powered up the Bose Performance sound system connected to his phone. It blasted out a bass-perfused, power-chorded rhythm, and the staccato-attacking lead guitar of a heavy metal Christian anthem, "Clear and Present Danger":

We must battle for the kingdom! Satan's on his way.
He's a clear and present danger. Get ready for the day.
We must fight against temptation.
We must resist his charms.
He's a clear and present danger. And we must take up arms!

Defner reached into the back seat, grabbed his black leather doctor's bag, opened it, and pulled out his otoscope, which he hadn't used since medical school. Keeping his hands low, he unscrewed the bottom cap where the batteries would usually go and pulled out a small pill bottle and a small spoon. He inserted the spoon into the vial. Looking around to make sure no one was around, he brought some white powder to his nose, sniffed, let out an "Ahh," and repeated it in the other nostril.

He reconcealed the cocaine in the otoscope and put it back in the bag. Yes, he had kicked the oxy habit. And really, he'd kicked the cocaine habit too, since he didn't use it every day, just when tired or stressed. Michael Jackson might have had his "Jesus Juice"—Defner had his "Christ Coke." Besides, sometimes he needed the extra boost.

His life was a perfect balance of devotion, the indulgence of frailty, and service to Christ. After all, Christ did not demand perfection, only acceptance as the Savior. So, a little cocaine, some pussy now and then —he luxuriated in his weaknesses, knowing he was saved.

He was headed out to Club 149, a Christian nightclub, to take out his frustrations on the dance floor, maybe even get lucky with a chick who was like him, saved but not perfect, and not without weakness of the flesh. The club was located downtown on Sixth Avenue. It had gotten its name from Psalm 149:3: "Let them praise his name with dancing and make music with timbrel and harp." The club had replaced the timbrel and harp with Christian dubstep, electronica, and disco.

He backed out of his parking lot and headed for the exit. Off to the left, he saw the garage elevator door open. Lange stepped out and headed toward what looked like a late-model Audi eTron. That fuckface would have an EV.

The dancing would have to wait. Defner slipped his car into a spot next to Lange's, got out, and positioned himself at the eTron's driver's door.

Lange approached. Defner did not move.

"Okay, Defner, what do you want?" he asked.

"Never do that to me again."

"What? Stop you from killing a patient?"

"I wasn't killing her."

"Look, shock is the pause in the act of dying, and lady's pause was over. She went asystolic while you were trying to get a chest tube in.

Not only did I save her life, I saved your ass from a morbidity and mortality review."

Defner's jaw clenched. "I served in the Marines with a combat tour in Iraq. Jesus is my lord and savior. I don't need you to save me from anything."

"Hallelujah and thank you for your service. Now get the fuck away from my car."

"You owe me an apology; I want it now."

"Apology? We just went over this. So once again—fuck off."

Defner grabbed Lange by the front of his shirt, spun him around, and slammed him against the car, hissing, "All the workers of evil say great things of themselves."

Lange just smiled at him. "Here's a quote for you: 'Do not envy a man of violence. And do not choose any of his ways.' If you want to trade Bible quotes, I can do this all night."

Watching Lange smile and hearing him quote the Bible infuriated him even further. Defner snarled and raised his fist. He would knock the shit-eating grin right off Lange's face.

Suddenly, crushing pain gripped his chest. He became short of breath and overcome with fear. Defner let go of Lange and clutched his chest, then fell against another car, then knelt to the floor, gasping for air. Lange stooped on his haunches in front of him.

Defner cried out breathlessly. "Keep away from me! Don't touch me!"

"Next time, you won't get off this easy. And you might want to wipe the coke out of your fucking nose."

Defner crawled away, gasping and using one hand to pinch and wipe his nostrils. He got up, panting, and stumbled out of the garage and back through the ambulance bay, ER, leaving that monster behind.

When he got to the ER, he cried out, "Get a cardiologist! I'm having a heart attack!"

Although Defner had treated countless coke-induced heart attack victims in the ER, like many physicians, he could never have imagined himself falling victim to the ills affecting others. And besides, he was cardiovascularly fit, without significant heart disease in his family. And if he died, they'd do an autopsy, and the tox screen would discover cocaine in his system. Fuck.

Because he was suffering from chest pain and a medical colleague, Defner's treatment was expedited. Within a few minutes, he was in a gown with an IV started and an EKG taken. A cardiologist, Dr. Sheldon Watkins of the Anchorage Heart Institute, was summoned to examine Defner.

Watkins examined the EKG. "Jason, you have mild tachycardia, but your EKG is otherwise normal. Tell me about your pain."

"Crushing, retrosternal, and radiation to my left shoulder, and a feeling of doom. No doubt it's cardiac."

"What were you doing when it came on?"

Defner hesitated. "I, uh, I was in the parking garage. Heading to my car."

He answered all of Watkins questions, informing him that he had no significant risk factors for coronary artery disease. Throughout the interview, Defner felt sweat beading on his face and soaking through his gown.

"As you know," Watkins said, "one can have a normal EKG while suffering acute MI or unstable angina. Maybe we should go have a look."

"You'll get no argument from me."

Twenty minutes later, Defner was lying supine on the imaging table in the cardiac catheterization lab. As Watkins donned a gown and glove, a nurse injected five thousand units of heparin, a blood thinner, through his IV to prevent blood clotting during the procedure.

After the technician prepped and draped Defner's right arm, Watkins inserted a needle in the right radial artery. Bright red blood jetted out in a pulsatile fashion. In rapid succession, Watkins passed a guide wire through the needle up the artery into the aorta, the large artery taking blood away from the heart. He withdrew the needle, made a three-millimeter nick in the skin, and with a few more passings of wires and catheters, cannulated the opening to the left main coronary artery with an AL1 catheter.

"Okay, Jason, hold your breath and keep still. Shooting!"

Defner held his breath. Machinery whirred, and he heard the beeping signal as the coronary arteriogram progressed.

Defner felt a warmth flash through his chest.

The process of whirring and beeping stopped.

"You can breathe now," Watkins said. He repositioned the catheter into the opening of the right coronary artery and repeated the process.

"Okay, Jason, let's see what we got," Watkins called out to a tech once he was finished. "Run them both."

The shot was displayed in extremely slow motion. The IV contrast filled a short main coronary artery, which branched into two: the left main coronary and the coronary circumflex artery. On the next run, the contrast filled the right coronary artery.

"Coronary arteries are normal. No lesions or spasm."

Defner closed his eyes, grateful.

"Okay, we're going to do a left ventriculogram. You might feel a rush."

Some mechanical whirring. As he looked at the monitor, he saw dye being injected into the left ventricle, the chamber pumping arterial blood out through the body. He felt a warm flush through his body and experienced a metallic taste in his mouth. He saw his ventricle fill with contrast, then contract, and push the dye out into the aorta.

"LV's moving normally, with excellent ejection fraction. Everything looks good."

How could everything look good? The pain had been real—crushing, terrifying. And yet the cath was negative. So, it wasn't the cocaine-induced coronary vasospasm. Was he imagining the pain? If there wasn't a medical explanation, had Lange played some Jedi mind trick on him?

Yes—but it had not been a Jedi Force. There was a more sinister one. The unholy force. Satan.

As if to refute Defner's dark ruminations, Watkins said, "Maybe you have myopathy or myocarditis of some sort. Let's do a biopsy." To the tech, he said, "Let's have the 5 French biopsy forceps."

21

AN AUTOPSY, INTERRUPTED

The autopsy viewing room was crowded with brass. Mayor Rotig, Police Chief Dell, District Attorney Strupinsky, and Dr. Zigler, the chief medical examiner, pressed close behind Becca as she worked the controls of the CT scanner. Eddie stood to one side with a few aides, watching the 3D reconstruction of Jack Peplow's head rotate slowly on the monitor.

"As you can see," Becca said as she moved the mouse to indicate the pertinent findings, "the bullet fragmented on impact. The largest piece lodged here, against the opposite side, with smaller fragments dispersed through the brain tissue."

"Can these fragments help identify the weapon?" the mayor asked.

"Possibly. Was a weapon recovered at the scene?"

"No," Eddie said.

"If the weapon is recovered," Becca said, "the ballistics lab might be able to compare the rifling marks on these larger pieces of the jacket. We'll send all the fragments we recover to the ballistics lab, of course, but you never know. Any other questions about the scan?"

No one offered any, so Becca led them down the hall, where Karl waited by the aluminum table. Jack Peplow's body lay stretched out, unremarkable except for the gaping, jagged-edged hole in the left side of his skull and the hair matted with blood and fragmented brain tissue.

As Becca gowned and gloved, Wally, the forensic photographer, finished taking pictures of Peplow's head from various angles.

"He's all yours."

Becca stepped up to the table. Eddie noted how the gown and mask focused attention on her eyes and the bruising. She took Peplow's head in her hands, rotated from side to side, and then started dictating into the overhead mic above the table. "The body is of a Caucasian male, normally developed, overweight, five feet eleven inches, 221 pounds. There is ecchymosis of the forehead. There is a large stellate laceration on the scalp. Underlying this is a large skull defect of the left parietal area"—she took out a ruler—"measuring six by ten centimeters."

From there, Becca described "fractures radiating in all directions from the defect," an "underlying defect of cerebral tissue," and "massive cerebral disruption and contusions." She also described "multiple irregularly shaped fragments of metal of varying sizes."

Rhonda, the receptionist, who was working late to greet dignitaries, entered the room.

"Uh, Dr. Raven?"

"What is it, Rhonda?" Becca asked.

"Mr. Brockman. He, uh, would like to see you." She was trying to keep it casual, but Eddie could see that she was stressed.

Becca let out a sigh. "Please tell him I'm not available. I'm in the middle of an autopsy."

"I told him that already."

"Uh—"

"I'll go see what that good old boy wants," Eddie offered.

"Thanks, Detective." Becca continued, "Well, ladies and gentlemen, we have the typical appearance of a high-velocity hollow-point bullet doing what it is designed to do—penetrate a body cavity, in this case the skull, and once inside the brain, expand, rapidly decelerate, and transfer its kinetic energy to form a pressure cavity with enough force to make the skull burst open, taking brain tissue and skull fragments with it. Zero chance of survival. You're welcome to stay and watch me pick out each metal fragment, but I think you have all the information you will need for your press conference."

Eddie headed out as she finished talking. When he reached the lobby, he found two guards standing in front of Brockman, who was pacing back and forth like a running back looking for an opening in the defensive line.

"Mr. Brockman, we don't want to call the police," one said, clearly trying to keep things from escalating. Brockman's past relationship with Becca was earning him special treatment from the guards. *Fuck that*, thought Eddie.

"I am not leaving here until I see Dr. Raven."

"You don't have to call the police; they're already here," Eddie said, stepping in front of the guards. "Mr. Brockman, I'm Detective Vaugner. You might remember we met a while back. Dr. Raven was clear. She wants you to leave. And now I am telling you to leave."

"This is none of your business." Brockman looked at him with the predatory stare of a successful manipulator not used to being denied. But the slight tremor in his voice, the way his hands kept clenching and unclenching, suggested a controlled rage.

"Sure it is. You're in a state office building, causing a scene, interrupting a forensic autopsy, and security personnel and a law enforcement officer have asked you to leave. You can either leave the premises or I'll call for backup, take you over to the station, and charge you with criminal trespass and disturbing the peace. Your call." He felt an urge to confront him about Becca's eye injury, but he didn't want to escalate the situation and further embarrass her.

Brockman's face turned red. He knew he had lost this round.

"Fucking one-legged gimp," he said as he stormed out of the building.

Eddie said nothing but followed Brockman out and stood at the front door. He watched Brockman walk to the parking lot and get into a late-model Lincoln Navigator SUV.

As the Navigator disappeared around the corner, Eddie mentally catalogued the warning signs for potential violent escalation in Brockman's behavior toward Becca. The narcissistic refusal to accept the breakup. Targeting Becca at her workplace. Showing overt hostility toward a police detective who stood in his way.

Becca had taken the right step in getting rid of him. But Eddie still felt a sense of foreboding. People like Brockman do not go away quietly.

Back in the lobby, Eddie pulled out his card and handed it to Rhonda. "My cell phone is on the card. If he comes back, first dial 911, and then call me."

The officials who were attending the autopsy exited the elevator to the lobby. As everyone left, Chief Dell pulled Eddie aside.

"Everything okay down here?"

"Yes, Chief."

"Okay, I don't have to tell you, they're going to be on us like flies on shit." He patted Eddie on the shoulder. "I know you're up for this."

Eddie went back to the autopsy room to reassure Becca and tell her to call him at any sign of trouble from Brockman, but Karl was alone. "Where's Dr. Raven?"

Karl shrugged. "Left."

22

CHURCH AND STATE

Later in the morning, after the autopsy and his encounter with Brockman, Eddie sat at his desk and typed "Gage Society" into his search bar. He found his way to the organization's landing page.

The website hadn't been updated to reflect the shooting.

Photos of Jack and Dana Peplow appeared with captions identifying them as Jack R. Peplow, MDiv, Executive Director, and Dana Harvey Peplow, MDiv, Managing Director. There was a graphic of a church steeple and Capitol dome separated by a wall, with the slogan: "Keep This Wall!"

At the bottom of the page was a sepia-toned profile of a nineteenth-century woman—Matilda Gage—accompanied by a quote:

United with the state, the church never rises above the merest superstition; united with the church, the state never rises above despotism. The most frightful periods the world has ever known have been those in which church and state have been united.

Eddie clicked the ABOUT link. A blurb explained that Matilda Joslyn Gage had been a prominent American women's suffragist, abolitionist, and freethinker, influential in the early women's rights movement. She distinguished herself with radical (for her time) critiques of religious institutions and passionate advocacy for the complete separation of church and state. She was also the mother-in-law of L. Frank Baum and had influenced him to portray female characters in Oz who were independent, powerful, and exhibited leadership qualities.

Next, Eddie read the blurb on the Peplows:

Jack and Dana Peplow met at Yale while pursuing their Master of Divinity degrees. Jack was interested in academics, and Dana was interested in becoming a pastor for the United Church of Christ. As they say, God works in mysterious ways and had other plans. Jack and Dana became alarmed at the increasing threat of religious influence over the government. They formed the Matilda Gage Society for the Separation of Church and State in America, more commonly referred to as the Gage Society, to combat this. The Gage Society's mission statement was derived from Gage's writings and soon grew from a small campus movement to a large national organization.

Eddie returned to his search results and found an article on the Peplows in the Yale Alumni Magazine, titled "Maintaining the Wall," with the subheading: "Jack Peplow '93 MDiv and Dana (née Harvey) Peplow '93 MDiv, keeping up the fight to keep God out of government."

The article repeated the biographical information from the website, but there was one passage Eddie found interesting:

"I am the executive director, and Dana is the managing director. Being the executive director means I sit on my keister while Dana does the work." In reality, that's hardly the case. While Dana handles administrative duties, Jack appears at public rallies, on campuses, and TV shows. Dana runs things behind the scenes.

The stress can be unbearable. Extreme religious groups vilify them, and they have lived with death threats most of their lives.

"No threats have materialized into action," says Jack.

"So far," Dana adds.

Next, Eddie searched for "Revus Roche America Salvation Church" and came across a three-year-old profile from the Anchorage Free Press, an alternative weekly: "Revus Roche Wants God to Be the Next President of the United States."

Headquartered on an expansive campus on Northern Lights Avenue, the America Salvation Church's modern cathedral was the largest in Alaska, with a spire reaching 150 feet toward the heavens. The only taller structures in Alaska were buildings dedicated to the other religion of Alaska—the upwards of 30 billion barrels of oil left to be extracted from of the National Petroleum Reserve Alaska and the Arctic National Wildlife Refuge.

The America Salvation Church campus also contained an executive office building, a daycare center, a K-12 parochial school, a security center, and the tax-free seven-bedroom, eight-bathroom, four-car-garage, 12,000-square-foot parsonage owned by the church—where its pastor lived.

It was often debated how Revus Roche, a former owner of a pesticide company with the motto "No one kills roaches like Roche!" became inspired to trade exterminating bugs for exterminating sin.

His supporters claimed he was moved by Matthew 5:14 to create a "city that is set on the hill" and make America "giveth light" and "shine before men and glorify our Father which is in heaven."

His critics claimed his spirit was more moved by a careful read of Publication 1828 of the IRS Tax Guide for Churches & Religious Organizations.

Roche's church began as a small storefront operation called the Alaska Salvation Church, which struggled to gain congregants. His early slogan, "fumigate with faith," conjured up allusions to prior exterminations of humans with Zyklon B.

But the World Trade Center attacks changed everything for Roche—9/11, and the growing fear of Muslims taking over the world, boosted membership.

On the advice of marketing experts, he gave up the pesticide references. The goal was now to make America one nation under the Christian God. The Alaska Salvation Church became the America Salvation Church, and rewriting the Constitution to make the United States the mecca of modern Protestant Christianity became its strongest selling point.

At first, this was regarded as a gimmick to attract a few fervent believ-

ers. However, as Roche's congregation grew, the church became more politically active and started backing candidates sympathetic to establishing a Christian theocracy. This drew the attention of Constitutional scholars and IRS agents.

The article then detailed the church's battle with the IRS over its tax-exempt status. There was no mention of Jack Peplow or the Gage Society.

Eddie leaned back in his chair. The Gage Society and the America Salvation Church were clearly ideological enemies, but was this rivalry motive enough for murder? He dimly recalled a quote from his college English class—a famous English king, though he couldn't remember which one—something like, "Will no one rid me of this meddlesome priest?" No direct order, yet it was enough to inspire knights to murder Thomas Becket.

And while Peplow wasn't a priest and Roche wasn't a king, Jack Peplow, MDiv, religious scholar and activist, had been killed while challenging religious authority.

23

PASTORAL CARE

James 5:14-15 reads: *Is any sick among you? Let him call for the elders of the church; and let them pray over him, anointing him with oil in the name of the Lord: and the prayer of faith shall save the sick, and the Lord shall raise him up; and if he have committed sins, they shall be forgiven him.*

The America Salvation Church used this passage to encourage its members to inform the staff of their own or a loved one's admissions to the hospital. They did this by calling the "confidential blessing hotline." The staff compiled a list for Roche. Studies of his congregation showed that donations increased by 13.5 percent from families he visited.

Roche entered the telemetry unit at PAMC with his two bulky bodyguards, who wore ill-fitting suits. The first patient on his list today was Mrs. Gwen Stevens, awaiting a heart rhythm procedure. On his way to her room, he spotted a familiar figure in pajama bottoms and a hospital gown, clutching an IV pole, about to turn into a room.

"Jason?"

"Pastor Roche. How did you—are you here to see me?"

"I'm here to see another patient. I wasn't aware you were in the hospital."

"Yes, I had what I thought was a cardiac event, but everything seems okay. I expect to go home today. Please, come in."

Jason was one of ASC's most prominent donors, so Roche would indulge him for a few minutes. Back in the room, Jason climbed onto his hospital bed, and Roche sat in a chair. The bodyguards assumed positions in the hallway. The TV was on but muted. A grim-looking talking head appeared above the chyron: "Deadly Shooting at the Hotel Captain Cook."

"Would you mind turning the TV off?" Roche asked.

"Not at all," Jason said as he clicked the TV off. "Just about that atheist who was gunned down."

Roche noted a slight scowl on Jason's face. "So what brought into the hospital, Jason?"

"Last night after work, I was hit with crushing chest pain."

"You mean like a heart attack?"

"Yes, but everything looks normal. My coronary arteries, my heart contractions—all normal. They took a biopsy, so we'll see." Jason lifted his gown to show the cardiac leads attached to his chest. "They've kept me monitored all night. No issues. I'm waiting for my cardiologist to come in and discharge me."

"Praise God, Jason."

"I've been taking comfort in Psalm 121:7. The Lord will keep you from all harm—"

"And he will watch over your life," Roche interjected. "So your heart's fine. Any idea what it was, then?"

Jason nodded slowly and frowned. "Oh, yeah, a very good idea."

"What is it?"

"Do you believe Satan walks among us?"

"If not in body, certainly in spirit."

Jason raised a hand in front of his chest and clenched it into a fist. "I may have encountered him last night. Satan, or at least an agent." He gestured toward the blank TV screen. "Last night, I, uh, treated the wife who was brought in."

"Yes, a terrible thing. So, you saved her?"

Jason scowled. "You see, that's the thing. When she came in, it was obvious her left chest was filled with blood. The initial treatment is putting in a chest tube to drain the blood. Just as I was getting the tube in, Lange, this surgeon, pulled me away in a panic and cracked open her chest."

"Lange, you say? Would that be Grayson Lange?"

"You know him?"

"I've been referred to him. Having a bit of an esophageal reflux problem, and my gastroenterologist referred me to Dr. Lange to fix it."

"No, Reverend, anyone but him."

Roche was surprised by the venom in Jason's voice. "But I've been told he's the best."

"Not him, I'm telling you. Anyone but him."

Roche smiled. "Okay, Jason, why not him?"

"I ran into him in the parking garage after my shift. I asked for an apology for assaulting me in front of the whole ER. Not only did he refuse, but he also taunted me and mocked scripture. I was upset, so I grabbed him to teach him a lesson."

"I understand your feelings, Jason. But you assaulted the surgeon who saved the life of a woman shot in an assassination of her husband. We've talked about your self-control, have we not?"

"I'm sorry. But his blasphemy got to me. Besides, any surgeon could have done what he did."

Roche gestured to the TV, his voice rising slightly. "That's not the point. I'm going to be suspect number one in this shooting. You're lucky you weren't arrested. He's not pressing charges, is he?"

"I doubt it."

"Thank God for that, at least." Roche took a breath, trying to calm down. "So how does this relate to your chest pain?"

"Just after I grabbed him, I was struck by this horrible pain in my chest. But it was more than just pain. I felt the doom and unspeakable evil."

Roche snuck a quick peek at his watch. "Jason—"

"And Lange just stood there—stood there!—watching me as I was gasping for breath."

"You mean he did nothing to help you?"

"Not only was he not helping me, it was like he knew what was going on—and was in control of it. He even said, 'If you ever touch me again, you won't get off this easy.'"

Roche studied the doctor for a second.

"How would a surgeon cause this, do you suppose?"

"I don't know. But Satan—"

"Jason, are you on drugs again?"

"This is not about drugs."

"Answer me, are you on drugs?"

"Okay, I took one hit of coke. But I'm not"—he made air quotes—*on drugs*. I only do the occasional hit when I need energy."

"Before we summon up Satan, Jason, let's consider an alternative scenario. You did some cocaine, which is known to cause heart attacks, then became irrationally agitated and assaulted the physician who apparently saved a woman's life, and in your drug-fueled state, experienced chest pain."

"This wasn't the drugs. It was Lange."

Roche stood up and smiled, not wanting to offend Jason.

"I must continue my rounds, but we can talk more about this later. In the meantime, Jason, please stay off the drugs. It would be a shame to lose such a valuable member of our Church."

"Okay."

"Okay, what, Jason?"

"Okay, I'll stay off the drugs. Not that I'm really *on drugs*."

24

AN INVITATION

Eddie's desk phone rang.

"Detective Vaugner."

"Detective, this is Special Agent Sarah Cooper with the FBI, Anchorage office. Chief Dell asked us to reach out. I'll be the Bureau's liaison on the Peplow homicide. I understand you're the lead detective?"

"I am."

"I've been briefed on the basics, but I'd appreciate getting your take on it. Do you have time to meet today?"

"Actually, I'm headed out to interview the pastor of the America Salvation Church in about an hour. The Peplow family pegged him as the number one suspect."

"Yes, we're aware of the antagonism between the ASC and the Gage Society. Do you want me to come with?"

"Given who they are, it might be better if you stay in the background for now. These folks tend to get defensive around you 'deep-state feds.' I'd rather not spook them this early in the game."

Cooper chuckled. "Agreed. Let's meet up afterward, so we're not just voices on the phone. We can discuss what you find in my office."

"Sounds good. Say around four?"

"Looking forward to meeting you."

EDDIE HAD DECIDED to try an unannounced visit. If the Peplows' assumptions were right, it might give them less time to organize a story. Arriving at the America Salvation Church campus, Eddie and Chik encountered a two-lane entry. The right lane was reserved for church members and employees with IDs to open a barrier arm, while the left lane, adjacent to the guardhouse, was for everyone else. Two cameras surveilled the entrance. They stopped, and a guard popped his head out the window.

"God bless. How are you gentlemen today?"

Eddie held up his badge and ID. "Detectives Vaugner and Uttaq, from the Anchorage Police, here to see Pastor Roche."

"Do you have an appointment, sir?"

"No, we don't."

"Are you carrying firearms?"

"We're cops."

"One second, please."

The guard went to his desk, picked up a phone, and punched a button.

"Hi, this is Gus at the main gate. I have two police officers here to see Pastor Roche... Really?... They said they didn't have an appointment... Oh, I see. I'll send them over." The guard hung up, and raised the arm gate.

"Welcome to the America Salvation Church. Apparently, they were expecting you. Follow the signs to the Executive Office Building."

"Expecting us,"scoffed Chik as they pulled through the gates, "They expected to be suspects."

So much for the surprise element to their visit, thought Eddie.

They followed the signs to the executive office building, passing two security cars. This campus was well-guarded. A group of elementary school-aged children cavorted in a playground.

After parking and ignoring the sign that read, *Visitors: Absolutely*

No Firearms Allowed in This Building!, they entered a well-furnished lobby with a high ceiling.

Above were two second-story balconies across the room from each other, each holding a guard dressed in paramilitary uniforms armed with assault-style weapons. Eddie recognized the Operational Camouflage Pattern, otherwise known as Scorpion V2. On the right shoulder of each uniform was a patch of the Salvation American Flag, with thirteen red and white stripes and a blue canton holding a double circle of fifty stars surrounding a white cross. On the left shoulder, a curved patch read "ASC Security Force" and below, a rank insignia. Beneath the rank insignia was a patch with the word "JERICHO." On the left chest, "ASC." Religious fanatics playing soldiers with an insurrectionist vibe, Eddie thought.

Eddie and Chik approached a woman sitting by a large, curved reception desk. She looked up at him and smiled. Behind her, two expressionless men in blue blazers and gray slacks sat on stools manning a conveyor X-ray system, and a walk-through metal detector guarded access to the rest of the building.

The woman behind the desk flashed a smile of perfect white teeth. "Are you the police detectives?" Veneers, thought Eddie.

"We are," he said, flashing her his badge. "Detectives Vaugner and Uttaq. We're here to see Mr. Roche."

"Pastor Roche told us to expect someone from the police department and to notify him immediately, no matter where he was or what he was doing. Terrible business, that killing."

She picked up the phone and punched a few buttons.

"Hi, Sally. This is Gretchen here at the front desk. I have Detectives Vaugner and Uttaq from the APD out here to see Pastor Roche... Yes... I presume so, but he didn't... Yes, very good."

She hung up. "Sally will be right out.

A door next to the security apparatus buzzed, and a woman came through. Her plain navy-blue dress and sparse makeup failed to conceal her curves, sensual walk, and full lips.

"Hello, Detective Vaugner. I'm Sally, Pastor Roche's executive assistant. I'll take you to see him now. If you would, please step through the metal detector."

"We have firearms, and I have a below-the-knee prosthesis."

"We have a strict firearms policy, Detective, none in the building."

Sally gave Eddie a bureaucratic smile, indicating she was not budging. Eddie smiled back. Clearly a power play.

"Okay, tell Pastor Roche I'll give him the opportunity to come downtown and be interviewed in one of our secure interrogation rooms on video. It shouldn't take more than half a day or so, but he'll feel absolutely safe. Heck, we can even throw in a subpoena and make it all official-like, as if he's a real suspect. Have a nice day. Let's go, Chik."

As they turned to leave, Sally said, "Please, give me one second."

She headed back in. When she returned a few minutes later, she escorted Eddie and Chik through the side door to Roche's office.

"Pastor, I have Detectives Eddie and Uttaq to see you."

Roche stood up to greet them. He wore a tailored dark gray suit, white shirt, and black-and-white striped tie. There was a lapel pin: an American flag with a white cross instead of stars in the blue union. Unlike any of the apostles, he kept his hair immaculately trimmed and gelled into place, with every strand occupying its precise designated position. The graying sides of his hair made him look like a Just for Men poster child.

The pastor stood up behind his desk and flashed a smile. Veneered teeth seemed to be endemic to the America Salvation Church.

"Sorry about the firearms to-do. We train our employees to be vigilant." He held out his hand across the desk. Eddie shook it—a warm, firm handshake from a self-assured man.

"Thank you, Sally," he said. Sally left, and Roche continued, "Terrible business, this killing. If you don't mind, I'm under strict instructions not to say a word until— Ah, here they are now."

Two men entered the office. One was a suit in his forties. He was introduced as Kevin Oslager, the in-house attorney.

The other was Dmitri Saparov, a crewcut, possibly sixty, in black slacks and a bush-style khaki overshirt with double-breasted pockets and epaulets. Eddie detected a slight bulge on his left hip. Carrying, no doubt. He appeared fit. He had the intense gaze and alert posture of a man who could immediately assess situations and take action. Not to be underestimated.

"Kevin's here to make sure I don't step in it, you know, from a legal standpoint," Roche said. "Truth be told, he told me not to speak to you at all, but not cooperating with our fine law enforcement officers wouldn't seem very civic-minded."

No mention of why Saparov was there.

Roche glanced over at Oslager, who gave an almost imperceptible nod. Saparov cracked a thin, confident smile. The pastor reached for a roll of Tums from his desk drawer. He popped two tablets, then two more. Nerves could turn up the acid.

"Now, Detectives, I am not surprised, of course, to see you here, and in fact, I was telling Kevin and Dmitri I would be astonished if you didn't put me on the top of your list of" —he made air quotes—"'suspects.' So, let's get down to brass tacks."

Roche sat back down behind his desk, took a paper from a drawer, and held it in front of him. He put on a pair of readers and smiled. "Mr. Oslager has given me a list of statements he has permitted me to tell you, after which I'll answer one or two questions."

Oslager and Saparov chuckled sycophantically. Eddie noticed their subtle sneers. Underlings who knew they were smarter than their boss but had none of his power?

"First, neither I nor any member of the executive council of this Church suggested, planned, or hinted Dr. Peplow was to be in any way harmed, threatened, or intimidated while he was in Anchorage. Second, no member of this Church, or any of its employees, or anyone on the executive council or security staff has come forth with any knowledge of a plan for this killing, either before or after the fact. Third, instead of wanting to assassinate Mr. Peplow, we invited him to address our church and debate me over the separation of Church and State. This debate was tentatively scheduled for the day after he was gunned down."

"He turned you down," Eddie said.

"I'm sorry?" Roche said.

"Peplow's family said Mr. Peplow turned down your invitation to debate him."

"Oh. I don't believe I was notified of this. May I continue?"

"Go ahead." Eddie and Chik exchanged this-guy-is-bullshitting glances.

"Finally, I would suggest our fine law enforcement organizations consider the possibility this was a false flag operation carried out by our enemies to foster suspicion and distrust toward our Church."

He was a smooth talker. Eddie could see why this man was able to attract a following.

"Who do you think would kill a man and blame it on you?" Chik asked.

Saparov shifted in his seat.

"We would investigate anyone you believed would go to these lengths to frame you," Chik continued.

"I'm sorry, I don't have anyone specific in mind," Roche said. Then he smiled. "Other than the government, of course."

"You have quite the security force," Eddie noted. "Surely some of them are ex-military, perhaps a few snipers in the mix."

Saparov chimed in, speaking with a Slavic accent. "I can assure security force not involved." Roche held up his hand to cut the man off.

Oslager stood up. "Okay, Officers, I believe Pastor Roche has been very cooperative, but I don't think there's much more to be gained by further questioning."

Roche smiled at the detectives.

"Look at Kevin, getting all lawyerly. And for the amount of money I pay him, I should listen to him. Otherwise, what's the point?"

Eddie and Chik rose to their feet, followed by Oslager and Saparov. Roche remained seated. Eddie took it as a sign of power and polite disrespect. Maybe even a "fuck you, catch me if you can."

"Is this where you tell me not to leave town?" Roche asked, grinning.

"No, Mr. Roche. You can go wherever you want."

As Eddie started to leave, the pastor extended an invitation.

"Detectives, one second. If I may, Mr. Oslager?"

Oslager shrugged.

To Eddie, this whole interview was a carefully rehearsed display of bullshit, right down to this staged moment of spontaneity.

"I would like to invite you to our service this Sunday. Perhaps it would help your investigation to see what we're about. We're not the religious nuts the liberal atheistic press and Jack Peplow have made us out to be."

"Jack Peplow and his wife were ordained ministers," Eddie said. "With Divinity degrees."

"Academics, posing as Christian," Roche countered.

"Okay, Pastor," Oslager said. Eddie expected Oslager to follow *the script.*

Eddie considered it. *Maybe a little operational intel would be useful.* He looked over to Chik, who remained inscrutable.

"Let me tempt you both. If either one of you attends this Sunday's service, we'll donate $10,000 to the Anchorage Police Health and Welfare Fund."

Eddie and Chik exchanged glances. Chik shook his head.

"I can't make it," Chik said.

Despite this being cartoonishly manipulative and close to a bribe, Eddie remembered the thousands of dollars the Fund had provided when he lost his leg.

"That's an offer I can't refuse," he said.

"This Sunday,I'll be addressing the Peplow killing, so this would be part of your investigation, eh?"

"I'll be there," Eddie said. "I might bring my son, Daniel."

"How old is he?"

"Eleven."

"We have a children's program that runs concurrently."

"He'll sit with me."

"No problem." Roche pulled a card from a holder on his desk, and as he scribbled something on it, he said, "I'll tell security to look out for you. Give them this card, and they'll whisk you right through security. No screening. We'll have two seats up front for you."

Sally showed up to escort the detectives out. Eddie figured she must have been wired into the room.

AFTER THE INTERVIEW, Eddie dropped Chik off at headquarters. He agreed to type up the interview while Eddie headed to Agent Cooper's office at the FBI building. After showing his ID, he was buzzed through.

Cooper's office was sparsely furnished with basic office furniture and a desktop computer. There was one personal item: a photo of Cooper and a woman of about the same age, both in waders and wearing automatic inflatable life jackets that provided safety and maneuverability, standing in a river, each holding up a silver salmon. They were beaming at the camera, with snow-streaked mountains rising behind them. They looked like serious Alaskan anglers.

Cooper herself matched the room's utility: medium height, solidly stocky, dressed in a plain dark suit, her graying hair cut efficiently short. She spoke plainly, not in the bureaucratic language he'd come to expect from faraway feds, and she had friendly eyes.

Eddie immediately felt comfortable with her and asked the question most often heard in the forty-ninth state: "What brought you up to Alaska?"

"The stork," she replied. "I was born and raised in Kenai and dreamed of joining the FBI since I was a kid." She went on to tell Eddie how she had enrolled in the FBI straight out of law school and was now a special agent in the Criminal Enterprise/Violent Crimes Division.

After Eddie recapped his meeting with Roche, Cooper said, "Of course he'd deny it, but the interesting person isn't Roche so much—he seemed exactly what you'd expect—polished, practiced, full of bullshit. Or the lawyer. But why was the head of security there? What was his name again?"

"Agent Cooper, you're reading my mind. Dmitri Saparov. My guess is he was there to find out what we knew. Maybe the brains of the whole operation."

"Enough with the Agent Cooper; call me Sarah. With an Eastern European accent, you said? I'll background-check him and see what turns up. Give me a few days."

They chatted some more, and Eddie left with the impression that Cooper could be trusted. She seemed interested in being helpful and clearly had no plans to take over the investigation.

Back in his car, Eddie's cell phone buzzed. It was an incoming text message from Becca:

Thank you for the other evening—with Jim.

Eddie punched in a reply: *Do you want to talk about it?*

Not right now, too embarrassed, she said.

Let me know if you have any more problems.

There was a slight pause after his message before her response.

BTW, in case it wasn't clear, I'm no longer seeing him.

Eddie's heart skipped a beat at the last message. Brockman was out. He felt a glimmer of— *Oh, forget it.*

He texted back a thumbs-up.

25

A SHOW OF FAITH

Cars jammed the expansive America Salvation Church parking lot.

"Wow, Dad," Daniel said. "This puts the Redeemer to shame."

Inside, the security presence was even more pronounced than on Eddie's previous visit. Uniformed security guards stood by scanners and metal detectors in the chapel's main lobby, and armed guards kept vigil from balconies. Off to one side, a large portrait of Jesus embracing the America Salvation Church flag greeted congregants. On the other was an alcove with a sign that read, "No Firearms Allowed in the Chapel. Please Check Firearms Here."

"For people who believe God is protecting and waiting for them in heaven," Daniel joked, "they sure seem scared of getting there sooner."

Eddie smiled and put his finger to his lips. The boy could be unfiltered, but he didn't miss much.

A uniformed security guard motioned for Daniel to walk through a detector.

"Step forward, please," he said.

"Hold on," Eddie said. He handed a security guard the business card Roche had given him. The guard looked at it.

"Wait one moment, sir."

He picked up a walkie-talkie and pressed the button. "I have a level-three clearance."

It crackled back, "Roger. On my way."

Within seconds, a man in gray slacks and a blue blazer approached. His name tag read "Brother Robert Erickson, Augusta, Maine." He asked Eddie for identification. Knowing these types responded to authority, Eddie showed him his police ID and badge, not his driver's license. Brother Erickson escorted them through a side entrance.

"That must be quite the prosthesis. If I didn't know you had one on, I don't think I could tell by your gait."

"It's a carbon fiber socket with a LimbLogic vacuum pump and an ElanC microprocessor foot," Daniel said. "Top of the line."

As they walked down a curved corridor approaching the chapel, Eddie could hear a choir singing: "...from the mountains to the prairies, white with foam..."

"Wow," Daniel said as they entered the cathedral. "This place is huge."

"Twelve hundred congregants on the main floor and another six hundred on the balcony," Erickson said. "The place is filled to the rafters, and we have an overflow crowd in the gymnasium with a video feed. A lot of people want to hear what Pastor Roche is going to say about the Peplow shooting."

Eddie noticed a separate section to his left, elevated slightly above the main congregation. There, Dr. Defner and about sixty other members sat in what appeared to be leather recliners, their jewelry and designer clothes gleaming under the lighting.

Daniel followed his father's gaze. "Why do they get special seats?" he whispered.

"My guess is they're the big donors," Eddie said. *And a little more saved than the hoi polloi.*

Facing out from the chancel, three massive ultra-high-definition LCD screens side by side in portrait orientation, each displaying the image of the Salvation American Flag waving gently against a blue-sky backdrop. The choir was not quite the Mormon Tabernacle Choir, but it numbered at least twenty to thirty. As in the lobby, armed security forces watched from above, pacing in small balconies along the sides.

Erickson led them to two aisle seats in the front row marked "Reserved."

"Enjoy the service, and God bless," he said.

Four armed security personnel carrying automatic rifles walked out onto the large open stage and positioned themselves at each corner of the stage.

One guard stepped forward and shouted toward the congregation. "Area secured!" In his mind, Eddie rolled his eyes.

Security theater, he thought, but the siege mentality served religious demagogues. It instilled followers with a sense of righteous defiance and purpose and probably encouraged financial donations.

Timed to coincide with the final line of "God Bless America," the Reverend Revus Roche, wearing a suit and sparkling gold cufflinks in the shape of a cross, walked out onto the large open stage, smiling and holding his hands up in front of him, palms together. One could barely make out the subminiature wireless headset he wore. The flags on the screens dissolved into his live image.

The audience applauded as Roche strutted around the stage before taking his place in the middle. He didn't stand behind a podium.

He held his hands up, and the audience came to a reverent hush. Roche paused, allowing the silent adoration of the congregation to flood over him.

"A brief historical note," he said.

On each screen, Irving Berlin's image faded in, peering out at the audience through round horn-rimmed glasses.

"The composer of this wonderful song, 'God Bless America,' Irving Berlin, was born Israel Beilin, a Jew."

The congregation murmured.

The image dissolved into another of Irving Berlin, his wife, and two children. The focus of the picture was Linda Louise Berlin, an infant at the time of the photo. All eyes in the family beamed down at her, held by her mother, reminiscent of the Adoration of the Magi scene.

After a beat, Roche continued, "A Jew who—praise the Lord— raised his children as Christians and saved them from an afterlife of eternal damnation."

The audience's applause had barely faded before Roche seamlessly shifted tone.

"And good morning, everyone. Hello, and God bless to our regulars, to those of you who are new, and to those of you who—ahem— have not been here for a while. As we do every Sunday, we'll start by affirming our faith in America's divine purpose by reciting the Salvation Preamble to the United States Constitution."

On each screen, the first segment of the Preamble of the US Constitution appeared—a golden scroll on a red background with black script in the same style used in the original document.

Repetition of a phrase embodying an idea—a key tool used by cult leaders.

Roche and the congregation recited together:

"We, the People of the United States, in order to form a more perfect union, establish justice, ensure domestic tranquility, provide for the general welfare, and secure the blessings of liberty to ourselves and to our posterity..."

A phrase, as if descending from heaven, floated down from above to insert itself, and the crowd recited along.

"...guided by the Holy Scriptures, recognizing the law of God as the paramount rule, acknowledging that Jesus is the Messiah, the Savior, and Lord of the world..."

The phrase settled into the preamble, and the congregation continued:

"...do ordain and reestablish this Constitution for the United States of America."

The crowd again broke out into applause and "amens."

Roche held up his hand, and they came to a hush.

"Today, I'm going to talk to you about the separation of church and state and about Satan. But first, I want to comment on current events."

This was not so different from the Catholic Church, thought Eddie. The Introductory Rites were armed guards entering the stage. The

liturgies were replaced by a reading of a new preamble to the Constitution conducted by Roche. And now, he was going right into the
sermon.

Jack Peplow's image, a screenshot from the Gage website, appeared
on each screen. A few hisses and muted boos emanated from the
congregation. Eddie watched with disgust as Roche encouraged his
flock's contempt for a murdered man with a smile.

"Judging from the reactions I hear, many of you recognize this
man as Jack Peplow, the founder of the anti-Christian movement
known as the Gage Society for the Separation of Church and State in
America, a subversive group trying to tear Christianity from the fabric
of American life."

More hisses and boos. Eddie glanced down at Daniel, who was
playing Fortnite with the sound off while still following the sermon.

"Earlier this week, he was gunned down in front of the Captain
Cook Hotel."

At least half of the audience applauded.

"Now, now. Let's not applaud violence." A sly grin belied his
sincerity. "As you might expect, the police have already contacted me
as a person of interest."

More boos.

"I have cooperated with the investigation, and I will continue to. I
would expect each of you and all my staff to do the same. If the police
contact you, think what you want, but please act nice and cooperate
fully with them."

The crowd murmured. Roche smiled down at Eddie.

Shit! He's going to introduce me to the congregation!

But Roche just continued. "As God is my witness, I want to assure
everyone in this congregation, and all our brothers and sisters all over
America, that the America Salvation Church had nothing to do with
the planning or carrying out of this execution. In fact, as many of you
know, I invited Mr. Peplow to address this congregation and to engage
in a debate with me."

No mention of Peplow turning him down. Big surprise. Demagogues often used omissions, half-truths, or outright lies to convince. They knew their followers didn't really care if they were lying. Eddie smiled to himself, recalling George Costanza's famous Seinfeld line: "It's not a lie if you believe it." He then paraphrased it: *Belief is more important than truth.*

"As a matter of fact, much of what I am going to talk about today was what I would have presented in the debate. But first, let's bow our heads and give a silent prayer for Mr. Peplow—an ordained Protestant minister, misguided, but nonetheless a man of God—and for his surviving wife, who was wounded in the shooting but fortunately survived, and for the entire Peplow family."

Silence swept across the congregation as every head bowed. After a long minute, Roche's "Amen" broke the quiet. The responsive *Amen* rippled through the crowd.

He lifted his head and adopted a more defiant tone. "So. What about God and the Constitution, this so-called separation of Church and State?"

On the middle screen, the preamble dissolved into an image of Abraham Lincoln.

"President Lincoln, what have you to say to this congregation?"

There was a slight delay as the animation cued up. Eddie watched Roche maintain a thin, irksome smile. He coughed, slipped his hand into his suit pocket, and pulled out a roll of Tums, quickly popping a few from the package into his mouth.

Lincoln's image began to animate as he spoke in a high-pitched voice. "We have grown in numbers, wealth, and power, as no other nation has ever grown. But we have forgotten God." Eddie briefly wondered how they knew what his voice sounded like.

Several *Amens* rose from the audience.

Daniel looked up from his phone and leaned over to his father. "That generative AI is pretty cool."

Roche said, "Well, Abe, things haven't improved much."

Applause filled the room. Roche held his hand up, the applause abated, and Abe continued, "Those nations only are blessed whose God is the Lord."

More applause from the audience. On the right screen, the image of Thomas Jefferson faded in.

"What say you, President Jefferson?"

Jefferson's avatar intoned, "The Bible is the cornerstone of liberty."

More "Amens" from the audience.

George Washington appeared on the right screen.

"And George Washington, founder of our country, do you shirk from God?"

Washington declared: "It is impossible to rightly govern the world without God and the Bible."

The congregation erupted in cheers, *Amens*, whistles, and applause.

The images of Lincoln, Jefferson, and Washington peered out to the crowd as Roche exhorted the congregation, "Search the Declaration of Independence! Search the Constitution! Search the Bill of Rights! Nowhere will you find the phrase *separation of church and state*. No, ladies and gentlemen, the separation of church and state is a lie foisted on this country by liberal atheists who want to turn Americans away from God and our Lord Jesus Christ!"

The crowd erupted in applause.

Roche let the applause die down, then picked up a Bible from the podium.

On the screen, CGI Bible appeared, opened to Second Corinthians, and zoomed in to chapter 4, verse 4.

Roche recited the scripture: "'The god of this age has blinded the minds of unbelievers, so that they cannot see the light of the gospel that displays the glory of Christ, who is the image of God.'"

He pointed at the monitor with the Bible. The g in "god" began to glow.

"The god of this age." Did you notice 'god' is spelled with the small *g*?"

The word turned from black to red.

"The small-g god signifies Satan, and it is Satan who has blinded the unbelievers! There is no better way to blind the unbelievers than to separate the church from the government, faith from governance, and God from the governed!"

The congregation applauded.

"And make no mistake. Satan is loose in the world. Here. Walking among us. We see him in the headlines every day. In cataclysms of nature. In global Islamic terror. The so-called Islamic terror is not just the work of misguided Muslims but the work of Satan himself."

A large "9/11" appeared on the screen, superimposed on a composite image of each of the Twin Towers being hit by a jet.

"Take the numbers 9 and 11. Add the ones together, and you get two. Then multiply the nine, and you arrive at 18."

Next, the image zoomed down to a split screen, and next to it appeared an image of Satan and the numbers 6-6-6.

"Now take the mark of the beast, six, six, six. Add those numbers, and you arrive at 18!"

The number appeared superimposed over both images.

The congregation gasped collectively.

Vaugner felt his stomach turn at Roche using such a tragedy to manipulate gullible believers.

"Yes, the signs are everywhere!" He paused for effect. "So we must be vigilant. Darkness is upon us. And do be careful. As it is stated in Matthew: 'False Christs and false prophets will appear and perform great signs and miracles.' And in Corinthians: 'Satan masquerades as an angel of light.' And when the world needs a beacon, it is more likely to follow a false light. So do not be fooled. Do not be seduced by bearers of false light or miracles wrought through Satan. Only the light of our Savior will save us, and from nowhere does the light of our Savior Jesus Christ shine brighter than America, this ONE NATION UNDER GOD. We must fight to turn America back to Christ and make this country a Christian nation, bringing the true light of salvation to the world!"

The congregants erupted into cheers and gave Roche a standing ovation. Eddie looked over the audience. All eyes were fixed on their pastor. Then he looked up at the donor section. Dr. Defner, the emergency room physician, was up on his feet, vigorously clapping, as transfixed as the rest of them.

Roche's eyes glowed with righteous triumph. He held up his hands. "One more thing. One more thing."

The audience hushed.

"A trial is about to begin—a trial of good versus evil, of light against darkness. The United States government is building a case to revoke our tax exemption status and has accused this church of being a political organization. It is not politics to turn to Christ! It is not politics to fulfill God's destiny and to turn our nation back to the concepts of our Founding Fathers to make this country a Christian nation! It is simply a commitment to our faith and manifest destiny to be the light of the world, the city on the hilltop, as Matthew spoke about."

"Amen!" sounded from the audience. Ushers brought collection plates. Daniel nudged his father and pointed to one.

"Look, Dad, they take credit cards." The silver plates had modern card readers attached to their sides, with preset donation amounts from $5 to $100—convenient tap-to-pay technology for the digitally inclined faithful.

"Should we donate something?" he asked.

"No, son."

Daniel frowned, clearly disappointed he couldn't try out the cool donation plate.

"And on top of this, because of our beliefs, we are chief among suspects in the ghastly murder of Jack Peplow. One can only imagine the legal expenses we will incur defending ourselves from false accusations, whether in a criminal proceeding or taking others to court for calumnies regarding this terrible crime."

More murmurings from the crowd.

"So we prepare for legal battles. This will take money. Lots of money as we fight the massive resources of secular groups and the mainstream liberal media. So, I ask all of you to give generously today. We need to keep the slanderous wolves at bay. And with your prayers and your donations, we will. God bless us, and God bless the United States of America!"

Roche stood on the stage for several minutes as the audience applauded him. The choir broke out into "Onward Christian Soldiers."

He held his hands up again, waved at his flock, and left the stage.

As the choir sang, a rolling stage was brought out, upon which a local Christian heavy metal band stood. "Hello, everybody! We're the Cross Brigade." They broke into an anthem:

We're Sol-jahs of the light, we stand as one
Our battle's fought till victory's won
With faith our shield and truth our sword
We Sol-jahs march to heaven's chord!

"Ready to go, son?"

"Sure, Dad."

A voice called out as Eddie and Daniel crossed the lobby on their way out of the church.

"Detective Vaugner!"

Eddie turned around. It was Sally, sensuous as ever.

"Pastor Roche asked me to deliver this to you."

She handed him a check. It was for $10,000 and made out to the Police Officers Peace Association. "He apologizes for not delivering it personally, but he did ask me to say he hopes you see him and our wonderful mission differently now."

He held up the check, smiled, and said, "Thank you."

EDDIE AND DANIEL decided to have brunch at Gwennie's on Spenard Road. They both liked its enormous servings and Alaskan decor. On their drive over, Daniel tapped his phone furiously.

"Ha!"

"What, Daniel?"

"Jefferson never said, 'The Bible is the cornerstone of liberty.' It's a fake quote that popped up years after Jefferson died. Let me check some more stuff. In fact, here it says Jefferson said, 'I have examined all the known superstitions of the world, and I do not find in our particular superstition of Christianity one redeeming feature.'"

Daniel thumb-typed on his phone.

"And Washington never said, 'It is impossible to rightly govern the world without God and the Bible.' He said, 'It is impossible to govern the universe without the aid of a Supreme Being,' not about having a Christian government. And it says here, 'Washington used generic terms like Providence, Divine Providence, and Almighty Being rather than specifically Christian language. His private correspondence lacked typical Christian theological expressions, and he didn't take communion and would leave church services before communion was served.'"

"What about Lincoln?"

More typing.

"Okay, he got that one right, but Lincoln also said, 'The United States government must not undertake to run the churches. When an individual, in the church or out of it, becomes dangerous to the public interest, he must be checked.'"

Listening to Daniel methodically fact-check Roche, Eddie felt a surge of pride—his son was a chip off the old block. Whatever was responsible for Daniel's IQ was up for debate. But the boy's skepticism, his bullshit meter, or whatever you wanted to call it, Eddie would happily take credit for that.

26

CHEVY VAN

"Hey Eddie, this is Jim Boyd from Robbery. I'm down here at the crime lab garage with something interesting. They just brought in a 1995 Chevy van that was found abandoned."

"What makes it interesting?"

"A Wilson Combat rifle with a scope and suppressor in the back, with the rear window removed. I'm thinking of the Peplow case. That's yours, right?"

"Jim, you're back on my Christmas card list. I'm on my way." Eddie hung up and called Cooper.

FIFTEEN MINUTES LATER, he found Boyd and Cooper in the crime lab's examination bay with a lean, crew-cut man. Cooper introduced him as Agent Mike Reeves with the ATF.

Eddie walked over to the van and noticed that the right rear window had been cleanly removed, not broken out.

"What's the story?" he asked.

Boyd referred to his notes. "Found off Point Woronzof Road near the end of runway 15. Keys in the ignition, no prints on the steering wheel or door handles."

"Do we have an owner?"

"Ted Murat. Owns Murat's Used Cars on Old Seward. Says he loaned it to 'friends of friends' from Kazakhstan for sightseeing. Five hundred cash, no paperwork."

"Kazakhstan," Cooper said. "On that background check, the preliminary findings indicate that Saparov immigrated from Kazakhstan and was naturalized in 2010. I'm hoping we'll get something back from NNCP by the end of next week."

"Murat seemed nervous—no, spooked—when I talked to him," Boyd added. "Didn't even ask when he'd get his van back."

"You'll need to follow up there with a photo of Saparov. My guess," Eddie said, completing the sentence in a cheesy Slavic accent, "'I never see this guy.'"

Eddie pictured the scenario—no overt threats, just the understanding: nice family, shame if something happened, would you mind renting us a van, five hundred cash. Pure Godfather.

Over at the stainless-steel examination table, a Wilson Combat Super Sniper rifle, still attached to its Leupold scope and suppressor, rested on white paper.

"High-end equipment," Reeves said, snapping on gloves. "Twelve thousand altogether. The rifle alone is six grand." Turning the paper without touching the rifle, he photographed the serial numbers on the gun, scope, and suppressor. "I'd bet my pension it's stolen. I'll start the trace, but don't hold your breath."

Eddie turned to a lab tech. "I need ballistics compared with the Peplow fragments, like, yesterday."

"On it," the tech said, whisking the rifle away.

"No attempt to ditch the rifle," Reeves said.

"Why take it out of the van and risk a witness spotting you?" Eddie said.

Cooper sighed. "Professional hit team's looking good right now."

"With Kazakh connections," Eddie added.

"In and out on multiple flights as solo travelers, staggered departures, domestic from Anchorage, then out of the country. Multiple passports," Cooper said.

"And someone local to organize it. Like Saparov."

Cooper shrugged. "Who works for Roche."

27

BIRTHDAY WAFFLES

Eddie studied his face in the bathroom mirror. "Happy birthday, old man," he said to his reflection. Thirty-nine. The cusp between young and middle age. Still young enough to get a master's in public administration but old enough to know doors would start to close soon. He and Anne had planned to have another kid by this time. Now, all he wanted to do was keep his only child alive.

Like every morning, Eddie cracked open Daniel's bedroom door. Not in his bed. Down the hall, Eddie knocked on the bathroom door. No answer.

"Daniel?"

Still no answer. Eddie opened the bathroom door, trying to ignore the dreadful feeling creeping up on him. No Daniel. He looked around. No blood, no vomit, or other signs of distress. Thank God, but where was he?

Eddie headed downstairs. Living room. Den. No Daniel.

He crossed the hall to the kitchen. Then his jaw dropped.

"Oh my God."

A flour bomb had gone off, with cracked eggshells on the counter and bowls everywhere. And in the middle of it all, Daniel stood triumphant with a big white flour smear—a badge of culinary honor

—on his blue polo shirt. The aroma of waffles and coffee filled the kitchen.

"Happy birthday, Dad! I made you breakfast."

Eddie scanned the disaster spread out before him.

"Wow, Daniel, this is— Wow!"

"Have a seat, Dad."

Daniel had cleared a place setting on the counter with a knife and fork, butter, syrup, and a coffee cup. Eddie sat down. Daniel went over to the oven and, using an oven mitt, pulled out a plate with waffles on it. He placed the plate in front of Eddie.

"Careful, Dad, the plate is hot. Here's some syrup."

Eddie poured some over the waffles. "Looks good."

Daniel grabbed a can of whipped cream, held it upside down over the waffles, and pressed the nozzle, piling it up in a spiral.

"Dig in, Dad. A few carbs on your birthday won't hurt. I made coffee, too."

As the boy grabbed the coffee carafe, Eddie passed his fork through the whipped cream and tried to cut through the waffle—too hard. He picked up a knife and sawed through it, forked a piece into his mouth, and chewed.

"Mmm. Good, Daniel. Love the crunch."

Daniel poured his father a cup.

"Thanks!"

Another voice rang out. "What on earth?"

Gertie, wearing backless slippers and a bathrobe, shuffled into the kitchen.

"Why—"

Eddie cut her off. "Look, Mom. Daniel made me a birthday breakfast!"

Gertie picked up on Eddie's interruption. "How thoughtful of you, Daniel."

"Don't worry about the mess, Grandma. I'll clean it up."

"You'll do no such thing. You go get cleaned up and get to school on time. Now scoot."

"Hold on, son," Eddie said as he stood up and held out his arms. "Give me a hug."

Daniel came over to his father to receive a hug and a "Thank you."

"Sure, Dad."

He left the kitchen, and Gertie went to Eddie and kissed him on the forehead. "Happy Birthday, son. Thirty-nine. Just like Jack Benny. You know who he is?"

"Thanks, Mom. Yes, I know who Jack Benny is. The cheapskate with the violin who claimed he was thirty-nine years old as a running gag until the day he died."

Gertie started cleaning up. As he chewed on his next waffle bite, he put down his knife and fork and started crying. She dropped her sponge, dried her hands on a dish towel, came over to him, and cradled his head.

"When he wasn't in his bed, I thought he was in trouble." Eddie waved a hand, indicating Daniel's preparation of breakfast. "This didn't even occur to me."

"It's understandable. But if Daniel were in trouble, he would come to you."

Eddie let out a tearful chuckle. "Maybe, but more like Daniel would wait and confirm things twice."

She smiled. "You have a point there."

"I don't want to lose him, Mom, or the world to lose him. I want him to be thirty-nine someday. He's such a kind and wonderful boy. So curious and eager to learn. He deserves a full life."

"I know, Eddie. I know. And who is to say he won't have one?"

Eddie's cell phone went off. He pulled it from his pocket. Caller ID indicated Providence Alaska Medical Center. "It's Prov," Eddie said.

"Vaugner."

"Hey, Detective, this is Rita. I'm just calling to let you know Ms. Peplow is awake and is anxious to talk to you. I showed her your card."

"That's good news."

"She's in Room 433 on 4-North."

"Got it. I'll be there in about twenty minutes."

"No problem. Just be easy on her. She still gets short of breath easily."

"Will do." He ended the call.

"What's up, son?" Gertie asked as she started cleaning up Daniel's mess.

"Dana Peplow's nurse says she's ready to talk to the police."

It had been eight days since the Peplow assassination—just as Lange had predicted.

Like Daniel, Dana Peplow had been given another chance at life.

28

NDE

Eddie found Dana Peplow sitting up in bed with an oxygen cannula in her nose and a cast on her left arm. A younger man and woman were in the room as well, the man on the windowsill and the woman in a chair.

"Mrs. Peplow?"

"Yes. Please call me Dana."

"I'm Detective Vaugner from the Anchorage Police Department, Homicide division."

The man stood up. "Hi, Detective, I'm Jack, and this is Helen; we spoke on the phone."

"Let me just save this," Dana said, clicking a few keys on her laptop. "You would not believe the paperwork involved when your spouse dies."

"You have my sincere condolences."

"Oh my god. You're a homicide detective. Of course you would know."

She closed her laptop and then turned off the TV with the remote. Helen settled into the chair by the window while Jack remained standing near the foot of the bed.

"Now, how can I help you, Detective?"

"Well, first, how are you?"

"Not too bad, all things considered. A little short of breath, but Dr. Lange said I will improve over time."

"Good to hear. Let me assure you, we'll do everything we can to bring the people who did this to justice."

"Revus Roche," Jack said, "have you interviewed him yet?"

"I'm not going to discuss specifics of an ongoing investigation," Eddie said. "But I can tell you we're pursuing every lead thoroughly and interviewing all suspects."

"You have questions for me, like, what do I remember, I suppose."

"What you remember is always a good place to start."

"As far as the shooting and afterward is concerned, I remember walking out of the hotel. There was this young man who approached Jack for an autograph. At first, I thought it was cool. Jack had signed a few books at lectures and bookstore appearances, but this was the first time he'd ever been approached on the street. And in Anchorage, Alaska, of all places."

We're a bunch of bumpkins up here, you know, Eddie thought.

"But then something about the fellow, the way he talked. He had an accent, maybe Eastern European? And the way he looked around made me nervous. It all seemed—what's the word?—perfunctory. Then nothing, until— Do you want to hear about Dr. Lange bringing me back to life in the emergency room?"

"Mom," Helen said softly, reaching for Dana's hand. "You don't have to. She had one of those near-death experiences."

"Yes. You would call it an out-of-body experience."

"I get you and your family strongly suspect Pastor Roche," Eddie said, "but do you all have other known enemies? Any recent threats? We don't want to have tunnel vision on this."

"Detective, we would get an occasional crank call or death threat, but nothing ever came of them over the years. However, we kept a log of them, which I will happily provide to you once I'm home."

"That would be great. We're liaising with the FBI, so I'll probably turn most of it over to them."

"Nice to know you have the FBI helping you, Detective," Helen said.

"Mrs. Peplow, uh, Dana, I have a delicate issue to bring up. Perhaps your kids could step out."

"You're going to ask if Jack was sleeping around. There's no need for them to leave."

"Okay, well, roughly 70-80 percent of homicides involve either financial motives or intimate partner relationships. So, I need to ask, any possibilities of extramarital affairs or financial problems?"

"Really, Detective—" Jack started.

Dana raised her hand. "Be quiet, son. I understand and appreciate your thoroughness, Detective. We weren't rich, but we were comfortable and debt-free. And, of course, with internet hookups and all, who can say with absolute confidence their spouse is faithful? But I never had any reason to suspect. I handle all our finances, write the checks, pay the bills, and go through the credit cards. We work together in the same office, live in the same house, travel together. If hanky-panky were going on, financial or otherwise, Jack would have been the greatest sleight-of-hand artist who ever lived."

Dana's eyes started to form tears. "Besides, we loved each other."

As Dana reached for some tissues, Lange entered with two young doctors wearing crisp white coats over their scrubs. Residents, presumably.

"Good morning, Mrs. Peplow. Are you okay?"

"Here's my savior, Dr. Lange. Yes, I was just telling Detective Vaugner how much my husband and I loved each other."

She dabbed some more tears from her eyes then said, "Detective, do you know Lange is an anagram for angel? That's what Dr. Lange is to me, my angel."

"I can see why," Eddie said.

"I was just about to tell Detective Vaugner about you bringing me back to life. I know you've heard this, Dr. Lange, but maybe your residents would be interested."

"Mom," Jack said with gentle affection, "maybe we should let Dr. Lange examine you first?"

"No, you go ahead, Mrs. Peplow," Lange said. Eddie took note of Lange's emotional intelligence.

Her eyes lit up. "One minute, I was leaving the Captain Cook hotel, and the next, I was hovering above myself in the emergency room. I had no idea what had happened. Above me, there was that bright white tunnel of light everyone talks about, with angels looking down. Below, I saw my body on the stretcher. This other doctor was trying to put in a chest tube when my heart stopped. That's when Dr. Lange pulled him aside and cut open my chest. All this blood gushed out, and then Dr. Lange reached inside. And even though I was floating above, I could feel his hand squeezing my heart. Even more amazing, perhaps, there was absolutely no pain."

Jack and Helen watched their mother with quiet smiles.

Eddie looked over at Lange. "And that's what happened?"

The doctor nodded. "Pretty much."

"When he grabbed my heart, this sensation went through me, and I knew I would survive. The angels faded, I fell back into my body, and the next thing I knew, I was in intensive care."

"Rodriguez," Lange said, as he smiled warmly at Dana, "what's the explanation for near-death experiences?"

The female resident straightened. "Several theories about NDEs, but most involve glutamate blocking N-methyl-D-aspartate receptors in the brain, causing a dissociative state."

"Correct. Davis, can drugs cause this?"

The other resident answered. "Yes. We can see the same or similar reactions with ketamine, LSD, psilocybin, DMT, and a few others."

Eddie frowned. Mrs. Peplow's spiritual moment reduced to brain chemistry.

"Dr. Lange," Dana interrupted, "I wasn't near-dead. I was dead-dead. Why, Detective, you might say I was a temporary homicide victim."

"Mom," Helen said, with a mix of exasperation and fondness.

"Anything else, Mrs. Peplow?"

"I don't know. Am I still a Mrs. Peplow? I don't have a husband anymore."

"Oh, Mom, of course you are," Helen said.

"Revus Roche, Detective. Revus Roche," Jack Jr. said. "He's my dad's killer."

Eddie stood up. "If you hear anything or recall anything else, please call me. My cell phone number is on the card." He nodded to Dr. Lange. "Thank you, Doctor."

"Another thing," Mrs. Peplow said. "There was a boy in the tunnel, about eleven or twelve years old, I would say, smiling at me."

Eddie gulped. The same age as Daniel. He noticed Lange's brow furrow for just a moment.

"A patient in the NDE state can experience random visual and auditory events not only relevant to their own lives," Lange said, "but to others' lives as well. That's why some of these events get so much traction."

"Oh, pooh," she replied.

Eddie reached into his coat and pulled out his business card holder. He set one on Dana's Mayo stand and gave one each to Jack and Helen. "Here's my card. If you have any questions or think of anything you consider helpful, email or call me. My cell phone is on there. I hope you continue to recover."

Jack Jr. took out his wallet and fished out his own card. "Here's mine if you need to call me. My cell number is on it." Eddie glanced at the card: *Rev. Jack T. Peplow, M.Div., Pastor, Unity Garden, A Nondenominational Christian Church.*

ON HIS WAY back to his car, Eddie got a call from Agent Cooper. She had info on Saparov, if he cared to drop by.

29

THE KAZAKH

After meeting Cooper in her office, they gathered in a conference room with her supervisor, Assistant Special Agent in Charge Martin Chen, a tall, thin Chinese American man. The 4:00 p.m. sun cast long shadows, and the snow on the Chugach Mountains glowed a brownish orange against the darkening sky—hints of longer days to come.

"Okay folks," Chen said, "where are we on the Peplow case?"

"Sarah, I cc'd you on the ballistics of the fragments recovered from Peplow. Ballistic match to the rifle recovered in the van," Eddie said.

"And I've got the ATF trace on the weapon," Cooper added. "Reported stolen from a gun store in Lexington, Kentucky, eight months ago."

"Probably went through a few sales with crypto," Chen said. "Little chance of putting names to this weapon."

"The van was wiped clean, too," Eddie said. "No prints on the steering wheel, door handles, or the rear door window, which was removed. No doubt the few prints on the dashboard and side windows will turn out to be from randos."

Cooper nodded, then turned to her laptop, which was connected to a projector. The screen flickered to life, casting a blue glow across their faces. "Which brings us to this," she said, pulling up a series of documents. "We have one Dmitri Saparov, born in 1963 in Almaty, Kazakhstan, of ethnic Russian parents. After military service, a career in state security services—KGB or military intelligence—from 1985 to 1991, rising to a midlevel position. We can't find any details on exactly what sort of work he did."

A grainy photo appeared on the screen: a younger Saparov, his face harder but with the same confident smile.

"No record of any religious activity during his entire Soviet-era career—which makes sense, given his position. In 1994, three years after the Soviet collapse, he surfaces as an immigrant to the U.S. as a devout Christian."

Cooper clicked through several documents. "Anyway, in 1995, he wound up in Coeur d'Alene on an R1 religious worker visa, employed as an assistant pastor and head of security for Grace Christian Mission; apparently, he was their go-to guy on the evils of big government's anti-Christian evilness. About two and a half years later, he was granted a Special Immigrant Religious Worker Green Card, EB-4 category, and five years later was naturalized."

Eddie gave a cynical smile. "Traded Marx for Jesus. How in the hell do you become a U.S. citizen while you're working for what is basically an antigovernment organization?"

"You get away with a lot in the name of religious freedom. Besides, bureaucracy doesn't always connect the dots. Saparov built a reputation in evangelical circles, moving between megachurches in Idaho and Washington. In 2016, he joined ASC as head of security and started the whole JERICHO security operation."

"A thought just came to me," Eddie said. "For someone who didn't come to the States until around '95, his accent is surprisingly mild. I'd expect someone born and trained in Kazakhstan to have a thicker accent after spending most of their life there. I mean, look at Arnold Schwarzenegger; he hired an accent removal coach and still couldn't get rid of it."

Cooper exchanged a glance with Chen. "Could mean he had extensive language training in the Soviet era," she said.

"Or some people just have different aptitudes and motivations for minimizing their accents," Chen countered.

Cooper shrugged. "Assuming Saparov was involved in the Peplow shootings, we have two options. Saparov, who is running JERICHO like a paramilitary operation, could have recruited from inside for his team or gone outside using contacts from his old spy days. With the discovery of the van, I would guess the latter. Too much of a coincidence. I think whoever pulled the trigger is enjoying a shubat in Astana."

"Shubat?"

"Yes, fermented camel's milk. A traditional Kazakh drink. I came across the term in my research."

"So, we have a man with a perfect profile and background to arrange an assassination," Eddie said.

"Who is confident he'll get away with it," Chen added.

ON HIS WAY HOME, Eddie considered the case. He found himself sympathizing with the Peplow children. Roche was certainly the most promising suspect. But like a mob boss, there were layers between him and the shooting. This was going to be a tough nut to crack.

Eddie's phone went off. It was Becca.

"Hi, Becca. What's up?"

"Another mitochondrial injury. Can you come by my office?"

"Sure, I'm in the car now. Be there in ten minutes."

30

MORE MYSTERIOUS
MITOCHONDRIA

Eddie met Becca in the conference room. She was setting up the projector.

"Hi, Eddie."

"Hi." He studied her face. The bruising around her eye had faded to a thin sliver of yellowish brown underneath the lower lid. "Your eye looks like it's recovering okay."

"Thanks."

"Any contact from Brockman?"

"Just a few text messages. I've blocked him."

"Are you safe?"

"Yes, I think so."

"Let me know if he gives you any trouble."

"I'm sure it will be okay. You ready to get started?"

Clearly, thought Eddie, this was uncomfortable for her. Her affect had flattened, and she seemed to have lost enthusiasm and energy.

Becca opened her laptop and punched a few keys. Three images of what Eddie now recognized as mitochondria appeared side by side.

"The middle one is normal. The left is from Father Dracule. On the right is our new finding." She paused, letting Eddie study them. "This came from a heart muscle biopsy. The inner membranes are thickened. Not completely disrupted like Dracule's, but not normal."

She was reciting facts dryly, not engaging in a Socratic manner, unlike the last time she reviewed mitochondrial findings. Maybe it was because Daniel wasn't here, but clearly, she was depressed. She hit the forward arrow button. A less magnified view of the mitochondria came up.

"This is a wider view showing several heart muscle cells." She pointed to various mitochondria. "Some mitochondria are normal, and some appear damaged. Here's an example of mitophagy—where a mitochondrion is undergoing degradation—and here's a mitochondrion replicating, making up for injured ones."

"So, a milder injury?"

"Yes. And from a living patient in Anchorage who experienced chest pain."

"Okay."

"One of the mitochondrial experts to whom I sent the Dracule specimen asked, and I quote: 'What the hell is going on in Alaska?' At least they're less likely to think this is artifactual."

"Is this the same injury? I mean, is it using the same mechanism?"

"It could be."

"Who is the patient?"

Becca unplugged her laptop and tucked it under her arm, signaling the meeting was over. Eddie thought he might be overreading the situation, but she seemed to want to cut things as short as possible.

"No clue. HIPAA laws and patient confidentiality, you know. The only information I received with the specimen is from a thirty-three-year-old otherwise healthy patient treated at Prov. But there was no identifying information."

"Can we find out who the patient is?"

"Dr. Sheldon Watkins, a cardiologist at the Anchorage Heart Institute, submitted the specimen. Perhaps I could find out through him. I'll call him and see if the patient will talk to me."

"If you do get a hold of the patient—"

"—we can interview him together."

"Yes."

Becca and Eddie walked out of the conference room into the hall together and paused in the hallway.

"Hey, if Brockman gives you any trouble, call me."

Becca sighed. "I know how to pick them, huh?"

"What can you do?" Eddie said. "Sociopaths can be very charming."

Becca turned and Vaugner watched her walk toward her office.

And very dangerous.

31

HEALTH CRYSTAL

"No, Grandma," Daniel shouted, "to the right! Fire! The red button! Now!"

"Oooh, I got him."

Eddie entered the den and took in the theater of operations. Taking a break from Fortnite, Daniel was supervising Gertie on a first-person, blood-and-guts shooter zombie game. Gertie sat on an ottoman, holding a controller with both hands. Daniel jumped up and down on the sofa behind her. On the sixty-five-inch LCD screen, a POV machine gun was streaming bullets at approaching zombies on a deserted farm.

"Quick, Grandma! Cycle to the flamethrower! Press the Y button!"

"Oooh!" Gertie cried.

A flamethrower replaced the machine gun. A flame shot out, frying a group of approaching zombies. Gertie shouted, "Take that, you brain-eating monsters!"

"Hi, Dad! Grandma's up to level three! She's killing zombies left and right." He bounced twice on the sofa and jumped over to him. Eddie caught him, hugged him, and put him down.

Watching Daniel coach his grandmother through the digital apocalypse, Eddie wondered if these moments were the real miracles—the small daily acts of carrying on.

"You didn't think I could do this, did you? In my day, I could play a mean game of Pong," Gertie said.

His mother's grim determination at the controller echoed the same determination she'd shown in facing every other challenge life had thrown at them—his father's abandonment, Anne's death, and Daniel's illness.

"As a law enforcement officer, I am shocked, shocked to find that vigilantism is going on in here," Eddie said in his best officiously indignant voice.

Daniel turned to face him. "They're zombies, Dad." He turned back around. "Grandma, look at your health. You better find a Health Crystal. There's one in the silo."

"Will do."

If only I could find a health crystal for Daniel.

Gertie navigated across a parched cornfield toward a bombed-out silo. "Watch out, Grandma!"

A huge zombie suddenly appeared and took a swipe at the POV shooter. The screen turned red, and a black GAME OVER zoomed in.

"Grandma, you gotta cycle to the plasma gun for Boris."

A pulsating message appeared: *Life regenerating.*

There was a whooshing sound, and the black screen faded into the farm. The regenerated POV character looked over the barrel of a shotgun. Zombies appeared, and blasting ensued.

"Now remember, Grandma, when you see the silo, cycle to the plasma gun so you're ready for Boris."

Eddie's phone sounded. He walked into the kitchen to escape the noise. "Hi, Becca."

"Hi, Eddie." Her voice was still flat, like she was just going through the motions. Eddie felt like screaming, *Snap out of it!*

"The person with the disrupted cardiac mitochondria called me. A doctor, Jason Defner."

"The ER doctor at Prov."

"You know him?"

"I've met him. He bears a remarkable resemblance to an asshole. You'll see, a real piece of work."

"He did seem a little edgy. Anyway, I've made arrangements to interview him on Monday at 11 a.m., assuming you can make it. In the conference room here. If not, I can call him back."

"I'll be there."

Becca could use a health crystal, too.

32

THE BEAST

They had agreed Eddie would arrive ten minutes before Dr. Defner's eleven o'clock appointment. Becca had already set up her laptop and projector in the conference room.

They sat in awkward silence.

"Any issues with Brockman?"

Becca sighed. "Eddie, I appreciate your concern, but please stop bringing up Brockman."

"No, you're right. I was—"

"I don't want you to think about Brockman every time you look at me. I don't want to be defined by him in your eyes. Please."

"So, Becca." He paused for a beat. "Who's this Brockman you keep going on about?"

They both laughed.

Dr. Defner arrived at eleven sharp. Rhonda, the receptionist, showed him into the conference room. He was wearing jeans and a black blazer over a black T-shirt. The shirt featured a horned beast's skull with the right side of the face torn away, leaving a jagged void. *Beast Slayer* appeared below in Gothic font, with *Revelation 13:1* underneath. He showed no sign of recognizing Eddie. Becca approached him and held out her hand.

"Welcome, Dr. Defner. I'm Rebecca Raven, medical examiner."

They shook hands. "This is Detective Vaugner with the Anchorage Police Department." Eddie kept his seat and nodded.

"Wait," Defner said. "Why is a cop here? Has Lange pressed charges?"

"Dr. Lange, the surgeon?"

"Do I need an attorney?"

"Dr. Defner," Becca sad, "we're interested in talking to you because the novel mitochondrial findings of your myocardial biopsy resembled the post-mortem findings of another forensic case I'm working on. I was hoping you could give me some insight. Detective Vaugner is here at my request since he's conducting the death investigation. I thought doing this with one interview would be more efficient."

Not wanting to spook Defner or make him defensive, Eddie held off on asking him what had made him think Lange might press charges. Instead, he said, "I wouldn't be here if Dr. Lange had pressed charges. I'm a homicide detective."

"Okay," Defner said. "Fine."

Beads of sweat were forming on the man's brow.

"You seem hot. Would you like to take your jacket off?" Becca asked.

"Yes, thank you."

"There's a hook by the door."

Defner slipped off his coat and turned to hang it up, revealing a passage from the Book of Revelation printed on the back of his T-shirt:

And I saw a beast rising out of the sea, having seven heads and ten horns, and on his horns ten crowns, and on his head a blasphemous name.

"Perhaps you could relate the events surrounding the cardiac event?" Becca asked.

"Okay, fine. Lange and I had a disagreement about a case earlier."

"What sort of disagreement?"

"It was about the Peplow woman, the wife of the guy who was shot at the Hotel Captain Cook. You know what I'm talking about?"

"Yes, we're familiar," Eddie said.

"She arrived at the ER in extremis with a gunshot wound to the left chest. As I was trying to put in a chest tube, Lange pulled me out of the way. Totally inappropriate."

"Why did he pull you out of the way?" Eddie asked.

"She flatlined. Lange panicked and grabbed me from behind, I might add. Basically assaulted me."

"What happened when Lange pulled you out of the way?"

"He cracked her chest and clamped the hilum—the structure where the blood vessels leave the heart and go to the lung."

"So Lange saved her life," Eddie said.

"Yes, but I would have done the same thing in another second. What he did wasn't a big deal."

Eddie noted how Defner's account corresponded to Dana Peplow's out-of-body recollections.

"What happened in the parking lot?" he asked.

"When I saw him, I called him on his unprofessional behavior and demanded an apology. He laughed at me and accused me of trying to kill the patient. He even blasphemed the Bible. I don't mind telling you, that set me off, and I got into his face. And as I did, I was suddenly overcome by severe chest pain and shortness of breath so bad I collapsed to the ground. After a few moments, I picked myself up and got to the ER."

"Okay," Becca said. She looked at Eddie. "Detective?"

"No, I'm good. Continue."

"Have you seen the micrographs of your mitochondria?"

"No, but Watkins described them to me."

"Okay, let's look at them."

Becca hit a key to wake the laptop from sleep mode. "Just for review, here's a micrograph of a normal mitochondrion. Focus on the cristae."

"Okay," Defner said.

She clicked to the next slide. "Here's your biopsy. The red arrows are pointing to gaps in the cristae. It's subtle, but these are definitely real and not artifacts."

"Yes, I see."

She clicked again. "Here's a micrograph taken from a dead person. This is the case Detective Vaugner is working on. Notice the cristae. Complete disruption. This is a fatal injury."

"And as Dr. Watkins may have related to you, mitochondrial experts have not seen this before."

"Can you give me more information on the other patient, the dead one, Dr. Raven?" the doctor asked.

"I'll defer to Detective Vaugner," said Becca.

Eddie stepped in. "I can tell you the patient was an eighty-two-year-old priest who, despite his age, seemed to be in good health. His mitochondrial lesions were in his brain."

"Two men of faith, each struck by an unexplained mechanism. For the old man, it was fatal. Maybe a matter of age. Or his faith. He was a Catholic, you know. Did Lange know the priest?"

"We have no information on that," Eddie said, even though his thoughts were turning toward the bearded man from the surveillance video. Could that have been Lange in disguise, covering up the scar that makes him stand out?

"Maybe you should find out," said Defner.

Eddie ignored the comment tell. "You asked if Lange pressed charges. Why would he press charges for you yelling at him?"

Defner shifted uneasily in his seat. "I was upset. I grabbed Lange by the shirt."

"You grabbed him by his shirt. Did you hit him?"

"No, just pushed him."

"That's battery. You're lucky he didn't press charges."

"I wanted to make a point. I wasn't going to hurt him. Besides, he did the same to me in the trauma room."

He did it to save a woman's life; you did it over a bruised ego.

"I understand," Eddie said aloud.

"Okay, we're just here to get at some medical truths," Becca said, redirecting the conversation. "Shall we continue?"

Eddie nodded. "By all means."

"You said you picked yourself up and went to the ER. Did Lange not assist you?" Becca asked, looking over at Eddie.

"No. He stood over me and told me never to touch him again, or he wouldn't let me off this easy. It was like he was telling me he'd caused it."

"Have you ever experienced pain like this before?" she asked.

"No."

"What about risks for cardiovascular disease?"

"None. I do not smoke; I drink only occasionally. My last total cholesterol is 154 milligrams, with an LDL of 60 and an HDL of 90. As commanded by 1 Corinthians 6:20, I glorify God in my body, eat well, and work out regularly. There is no family history of heart disease. Both of my parents are in their seventies and in perfect health."

"Very good. I see from the tattoo on your forearm that you were in the service. Did you see combat?" Becca asked.

"Yes, I was a medic in Germany, at the military hospital in Landstuhl. I treated the results of combat. I became interested in becoming a doctor during my service."

"Do you suffer from post-traumatic stress?"

"No."

"Do you take any performance enhancers? Anabolic steroids?"

"No. Never."

"Are you on any medications?"

"No."

"Any cocaine, meth, or other amphetamines or other stimulants?"

"No."

"What about travel? Have you been out of state or country lately?"

"Not recently. I was down in Idaho over a year ago, but no travel since."

Eddie jumped in again. "As an ER physician, do you have any idea how Dr. Lange, or anyone else, could have caused this injury? What would the mechanism be?"

"I don't know. But I felt an evil presence as Lange stood over me, doing nothing."

"As you must know, Dr. Defner," Becca said, "feelings of doom are common in patients suffering cardiac chest pain."

"This was more than doom; this was Satanic. Evil. Besides, my cath was normal."

"People who have anxiety reactions can experience chest pain indistinguishable from cardiac-caused chest pain," Becca said.

Eddie was getting irritated. "You assaulted Lange after he intervened and saved a woman's life. Who was being evil?"

Defner glared at him. "Are we done here, Dr. Raven?"

"I'm good," Becca said. "Detective Vaugner?"

"No further questions."

Becca stood. "Thanks for coming in."

The doctor got up, put on his jacket, and headed out the door. He paused and turned to face Becca and Eddie.

"You can think I'm crazy, but I know Lange did this to me. Maybe he should be your main suspect in the death of the priest."

Eddie smiled. Becca said, "Thank you, Dr. Defner."

The man looked like he wanted to take a parting shot, but he thought better of it and left the room.

"What do you think?" she asked.

"I guess I should interview the evil Dr. Lange."

IN THE PARKING lot outside the medical examiner's office, Defner climbed into his Corvette and sat rigidly behind the wheel. He reached for his doctor's bag. *What if they go to Lange, and he tells them he saw coke in my nose?* Fuck it. He couldn't prove anything. Defner decided he would have to stay clean a while, in case they hit him with a surprise drug test.

"Fucking Lange," he hissed. He put the bag back in the back seat.

33

CLOSE TO THE VEST

Back in the office, Eddie googled "Grayson Lange M.D. Anchorage, AK." He scanned a patient review site. Words and phrases like "caring," "listened to me," "made me feel at ease," "compassionate and competent," and "saved my life" were common. One three-star review was from a patient from Fairbanks who was miffed that Lange was out of town when she tried to make an appointment while visiting Anchorage.

In addition to garnering rave reviews about his medical skills, Lange had carved out a reputation in the extreme adventure world. Apparently, he tackled everything from skiing and mountain climbing to free climbing and BASE jumping. Between death-defying feats, he enjoyed typical Alaskan pursuits like flying, fishing, and snowmachining. One photo in particular caught Eddie's attention: Lange holding his gathered parachute at the bottom of Norway's Kjerag Cliff. Not only because of where he stood, but also because of the way the oblique sunlight threw his scar into sharp relief.

He came across a 2019 Anchorage Daily News profile titled "The Adventurous Dr. Lange: Saving Lives. Risking His Own?" It featured two photos of him, one in scrubs and one in a ski outfit, holding up a pair of skis.

He took a gap year between college and medical school to summit Mount Everest in 2007 when he was twenty-two. "It was a bucket list item and seemed like the best time to do it. If I were to be swept away by an avalanche or fall into a crevasse, I didn't want my last thoughts to be, 'After all that time, money, and effort going to med school!'"

Later in the article, Lange dismissed suggestions he was reckless by nature: *"I prepare for every adventure and train hard."*

One detail in particular caught Eddie's eye.

Asked why he chose to practice in Anchorage, Lange replied, "Not only was I raised here, but my life was also saved here." In the mid-nineties, when he was six and living in Talkeetna, he lost his family in an accident. He was the only survivor. "I was flown to Anchorage, to Providence, where my office is now. Surgeons saved my life, and that's what inspired my career choice. One of the biggest thrills of my life was coming back here as a surgeon and assisting Dr. Keller, the surgeon who saved my life just before he retired."

"Also, Alaska remains one of the few places left in America where a surgeon can have a solo practice and not be part of a large group. With my lifestyle, it was important for me to be my own boss and make my own schedule."

Eddie navigated to Lange's surgical practice website. His office was on the Providence campus, hours 9 a.m. to 5 p.m. He dialed the number.

"Dr. Lange's office. This is Cheryl."

"Hi Cheryl, this is Detective Vaugner from the Anchorage Police Department. I'd like to talk to Dr. Lange in the next day or two."

"As a patient or a detective?"

"Detective. It's about a case I'm working on."

"I can give you thirty minutes at one o'clock this Thursday."

"I'll take it."

LATER THAT AFTERNOON, Eddie was standing at the doorway of the office of the Homicide Division's commander. Sergeant Polkovich was on the phone but waved him in and gestured to a chair.

"It's her wedding, dear. If she wants the salmon instead of the chicken, get the salmon. Yes, I know what it costs... Just get the salmon. No, fuck it, get the chicken and the salmon. I gotta go, Eddie's here... Okay... Okay... Love you too."

He hung up and rubbed his temples. "Jen says hi. Not that I don't love mine, but you should thank God you don't have a daughter."

Eddie smiled. *There's not much I feel like thanking God for these days.* He simply said, "Yeah, I hear that."

"Anyway, Eddie, I called you in because I was looking at the murder board."

The murder board tracked all open homicide cases. It had evolved from an actual blackboard to a whiteboard and was now maintained as a spreadsheet on the homicide division intranet.

"Why is this dead priest on here?" Polkovich asked.

Clearly, the sergeant hadn't read the case notes. Eddie outlined the evidence: the kicked-in confessional door suggesting someone had held it closed, surveillance video showing another person walking with the priest near his estimated time of death, the inexplicable cause of death, the priest's false identity, the castration, and the scars compatible with old stab wounds.

Eddie understood Polkovich's position. Homicide clearance rates were closely monitored nationwide, and with rates declining, chiefs of police pressured division heads to "get them cleared." Anchorage's 66 percent clearance rate—twenty-two solved cases out of thirty-three homicides the year before—had beaten the national average, but in a small city, even one or two unsolved murders could tank the statistics. Both the police chief and the mayor watched these numbers closely.

"We can't verify his identity or background before the '90s. No state or federal ID. No fingerprints or DNA in any database. Like he dropped in from a UFO."

"He was hiding a past life," Polkovich said. He drummed his fingers on the desktop, eyes darting between Eddie and his computer screen. "But no family pushing for answers, no clear evidence of foul play, nothing in the news, and frankly, no political pressure to solve it."

"That's right."

Polkovich's phone buzzed. "Shit, it's Jen again." He picked up. "Hey, hon, one sec."

As Eddie stood to leave, the sergeant added, "Okay. Use your judgment. Obviously, the Peplow case is your priority."

Walking back to his office, Eddie wondered why he hadn't mentioned the Lange connection or his upcoming interview. Was it the tenuous connection? His admiration for the doctor? Fear that Polkovich would shut down the investigation? Instinct? Probably all of the above.

34

OFFICE VISIT

"Detective Vaugner?"

"That's me," he said to the woman at the desk.

"Dr. Lange is just finishing up with a patient."

"No problem."

Eddie paced around the waiting room of Lange's office on the PAMC campus. A Danish modern motif. Alaska-themed art on the walls. A six-foot-wide panoramic image of Denali dominating the Alaska Range, taken by Alaskan photographer Myron White. On the opposite wall, a giclée by John Gause titled "Awaiting a Wind" of Captain Cook's ships, the HMS *Resolution* and HMS *Discovery*, in calm waters in Prince William Sound, with the sun low in the sky over purple and white mountains. A David Boxley Tsimshian mask. *Jesus, those go for five grand.* In one corner, a locked mahogany and glass cabinet displayed baleen baskets of various sizes and shapes. Another few thousand bucks.

"This is quite an art collection you all have here," Eddie said.

"Yes, isn't it? Everything you see in here is a gift to Dr. Lange from patients."

"What does the mask represent?"

"A killer whale."

"Oh."

Lange, dressed in blue scrubs, emerged from the back of the office suite accompanied by a middle-aged woman. A nurse followed behind and sat at a back desk.

"Cheryl, we're all done with Mrs. Charles. No need for further follow-up."

"Okay," Cheryl said.

"Thank you, Dr. Lange. You and the entire office. You guys are the greatest."

As the woman walked out through the waiting room, she beamed at him. "You're in good hands," she said.

Eddie smiled back at her. "Good to know, ma'am," he replied as she left. *Hmmm,* thought Eddie. *I'm not exactly getting a murderer vibe here.*

"Detective," Lange said. "Come on back."

He followed Lange into his office. The doctor took his seat behind a large, L-shaped desk and asked Eddie to have a seat as well.

Diplomas and certificates hung on the wall behind his desk. Stanford Medical School, residency training certificates, American Board of Surgery certification. On another wall, a world map was dotted with stick pins on every continent except Antarctica, most over mountain ranges. Eddie assumed these marked the locations of his adventures. Scattered around—hanging on walls, sitting on top of bookshelves and credenzas—were photographs of Lange, either alone or with groups, geared up. On one wall, a framed ten-by-twelve photograph of Lange standing on a mountaintop, holding two thumbs up, with an expanse of white peaks off in the distance below him and blue sky above. Eddie assumed this was his Mount Everest summit. On a bookshelf at a right angle to his desk, he saw a faded, small-framed photograph of a boy, about twelve years old, standing on a porch, smiling and squinting in the sunlight. It reminded Eddie of the picture on Daniel's nightstand.

"How is the Peplow case going?" Lange asked.

"Slow, but I'm not here about the Peplow case."

"Well, how can I help you, then?"

"The incident involving Dr. Jason Defner in the parking garage two weeks ago. What can you tell me?"

Lange raised his arms and clasped his hands behind his head. Once again, Eddie noticed the 2-3-1-6 tattoo on his left forearm.

The doctor chuckled. "Why is a homicide detective asking questions about a fracas I had with Defner?"

"It may have a bearing on another case we're working on. I got Defner's version; now I'd like yours."

Eddie studied Lange's reaction. All he saw was a shrug. "Okay, as you know, Mrs. Peplow came in with a gunshot wound to her chest, very close to death. Defner was having trouble putting in a chest tube, and she flatlined and he was floundering. I asked him to move away. He refused, so I pulled him out of the way to perform an emergency thoracotomy."

"As Mrs. Peplow related in her near-death experience."

"Yes. From there, we went to the OR, and, as you also know, I removed her left lung. Later that evening, heading to my car—shortly after seeing you, as a matter of fact—I found Defner standing at my car's driver's door, demanding an apology for pulling him away from Mrs. Peplow. In so many words, I told him to fuck off and get out of my way. We went back and forth"—Lange let out a small chuckle—"even traded Bible quotes. This really set him off, and he grabbed me by the front of my shirt, spun me around, and slammed me against the car, then raised his hand to hit me. Suddenly, he let go and clutched his chest. He fell against another car, slumped, and fell to the ground."

"He said you did nothing to help him."

"He told me to stay away from him. Besides, there wasn't anything I needed to do for him."

"How do you mean?"

"He was in distress but alert, breathing, and moving under his own power."

Eddie looked down at his notebook. "Defner stated you said, 'Touch me again, and you won't get off this easy.'"

"When he was in my face, I noticed some white powder in his nostril. If cocaine was causing him to be overly aggressive and he flunked a drug screen, he would have been fired, his license suspended or revoked, and left with a criminal record for assault and battery. I'd say I let him off easy. And, of course, cocaine can cause chest pain, even heart attacks."

"He also said you just got into your car and drove off."

"Yes, Defner had gotten up and was walking back toward the hospital under his own power. No reason for me to stay."

"You weren't concerned about him?"

"Whether Defner lives or dies is of no concern to me. Besides," Lange joked, "he has a glorious afterlife with Jesus waiting for him."

Eddie jotted a few things in his notepad.

"He believes you caused his heart attack, or whatever it was. He underwent a cardiac cath and biopsy."

"Defner believes a lot of crazy things. He's part of that America Salvation Church."

Eddie noted the surgeon showed no curiosity about the biopsy.

"He had some mitochondrial damage, which appears to be low-grade and reversible."

"The cocaine, I guess."

"The mitochondrial experts don't think it was drug-related."

"I don't know what to tell you. I'm just a dumb surgeon."

Eddie pulled out his phone, brought up an autopsy photo of Father Dracule's face, and showed it to Lange. "Do you know this man?"

The doctor studied the photograph. Eddie detected no anxiety, nor any sign that he recognized Dracule.

"This is a corpse. With a freaked-out expression. Not familiar. Was he a patient of mine?"

After a beat, Eddie replied, "Not that we're aware. His name is Father Dracule Vincent."

"Why are you asking me if I know him?"

Eddie took the picture back and pocketed it. "He had mitochondrial injuries similar to Dr. Defner's, except fatal."

Lange shrugged. "Sounds potentially interesting."

The photograph of the little boy caught Eddie's eye again.

It seemed out of place in the office, which was otherwise filled with mementos of heroic adventures and professional accomplishments.

"The little boy, who is that?"

"My older brother, Tommy. He died shortly after that photo was taken. I was six then."

Eddie looked from the photo to Lange's scarred face. Then it clicked. Talkeetna.

"Wait, are you the survivor of the Gower family murder in Talkeetna back in the mid-nineties?"

"1996. And yes, I am."

"You were the only survivor."

"Yes, unfortunately."

"You changed your name."

"I took the last name of my adoptive parents. I didn't want to be identified with one of the worst family murders in Alaskan history."

Eddie tapped his lips with his fingers, looking at the scar on Lange's face.

"What about the scar?" he said as he stroked his own cheek. "I mean, speaking of being identified with a murder, how do you explain that away?"

"Most people don't ask about it, and if they do, I tell them it was from an accident."

"Ever think of growing a beard?"

"No." Lange laughed. "Besides, it tones down my good looks, so I'm not just a pretty face."

Eddie smiled and nodded. Lange didn't seem fazed by the beard question. He closed his notebook and pocketed it. "Dana Peplow seems to be doing okay. She calls me from time to time. Do you hear from her?"

"Yes, regularly, and she's doing great. She's lost some weight. Not requiring oxygen. She's frustrated about how the case is going. But you probably know that."

"Yes, I do. We're all frustrated."

Eddie stood up and held out his hand. Lange shook it. His hand was warm and dry. *If Lange killed Dracule, he may be one of the most composed subjects I've ever interviewed.*

Eddie took another glance at the photo of Tommy before leaving.

"I have to say, what you've made of your life—it's an inspiring story."

"Yes, I was lucky."

AFTER HE LEFT Lange's office, Eddie waited for the elevator. The right elevator door opened. Eddie stepped in. As the door closed, he saw Reverend Roche pass in front of him in the hallway, heading in the direction of Lange's office. Eddie pushed the open door button. He waited a second and rubbernecked down the hallway to see the pastor enter Lange's office.

35

DIEU LE GUÉRIT

Cheryl handed Reverend Roche's chart to Grayson.

Sitting at his desk, Grayson flipped the chart open and read through it quickly. Symptoms of esophageal reflux. Failed medical therapy. Referred by gastroenterologist Sam Olsen, MD.

"He's ready. He had his bodyguards in there with him, but I told them to stay in the waiting room."

"Anchorage can be a small town sometimes."

"What do you mean?" Cheryl said.

"Detective Vaugner, who is investigating the Peplow assassination, was just here, and Pastor Roche, the main suspect, is my next patient."

"What can I tell you? He wanted his surgery yesterday, so I reserved a spot on the schedule for a lap Nissen next week."

ENTERING THE EXAM ROOM, Grayson found Roche sitting on the exam table, clad in socks, underwear, and a patient gown with an opening in the front. The reverend flashed him a tense smile, typical of Type A personalities forced into the nondominant role.

"Hi, Doctor. I left my shorts on. Is that okay?"

"Not a problem."

There is a medical art known as *Augenblick*, which is German for "the blink of an eye." It's the ability of the physician to assess a patient at a glance.

Preternatural white teeth: veneers. Lack of forehead wrinkling and arched eyebrows: Botox injections. An unnatural brow line and hair follicle distribution: hair transplant. Hollowed-out eyelids: over-aggressive blepharoplasty. Faint scar with beard line close to the ear: facelift.

The open gown revealed several faint scars, each about a quarter inch, with areas of slightly rippled skin indicating liposuction. A pinky diamond ring. Manicured fingernails. Silk boxer shorts.

Despite his practiced calm, the masseter muscles in Roche's jaws rippled, and his knees jiggled back and forth constantly. Tells of tension beneath his polished and confident exterior.

Even his diagnosis, GERD, supported Grayson's impression of his patient. The disease was most common in competitive, achievement-oriented, impatient, controlling individuals with aggressive and hostile personality traits.

Grayson's blink-of-an-eye assessment of Roche: a vain, controlling sociopath.

"Dr. Lange, before we get started, do you know who I am?"

"You're the head of the America Salvation Church. Pretty much everyone in Anchorage knows who you are."

"Good. So you must know I am suspected of the assassination of Jack Peplow."

Grayson shrugged. "Yes, it's a hot story right now."

"You also should know that one of my prominent church members, Jason Defner, the ER physician, suspects you of causing some sort of heart incident a few weeks ago."

Grayson smiled. "And how does he suppose I did that?"

"He thinks you're an agent of Satan."

Grayson chuckled. "You want an agent of Satan operating on you?"

"Jason is a man of faith, but sometimes I think he has a bit of PTSD from his time in the service. I am here because I asked Dr. Olson to send me to the best surgeon in Anchorage."

"There are several others who would do a fine job."

"No, I always go with the best. I just wanted to clear the air and know if any of this causes a problem with you operating on me."

Grayson smiled again. "My practice has a contract with the Department of Corrections. I treat all sorts of ne'er-do-wells. Convicted thieves, rapists, and other murderers. Treating you will not pose a problem for me, even if you are the head of a megachurch."

Roche guffawed. "Touché, Doctor." If he caught *other murderers*, he didn't give an indication.

"Tell me how your reflux symptoms are interfering with your life."

"I have frequent bouts of heartburn. I often wake up at night coughing. And the pills aren't helping much anymore. Dr. Olsen says I have chronic inflammation of my esophagus, which, if not treated, may lead to cancer."

Grayson nodded. "You may have heard this before, but I will go through it again, so you know where I am coming from regarding your treatment."

"Fire away, Doctor. Repetition is the key to learning."

"As you probably know, GERD, gastroesophageal reflux disease, is a condition in which the physiological sphincter between the stomach and esophagus malfunctions and allows acidic gastric contents to reflux up into the esophagus. Your heartburn is from acid-induced inflammation of the esophagus, which doesn't have the protective lining the stomach does. The coughing at night indicates the reflux is so severe that the stomach contents are going all the way up the esophagus and spilling into your trachea. In your case, it has caused Barrett's esophagus, a chronic inflammatory state of the lower esophagus. And yes, this is a risk factor for esophageal cancer, so it's imperative to get this under control. You with me?"

"Yes, you're doing a great job of explaining things. I like that."

"The operation I would perform for this is called the laparoscopic Nissen fundoplication, and it's the gold standard for treating patients like you who have failed medical therapy. This operation involves wrapping the upper part of the stomach around the end of the esophagus. This creates a new sphincter to stop the reflux. We do this laparoscopically—a minimally invasive approach. We make four small half-inch incisions and use special instruments to perform the wrap. Most patients can go home the same day. You'll be restricted to a liquid diet for one to two weeks, then soft foods, and finally a regular diet."

"Doesn't sound so bad. It will be nice to sleep through a night without waking up with severe heartburn and coughing."

"Even after this operation, Dr. Olson will have to monitor you closely."

"Yes, he told me."

Grayson opened the gown, removed his stethoscope from his lab coat pocket, and listened to Roche's heart and lungs. When he was done, he pocketed the device.

"Did you hear this one?" the reverend asked. "A man died and went to heaven. While standing at St. Peter's gate, he saw this old man with a long white beard running around wearing a white coat and a stethoscope around his neck. The man asked, 'Who's that?' St. Peter answered, 'Oh, that's God, he likes to play doctor.'"

Grayson smiled. "Yes, I've heard it. Lie down, please."

Roche lay down, and Grayson started palpating his abdomen.

"Do you play God, Doctor?"

He pressed down on Roche's abdomen—upper and lower, left and right. The reverend held his breath and tensed up. He seemed uncomfortable being the supplicant, even though Grayson's hands were warm and his palpations gentle.

"Do you know who Ambroise Paré was?" Grayson asked.

"No, I haven't heard that name."

"Ambroise Paré was a barber-surgeon of the sixteenth century in France, a surgeon to several kings. He's considered the father of modern surgery. He is famous for saying, *Je le pansai, Dieu le guérit*, which means 'I bandaged him, God healed him.' Today, surgeons have adopted and economized the sentiment by saying, 'I cut, God heals.'"

"Well, it's nice to know you're a man of God."

Grayson just smiled.

"You are a man of God, aren't you?"

"Aren't we all God's children, Pastor? Cheryl tells me you are scheduled for next week. Any questions?"

"How did you get that scar on your face, Doctor?"

Grayson knew the inquiry was not born out of empathy or even curiosity. Roche was doing his sociopath thing—trying to probe for weakness to establish dominance.

Grayson batted the question away. "A childhood accident."

It was all Roche was going to get. Grayson opened the door. "I'll see you soon," he said, stepping out. "You can get dressed. Cheryl will have some paperwork and instructions for you."

"Okay, Doc. You cut. God will heal."

"Indeed, He will."

Grayson saw Roche smile with self-satisfaction, as if the killer had won the upper hand.

36

THE GOWERS

Eddie blinked at the computer terminal a few times, then looked at the acid-free box of original case files on the table in the middle of the windowless reading room. White cotton archival gloves rested on top of it. The Alaska Bureau of Investigation had already pulled the Gower murder files for him—nearly thirty years old but preserved under statute 12.36.200, which mandated evidence in homicides be kept for fifty years.

Flipping through paper would be easier than navigating scanned documents in a database.

He pulled on the gloves and lifted the lid off the box, and his nose caught the musty odor of archived documents that had waited patiently in a storage facility for some thirty years. He flipped through several binders until he found the executive summary submitted by Sergeant Robert Oakes of the Major Crimes Section, Alaska Bureau of Investigation, a division of the Alaska State Troopers. He began reading.

ALASKA BUREAU OF INVESTIGATION
MAJOR CRIMES SECTION

Case File: 95-0115-H

DATE: January 21, 1995

REPORTING OFFICER: Sgt. Robert Oakes

INCIDENT TYPE: Multiple Homicide

LOCATION: 13925 Red Tail Road, Talkeetna, AK

STATUS: Open

INITIAL FINDINGS:

On January 15, 1995, at 2319, state 911 operators received a call from Richard Gower, brother of John Gower, reporting a mass shooting at the residence of John Gower at 13925 Red Tail Road in Talkeetna, Alaska.

Police and EMS officials arrived at the scene to find Richard Gower distraught, crying, "They're all dead."

VICTIMS:

Inside the residence, three members of the family were deceased:

1. John Gower, aged 45

2. Alice Gower, aged 36

3. Thomas Gower, aged 12

A fourth victim, Grayson Gower, aged 6, was found alive but in critical condition. Grayson was resuscitated at the scene by EMTs and evacuated by helicopter to Providence Alaska Medical Center, where he underwent emergency surgery. He has provided a limited eyewitness account due to unconsciousness/traumatic amnesia.

AUTOPSY FINDINGS:

1. John Gower:

   - COD: Exsanguination from shotgun blast to left flank

   - Disruption of iliac artery and vein

   - Death not instantaneous

2. Alice Gower:

   - COD: Massive cerebral trauma from shotgun blast to face

   - GSR: present on hands and arms

3. Thomas Gower:

   - COD: Massive cardiac injury from shotgun blast to chest

   - Evidence of recent sexual assault

- *Trauma to anus and rectum*
- *Gross hemorrhage and fecal contamination noted*

CRIME SCENE RECONSTRUCTION:

The following reconstruction is based on witness statements (Grayson Gower) and crime scene evidence:

At approximately 2200 hours on January 15, 1995, Grayson Gower awakened by sounds of his brother crying. Witness statement as follows:

"Tommy was bent over the back of the sofa, and my father had his pee-pee in his butt. Tommy was crying, 'Please stop, it hurts.'"

Grayson reports yelling at his father to stop. When ordered to return to bed, he instead went to the kitchen and acquired a six-inch filleting knife. He has no further recollection of events.

PRELIMINARY SEQUENCE OF EVENTS:

Initial theory suggested:

1. Grayson, wielding knife, assaulted father.

2. Father overpowered him, took the knife, and inflicted near-fatal abdominal wounds (see operative report).

3. Mother (Alice Gower) entered with Winchester Model 1897 shotgun.

4. Mother fired at Mr. Gower, causing flank wound.

5. Struggle for weapon ensued.

6. Weapon discharged into ceiling during struggle.

7. John Gower took weapon from Alice Gower, shot her and Thomas.

8. John Gower died of wounds.

WEAPON DISCHARGE SEQUENCE:

Four confirmed discharges of shotgun:

1 . John Gower (left flank).

2. Ceiling of living room (confirmed by buckshot pattern).

3. Alice Gower (facial wound).

4. Thomas Gower (chest wound).

CRITICAL INCONSISTENCY:

Absence of GSR on John Gower's hands/arms.

Procedural error noted: Richard Gower not tested for GSR at scene.

TIMELINE OF EVENTS:

2200: Initial incident begins

2221: Call from John Gower residence to Richard Gower

2315: Richard Gower arrives (40-minute delay reported)

2320: 911 call placed

2335: State Police/paramedics arrive

2340: Rev. Cyrus Chase arrives

WITNESS STATEMENT - RICHARD GOWER:

The following is the reconstruction of Richard Gower's events based on his interview:

- Received emergency call from brother at 2221.

- Delayed arrival by 30 minutes due to car trouble.

- Found all victims upon arrival.

- Checked for vital signs on all victims. Detected no breathing or pulses.

- Made 911 call at 2320.

- Also contacted Pastor Cyrus Chase.

- Unable to produce ID when requested, states he left house in a rush. Identity attested to by Pastor Chase

- Expressed shock at Grayson's survival.

- Quote: "miracle from God like Lazarus rising from the dead."

SUBSEQUENT INVESTIGATION:

Richard Gower's whereabouts unknown after incident:

- $500 ATM withdrawal night of murders.

- Additional $500 withdrawal following morning.

- Remaining balance: $330.

- Richard Gower's vehicle never recovered.

- Multistate search yielded no results.

- No forwarding information provided.

Case remains open.

·   ·   ·

AFTER FINISHING THE ORIGINAL REPORT, Eddie moved on to the first supplemental report.

ALASKA STATE POLICE
   SUPPLEMENTAL INVESTIGATION REPORT
   CASE #: 95-01-0142 ORIGINAL DATE OF INCIDENT: January 15, 1995
   SUPPLEMENT #: 2
   DATE OF REPORT: January 29, 1995
   LOCATION: Gower Residence, 13925 Red Tail Road, Talkeetna, Alaska
   REPORTING OFFICER: Detective Sgt. Robert Oakes, Major Crimes Section
   SUBJECT: Background Investigation - Gower Family
   SUBJECT BACKGROUND INFORMATION
   FAMILY INFORMATION
   COMMUNITY INTEGRATION
   Interviews with neighbors (see attached statements) indicate minimal community interaction outside church activities. The family described as "pleasant but private" by multiple sources. Pastor Cyrus Chase reports John Gower was "devout" and had previously considered entering Catholic priesthood before converting to Second Advent faith.
   CHILDREN'S RECORDS
   NOTE: Interview with midwife Lilly Gill (01/27/95) confirmed she delivered both Thomas and Grayson Gower, as well as most of the children of the Second Advent Church, as an independent healthcare provider and completed standard birth documentation. Gill described the Second Advent Church as "weird and private" and very devoted to Pastor Chase. Pastor Chase attended most of the births in his church. When asked about Grayson, Gill said Grayson always seemed "bright and special," although she had limited interaction with him and the other children, mostly just occasional run-ins at the supermarket, bakery, gas station, and similar situations. (See Attachment 11 for full transcript)

VICTIM STATUS UPDATE

GRAYSON A. GOWER remains in critical but stable condition at Providence Alaska Medical Center, but remains unable to provide additional details beyond initial statement. Attending physicians report remarkably quick improvement given the severity of injuries.

SEARCH FOR RICHARD D. GOWER

Efforts to locate RICHARD D. GOWER continue. Subject's bank account shows no activity since withdrawals on January 15-16, 1995. Subject was a self-employed handyman and worked irregular schedules. Frequently took extended periods off. Customers reported his work as solid and reliable. He had not filed a 1040 (Schedule-C) statement in three years.

Investigation has revealed no apparent motive for the assault beyond subject's witness statement regarding sexual abuse. No financial stressors, history of violence, or other typical precipitating factors have been identified. The lack of photo identification for John Gower and limited community engagement outside religious circles suggests a pattern of social isolation that may be relevant to understanding family dynamics. Inconsistencies in witness accounts regarding family history and birth records warrant further investigation.

Detective Sergeant Robert Oakes, Major Crimes Section, Alaska Bureau of Investigation

EDDIE FOUND the note on Lilly Gill interesting. He skimmed through the next two supplemental reports—routine updates on unsuccessful searches for Richard Gower, interviews with church members that yielded nothing, and dead-end inquiries to transportation hubs. The only information of note tracked Grayson Gower's continued recovery. Supplemental Report #2 documented the boy regaining consciousness and providing limited testimony. Report #3 noted his transfer from intensive care to a regular pediatric ward, with physicians expressing surprise at his resilience despite the severity of his wounds. By Supplemental Report #4, filed six weeks after the murders, the case was clearly growing cold.

ALASKA STATE POLICE

SUPPLEMENTAL INVESTIGATION REPORT CASE #: 95-01-0142

ORIGINAL DATE OF INCIDENT: January 15, 1995

SUPPLEMENT #: 4

DATE OF REPORT: March 1, 1995

LOCATION: Gower Residence, 13925 Red Tail Road, Talkeetna, Alaska

REPORTING OFFICER: Detective Sgt. Robert Oakes, Major Crimes Section

SUBJECT: Update on Search for Richard D. Gower / Status of Grayson Gower

SUMMARY OF INVESTIGATION

This report documents ongoing efforts to locate RICHARD D. GOWER (W/M, DOB 06/17/1952), who remains a person of interest in the homicide investigation of John, Alice, and Thomas Gower.

INVESTIGATIVE ACTIONS

The following actions have been taken in attempts to locate subject RICHARD D. GOWER: [See supplemental reports]

CONCLUSION

After six weeks of intensive search efforts, the whereabouts of RICHARD D. GOWER remain unknown. Investigation into the homicides continues with subject remaining a person of interest.

STATUS OF GRAYSON GOWER

GRAYSON A. GOWER was discharged from Providence Alaska Medical Center on February 7, 1995, following substantial recovery from his injuries. Subject has been placed with licensed foster parents Edward and Margaret Lange of Anchorage under Child Protective Services supervision. The Langes have initiated formal adoption proceedings. Medical staff indicate subject will require ongoing physical therapy and psychological counseling. CPS case worker Judith Reynolds reports the subject is adjusting adequately to his new environment, considering the circumstances.

Detective Sergeant Robert Oakes Major Crimes Section, Alaska Bureau of Investigation

CC: District Attorney's Office AST Captain James Reeves FBI Liaison Office

EDDIE FLIPPED through several more supplemental reports, each filed at increasingly wider intervals. Supplemental #5, dated April 19, 1995, was little more than a form acknowledging routine database checks. While #6 from August noted a possible sighting in Fairbanks, it proved to be a mistaken identity. By Supplemental #7 in February 1996, the investigation had been downgraded to inactive status, with no new leads or evidence. The case's final entry, Supplemental Report #8 from January 1997—two years after the murders—contained only a notation that Richard Gower's information remained in NCIC and periodic database checks would continue per departmental policy. There were no further mentions of Grayson's condition or recovery; the Bureau had evidently determined that the surviving victim's welfare fell outside their investigative purview once he was legally placed with the Langes.

There were several medical reports in the file. Eddie's eyes landed on the photocopy of the handwritten post-op note by the trauma surgeons.

IMMEDIATE POST-OPERATIVE NOTE DATE: 01/16/1995
   PATIENT: Gower, Grayson
   PREOPERATIVE DIAGNOSIS: Multiple stab wounds to abdomen
   POSTOPERATIVE DIAGNOSIS: Multiple lacerations to small bowel, liver lacerations to segments VII and IVa,
   PROCEDURE: Emergent exploratory laparotomy, repair of multiple enterotomies, repair of liver laceration.
   SURGEON: Robert Keller, M.D. ASSISTANT SURGEON: Ralph Dawes, M.D.
   ANESTHESIA: General endotracheal, Jeff Portman, M.D.
   EBL: 1200cc REPLACEMENT: 4U PRBC, 2U FFP, 1U PLT, 2500cc crystalloid

DRAINS: Two #19 Blake drains to RUQ and pelvis, Foley catheter
DISPOSITION: PICU, critical condition, intubated, on pressors

THERE WAS an op note from the plastic surgeons two days later, describing the repair of the face and neck wounds. They noted no apparent injuries to the "facial nerve or parotid gland structures."

Flipping through more documents, Eddie landed on a social worker's report, typed on letterhead stationery:

CASE #: CPS-95-0437 CHILD: GOWER, Grayson A.
 DOB: 11/04/1988
 DATE OF ASSESSMENT: 07/15/1995
 CASEWORKER: Ellen Mortensen, MSW
 SIX-MONTH ASSESSMENT SUMMARY
 Grayson Gower is a six-year-old white male who was a victim of attempted murder by his father and witnessed the murder of the rest of his family. Grayson has shown remarkable resilience. He is emotionally reserved but does not exhibit many signs of stress typically seen in these situations, including hyperactivity, bedwetting, anxiety, or sleep disorders.

Grayson still refers to his brother in the present tense: "I don't like broccoli, but Tommy will eat it." He asked for pictures of Tommy, and several were retrieved from his home. He never mentions his mother or father.

Grayson relates well to his Anchorage foster parents and foster siblings. He does not exhibit cruelty, and he plays with them in very cooperative ways.

Regarding school, Grayson appears to be very intelligent, exhibits a keen interest in learning, maintains focus, and enjoys participating in group events. He will often help other children who are having difficulty. He is currently reading at a fourth-grade level.

In terms of permanent placement for Grayson, the only known living relative is Richard Gower, the brother of John Gower. Richard Gower is a self-employed carpenter and an independent contractor with various construction firms in the Matanuska Valley. Richard Gower left Talkeetna shortly after the murder and left no forwarding information.

RECOMMENDATIONS

1. Continue placement with Edward and Margaret Lange, who have expressed interest in adoption.

2. Begin formal adoption proceedings, as Richard Gower cannot be located after reasonable efforts.

3. Continue quarterly progress reports until adoption is finalized.

4. Maintain twice-monthly therapy sessions with Dr. Rebecca Klein.

Ellen Mortensen, MSW Child Protective Services Anchorage Regional Office

Eddie searched "Richard Gower" on his phone. The search yielded many Richard Gowers—artists, CEOs, and mariners of the past. He refined the search by adding "Talkeetna"—nothing.

He put his elbows on the tabletop and rested his chin on his gloved fists, eyes blurring at the documents. He had read enough. The bureaucratese, the technical language, could not blunt the unimaginable horror for a little boy.

Father Dracule—a castrated priest, possibly by his own hand. John Gower, a sex molester of children. *Do I have two ghosts or one?*

A theory of the case started to percolate through Eddie's detective brain. An identity switch, and a prey turned predator.

37

WHO'S BURIED IN TALKEETNA?

The next day, Eddie sat at his desk in the homicide office and logged into APSIN, the Alaska Public Safety Information Network, Alaska's criminal database system. It was connected to the FBI's National Crime Information Center and other state databases. He waited as the system searched through records. After several minutes, the results for both John Gower and Richard Gower came up empty. Neither man had ever been arrested.

Chik sat down at his desk next to Eddie's. Eddie looked up from his computer and stared at his friend.

"What's up?" Chik asked.

"Are you familiar with the Gower murders up in the valley? 1995?"

"In Talkeetna, a man killed his entire family and was shot and killed in the process."

"Not quite his whole family. Your surgeon, Grayson Lange, formerly Grayson Gower—the youngest son, who was six at the time —was the only survivor."

Chik took it in for a moment. "That's where his scars come from?"

"Yes." From there, Eddie refreshed Chik on the details of the Gower murder.

"So, where are you going with this?" Chik asked.

"The dead priest, Father Dracule. I think he could be John Gower, Lange's father."

"What?"

"Hear me out. John Gower, born in 1946, would be seventy-eight years old, about Father Dracule's age. Meanwhile, it appears Father Dracule is a false persona. John Gower was part of a religious cult in Talkeetna, but was raised as a Catholic. Becoming a priest would be a comfortable false identity for him. John Gower was a child molester. Father Dracule may have castrated himself. Did he do it to reduce unwelcome sexual urges?"

"Hmmm..."

"Meanwhile, on the video, we have an unsub who is roughly the same height and build as Dr. Lange."

"Whoa."

"Yeah, whoa."

"So, who's buried in Talkeetna?"

"The brother, Richard. It was John, not Richard, who met the police, and Richard who was dead at the house."

"Go on," Chik said. "I think I know where you're going."

"John Gower called his brother Richard out to his home, and when he got there, shot and killed Richard, and managed to pass himself off as Richard while the authorities assumed it was John dead at the scene."

"The old fratricide angle, eh?"

"Oldest murder on record."

"But Richard—or John—called 911. The police interviewed him at the scene."

"Yes," Eddie said, "but would they know who was who?"

"Brothers can look alike."

"So, John assumes a new identity after the killing. A lot easier to do back in the '90s, before Facebook, Instagram, and cellphones—especially if you didn't have a criminal record."

"What about the pastor—Cyrus somebody—you said he showed up at the scene and identified John and Richard Gower?"

"Cyrus Chase. Maybe he was in on the cover-up."

"Why would he?"

"Sarcasm alert. Why would a church cover up a scandal?"

Chik shrugged. "Point taken. Especially a cult."

"So jump forward twenty-some odd years, and the bearded suspect in the video?"

"Dr. Lange, in disguise," said Chik.

Eddie pursed his lips and tapped his fingers together a few times.

"There's only one problem," Chik said, "how would Lange have killed the priest? What's the mechanism?"

Eddie shrugged. "I don't know, but what about what your father-in-law Inuksuk said, that Lange has a power?"

"So now we're talking, what, spells and miracles?"

"Seems crazy, I know. And if Lange has this kind of power, he should be the most famous or richest person in the world. Or at least be leading a cult of thousands."

"I don't know if that's necessarily true," Chik said.

"What do you mean?"

"Look at Jesus. Not only resurrected Lazarus but supposedly rose from the dead in some backwater province of the Roman Empire. Took three hundred years for that to catch on. And some two thousand years later, two-thirds of the world doesn't believe it or care. And the other third took a lot of convincing, and most of those can't even agree about what he was about."

Eddie chuckled. "So we're comparing Grayson Lange to Jesus Christ now?"

"Nah," Chik said with a smile. "Just saying that just because something 'supernatural' has happened, it might not exactly 'change the world,' or even be noticed by much of it." He punctuated the words with air quotes.

"Maybe he doesn't want to end up like Jesus, nailed to a cross. Or maybe not everybody wants to rule the world," Eddie said, sing-songing the lyric from the Tears for Fears song.

"Maybe being a surgeon is enough for him," Chik said.

Eddie pondered Chik's statement for a moment, then dialed the medical examiner's office. They connected him to Becca.

"Hi, Eddie." Her voice was professional and neutral.

"Hey." There was an awkward pause. "How are... things?"

"Fine. What can I help you with?" Her tone was friendly but remained guarded. *Or am I just overreading things?*

"Yeah, okay. Well, I need a DNA kinship analysis using the DNA from a cold case."

"Sure. How cold?"

"January 1995. Triple homicide in Talkeetna. John Gower, case number AK343-774. Died from a shotgun wound to the iliac vessels."

Eddie heard Becca's keyboard clicking. "One sec, I need to access a different database... Okay, got it. Gower, John L. What exactly are you looking for?"

"Was anything sent for a DNA profile?"

"Let's see here... No record for a DNA profile."

"Why not? It was available by '95, wasn't it?"

"Do you know if John Gower had prior military service or criminal records?"

"Negative. No service, no priors."

"So, in '95, they would have had to send DNA cases to the FBI lab in Quantico. The wait time was over a year, unless you had a high-profile case. Plus, there really was no point, since John Gower wouldn't have a DNA profile on record. I mean, he didn't even have fingerprints in the database. Not only that, CODIS didn't go national until 1998, three years after the murders. Of course, now we run our own DNA profiles at the Scientific Crime Detection Lab, so the process is a lot quicker. We can have the results for a cold case in six to eight weeks."

"Any preserved tissue samples we could run DNA on?"

He heard more typing. "Yes, we have blood cards and some paraffin blocks. We can use those for DNA analysis. Who is the second person?"

"Father Dracule."

"You think Father Dracule and this John Gower are related?"

"No, I think Father Dracule *is* John Gower, and the person buried in Talkeetna is his brother."

"Body switch? Sounds intriguing. What's the theory?"

"Well, it involves Dr. Grayson Lange, the surgeon."

"The one who had the run-in with Dr. Defner?"

"That's the one. Turns out he was born Grayson Gower, and he's the sole survivor of the Gower family murders."

"So you think he had something to do with the priest's murder?"

"It's a scenario."

"Jeez. Okay, send me the paperwork. I'll keep an eye out and call you as soon as the report comes in. It'll take a few weeks."

38

THE SCIENCE FAIR

The Alaska Airlines Center, situated next door to the campus of Providence Alaska Medical Center, buzzed with the energy of dozens of middle school students explaining their projects to circulating judges of the Alaska State Science and Engineering Fair. Eddie and Gertie found a seat in the stands within earshot of Daniel's display. Daniel stood confidently by his three-panel display board, above which was the title: *Einstein's Relativity in Everyday Life*.

Wait, was that Becca? She had joined the small crowd around Daniel's display. What was she doing here?

Becca turned and noticed him. A card attached to a lanyard around her neck identified her as a judge. She smiled and gave him a small wave. He waved back. She walked over and sat next to Eddie.

Seeing Becca reminded Eddie how the Dracule case had stalled. And the Peplow investigation wasn't proceeding any better. Cooper's leads on the assassins had all dead-ended, the van sat in impound stripped of evidence, and the rifle's history led nowhere. No one really cared about the Dracule case, but the brass was getting impatient about Peplow. A high-profile shooting with no arrests embarrassed the politicians and made the department look bad. It wouldn't be long now before the knives came out.

"Gertie, this is Dr. Raven, one of the assistant medical examiners."

"Nice to meet you," Gertie said. "In case you couldn't tell, I'm Eddie's mother."

"Nice to meet you, uh, should I call you Gertie?"

"Why not? Everyone else does, even my own son."

"Daniel's exhibit looks very impressive," Becca said.

"Yes. So, you're a judge?"

"Yes, Dr. Zigler was going to judge some of the medical exhibits, but came down with a cold and asked if I could step in."

After a beat, she said, "I was going to call you Monday. Sadie at the lab told me all the biological samples from that Talkeetna case—the Gower murders—were lost in a '98 fire at the old evidence facility."

"Well, shit."

"Faulty wiring, apparently. Lost everything in one of the biological storage areas. It was a defense attorney's dream. A number of cases got thrown out because of it."

"So Father Dracule's tissue is all we have to work with."

"Are there bodies buried somewhere? You could always try for an exhumation."

"I don't think I have a strong enough case at this point."

Eddie briefly imagined filling out a request stating he believed the suspect, Grayson Lange, MD, had caused the death of Father Dracule by employing some Vulcan mind meld.

"There's one other thing I could do," he said. "I could have you run a DNA test on Lange and the priest."

"Yes, you could. Do you have some of Lange's DNA?"

"No. I guess I'll have to ask him for a voluntary sample."

"Good luck."

Over in the exhibit area, three judges gathered to evaluate Daniel's project.

"Here we go," Eddie said.

The first judge was Dr. James Chen, a quantum physicist from UAA. Next to him stood Sarah Blackwood, a retired high school physics teacher. Her silver hair was pulled back in a neat bun, and she took careful notes on a small pad. The third judge was Dr.

Marcus Whitman, the assistant director of the Alaska Science Center.

"What do you have for us today, Daniel?" Dr. Chen asked.

"Hi, judges. My exhibit tries to show how relativistic effects are all around us, from GPS to the color gold and mercury."

He began with his GPS model. For his exhibit, he had sawed a twelve-inch globe of the earth in half, glued it to a poster, and glued four photos of GPS satellites around it.

"GPS satellites move at 14,000 kilometers per hour and orbit 20,000 kilometers above Earth. Their atomic clocks are incredibly accurate, but Einstein's theories affect them in two ways. Special relativity makes their clocks tick slower because of their speed, while general relativity makes them tick faster because of weaker gravity up there. The net effect is their clocks run 38 microseconds per day faster than Earth time."

Daniel pushed a button on the laptop sitting on the exhibit table. A red panel and a green panel started ticking off numbers. "I've written a program that simulates the atomic clocks in the GPS satellites in real-time as they orbit Earth. The green panel represents a satellite whose clock is adjusted to run at exactly 10.22999999543 MHz to adjust for relativistic effects, and the red panel one with its clock set to run at 10.23 MHz."

At thirty seconds, he pushed a key to pause the program. The red panel showed an error of 11.36 km, while the green panel showed zero error. "By slowing the satellite's clock by the right amount, we maintain synchronization and accurate position to within three meters."

"So why does time for an object slow down the faster it moves?" Dr. Chen asked.

"Ha! Trick question, right? We don't know why that is. It started out as an abstract mathematical calculation when Einstein discovered that the speed of light is constant. But now, we use relativity to explain things and make GPS satellites work better. Although we can predict it and calculate for it, we haven't figured out why. Not yet, anyway. So far, only God knows why we have relativity and gravity."

"What about the space station?" Blackwood asked. "Does it have to adjust its clocks?"

"Not really, actually," Daniel said. "The space station orbits at a much lower altitude than GPS satellites, averaging 400 kilometers above the Earth versus 14,000 for the satellites. But it travels roughly twice as fast to stay in orbit, around 27,500 kilometers per hour. The combined relativistic effects make the ISS clocks slower than those on Earth, whereas GPS clocks run faster. And relativity effects on the space station are much less. The total time slowing on the ISS since it first went into orbit 26 years ago is about 235 milliseconds, or nine milliseconds a year."

"Very good," Dr. Whitman said. "What about the Moon?"

"Yes, time moves 58.7 microseconds a day faster on the Moon than on Earth, mostly due to general relativistic effects of lesser gravity, so after a year, a clock would be 20.5 seconds faster than on Earth. Today, scientists at NASA are working on standard lunar time, called Coordinated Lunar Time. We'll need this when more and more missions and instruments wind up on the Moon."

"Let's move on to the next panel, then," Dr. Chen prompted.

Listening to Daniel talk about relativity and time dilation, Eddie recalled that moment in the video lab with Chik and Stanley. Ten seconds of static, ten minutes of unaccounted-for action. Stanley talking about the Church going through a relativistic time glitch. If weird things happen to satellites, why not here on Earth? Whew, boy. Daniel was right—spooky action. *Or am I just spooky speculating?*

Daniel moved to his second display, a poster that depicted the characteristics of gold and listed its atomic statistics and structure. Under that, Daniel had taped a gold wedding band, a silver crucifix, and a set of platinum earrings.

"Where did you get that jewelry, young man?" Blackwood asked.

"From my mom."

"Oh, she must trust you very much."

"My mom died four years ago in a car accident."

"Oh, I'm terribly sorry, Daniel."

"It's okay. My grandmother lives with us now." Daniel held up a black box with a USB cable coming out of it. "I would like to start by using this spectrograph I made using an old webcam from which I removed the infrared filter and a DVD fragment I attached to the webcam. The microscopic pits on the DVD act as a diffraction grating, which splits light into its individual colors when a light source passes through it.

"After securing the DVD fragment over the webcam lens, I angled the webcam inside the wooden box at approximately thirty degrees to the line of incoming light. This angle is crucial for ensuring the light is diffracted and then reflects off the DVD properly, producing a clear spectrum. I painted the inside of the box flat black to prevent any surrounding light from interfering with what we observe, and I created a narrow slit at one end for light to enter, which helps concentrate the incoming light."

With excitement building, Daniel transitioned to the demonstration. "Now, I'll show you the spectrum of white light using my spectroscope. This is a 5,400-kelvin light bulb that acts as a black body emitter, which means it emits all wavelengths of visible light and illustrates the full spectrum."

He turned on the blackbody bulb, and the warm glow filled the space, illuminating the setup. As the light entered the spectroscope, the colors of the spectrum spread across the screen. "This is the complete spectrum of white light coming from the blackbody emitter, revealing all the wavelengths. Notice here, you can see there is blue light in the spectrum."

"Now, let's see how gold interacts with light." Daniel held up a setup consisting of two clear microscope slides taped together that held a very thin piece of gold leaf between them. "I'll now place this gold leaf across the slit of the spectrograph." On the screen, the spectrogram changed. "Now, notice how much of the blue light is absent from the spectrum. This is because gold absorbs blue light. When blue is absent from white light, it will appear yellow to us. And what you see here is due to relativity. One more thing. If you look closely here," he said, emphasizing the spectrograph, "you can see that UV light is present in gold's spectrum as well."

He removed the gold foil setup and replaced it with a similar device made with silver foil. "Now look. The blue light has returned, but notice that much of the ultraviolet light is missing."

Daniel paused for dramatic effect. "What we see here can be explained by relativity. Gold has the atomic number 79, meaning it has 79 protons and 79 electrons. The stable isotope of gold also has 118 neutrons, making gold a fairly heavy atom. Because of the size of the nucleus, the electrons have to move very fast. The inner electrons around gold atoms move so fast—about 58 percent the speed of light—that they experience a mass increase, as predicted by Einstein's theory of relativity. This mass increase makes the electron orbitals contract or get closer to the nucleus because electrons with higher mass are more attracted to the nucleus. This causes the outer gold orbital, the 6s orbital, to contract and move closer to the 5d orbital. Because the orbitals are close, the amount of energy required to make the electron jump to the next orbital is found in the blue light frequency. So, gold tends to absorb photons in the blue light range and reflect all these others. And this makes gold look bright yellow. Platinum and silver, on the other hand, with their smaller nuclei, don't contract the electron orbitals as much, so their orbitals are farther apart and require higher energy light to jump an electron to the next higher orbit. It turns out higher-energy ultraviolet light is needed to do this, as you see here with the silver spectrum. So silver and most other metals absorb UV light and ignore the lower-energy blue light, so all visible light is reflected, giving silver and other metals their silvery appearance."

"What about white gold? How is that made to be white?" Whitman asked.

"Most white gold is alloyed with palladium or nickel, though palladium is becoming more common because some people are allergic to nickel. When we add palladium, something fascinating happens at the atomic level. Palladium's 4d orbitals overlap and interact with gold's 5d orbitals, creating hybrid molecular orbitals. This hybridization increases the energy gap between gold's 5d and 6s orbitals. Remember, gold absorbs blue light because the gap between these orbitals matches blue light's energy. Well, when we add palladium, the new hybrid orbitals create a larger energy gap. Now, it takes more energy to excite electrons across this gap, so the alloy is more interested in UV light than blue light. The exact shade depends on the ratio of gold to palladium and whether other metals, like silver, are also added to the alloy. This also explains why 24-carat gold is more yellow than 18-carat gold, and so on."

The judges nodded. "Continue, Daniel," Dr. Chen said.

As Daniel moved to his mercury panel and his explanation of why mercury was a liquid at room temperature, Eddie looked at Becca. She sat perfectly still, her eyes fixed on Daniel, her lips clenched and her face stern with concentration. The vigilance in her eyes had given way to curiosity. She seemed free from the weight of the memory of the Brockman beating and whatever hell she was going through now.

When Eddie refocused on Daniel, he was finishing up.

"Oh, and I almost forgot, although relativistic reasons for mercury being liquid have been a theory since the 1960s, it wasn't proven mathematically until 2013. The proof required a lot of computing power."

"Very good, Daniel," Dr. Chen said. "Thank you for this most interesting exhibit." The judges moved on, and Daniel bounded over to where his father, his grandmother, and Becca stood.

"That was wonderful, sweetheart," Gertie said, giving him a quick hug. "I even think I understood part of it."

"Thanks, Grandma." Daniel smiled when he saw Becca standing with them. "Hi, Dr. Raven. You're a judge?"

"Hi, Daniel. Yes, I judged the medically related exhibits."

"We're going to the Glacier Brewhouse after the award ceremony," Daniel said to her. "Would you like to come? If it's okay with Dad?"

"Of course it is, but Dr. Raven may have other plans," Eddie said.

Becca hesitated as if weighing her options. "Yes, Daniel, I'd love to join you. Oh, I've got to go; the judges are meeting. What time are the reservations?"

"Five," Eddie said.

The judging was complete, and they were waiting for the awards ceremony to begin. As Eddie mulled over the Lange case and the loss of DNA evidence, he noticed Dr. Chen chatting with his fellow judges near the staging area. The physicist seemed jovial and approachable, so Eddie made his way over.

"Dr. Chen, hi, I'm Eddie Vaugner, Daniel's father."

Chen looked up with a warm smile. "Oh yes, he's a bright boy. Very nice exhibit."

"Thank you. Listen, I'm a homicide detective with the APD. Could I run something by you?"

"Uh, sure."

"I have a case where a death was caused by mitochondrial damage by an unknown mechanism."

"I see."

"Okay, this is going to sound crazy, but could someone's mind cause mitochondrial damage to another person? I don't know, some sort of spooky action?"

Dr. Chen smiled. "Spooky action. That's a very interesting question, detective. You probably know Einstein used that phrase— *'spukhafte Fernwirkung'*—as a scoffing term to describe quantum entanglement, which he found disturbing at first but then came to accept. But mitochondrial damage from consciousness interaction? You're asking about something even more exotic."

He set down his briefcase, clearly intrigued. "You're actually touching on some fascinating theoretical territory. Tell me, where was the damage?"

"In multiple areas of the brain."

Chen's eyebrows rose. "Interesting. You see, mitochondria aren't just cellular batteries,—they're quantum machines. They use quantum tunneling for electron transport, maintain quantum coherence despite cellular noise. Some researchers believe consciousness itself emerges from these quantum processes. If that's true, then theoretically—and I stress theoretically—someone with the right neural architecture could influence another person's quantum biological processes."

"So, it's possible?"

Chen chuckled. "In quantum reality, what isn't? Theoretically possible, yes. It hasn't been demonstrated yet, so proving it in a court of law is your basic no way, José situation, I would imagine."

"So we have this recording. There is a time glitch. An event that took as long as 10 minutes seems to pass during a 10-second static pattern on the recording."

The professor stroked his chin and blinked a few times. "Like the local relativistic effect in GPS satellites in your son's exhibit. We can see them orbiting in our time, but they're experiencing their own time. Now imagine that same principle, but compressed into a confined space—say, a closet. From the outside, ten seconds pass. Inside that localized field? Could be ten minutes, an hour, who knows? Like someone using entanglement to pull the quantum plug on cellular function."

"But GPS satellites are moving. The closet was standing still."

"You don't need motion for relativistic effects. Intense gravitational fields cause time dilation too—that's the general relativity your son mentioned. But here's where it gets weird: in theory, any sufficiently warped spacetime could create a time differential. A localized quantum field of sufficient intensity could theoretically warp space-time in a small area. No GPS satellites needed—just an intense enough field distortion."

"And that could cause static on a video recorder?"

"Think of it like when you put a magnet near an old TV and the picture distorts. But instead of a magnetic field, you're dealing with a fundamental distortion of space and time itself. The camera's magnetic tape would go haywire trying to record through that kind of field distortion. It would capture gibberish—static—while inside the field, time is moving differently."

"I understand the words, Professor, but I don't understand what you're saying."

Chen chuckled. "Don't worry about it. As your son said, no one understands relativity. We just observe it and calculate for it. And as for your scenario, I'm just throwing spitballs against the wall—it's what we physicists do—then see what sticks."

. . .

THE AWARDS WERE PRESENTED in the school auditorium. Based on the quality of the exhibit, presentation skills, and understanding of the subject, Daniel won first place in physics.

JUST AFTER 5 P.M., Eddie sat with his son and mother at the restaurant. Eddie spotted Becca at the hostess stand and stood up to wave her over. When she saw him, her face broke out in a smile. She made her way to their table and slid onto the bench beside him.

"This is nice. This is my first time here." Becca looked around, taking in the lodge-like atmosphere of the restaurant. The dining area was a great room with exposed beams, trusses, and ductwork, featuring a large stone hearth in the center and an open kitchen busy with cooks and their assistants getting meals out, while an expediter checked food quality and accuracy as orders went out to the dining room.

They had a booth in front of the hearth. Off to one side was a large bar with multiple brews on tap and, as one would expect in a brewhouse, a glassed-off room with large brewing tanks, all stainless steel and brass.

A server came over and took their orders. Daniel ordered a Coke, Eddie asked for water, and the others followed suit.

"Congratulations again, Daniel," Becca said. "That exhibit was really impressive."

"Thanks! Were the medical exhibits interesting?"

"Some of them. There was one on antibiotic resistance that was quite good."

Gertie smiled. "So, how do you like Alaska, dear? Baltimore to Anchorage is quite a change."

"I love it, actually. The summer—all that daylight."

"And this is your first Anchorage winter?"

"Yes, although I'll have to admit, it's not as severe as I thought it would be. Temperature-wise, it's not that different from Baltimore, just longer and darker."

"Yes," said Daniel, "It's because the Alaska Current, which is part of the Pacific Current. It brings warm water, which makes Anchorage winters much milder than in Fairbanks, located in the interior. Oh, and the Pacific current is fed by the Kuroshio Current coming up from Japan."

"Like the Gulf Stream in the Atlantic, warming much of Europe."

"Exactly," said Daniel.

"Did you grow up in Baltimore?" asked Gertie.

"Yes, but my parents retired to the Eastern Shore a few years ago. St. Michael's. They have a place right on the water."

"Oh, that sounds lovely. Sometimes, I wouldn't mind living in a warmer place. At least for the winter, I'm getting tired of these winters."

"Where would you go?" Becca asked.

"Oh, I don't know. Somewhere I could walk outside in January without three layers and boots. Maybe Arizona. Or New Mexico. I have a friend who moved to Tucson. She sends me pictures of her patio— cactuses, sunshine, sitting outside in a t-shirt on Christmas Day."

"Grandma, Tucson can get chilly in the winter, it's at a high elevation. You'd be better off in Phoenix."

As they chatted on, Eddie watched the exchange with quiet satisfaction. Gertie had that effect on people—drawing them out, making them comfortable.

But just as Becca was starting to relax, her eyes sparkling, her shoulders soft, her smile growing warmer, she suddenly froze.

"Oh God." Her face went blank. She blinked a few times as something beyond the table caught her off guard.

"What is it?" Eddie asked.

"Jim just walked in. What's he doing here?"

Eddie turned to watch as Brockman sat at the bar and ordered a drink, deliberately not looking their way. The same flat smile concealing hostility stretched across his face, but now his unsympathetic eyes held the wounded pride of a predator.

"Did he know you were coming here?"

"No. I don't communicate with him. I blocked his number and stopped responding to his emails weeks ago."

"We should check your car for a GPS tracker. These guys often plant them in the wheel wells or under the bumper."

"I'm sorry, I need to leave," Becca said, gathering up her coat and purse.

"Let me take you to your car. Wait here, you guys."

"Wow," Daniel said, "this is kind of weird." He took out his phone to play Fortnite.

"Sometimes adults have weird problems, sweetheart," Gertie said.

Becca fished around in her purse. "Let me leave you some money."

"Stop," Eddie said.

"I'm so sorry," Gertie said.

As they left the restaurant, Eddie looked over at Brockman. He was sipping on his drink, avoiding eye contact.

In the parking lot, Eddie started running his hand along the right rear wheel well of Becca's car.

"What are you doing, Eddie?"

"The most common place would be the wheel well or on the underframe, quick access." He moved to the right front wheel well. "Bingo." He pulled out a small black box.

The restaurant door swung open. Brockman walked out, looking down at his phone.

"Hold it right there, Mr. Brockman," Eddie said.

Brockman looked up. Seeing Eddie, he tapped his phone and pocketed it.

"You're tracking me?" Becca asked.

"I have no idea what you're talking about."

Eddie held up the tracking device. "This is a Class A misdemeanor under Alaska Statute 11.41.270. It's illegal to place a concealed tracking device on someone else's vehicle without their consent. You could be jailed for one year or fined up to one thousand dollars. I could arrest you on suspicion right now."

"You can't prove I did it," Brockman said.

"Would you like me to take you in now and see what our forensics team can prove?" Eddie took his cell phone out of his pocket.

"Please don't, Eddie," Becca said quietly.

Eddie stared at Brockman for a long moment, then nodded slightly to her. "You need to file for a restraining order first thing Monday morning. The forms are online."

He turned back to Brockman.

"Get the fuck out of here and stay away from her."

Brockman opened his mouth as if to argue, then thought better of it. He backed away slowly, crossed the street, got into his car, and drove off.

Becca let out a shaky breath. "Thank you. What a joke. I told you not to define me by my relationship with him, and now this."

"Hey, don't apologize. You're moving on. He's following you."

"Like an albatross."

She leaned against the driver's door, hands trembling slightly as she held her keys. "You have a lovely family. I'm sorry they had to see something like this."

"We've been through worse. They're tough."

She hesitated, then reached up and pecked him on the cheek.

"Monday morning, restraining order," he said. "And get your house swept for bugs."

"I will." She managed a weak smile. "Thank you, Eddie."

As she drove off, Eddie touched his cheek where she'd kissed him. It was the first time he'd felt a woman's kiss in four years.

39

HOME INVASION

At 6 a.m., Grayson stood at his bedroom window, naked, looking out at the lake.

A woman's husky voice said, "Hey you."

Grayson turned to face Jennifer, who was in bed, up on one arm, smiling at him. She, too, was naked.

"Good morning, you."

"You're beautiful, Grayson," Jennifer said, admiring his form in the light coming from the full moon.

"Except for the scars." He looked down at his abdomen. The oblique light gave the scar there a furrowed appearance.

"No, they're like afterthoughts from an eccentric sculptor who didn't want his work to be too perfect."

Grayson smiled and walked over to her. She took him in her hands and lifted him into her mouth, and he responded. She sucked him for a few moments, then lay back and threw the covers aside.

"Fuck me, Grayson."

Later, Jennifer was in the shower, and Grayson was reclining on one of the two Ekornes loungers in the living room, reading *The Left Hand of Darkness* by Ursula K. Le Guin, when the doorbell rang. He put the book down and picked up his cell phone to tap his Ring app.

The image of Detectives Vaugner and Uttaq standing at his front door appeared on the screen.

OUTSIDE, Eddie and Chik stood at the door. Lange opened it with a puzzled look on his face.

"Hi, Doc," Chik said. Eddie thought he detected a sheepish tone— maybe Chik felt awkward treating his surgeon as a person of interest.

"Hello, gentlemen." Eddie noted Lange's voice was pleasant, but his face had a hint of what-the-fuck-are-you-doing-here?

"Could we come in?"

"Sure."

Once inside, Lange invited them to hang their coats on hooks in the foyer. In true Alaskan custom, Eddie and Chik slipped off their shoes and padded into the living room in stocking feet.

"How are you doing, Detective Uttaq?"

Chik gave his abdomen a tap. "Great, like it never even happened."

"And your father-in-law, how is he doing?"

"Doing very well, thanks. Still singing your praises."

Eddie noted the irony. A shaman from Greenland via Denmark was singing Lange's praises, while Eddie was taking his DNA to rule him out as a murder suspect.

Lange's home was a typical late-'70s Anchorage, but remodeled. Open concept. Deep leather chairs in warm beige tones faced the expansive lake view. Alaskan paintings and sculptures. A few abstract paintings thrown into the mix, but those had a warm palette. Very similar motif to his office. The kitchen was designed for someone who enjoyed elevated cooking and dining—high-end appliances and a shelving unit filled with cookbooks.

Everything here whispered peace. Earned peace, deserved peace, and needed peace.

The morning sun spilled through the wall of windows. A Cessna Skylane sat on skis on frozen Campbell Lake, its blue and white paint gleaming.

"Nice plane, Doc," Eddie said. "Skylane?"

"Yes. What brings you guys out here today?"

"We'd like a DNA sample from you," Eddie said.

"A DNA sample? Why?"

"I know this might sound far-fetched, but because of the similarities in the mitochondrial injuries between Dr. Defner and Father Dracule, I did some further investigation. There are parallels between your father and Father Dracule."

"Wait, are you saying I'm a suspect in a death investigation?"

"I wouldn't say suspect. A person of interest, more like."

Lange's expression indicated he was genuinely surprised, and a little peeved. "My father died years ago. I'm not related to any priest."

"That's where the DNA sample comes in. This would merely confirm it, and we can tick it off the list. And we thought it would be better to do it here at your home, where it's more private. Purely voluntary, you understand. You may refuse, of course."

"Did you bring a kit?"

"Yes," Chik said.

A woman dressed in spandex shorts, a T-shirt, and training shoes came into the living room, her hair still damp from a shower. Eddie took in her long dark hair, light hazel eyes, and full lips. Her breasts filled the T-shirt well, her nipples forming little white mounds through her support bra, and her legs and feet were lean and muscular.

"Hello," she said.

"Dr. Dawson," Lange said, "meet Detectives Vaugner and Uttaq from the Anchorage Police homicide department. They want my DNA. Dr. Dawson is a friend of mine up from Seattle."

"What kind of doctor, ma'am?" Chik asked.

"Jennifer. Infectious diseases."

"Jennifer's an associate professor at the University of Washington School of Medicine," Lange added.

She moved with the effortless grace of an athlete, her build suggesting someone who could keep up with Lange's adventures. And a doctor, up from Seattle? It gave Eddie the impression these were two accomplished people who had found a way to share their lives without consuming each other. He wondered if he would ever find companionship again or—

Focus, Vaugner!

"DNA? Tell me you're not a criminal, Grayson," Jennifer teased. "I was just beginning to like you."

"No, ma'am, nothing like that," Chik said.

"They want to make sure a dead priest is not my father."

"Your father died years ago, didn't he?"

"Yes."

"But they don't believe you?"

"Yes, we believe him, ma'am," Eddie said. "We just need to confirm. You know, the old trust and verify."

Eddie reached into his jacket pocket and pulled out a consent form, folded in half along its long axis. Lange took it and started reading it.

"Maybe you should consult with an attorney first," Jennifer said, "before your DNA winds up in a national database."

"Oh no, ma'am. This is an elimination test. Since we're using it to eliminate Dr. Lange as a suspect, we won't enter his DNA profile into any state or national databases—this is strictly a one-time comparison test against the evidence we found at a potential crime scene."

"You can do that?" Jennifer asked.

Her concern about the legal implications of DNA samples, combined with her apparent knowledge of Lange's past, indicated an established relationship and genuine affection. She and Lange seemed to have the comfortable chemistry of two people who knew exactly what they wanted from each other.

"Absolutely. Scout's honor. Collecting DNA as an elimination tool doesn't meet the criteria for entry into CODIS." Eddie left out two other requirements: the sample needed to come from a confirmed crime scene, which Dracule's death wasn't, and reasonable evidence that the DNA was from a perpetrator, also lacking. He knew he might be hunting snipe.

"What do you think, Grayson?" Jennifer asked.

"If I don't, they'll just skulk around to swab some DNA content off a paper cup or beer bottle."

Eddie smiled and shrugged.

"Okay, to save you the indignity of rooting around in my trash, I'll do it."

"We appreciate that, Doc," Chik said.

Lange finished reading the document and signed it. Chik took it from him and filled in the other information required on the form.

"Doctor, have you engaged in kissing or oral sex in the past hour?"

Jennifer smiled. "No, not in the last hour."

Vaugner looked at Lange with an inquisitive smile.

"What she said," Lange replied.

Eddie slipped on some nitrile gloves and removed two cotton swabs from their package.

"Open your mouth, please, Doctor."

Grayson opened his mouth. Eddie held the two swabs together and rubbed them firmly against the inside of each cheek for thirty seconds. He held the swabs upright to air dry while Chik labeled the collection tube with case number, date, time, and subject information. Once they were dry, Eddie placed both swabs into the sterile collection tube, sealed it, and slipped it into an evidence envelope and sealed it. He signed across the envelope's seal, documented the chain of custody details, and secured everything in his briefcase.

"Thanks, Doctor," Eddie said. "This will help us from going down a rabbit hole."

"No problem," Lange said. "Anything else?"

"No, we're good," Eddie said.

"Sorry to disturb you guys," Chik said.

Grayson escorted Eddie and Chik to the door and showed them out.

On the way to their cars, Chik asked, "What do you think?"

"Dr. Lange seemed appropriately annoyed and not too worried," Eddie replied.

"That's good, isn't it?"

Eddie surprised himself by saying, "Yeah, I think it is."

40

DEUS EX UBI?

Several days after collecting Lange's DNA, Eddie's desk phone rang. The screen indicated it was the reception desk.

"Hey, Doris."

"Hi, Eddie. I have a Revus Roche down here, wanting to see you."

"Really? What does he want?"

"To talk to you. That's all he would say. And, uh, he's acting kind of weird. I have a couple of patrolmen down here."

"Is he acting violent?"

"No, just weird, like he's got bugs or something. Plus, he's all disheveled and smells bad."

"Okay, have the men get him to Interrogation 2. I'll be down in a minute." He hung up the phone.

Chik looked over at him quizzically.

"It's Revus Roche," Eddie said. "He came in downstairs wanting to speak to me. Doris says he's acting"—he made air quotes—"weird."

"Wanting to speak to you is always weird. I mean that in a good way."

Eddie and Chik hustled down to the interrogation room. They first watched Roche from the observation room. Gray-black stubble darkened his face, and unkempt hair stuck out at angles. His wrinkled suit hung loose, his tie was missing, and his shirt was marked by a brown stain. He swatted at invisible objects, muttering, "Get away from me," and frantically brushed at his clothing.

"Been like that since he arrived," the patrolman said. "Like he's on a bad acid trip."

"Do people even do LSD anymore?" Eddie asked.

"No clue, but I can ask Non arcotics," Chik deadpanned.

"I'm going in. Turn on the recorder."

Eddie entered the room and was immediately hit by the pungent stench of body odor.

Roche looked up, relief flooding his face. "Thank God you're here."

"Hold on, Mr.—uh, how do you like to be addressed?"

"I don't care, just make this stop. Pastor's fine."

"Okay, Pastor, what brings you to the station?"

Roche made a brushing motion down his sleeve, then swiped at his cheek repeatedly. "I'm here to confess."

"Okay. This interview is being recorded, just so you know."

"That's fine."

Eddie stated his name and badge number, Roche's name, and the date/time for the record, then said, "Confess to what?"

"Don't you need to read me my Miranda rights first?"

"Miranda rights only apply when you're under arrest or—"

Eddie reconsidered.

"You know what, Pastor Roche, you're right, I should." No telling where Roche's mind was. He could recant, or a defense attorney could argue that Eddie was taking advantage of an ill man. So Eddie mirandaized him and then asked, "Do you know where you are?"

"Yes, I'm in an interrogation room at the APD headquarters."

"What day of the week is it?"

"Wednesday. Look, I know I'm acting strange, but I'm not crazy. I am fully aware of what's going on and what I'm doing and that I'm hallucinating."

"Okay, Pastor, tell me why you're here."

"I'm here to confess to the murder of Jack Peplow."

"You killed Jack Peplow."

"We, not myself. I instigated the assassination effort and paid for the assassination team."

"So you had him killed. Why should I believe you?"

"Come on, Detective. I'm the number one suspect, am I not?" He rubbed the left side of his face compulsively. "Surely you can't be surprised."

"I'm not surprised you did it; I'm surprised you're confessing."

"You know, I am too. But something in my mind clicked and told me to get right in the sight of the Lord." Roche swatted again. "Get the fuck off me."

"Pastor Roche, are you seeing things?"

"Sometimes I think I see insects flying at me or crawling on me."

"Weren't you in the extermination business before you got religion?"

"Yes." He ducked and raised his hands. "Jesus, God! Do you mind if I stand up?"

"No, go ahead."

He stood up and waved his arms around. "I know there's nothing there, but I can't help it." He brushed more imaginary critters off his jacket. "Get off me!"

Eddie had a hard time believing this man had suddenly developed a conscience. Something made him snap.

"Okay, do you want to tell me how you arranged the murder of Jack Peplow?"

As he paced, he said, "I ordered my security chief, Dmitri Saparov —you met him in my office—to arrange it." Roche stopped, took a deep breath, and suddenly, the fidgeting stopped. He seemed calmer. He held up his hands and look at Vaugner.

"You see? No more bugs."

"Uh, that's great, Pastor, but I never saw any in the first place."

"Oh wow. It's like a release—like I'm free. Expiation, Detective, sweet expiation. It's a wondrous thing."

He stood almost motionless, head tilted up, arms outstretched, eyes closed, reveling in his relief. It reminded Eddie of the poster from the Shawshank Redemption, without the rain.

"I'm sure it is, Pastor. Would you like to continue?"

He smiled at Eddie, then sat back down. "Killing Jack Peplow when he came to Anchorage was an opportunity for the church. Dmitri did the hiring, and I provided the finances. No one other than he and I knew about this."

"Do you have proof of this?"

Roche pulled out his phone. "I have confidential recorded conversations with Saparov. Encrypted here on my phone. These have my instructions to Saparov and him agreeing to plan the assassination. I also have backup records in my bedroom safe at home."

"Can I have your phone?"

"Sure. I won't need it anymore." He handed Eddie his phone and showed him how to access his conversations with Saparov, his payment details, and the entire operation laid bare in his Dropbox account under the label "POCONVO." Eddie carefully printed the access codes onto his business card, confirming each one with Roche.

"Give me a few minutes."

Eddie took the phone and the codes to Chik in the observation room.

"Chik, can you run this over to Stanley?" Eddie said, handing him Roche's phone and the note with passwords. "It's got encrypted audio files that could nail Saparov."

"Then get a search warrant for Roche's place, but we'll hold off until Saparov has been arrested."

Chik took the phone. "I'll have Stanley clone it first, so we don't risk losing anything on the original."

"Good idea. Drive with lights and sirens."

Chik nodded and headed out. "Lights and sirens. I love playing cop."

After he left, Eddie called Stanley and explained the situation.

"And I need this yesterday, today, in a few hours," Eddie said. "We may lose a suspect if any of this gets out."

"Since we have codes, I can do it, but you owe me one."

"Thanks, Stanley—and tell Chik to give you a kiss for me."

Eddie went back into the room to continue his questioning.

"Okay, so what was the plan?" Eddie asked.

"Saparov was to make sure the Peplows were killed in public when he came to Anchorage so there would be no doubt it was an assassination. Other than that, I was to know nothing. He did not want me knowing who he hired or how he hired them. Compartmentalization, he said."

"Why kill him here in Anchorage? Why not kill him in DC, where he lives, or some neutral town?"

"Ah. You are operating under the wrong assumption."

"What assumption is that?"

"You think I had him killed because of his advocacy for separation of church and state."

"He was going to advise the U.S. attorney here regarding its case against your church engaging in political activities to change America into an officially Christian nation. So yeah."

"Come on, Detective. You honestly think America will ever become an officially Christian nation?"

"Not sure that's the point. He advocated for churches like yours that engage in political activity to lose tax-exempt status."

"Ah, a monetary motive. Now you're getting closer to the truth. But no, we were not worried about losing our tax-exempt status. We don't endorse a particular candidate. In the entire history of the IRS, as far as I know, only one politically active church has ever lost its tax-exempt status, back in 1992 for publishing a full-page anti-Bill Clinton ad."

"Okay, so why did you have him killed?"

"Our numbers were falling here in Anchorage. While we were still profitable, our congregation was down by 15 percent, and our donations were down by twenty. We were trying to open a satellite church in Idaho, outside Coeur d'Alene, but we were having trouble finding enough members down there. The trend was clear, and we could see the writing on the wall."

Roche leaned forward. His eyes gleamed with pride. "The genius of the plan, if I may say so myself, was to get ourselves suspected of killing Peplow but leaving no way for anyone to prove it. As you saw in my sermon, this allowed us to set ourselves up as advocates for religious freedom and victims of government persecution. The Peplows needed to be killed in Anchorage. We wanted the suspicion directed toward us. We milked it. You heard my sermon, no? It worked beautifully. Millions of dollars have come into America Salvation Church, and our membership is up. It was quite a return on investment."

"You see killing someone as an investment?" *Dumb question. People murder for a pack of cigarettes or disagreements about who the best quarterback in NFL history is.*

"Read your Bible, Detective. God has killed millions to punish people for shirking faith or to reward others for keeping theirs. And some of the killings seem whimsical. Remember what happened to Herod—not the Great, but his grandson? Acts 12:23. 'And immediately an angel of the Lord struck him because he did not give God the glory, and he was eaten by worms and died.' In biblical terms, killing is often a means to an end."

"I can't argue with you there," Eddie said.

The pastor smiled at him. He seemed at peace.

Eddie studied Roche. Then a recollection crowded in. Roche heading into Lange's office. And now hallucinations and confession out of the blue. No. Couldn't be. Could it?

"You're a patient of Dr. Lange's?"

"Yes, I am."

"What are you seeing him for?"

"I had a severe case of esophageal reflux. He operated on me to fix it."

"When was the operation?"

"Three weeks ago."

"How did things go after surgery?"

"Perfect. I went home the same day. I'm already back on a regular diet and ahead of schedule, and no more heartburn. Dr. Lange did a great job. I'm glad I stuck with him."

"What do you mean, 'stuck with him'?"

"Oh, this Dr. Defner in my congregation. He's a devoted member and a great donor, but a little, let's say, PTSD-y. Has this notion that Lange is, uh, evil. But I must say, I found him quite pleasant to deal with."

"How did you come to be his patient?"

"My gastroenterologist referred me to him. Why are you asking me about Dr. Lange?"

"Did you know he was Dana Peplow's surgeon?"

"Yes. In fact, I asked him if my being a suspect in the Peplow shooting would affect his ability to treat me. He said he treats other murderers and ne'er-do-wells from the prison population all the time, so there would be no problem with me. We had a chuckle. He even suggested if I was uncomfortable with him as my surgeon, he could recommend other surgeons who could do the job."

"But you stuck with Lange."

"Yes, I wanted the best."

Eddie nodded, trying to convince himself it was just a coincidence. Not like Anchorage has a million surgeons.

"I'm going to start typing this up. Say, are you hungry? Thirsty? I can have something brought down."

"I haven't had anything for twenty-four hours. I could eat."

Eddie excused himself and opened the interrogation room door. "Hey, Rodriguez, get him something to eat or drink, will you please?"

"Roger."

BACK IN HIS OFFICE, an hour later, Eddie and Chik were at their desks when Eddie's phone chimed—a text from Stanley.

Check your email. PW: R1O2x!

Eddie went to his email and opened Stanley's message, which had a password-protected audio file attached.

"Let's hear what we got," Eddie said. Chik brought their chairs closer. The digital audio player opened on his screen.

. . .

ROCHE: "AND YOU KNOW SOME GUYS?"

SAPAROV: "Oh, yes, some boys back in Almaty."

ROCHE: "It needs to be public. Very public, while they're here in Anchorage. I want everyone to know Jack Peplow and his wife were assassinated."

SAPAROV: "His wife?"

ROCHE: "She's part of their organization, so her too."

SAPAROV: "Two shots—more risky, but they can do it for the right price."

ROCHE: "Whatever it costs. Money is not a problem. It just can't be traced to us."

SAPAROV: "These men are professionals. Fake passports from multiple countries. In and out like magic."

ROCHE: "Good. I want them to suspect us, but never to prove it. Along those lines, I don't want to know anything about the operation. Use the crypto account to pay them."

SAPAROV: "This will be fun—like good old days."

EDDIE WALKED UP to Sergeant Danek's office and knocked on his door jamb. Danek waved him in.

"What's up Eddie?"

"Remember Pastor Roche?"

"Yeah, the head of America Salvation Church. He was on your list."

"He just walked in and confessed to the Peplow assassination."

"What?"

"Pastor Roche, he just walked—"

"I heard you. What made him do that?"

Eddie briefly weighed telling Danek about his potential Lange theory, if he could even call it that, but then came out with, "No clue, but we have corroborating evidence from his cell phone."

From there, they notified Chief Dell, who rushed to the interview observation room to get a look at Roche. To keep Roche's confession and detention confidential, Eddie suggested they keep him in the interrogation room and not book him until Saparov's arrest. Same for notifying the city attorney and the mayor. Dell agreed, and planned to call a press conference for 10 a.m. the next morning.

"I'll call the SWAT captain to plan the takedown," Danek said. He and Dell left.

Eddie had one more call to make. Dana Peplow.

"DETECTIVE VAUGNER?" Her voice was guarded.

"Yes. I have news, Mrs. Peplow. Can you keep a secret?"

"Detective, I'm an ordained minister. I am trained to keep confidences."

"We have an ongoing tactical operation, so this has to stay just between us."

"You have my word."

"We have Roche. He confessed."

"That son of a bitch! God bless you, Detective."

"I wish I could take credit, but he walked in and confessed."

"He just walked in?"

"Yes. And confessed."

"What made him do it?"

"I have no idea. He came in agitated and needing to get the murder of your husband off his chest."

"And you're sure he did it? This isn't some ruse or false confession?"

"We have records. It's a solid case, even if he recants his confession."

"It seems so *deus ex machina*, Detective. You have no idea what made him confess?"

Eddie hesitated, thought about Lange, but said, "Uh, not really. No."

"When can I tell the kids?"

"The announcement is scheduled for 10 a.m. tomorrow, which will be 2 p.m. your time. You can probably watch it on live stream—google KTUU Alaska's News Source. You can tell your kids after that."

"Oh my God, I'm busting at the seams."

After his call with Dana, he called Agent Cooper to bring her up to date.

41

GSW

After his phone calls with Dana Peplow and Cooper, Eddie and Chik joined Special Operations Commander Lieutenant Keith Vander and the SWAT team for the briefing. Vander, a twenty-year veteran of tactical operations, pulled up a Google Maps aerial view of Saparov's house in Shangri-La Estates, a development nestled in the foothills of the Chugach Mountain range in South Anchorage. The house sat far off from the road in a cleared patch in the forest.

Vander studied the layout for a few seconds.

"This is perfect," he said, indicating a switchback west of the house. "Driveway—three hundred feet long, curved, running through this dense alpine forest. Six SWAT team members will move down the north side of the driveway under forest cover. This will be a simple takedown as he leaves the house in his vehicle." He paused. "Now for the cool stuff. Tonight, we're going to use the RF SafeStop in tactical operation for the first time."

A few murmurs emanated from the crowd as he tapped his computer key to bring up an image of a matte-black Toyota Tacoma pickup truck with a large, light gray cabinet at the front of the bed, a large square at the rear, and an array of twelve-volt batteries at the near edge of the bed.

"This is the RF SafeStop. This large square at the back is the transmitter."

The next image showed a control panel under the truck's dashboard with various buttons colored red, yellow, or green.

"The SafeStop emits nonlethal, high-power radiofrequency pulses. Disables the vehicle's electronics and shuts down the engine. We'll position it here, just beyond this turn. Once he comes around in the line of sight, we'll fire it, and hopefully, the vehicle will shut down. DMV records show Saparov owns two vehicles, a 2024 Ford F-150 and a 2023 Mercedes CLA. It doesn't matter which—RF SafeStop will disable either vehicle."

"Chik and I want to be in on the raid," Eddie said. "Be the arresting officers."

"What he said," Chik added.

Vander considered things for a moment. "Okay. You guys can go down in the G2. You stay inside until SWAT has secured and detained Saparov, then make the arrest. Got it?"

"Yes, sir," they both said in unison.

"We'll find out from Roche when Saparov leaves for the office."

The SWAT team stood up. Vander raised his arms.

"Listen up! Saparov has extensive military and tactical training. Consider him armed and extremely dangerous. Level Four armor, double mag loads."

"CAMERAS UP," the tech announced. The Tacoma with the RF SafeStop slowly and quietly backed down Saparov's driveway. Following close behind, Eddie and Chik, wearing tactical vests, sat in the back of the Lenco BearCat G2 tactical vehicle, along with the six SWAT team members.

Two monitors in the G2 were set for six split screens, showing perspectives of each of the SWAT team members on foot.

The Tacoma with the SafeStop stopped short of the final curve to maintain a buffer from the house. The BearCat G2 stopped just behind it. The SWAT EMS MedCat vehicle and the tactical van were positioned at the top of the driveway.

Four SWAT team members exited the vehicles and flanked the north side of the driveway, taking cover in the woods. One moved forward and knelt at the front passenger side of the Toyota.

The final team member, Thompson, advanced just past the turn, hugging the tree line to avoid detection, keeping the garage door in line of sight. Everybody waited.

At 6 a.m., just as Roche predicted, Saparov's garage door rose. A late-model black Ford F-150 backed out, executed a Y-turn, and headed up the driveway.

"Here he comes," Vander said through the comms.

As Saparov's truck came up the driveway and made the turn into the line of sight, the tech inside the Tacoma activated the SafeStop by pushing buttons on a control panel. Almost instantly, the truck's engine died, and its lights went dark.

The SWAT team moved from the woods to the edge of the driveway, their weapons fixed on the truck's driver's door.

"This is the Anchorage Police Department!" boomed the loudspeaker. "Do exactly as instructed. Open the door and exit the vehicle with your hands raised, palms forward!"

"Hot damn, the son of a bitch worked," Vander commented in almost a whisper.

Saparov didn't move.

"Exit the vehicle now!"

The driver's door opened. Saparov turned slowly toward the SWAT team, raising his hands and smiling. In a blur of motion, his hands continued up to the truck's ceiling, then came down holding an assault rifle. Saparov dove to the ground, rolled into a kneeling position, and opened fire.

"Gun!" multiple voices shouted.

The scene on the monitors became chaos—weapons rose, the crack of multiple rifles, cameras jerking with each shot. Muzzle flashes sparked from Saparov's position as he got off a short burst before his body crumpled forward, hit by a dozen rounds.

Everyone froze in position. Saparov lay motionless, the assault rifle still in his hands.

Slowly, the SWAT team inched toward the man.

"So much for our arrest," Chik said.

He opened the rear door and stepped out of the vehicle. Eddie started to follow.

Incredibly, Saparov stirred and lifted his rifle. Without looking, he squeezed the trigger, shooting blindly, before the second hail of bullets riddled him.

Eddie felt a bullet hit the G2 door. Then he saw Chik fall.

He screamed, "Man down! Chik's been hit!"

Eddie leaped from the G2 and knelt over him. Thompson was the first to reach them. Quickly, he removed Chik's vest and cut open his shirt. There was a small hole in the left lower quadrant of the abdomen, just below where the vest reached. He took out a wound pack and placed it over the injury, applying firm pressure.

"Ouch," Chik gasped as they secured the wound dressing.

"I know it hurts, but we need to control the bleeding," Thompson said.

The MedCat screamed down the driveway. The medic jumped out and ran to the scene.

"Chik, are you okay?" he asked as he checked his pulse.

"I forgot to duck."

The question wasn't rhetorical—ABCs of trauma: airway, breathing, circulation. If a patient could talk, his airway and breathing were good. "Pulse palpable but rapid; we need to move." In other words, circulation, not so hot.

"You're too short to duck, Chik," Eddie said.

"Yeah, if I was you, I might have gotten my nuts blown off."

"You're going to be fine," Eddie told his friend, whose face was growing increasingly ashen. "MedCat's here."

They lifted him onto the stretcher. This was a scoop-and-run situation. The priority was getting him to the trauma center; every second counted.

They loaded Chik into the back of the MedCat. The driver immediately executed a three-point Y-turn to navigate out of the tight space behind the Tacoma and BearCat G2, then accelerated up the driveway past the command vehicle.

"You okay, man?" Eddie asked, sitting beside Chik in the vehicle as the medic worked to establish IV access.

"Not sure," Chik managed.

Eddie held his left hand. The skin was clammy to the touch. The medic started a large-bore IV in the right antecubital fossa while Thompson maintained pressure on the wound.

It seemed like hours, but only minutes had elapsed.

The medic radioed ahead: "Providence ER, this is APD tactical unit. Incoming GSW to the lower abdomen, through and through, officer down. Patient conscious but shocky, one large-bore IV started, running fluids. ETA four minutes."

Just as they turned onto Thirty-Sixth Avenue, blocks from the hospital, Chik lost consciousness.

"He's out. He has a pulse, but we may lose his airway. I need to intubate him," the medic said.

"Chik, stay with me!" Eddie shouted.

The medic reached into a drawer and pulled out a laryngoscope. From an open bin, he grabbed an endotracheal tube and ripped off its package. Quickly, he inserted the laryngoscope into Chik's mouth, inflated the balloon, and inserted the tube into his windpipe. He attached a breathing bag and started ventilating by squeezing the bag.

"Take the bag for a second, Eddie, ventilate him like this. He's breathing, so just go with him when he inhales. You got it?"

"Yeah," Eddie took the Ambu bag while the medic put his stethoscope over the right chest and left chest.

"We're good, equal breath sounds. I can take over."

"No, I'll do it," Eddie said.

"Sure, Eddie, you're doing fine."

CHIK STILL HAD a pulse when they pulled into the Providence ER.

They quickly transferred him from the MedCat's gurney to a trauma stretcher.

"I got this," a nurse said to Eddie. Eddie kept squeezing the bag. "Sir, you want to let go now? We've got this."

Eddie looked at the nurse pleadingly for a moment, then released his grip, and the nurse took over ventilating Chik. He stayed with Chik as the ER team rushed him through the double doors.

Lange was there, dressed in scrubs, indicating he was the surgeon who would be operating on Chik. Eddie was glad to see him, and Inuksuk's claim of Lange's healing power popped into his head. Eddie found himself hoping it was true.

They positioned Chik in the trauma bay; the SWAT medic gave a rapid report: "Through and through GSW lower left quadrant, one liter of fluid given, initial pressure 100/70, now down to 80/50, lost consciousness about two minutes ago."

The anesthesiologist listened to Chik's chest. "Breath sounds equal and bilateral." The ER team cut open his clothes with shears, established another large-bore IV, and began running more fluids. With Chik's clothes opened, Eddie could see the gunshot wound. It was about the size of a dime and situated two inches below and four inches to the left of his belly button.

"Let's turn him over," Lange said.

They rolled him over, revealing a larger wound. "Confirmed. It's a through-and-through wound," Lange said. "Okay, let's move."

As the healthcare team, led by Lange, rushed Chik toward the OR, Eddie wondered if he would see his friend alive again. A nurse gathered the waiting officers and directed them to the surgical waiting area, where they found Christina, Chik's wife, rocking back and forth with worry. The small Inuit woman jumped up when she saw Eddie.

"How's Chik? Is he dead?"

"No, he's alive. They're taking him to surgery now."

"Thank God."

For hours, police officers in uniform and plain clothes gathered with Christina. Chief Dell came down. Through the windows, the dusky gray of the incomplete Anchorage summer night bloomed into daylight under clear, pale blue skies.

Three and a half hours later, Lange entered in his scrubs, his expression neutral. Christina clutched Eddie's arm as everyone stood.

"Detective Uttaq made it through surgery and is stable. He's heading to ICU."

Collective sighs of relief filled the room.

"I'm his wife," Christina said. "Is he going to live?"

"Barring complications, he should recover fully."

Lange took her aside for a private conversation. When they finished, they shared a brief hug before he left. Christina returned to the group.

"The doc said he was shot through several loops of his small intestines, and the bullet nicked an artery and caused a lot of blood loss. Iliac artery, I think he said. They had to give him four units of blood. They'll keep him knocked out on the breathing machine for today. He said he needs to warm up and hopefully get the breathing tube out shortly after that. Maybe tomorrow or the next day, they'll see how he does. Not much else to do now, so everyone should go home and get some rest."

The room slowly emptied as people hugged Christina goodbye.

"Eddie, can you take me up to see him?"

"Of course," he said.

IN THE ICU, Eddie's badge got them past the two officers stationed outside Chik's room—standard protocol for officers shot on duty. Eddie saw Lange sitting at a computer station nearby, on the phone, and felt a rush of gratitude.

Inside, Chik was barely recognizable. His face was swollen, partially obscured by tape securing the breathing tube. The monitors showed steady vitals: heart rate 86, oxygen saturation 100 percent, blood pressure 115/82.

Lange finished his call and approached.

"How is he?" Eddie asked.

"Stable."

"Why is he so swollen?" Christina asked.

"From all the fluids we gave him during shock. It's normal—it'll resolve in a few days."

"Thank you again, Dr. Lange," Christina said softly.

42

WARRANT

At five in the morning, Eddie left the hospital and headed home to shower and shave. Coffee and adrenaline had kept him going. He and the CSI unit were to converge at Roche's house on the America Salvation Church campus to execute the search warrant before the press conference. At seven, with two patrol cars and a CSI van behind him, Eddie pulled up to the gate of the America Salvation Church.

A guard came to the window of the guardhouse. "Can I help you, gentlemen?"

"I'm Detective Vaugner, Anchorage Police. We have a warrant to search Pastor Roche's home."

"May I see it?"

Normally, Eddie would have produced the warrant even though it wasn't required, but he was tired and he didn't feel like fostering a collegial rapport with any employee of the America Salvation Church.

"Do you live with Pastor Roche?"

"Uh, no, of course not."

"No, you may not. The law does not require me to show a warrant to a private security guard, which is what you are, despite your Delta Force cosplay."

"But the house is on private church property."

"Doesn't matter. You cannot block access to a valid warrant, even on private property."

Eddie kept smiling to show the guard he was enjoying seeing him starting to melt.

"Before I let you in, maybe you should wait until I call Pastor Roche or the head of security."

Eddie was starting to feel sorry for the guy. It was beginning to seem he was more concerned about covering his ass than being deliberately officious. So Eddie gave him another out. Without telling the guard Roche and Saparov were not taking calls, he said, "You can call whoever you like, but you will be arrested if you attempt to impede a duly authorized police action. Open the gate, or we'll crash through it."

The guard muttered, "Yes, sir," sounding relieved to open the gate. As Eddie and the team went through, the guard picked up his walkie-talkie.

They drove a few hundred feet through the church grounds to approach the driveway of Roche's house. They parked in the driveway. Two patrolmen went to the front door to stand guard. The other two stayed with Eddie and the CSI team.

An America Salvation Church security van pulled up to the house. Two armed guards stepped out and swaggered up to Eddie as he punched the code on the garage door keypad.

"Hey, hold on there."

Eddie pulled out his badge. "Anchorage PD. We're searching this residence. Any attempt to interfere with our authorized action will result in an arrest, so back off."

"We'll need to see the warrant."

"You don't need to see shit, you're a rent-a-cop."

The guard considered his options for a second, then returned to his vehicle. Eddie saw him tap on his cell phone. Assuming the guard was calling Roche or Saparov, Eddie whispered to himself, "Leave a message, pal."

Leaving the two patrolmen to stand guard in the garage, Eddie and the CSI team entered the house through a mudroom, then into a well-appointed kitchen with top-of-the-line stainless steel appliances.

The house was open concept, with a sightline through a dining area into a large living room with a cathedral ceiling. A massive slate hearth was the focal point of one wall. Framed photographs of Roche with various members of Anchorage's elite political community and a few has-been actors sat on a live-wood mantel. Cushioned leather sofas, chenille-covered chairs, mission-style end tables, and coffee tables were arranged on a large oriental carpet costing three months' worth of Eddie's wages.

"I don't get it," one of the crime lab techs said. "Why give all this up and confess to a murder you got away with?"

Echoing Dana Peplow's earlier comment to him, Eddie replied with a hint of sarcasm, "The Lord moves in mysterious ways."

They moved up a spiral staircase, passing a large master bedroom with an ornate four-poster king bed and then heading into an office.

"Should be in here."

"Roger."

Eddie opened a closet door to find the wall safe. He took out his cell phone and read out the combination Roche had given him.

A CSI investigator opened the safe and removed several documents, including a passport and a flash drive.

Everything was just as Roche said.

Eddie pointed to a laptop on the desktop and a PC on the floor next to the desk.

"These too."

On their way out, as they went through the kitchen, Eddie noticed a few items stuck to a whiteboard with magnets. One of them caught his eye: a medical appointment card from the office of Grayson Lange, MD, FACS. A simple little appointment card. Anyone with a doctor might have one. He left it there.

43

PRESSER

At 10 a.m., reporters crowded the Anchorage Police Department press room. Mayor Rotig stood at the microphone, flanked by Chief Dell and District Attorney Jane Strupinski. Eddie remained in the background, standing expressionless and in stony silence behind the officials. These sorts of announcements belonged to people in public office and those wanting to run for one.

Mayor Rotig went first.

"Good morning. Due to the rapidly evolving nature of this case, we will issue a brief announcement and refrain from answering questions. Two months ago, a horrific shooting occurred —an assassination, no less—that took the life of Jack Peplow and severely wounded his wife, Dana Peplow. This was a black mark on our city. We promised we would not rest until those responsible were brought to justice."

A murmur swept through the room. The mayor waited for it to die down.

"This morning, it is with great relief and pride that I announce the Anchorage police have made an arrest in the case. I will now turn things over to Chief Dell."

Eddie smirked to himself. Of course, Rotig would leave Roche's name for someone else to utter—he didn't want to risk alienating the voters.

Chief Dell walked up to the podium. "Thank you, Mayor."

The Chief then read from a prepared statement. "Yesterday, Revus Harrison Roche, age fifty-seven, the pastor of the America Salvation Church, approached our department and voluntarily confessed to the murder of Jack Peplow and the attempted murder of Dana Peplow."

The crowd gasped and started to murmur.

Chief Dell raised his hands, waiting for quiet. "Based on the information Pastor Roche provided, we attempted to arrest Dmitri Stanislau Saparov, age sixty-five, at his home in South Anchorage. Mr. Saparov was the head of security at the America Salvation Church. Unfortunately, Mr. Saparov fired upon the arresting officers and was killed by return fire at the scene. One of our detectives is being treated for gunshot wounds at Providence Alaska Medical Center and is expected to recover fully. I'll now turn things over to States Attorney Jane Strupinski."

Strupinski strode to the podium. "Good morning. At this time, our office is preparing an indictment against Mr. Roche. I will remind everyone that a confession is merely one piece of evidence. The investigation to validate the details of Mr. Roche's confession is ongoing. We expect Mr. Roche to plead guilty at the arraignment to all charges filed. Our office will have no further comments until the investigation is complete and all legal proceedings have concluded."

The mayor returned to the microphone. "As many of you know, Mr. Roche leads one of the largest congregations in Anchorage. I want to emphasize that, as of now, the evidence indicates the Peplow assassination was arranged solely by Mr. Roche and his head of security, Mr. Saparov. We have no evidence that other church officers or members had any knowledge of or took part in this assassination. Thank you."

"Did Pastor Roche explain why he killed Jack Peplow?" a reporter shouted.

"Why did Roche confess?" another called out.

More questions followed as the officials left the podium. All were ignored. Eddie headed straight for his car in the Fifth Avenue parking lot.

"Detective Vaugner!"

He turned to see Richard Preski, a well-known reporter for the *Anchorage Daily News*, approaching.

Eddie kept walking.

"I'd like to ask you a few questions."

"We just had a press conference. Refer to your notes."

A birdie told me you're the lead detective—and the one Roche confessed to."

He wasn't known as Preski the Pest for nothing.

"No comment."

"I don't get it, Detective. I've been covering Roche and his fake church for years. If there was ever a man who could kill someone and show no remorse, it's Roche. I find it hard to believe he just walked in and confessed."

"No comment."

"So what or who got to him?"

Images of Roche walking toward Lange's office, the appointment card on the refrigerator door, Bearded Man, the time glitch, and Dr. Chen talking about right neural architecture influencing another person's quantum biological processes flashed through Eddie's mind.

"No comment."

44

ÂNGUAK

After four days in the ICU, Chik was transferred to the surgical ward, 4-North.

Eddie greeted the patrolman sitting outside his door. Entering the room, he found Chik in a sitting position on his bed, dozing. Several IV machines attached to poles with blinking lights were running fluids. A half-filled urine collection bag hung from the bottom bed railing. Green fluid ran from his nose through a nasogastric tube. A cup of ice with a plastic spoon sticking out sat on the nightstand. The television was tuned to local news.

"Chik?" Eddie said softly.

He opened his eyes. "Hey, Eddie."

"How are you feeling?"

"They have this hook-up in my back—an epidural. It delivers pain relief to the spinal cord area, so I'm not in much pain. Tired, though."

"You're really milking this, aren't you?"

"Yeah, I need some me time."

Several flower-filled vases lined the windowsill, with cards propped open beside them.

"Have any idea how long they'll keep you?"

"About five or six days, they said, if everything goes well. I have to fart to get out of here."

"That's never been a problem for you."

"Hi, Eddie." Christina entered the room with Inuksuk following close behind. She walked over and kissed Chik on the cheek. Inuksuk grinned at Eddie.

"How's my wounded hero?" Christina asked.

Chik rolled his eyes.

"He's doing great," Eddie said. "All he has to do is fart, and he's out of here."

"That's never been a problem for him," Christina said.

Inuksuk took an object from his pocket. It was about a half an inch thick and about as wide as his thumb, roughly triangular, rounded at the top with a gentle widening at the base. Its surface was smooth. There were subtle variations in its coloring, mostly ivory, but with deeper amber shadows collecting in its curves and along its edges. Two carefully drilled holes with rounded edges pierced the amulet: a larger one positioned toward the bottom and a smaller, eye-like opening near the top. Another hole, carefully drilled to intersect with the upper hole at a right angle, accommodated a thin silver chain.

"It's beautiful," Eddie said. "What's the material?"

Inuksuk handed Eddie the amulet.

"Walrus tusk," Christina answered.

The surface was smooth, and as he rotated it seemed to shimmer.

Eddie thought it might represent an animal, but he couldn't be sure. Inuksuk said something in Inuit.

He handed it to Christina, who put it around Chik's neck.

"Papa calls it a healing amulet," Chik explained to Eddie.

"Is this an Inuit thing?" he asked.

"I think it's a Papa thing."

"You can see the healing power surging through you," Christina said, her tone so dry it was hard to tell if she was kidding.

"It's that or the fentanyl," Chik replied, lying back and closing his eyes. Before drifting off, he said, "Hey, Eddie, I need to tell you something."

"Yeah?"

"I'm done. Twenty-four years in and getting shot. Enough."

Eddie studied his partner's face. "What do you mean, done? Like retire?"

Christina smiled and nodded eagerly.

Chik opened his eyes again. "Yeah. Christina has been wanting to move to Denmark. I think I'm ready to let her. She's been here for me; now it's my turn." He adjusted himself in the bed, the healing amulet sliding slightly on his chest. "Getting shot puts things in perspective, you know?"

"What the hell are you going to do in Denmark?"

"I don't know. Play more golf. Get serious about my game."

"You're moving to Denmark to work on your golf game? They even have golf courses in Denmark?"

"Yeah, with senior memberships. And the golf season there is longer than here. And in the winter, the flight from Copenhagen to the Canary Islands takes less time than it does for us to fly to Hawaii or Arizona."

"Sounds like you've thought this out," Eddie recalled that Chik, in addition to his savings and pensions, had some family money, so golf shouldn't be a problem for him.

"Yeah," Chik said..

"As long as you don't spend it all on green fees," Christina said.

"The department won't be the same without you."

"Yeah, well, maybe that's good. Getting too old to chase bad guys anyway."

"You're a homicide detective, Chik. You don't chase bad guys."

"Oh, yeah."

His eyes grew heavy, and he drifted off.

Christina squeezed her husband's hand as his eyes closed. Eddie watched the amulet rising and falling on his chest with each breath.

The door opened, and Dr. Lange stepped in. "Good morning, everyone."

Inuksuk stood up and beamed at Lange. The doctor went over to Chik and nudged him gently on the shoulder.

"Yoo-hoo, Chik. Time to wake up and go to school."

Chik's eyes fluttered open. "Oh, hey, Doc."

"The numbers look great. How's the patient feeling?"

"Not too bad."

"Can I see your stomach?"

"Sure." He lifted his gown to reveal a line of skin staples running vertically in his midline.

"Incision looks good; let's have a listen."

Lange took out his stethoscope and placed it on Chik's abdomen.

"I hear some rumbling, Chik. Passed any gas?" The doctor pocketed his stethoscope.

"Seems to be the question of the hour, but no."

"We'll get the epidural out tomorrow. That should help."

"What about the Foley?" Chik said, referring to his bladder catheter.

"Epidural first, then the Foley." Lange pointed to Chik's amulet and nodded warmly at Inuksuk. "*Ânguak*," he said, and gave him a thumbs-up. Inuksuk replied in Inuit.

"Tell your father I don't really speak Inuit. I know a few Inuit words, but I picked them up during some rotations at the Alaska Native Medical Center when I was a resident."

"He said his father made the ânguak for him, and now he is passing it on to me," Chik said.

"Tell him extra healing power is a good thing."

Chik translated for him, and Inuksuk replied. Chik translated: "He says, 'You're more powerful than any amulet. Thank you for saving my daughter's husband.'"

"It's my job, and you're welcome."

"Speaking of healing power, Dr. Lange," Christina said, "any idea when Chik can come home?"

"Let's see, I'm going to Europe in eight days, and I want Chik home long before then. I see him being discharged in around four to five days."

"What you got in Europe, Doc?" asked Chik.

"Getting in a little skiing before the season ends. Have a hot date with the north face of the Obergabelhorn."

"Have fun, but don't break a leg. Or should I say, break a leg?"

Lange chuckled, "Maybe I should borrow your amulet."

"Sure, you can take it."

"No, you keep it. Until you pass gas, at least."

The doctor looked at Eddie and smiled. If there was any resentment from Lange about the DNA testing, he didn't show it. The results were still pending.

Lange held up his hand and smiled at Inuksuk. "*Sulaaqqit*—tomorrow."

"Thank you," Inuksuk said in heavily accented English. "Much thank you."

A few moments after Lange left the room, Chik nodded off. Moments later, as Chik dozed, Eddie hugged Christina, shook Inuksuk's hand, and took off. Sitting in his vehicle out in the garage, Eddie took out his phone. He googled the *North Face of Obergabelhorn*. Wow. Several photographs showed a massive pyramidal-shaped mountain jutting up into a clear blue sky. The north face looked incredibly steep and intimidating. It seemed almost suicidal to ski that face.

45

WHERE GODS LIVE

Luca, the Swiss mountaineering guide Grayson had hired, met him and Jennifer in the Mont Cervin Palace lobby. They'd already spent several days at the hotel acclimatizing to the altitude, skiing the high slopes accessible from the Klein Matterhorn lift, which topped out above 3,800 meters. As with all his adventures, Grayson had planned this descent with meticulous attention to detail. He had been communicating with Luca via text and email for six weeks. When they finally met, they were like long-lost buddies.

Luca loaded the gear into the hotel's electric shuttle. Dawn was breaking. They drove to the Air Zermatt helipad, where they met Werner, the pilot of the charter Airbus H125 helicopter Grayson had arranged. Once their skis and other gear were loaded, they set out for the *Rothornhütte*, where they would spend two days further acclimatizing at the higher altitude.

The Rothorn Hut serves as a way station, offering accommodations for skiers and hikers. It was a fifteen-minute flight, passing by the Matterhorn, over the Trift Glacier and its menacing-looking crevasses, then over the Gabelhorn Glacier. Finally, the hut came into view—a primitive-looking stone structure festooned with bright red and white shutters, perched on a ledge in the jagged peaks of the Zinalrothorn in the Pennine Alps. They spent the day hiking, reading, admiring the view, chatting with other guests, and taking a nap. Grayson was the only skier whose destination was the Obergabelhorn. A few raised their eyebrows when they learned he was going to take on the North Face.

ON THE THIRD morning at the Rothorn Hut, Grayson awoke at 2 a.m., almost ready to begin the long grind upward. Jennifer lay beside him. He ran his hand along her thigh, under her T-shirt, toward her breast.

"Don't even think about it," she said.

"You're awake."

"Have been all night."

"I don't get one last quickie before I head out?"

"No, Grayson. Save your energy for the mountain. Besides, I don't want to jinx you. No last of anything, only later for everything." She rolled over and gave him a hug. She felt his erection. She bopped his nose with her finger. "You'll get more than a hug later."

OUTSIDE THE HUT, in the dead of night, Jennifer kissed Grayson on the cheek and patted his shoulders. "Take good care of him, Luca!"

Luca flashed Jennifer a wide grin. "*Ja, Frau* Jennifer. Like he's my *Bruder*!"

"And drink plenty of water, Grayson." Her voice made it clear she was worried about more than just his hydration status.

"See you at the top," Grayson said as he set out with Luca. Later, Werner was coming back for Jennifer to follow Grayson's descent in the helicopter. After a few steps, he stopped and turned around to wave to Jennifer one last time, but she had already gone back into the hut. He smiled and nodded, then hustled to catch up with Luca.

Grayson and Luca used touring skis with skins for the less steep initial glacier approach. When the terrain steepened, they transitioned to crampons and ice axes, strapping their skis to their packs. For the ascent, they both wore alpine touring boots that worked with both crampons and ski bindings. But these wouldn't provide the performance Grayson needed for his North Face descent. To save Grayson energy, Luca carried Grayson's alpine ski boots and high-performance downhill skis on his back during the entire climb, which went right on schedule.

FIFTEEN MINUTES FROM THE TOP, Luca pulled out the satellite phone. *"Werner. Wir sind kurz vor dem Gipfel. Eine Viertelstunde... Ja... Er ist gut in Form. Ya, ich sage es ihm."*

He hung up. "I told Werner we were close to the summit and that you were in good shape. And Jennifer wishes you good luck."

AT THE SUMMIT, Grayson switched to his alpine skiing gear: Nordica HF Pro 130 boots and Völkl M7 Mantra skis. The thumping sound of a helicopter's rotors approached. It was the Airbus H125. "Werner's here. And there's your woman," Luca said.

THE HELICOPTER BROUGHT Werner and Jennifer closer to the Obergabelhorn. This was Jennifer's first close-up, in-person look at the north slope. The massive, sheer white face looked more impossible than in photographs and videos.

She gulped. "Werner, it looks even more foreboding in person than in the photos."

"Ja, Frau Doktor," Werner said. "She's a monster. Fifty degrees in places, maybe steeper. Wind slab over old snow—very dangerous conditions."

"Call me Jennifer, Werner, or Jenn."

"Easier for me to say *Frau Doktor!*" They both laughed.

As they flew closer, Jennifer saw Grayson and Luca at the summit, two small black dots against an expanse of white. "Look, I see them!"

Fleetingly, she thought, *Why did I even agree to go on this trip?* She tried to suppress thoughts about a fatal fall and how she would get his body back to Anchorage.

GRAYSON SAW Jennifer in the front passenger seat. He held his ski poles up. Luca started packing up the other gear. He was going to take the south-southeast ridge down—a much tamer and safer route. Skiing down with the extra gear would not be a challenge for an experienced Alpine guide.

Grayson raised a ski pole, indicating he was ready. Werner rocked the helicopter to signal he was ready. Jennifer picked up her binoculars and zoomed in on Grayson. She could hardly see his face, but he looked... ready. Yes, he looked ready.

Luca patted Grayson on the back. "Okay, *Herr Doktor*, off you go now! *Viel Glück!*"

Grayson inched toward the precipice, gazing down the face he was about to descend. He closed his eyes. As he listened to the thump of the helicopter blades, he mentally rehearsed his jump turn.

He pictured a clock face. As he traversed, he imagined his skis perpendicular to the hand pointing at 12 o'clock, then jump-turning and landing so his skis would be perpendicular to the hand pointing at 4 o'clock, then completing the turn in the snow until the skis were perpendicular to the hand pointing at 6 o'clock, traversing in the opposite direction. On these slopes, it's not how fast or slow you go; it's about how well you can control your turns. You can't schuss or pizza-wedge your way down on the north slope of the Obergabelhorn.

He looked up one more time, threw Jennifer a kiss, and took three deep breaths. *Now comes absolution or condemnation. It's time for the mountain to judge me.*

He pushed off. As the mountain tried to pull him toward terminal velocity just a few feet into his descent, he initiated the first turn—the one that would set the pattern for his surviving the run.

He double-pole planted to let his arms help his legs, then boosted upward, completely unweighting both skis. Airborne for a fraction of a second, he rotated 120 degrees and landed with seventy percent of his weight on his downhill ski. He kept the downhill ski slightly behind the uphill ski, ankles flexed, body leaning forward to keep his center of mass close to the surface. He slipped sideways down the slope for a short distance, then he felt his metal edge bite as loose snow broke away from his edges, cascading down the face.

He traversed for a few seconds, then repeated the sequence in the opposite direction—plant, explode, rotate, land, weight on the down-hill ski, keeping his ankles flexed and his body leaning slightly forward to keep his center of mass as close to the surface as possible to prevent rearing back on his skis.

It was all nearly automatic, the technique ingrained from growing up and skiing the 2,000-vertical-foot double-black diamond zone on the north slope at his home resort at Alyeska, rated as one of the most challenging slopes in North America.

Each well-executed turn was a point in his favor, and the mountain was keeping score.

IN THE HELICOPTER, Werner watched intently through his side window.

"Perfect entry!" Werner shouted over the rotor noise. "And he turns well! *Kritisch!*"

"Oh my God!" Jennifer's excitement started to overtake her apprehension as she watched through her binoculars.

"See how he traverses? You can't go straight down a slope like this. Direct fall line not doable."

As she watched his perfect technique, Jennifer felt her jaw unclench.

"He's making it look almost easy!"

Werner laughed. "*Ja!* If you can't make it look easy, you have no business being out here!"

Grayson monitored his speed carefully, and at the end of each traverse, he scrubbed his speed with a slight uphill turn before committing to the next direction change. With each turn, loose snow broke away from his edges and skittered down the face in miniature avalanches.

WERNER BANKED the helicopter slightly to maintain position.

"He's doing alright, no?" Jennifer said, her breath fogging the window.

"*Ja!* Perfect technique! But see all that snow he's kicking loose?" Werner paused, studying the slope. "This whole face could slide."

"What do you mean slide?"

"Avalanche, *Frau Doktor*. Wind slab over weak layer. Very unstable."

"Too much information, Werner!" Jennifer's knuckles whitened as she gripped her binoculars.

GRAYSON APPROACHED the steepest pitch—fifty degrees of wind-scoured ice. This was prime avalanche terrain. Still, he skied rhythmically—plant pole, launch upward, twist skis 120 degrees, land on opposite edge, favoring the downhill ski on each traverse for crucial edge grip.

"*ACH*, here comes the bad section. Fifty degrees, maybe more."

"Should we be worried?" Jennifer asked.

"Always worried about a face like this, but he's doing well." They watched Grayson's short-radius jump turns. "*Sehr gut!* See how he never stays in one place? Don't give the slope time to break."

Jennifer noted the cascades of loose debris streaming down the face with each turn.

"All that snow he's moving... will it hold?" Jennifer said nervously.

"*Ja.* Probably. But you never know for sure."

. . .

GRAYSON FELT his edges chattering more intensely. He hit a patch of blue ice—diamond-hard and treacherous. His edges chattered and scraped, fighting for any grip. Ice chips cascaded into the void.

"*ACH*! *Blaues Eis*—blue ice—hard like concrete. This is the test now."

"What's blue ice?" Jennifer asked.

"See how his skis bounce and chatter? He fights for every bit of control." Werner watched intently. "Technique saves him—small movements, never fight the mountain. But by now, you can believe his legs are burning!"

AS HE SUCCESSFULLY MANAGED THE ice, the slope moderated. Grayson's jump turns gave way to dynamic parallel turns. But now his legs ached with the telltale fire of oxygen debt. In his physician's mind, he could picture his mitochondria—those tiny powerhouses essential for life—working overtime to produce ATP. But his metabolic demands exceeded the limit of his mitochondria to utilize oxygen, so the sarcoplasm activated anaerobic metabolism, trying to produce even more ATP. The byproduct of anaerobic metabolism is lactic acid, which made him *feel the burn*. But his form remained flawless.

Werner banked toward the landing zone.

"*Ausgezeichnet!* Not too bad for an *Amerikaner!*"

"He did it!" Jennifer shouted.

"*Ja*, but must stick the landing."

GRAYSON COMPLETED the final pitch with sweeping turns through softening corn snow. His hockey stop threw up a dramatic plume—the signature finish of a descent that had drained every ounce of energy.

THE HELICOPTER TOUCHED DOWN, its rotors kicking up snow. Grayson bent over, his arms on his knees, supporting his torso, taking deep breaths. As the lactic acid was metabolized, the burning stopped, and now it was just fatigue.

THE CRYSTALLINE SNOW settled around the helicopter. Werner smiled at Jennifer and motioned toward the door.

"*Geh!* Go celebrate with him!"

She nodded enthusiastically and jumped out into the bracing cold.

GRAYSON STEPPED out of his skis, smiling as Jennifer ran toward him, each stride kicking up snow. He could see the relief and amazement on her face.

He let out a "Whoooh!" When she reached him, she threw her arms around him, and her momentum, combined with his weakened legs from his descent, caused them to tumble into the snow.

"That was beautiful, Grayson! And terrifying!"

Werner approached.

"*Ausgezeichnet!* Perfect technique, top to bottom."

He extended an arm, offering them a hand up, and then gave Grayson a hug. "You skied like almost a Swiss—the highest compliment I give."

Grayson laughed, "Whew! That was fun!"

They headed back to the helicopter.

As they lifted off, Grayson looked up at the Obergabelhorn—"above the clouds," where the gods lived. They flew past the face, and he could see his serpentine tracks in the snow, fleeting proof the mountain had judged him and chosen absolution over condemnation.

"Ready for lunch? I'm starved!" Jennifer said.

Grayson laughed. "Epinephrine down, dopamine up! And then that more than a hug you promised me."

46

, EDDIE

At the initial hearing, the prosecutors charged Reverend Roche with two counts of solicitation to murder and denied bail. Local media aired specials on Roche's rise from struggling pest control contractor to wealthy megachurch leader, and pundits debated the American Salvation Church's future.

Against Roche's will, America Salvation Church's lawyers hired psychologists and psychiatrists to evaluate his mental state and hopefully get him off due to diminished mental capacity. All found him sane.

Throughout all this, Roche showed no remorse over his victim's death, no empathy for Dana Peplow's long recovery from losing a lung to the assassin's bullet; he shrugged off spending the rest of his life in prison. Eddie read one report in which a psychiatrist used a term—*la belle indifference*, a phrase coined by Sigmund Freud to describe the characteristic lack of concern that hysteria patients adopted toward their symptoms.

The psychiatrist, however, emphasized that hysteria is not psychosis. It's a defensive mechanism, a way to cope.

Despite the psychiatric characterizations of Roche's behavior,

Eddie couldn't shake the feeling that something wasn't right about all of this.

And that something was Lange.

First Dracule—possibly his father, if his theory was right. Now Roche, who was Lange's patient. Two sociopathic killers, both dead, both connected to Lange.

The prosecutors had built an airtight case—taped conversations between Roche and Saparov planning the operation, Cayman bank records confirming cash withdrawals to convert to crypto. Even if Roche recanted, they had him. The only loose end was the identities of the actual killers, and that information had been buried with Saparov.

But, as the lawyers in the Anchorage District Attorney's Office were high-fiving each other, anticipating Roche standing up in court and pleading guilty, and as Eddie was suspicious about the *confession*, Reverend Revus Roche, while lying peacefully on his bunk at the Anchorage Correctional Complex, Bible propped up on his chest, died.

THE JAIL WAS IN LOCKDOWN. A guard led Eddie past a row of cells, where inmates either lay reading or stood gripping the crossbars.

"Who died?" one prisoner called.

"Let's hope it's that faggot, Lipinsky!"

That was clearly the tier's favorite as guffaws and howls ensued.

Two guards flanked Roche's cell. Inside, the ACC superintendent, Jake Haskins, ended a phone call as Eddie approached.

"Hey, Jake."

"Hey, Eddie."

Roche lay face-up on the floor in his orange jumpsuit. His face was pale, with an endotracheal tube protruding from his mouth. One eye was closed, the other half-open, with an unfocused, mid-dilated pupil. Eddie knelt for a closer look—no trauma marks, rope burns, or contusions on the face or neck.

Pam Wilson, the commissioner of the Alaska Department of Corrections, entered. "Jesus, Jake, what the H-E-double hockey sticks?"

"What can I do? He dropped dead. Check that. He was lying in bed, so he didn't drop."

Though the space was designed for two inmates, Roche's protected status made him its only occupant. Everything was orderly: metal bunk beds bolted to one wall, both made, but the bottom one was mussed. A King James Bible with a red leather cover and gold lettering rested on top. A stainless-steel sink/toilet combo faced the beds. The furnishings were completed by two small writing desks with built-in swing-out stools, also fixed to the wall—a standard precaution against furniture being used as weapons. A notebook and a cup of ballpoint pens sat on one desk.

"What happened?" Eddie asked.

"Guards found him unresponsive on the lower bunk, Bible on his chest," Haskins said. "They got him to the floor, started CPR, and called 911. EMTs arrived in ten minutes, intubated him, and worked for another ten minutes. No electrical activity; end-tidal CO_2 is under 7. They said no one comes back from that, called it, and told me to notify homicide and the ME."

Jane Strupinski, the district attorney, appeared at the cell. "Eddie, what happened?"

"Found in bed, unresponsive, Bible on his chest. Looks like cardiac arrest. No obvious signs of violence."

"Jesus fucking Christ. Pardon my French." She had just lost a slam-dunk high-profile case.

"Any unusual events this morning?" Eddie asked Haskins.

"Nothing. Breakfast at seven, back in his cell by 7:45. Seemed in good spirits."

"Health complaints? Infirmary visits?"

"None we know of."

"Hostile encounters? Threats?"

"Nothing. He was segregated from the general population."

The CSI team arrived.

As CSI worked, Eddie canvassed the tier. Fifteen inmates gave him variations of "didn't see nothin'" with one "fuck you" thrown in.

Wolf whistles and foot stomping erupted down the corridor.

Becca, followed by two morgue attendants with a gurney, appeared around the corner. She was dressed in jeans, a flannel shirt, and a down vest, and she carried her satchel. She ignored the catcalls but smiled when she saw Eddie.

"Hello, everyone," she addressed the cell. "I'm Dr. Rebecca Raven, assistant medical examiner. Who's in charge?"

"That would be me," Harvey said, the lead CSI investigator.

"May I approach the body?"

"Be my guest," he said.

"He was found dead on his bed," Eddie added. "Moved to the floor for resuscitation, which failed, obviously. No obvious foul play."

Becca donned a cloth jumpsuit and paper shoe covers and then methodically studied Roche's visible surfaces.

"Agreed, no sign of physical violence. Can we remove the body?"

Harvey checked with his team. They all nodded or gave the thumbs-up.

The CSI photographer flashed one more pic and said, "I got what I need."

"Dr. Raven, can you get to his autopsy tonight?" Strupinski asked. "I need his cause of death out there immediately. I don't want religious nuts spreading conspiracy theories."

"Good luck," Harvey said dryly. "Fake moon landings, flat earth, shooter on the grassy knoll. We've got an unwitnessed death of a cult leader in a prison cell. This is conspiracy theory gold."

Eddie was sympathetic. Get the answers out quickly—it's a cover-up. Take time for a complete investigation—it's still a cover-up. If a nut wanted a conspiracy, there was going to be a conspiracy.

"Yes, how about seven o'clock tonight?" Becca said.

"I'll be there." Strupinski left.

As Eddie watched the ME attendants seamlessly move Roche into the body bag, zip it up, transfer it to the gurney, Becca came up beside him.

"Hey, Eddie."

"Uh, yeah?"

"See you at the autopsy?"

"I'll be there."

"Say hi to Daniel for me."

"I will—he asks about you."

"How sweet. We should all get together, huh?"

"Yes, that would be nice."

Eddie swallowed and hoped he wasn't blushing. Was there warmth there? A bit of affection? He felt a tingle of hope and fantasy spread through his body, even into his phantom limb. Or was he reading too much into that, as well?

Becca left shortly after, without either of them offering a definite plan to get together. Eddie sensed a wall.

47

THE WIDOWMAKER

Later that evening, the control room of the medical examiner's CT scanner was crowded with officials—a scene that had become all too familiar. Eddie stood with Becca, Dell, Strupinski, and the Anchorage Corrections brass, Haskins and Wilson, while Chief Medical Examiner Gerson Zigler bent his tall frame toward the monitor.

Two high-profile deaths in as many months, Eddie thought. First Peplow, now the man who'd ordered his killing.

The nude corpse of Revus Roche lay on the scanner. No dignity for the dead, not that he deserved any, thought Eddie.

Karl sat at the controls, fingers poised over the keyboard. Eddie glanced at Becca. She was handling the pressure well—calm, professional, despite the police chief and DA breathing down her neck. *That's my girl, except she wasn't. Jesus Vaugner, there you go again.*

"I've got it set to 140 kVp and 450 mA," Karl said.

"That should do it," Becca said.

Eddie watched her lean forward to check the settings, the fluorescent lights catching the auburn undertones in her hair. She'd pulled it back in a low ponytail, exposing the curve of her neck. *Jesus, Vaugner.*

Zigler addressed the group. "With corpses, we use a higher level of radiation. Typical settings for live patients would be 80-120 kVp and

100-300 mAs. We get much better images this way, and we can use thinner slices—one millimeter instead of the standard three to five...”

Eddie tried to focus on the technical explanation but found himself watching how Becca's fingers drummed silently against her thigh while waiting for the images. *This is pathetic. Completely pathetic.* “...It shows us much more detail, but the drawback is the scans take longer, around twenty minutes. Not that our patients are in a hurry to be anywhere.”

A few chuckles from the crowd. Eddie felt a poke at his side, interrupting his reverie. Sarah Cooper stood beside him and gave him a wink.

“Agent Cooper, what are you doing here?”

“That's what I want to know. Chen wanted me here to cross *t*'s and dot *i*'s, I guess. Never been a fan of autopsies.”

The machine cycled up, and Roche's body moved through the CT doughnut, one millimeter at a time. Eddie watched Becca step closer to the monitor, her shoulder brushing past his. Just that brief contact sent an unwelcome jolt through him. *This is insane. You're acting like a teenager.*

While the machine hummed, Cooper drew Eddie aside.

“Now that the major perps are dead, we're getting signals to stand down on the case.”

“And not go after the hit team?”

“Extradition from Kazakhstan is complicated, and with current diplomatic priorities, no one in Washington wants to push too hard on a case like this. Hell, the team could be part of the kleptocratic apparatus.”

He was trying to focus on Cooper's words, really trying, but Becca had just tucked a strand of hair behind her ear and—*For Christ's sake.*

“Eddie,” Cooper said, “are you listening?”

“Yes. So, foreigners entered our country, killed one of our citizens, wounded another, and we're talking diplomatic priorities?”

“Realpolitik, my man, realpolitik. But if you get any info we can act on, reach out to me.”

Karl announced, “We're getting good images now.”

Zigler stepped forward, his weathered hands gesturing at the screen, and resumed his running commentary. "The five most common causes of noncriminal nontraumatic sudden deaths, in no particular order, are one, arrhythmia..." Eddie's peripheral vision betrayed him—he tracked the tilt of Becca's head as she concentrated on the sequential cross-sectional images appearing on the monitor.

"...which is an electronic malfunction of the heart; two, acute coronary thrombosis or heart attack from a blood clot in a coronary artery; three, intracranial event, either occlusion or rupture of blood vessel in the brain; four, aortic or major blood vessel rupture; and five, PE, pulmonary embolism, blood clot to the lung." He paused as if remembering something. "Had a case last year where we found all five in one patient. Like he won the sudden death lottery."

Becca pointed to the monitor and took over. "On the images, we can see there is no fluid in the chest, abdomen, or cranial cavity, so we can rule out ruptured blood vessels. I don't see any thrombus in the main pulmonary vessels, so no PE." He realized he'd missed half of what she'd said, too busy watching the way her brow furrowed when concentrating. *Get. A. Grip.* "I don't see any blood or hypoattenuation in the brain, so most likely, there is no stroke. So, the two most likely possibilities are either cardiac arrhythmia or coronary thrombosis. Since he is a middle-aged white male, my money would be on coronary thrombosis."

Zigler nodded. "Agreed."

Attendants put Roche on a gurney to move him from the CT control room to the autopsy room. The entourage, Roche's last, followed.

As they rounded a corner, Eddie heard Strupinski say, "Dr. Zigler, a word?"

Zigler and Strupinski hung back. Eddie stepped around the corner but stayed within earshot. "Shouldn't you be conducting this autopsy yourself, given the politically explosive nature of the case? Anchoragites will want to know that the most experienced forensic pathologist performed the autopsy."

"Dr. Raven has exceptional expertise in cardiac pathology. She's probably better at cardiac pathology than I am these days."

"But—"

Zigler interrupted Strupinski. "Look, she's the best person for the job. I'd want her to do my heart if it were me on the table. You want this done right, don't you?"

Eddie felt a surge of pride at Zigler's words.

When they reassembled in the autopsy room, Karl took his usual place on the right side of the autopsy table.

"Okay, Karl," Becca said.

Karl started the Y-incision while she put on her apron and snapped on gloves.

"Should we do it Rokitansky, Virchow, or Letuelle?" Karl asked as he started peeling the skin and muscles away from the rib cage.

"Since our money's on the heart, I vote Virchow," Becca said.

The way she pronounced it—the soft V, the slight roll of the R. Eddie caught himself memorizing the sound. *This is completely inappropriate. She's cutting open a corpse, and you're mooning over her like an adolescent.*

Zigler stepped closer, gesturing in front of him. "There are three basic ways of performing an autopsy. The Virchow method removes each organ individually, one at a time, and examines it before proceeding to the next. The Letuelle method removes all the organs at once in one block by cutting through the upper windpipe and esophagus, the rectum, and then all the attachments. This way is much quicker. The Rokitansky is an in-between approach. Since we suspect coronary artery lesions and no doubt you people want to cut to the chase, the Virchow method, looking at one organ at a time, starting with the heart, is most appropriate here."

In a few minutes, they had the front part of the rib cage removed.

With a few deft strokes, Karl removed the heart from the chest and gave it to Becca, who set it on a side table. She pointed to curvilinear fat-covered grooves running vertically down the heart.

"You see here, here, and here? These are the main arteries of the heart. We have the main coronary artery arising from the left side of the aorta. After about an inch, it divides into the left anterior descending artery and the circumflex artery. These supply blood to the left ventricle, the main pumping chamber of the heart. On the other side here, passing in this groove between the right atrium and ventricle? This is the right coronary artery. It's the main supplier of blood to the right ventricle, the chamber that pumps the venous blood to the lungs." She showed the group at the top of the heart where the aorta, the main trunk of the body, came out. She pointed out the valves and showed them two holes tucked away in the valve cusps.

"This hole here is the ostium of the main coronary artery, and this one here is the ostium of the right coronary artery."

She put the heart down on the table and made a series of small transverse incisions on the surface of the heart into the coronary arteries, each incision a couple of millimeters apart.

"Ah. We have something here in the left anterior descending artery, the LAD."

She used a set of tweezers to gently spread apart one of the incisions she had just made.

"Look at this—like a thick yellow doughnut with a dark red jelly center? The thick yellow wall is atherosclerosis, a hardening of the artery, and the substance that resembles red jam is a fresh clot. It looks like the patient died of an acute thrombosis of a diseased LAD, left anterior descending."

She went through the rest of the coronary arteries.

"Looks like an isolated lesion. The rest of his coronary arteries look pretty clean."

"The widowmaker," Karl said.

"Widowmaker?" Chief Dell asked.

"The isolated lesion of the LAD," Becca said. "It's called the widowmaker because acute obstructions of the LAD often result in sudden death in men. This lesion killed James Gandolfini and Tim Russert, the news guy."

"Atherosclerosis is usually a diffuse process," Zigler added, reinforcing what she had said. "People tend to have atherosclerosis in all their coronary arteries, as well as in other arteries, like the carotid arteries leading to the brain and the arteries going to the legs. People who have a heart attack are twice as likely to have a stroke and vice versa. But his coronary arteries, other than this lesion, look clean. The LAD is notorious for this isolated lesion."

"You called it, Dr. Raven," Eddie said, looking over at Strupinski. Eddie felt a surge of pride—and something warmer than just professional admiration.

"You have your answer for the news conference," Becca said. "LAD blockage, known as the widowmaker, causes myocardial infarction, arrhythmia, and death. No need to stay for the rest unless you want to. We'll complete the full protocol, and if anything contributory comes later, I'll get a memo out tonight."

"Okay, that does it for me, Dr. Raven," Strupinski said. "Thank you for getting right on this."

"I guess I'll head out too," Chief Dell said.

"Excellent job, Becca," Zigler said. "I'll see our guests out."

Cooper gave Eddie a light punch in the arm. "That was fun. Not. I'll catch you later."

Now it was just Eddie, Karl, and Becca in the room. "At least it's not another mitochondrial problem," Eddie said.

"Well," she said, "actually, that's not quite true."

"What do you mean?" Eddie asked. As in, *are you fucking kidding me?*

"Mitochondrial dysfunction resulting in the production of reactive oxygen species may play an important role in the formation of atherosclerosis."

"Could you try again in English?"

"Mitochondrial damage can lead to oxidative stress, which increases the production of reactive oxygen species that damage blood vessel walls. This allows LDL cholesterol to penetrate the arterial wall, and things get worse from there."

"I see." *Was Grayson getting better at his mitochondrial lesions? Or maybe Roche just drew the same lot as Gandolfini and Russert.*

"Grayson operated on him for a hiatal hernia."

"Oh. That's potentially interesting. But let's take a look at his handiwork, shall we?"

She took a scalpel in her hand.

"May I, Karl?"

Karl laughed. "Go for it, Doc."

Eddie watched her gracefully extend Karl's chest incision down through the midline of the abdomen. With a few cuts of the scissors, she exposed the area where the esophagus meets the stomach. *She has no idea how graceful she is, even here, even doing this.*

"A Nissen fundoplication. Dr. Lange did a nice job. Symmetrical wrap, not too tight or too loose. Perfect, really."

She removed the stomach and esophagus and made a longitudinal incision along the length of the esophagus. "Oh yes. Definitely indicated." She pointed out a grayish area inside part of the esophagus closest to the stomach. "See this? Compared to the normal esophagus up here. Normal pink here, gray and scarred here. Healed chronic inflammation from severe reflux. If untreated, this can lead to esophageal cancer. So Lange may have spared him from a miserable death from esophageal cancer, at least."

And provided him with a quick one? thought Eddie.

Becca snapped off her gloves and hung her apron on a hook. As they wrapped up, Eddie realized something startling. For the first time since Anne's death, he'd made it through an entire autopsy without once picturing her on the table. Not even thinking about her. He'd been so distracted by Becca—her voice, her hands, the way she bit her lip when concentrating—that he forgot to be haunted.

The realization brought a moment of vertigo. He'd been dragging his grief around like chains on that guy from the Ebenezer Scrooge story. But Anne would have laughed at him for that. *You're using the chains,* she would have said, *because my ghost never rejects you.*

48

THIRTY DAYS

The morning following Roche's autopsy, Eddie, Chik, and some other detectives watched the Bureau of Prisons press conference from their desks. It was conducted by Wilson, Zigler, Strupinski, Public Information Officer Bertha Hansen, and Michelle Stone, Roche's panel attorney.

Hansen introduced the other four and then turned the podium over to Commissioner Wilson, who summarized the morning's events.

"Pastor Roche was awaiting sentencing after pleading guilty to arranging the assassination of Jack Peplow and the attempted assassination of Dana Peplow. He was found deceased in his cell at approximately 10 a.m. yesterday, lying on his bed."

From there, Strupinski and Zigler summarized the events and findings, including the resuscitative efforts and the findings at autopsy. Zigler showed a slide demonstrating the cross-section of Pastor Roche's left anterior descending coronary artery. "What you're seeing here is a thickened yellowish wall of the artery—cholesterol buildup."

As Zigler described Roche's coronary lesion, the intercom button on Eddie's phone lit up.

"Yes?"

"Detective Vaugner, there's a Dr. Defner here to see you."

"Defner? What does he want?"

"He says he has some important information for you."

"Put him in an interrogation room. I'll be down in a few."

WHEN EDDIE ENTERED the interrogation room, Defner was seething.

"You put me in an interrogation room like a suspect?" the doctor demanded when Eddie entered.

"This is where we conduct all our interviews, suspect or not. What can I do for you, Doc?"

"Are you aware Lange operated on Pastor Roche?"

"Yes, I am."

"Have you interviewed him?"

"No, why should I?"

"More than likely, he was responsible for his death."

"What makes you say that?" Eddie did not like Defner. Even worse, he hated the idea that he might share the same theory as this religious nutjob.

"Are you aware of the significance of Roche dying just over thirty days after Lange operated on him?"

"Why don't you enlighten me?"

"If a patient dies within thirty days of a procedure, it is considered a postoperative mortality, and it must be reported, no matter what the cause."

Eddie blinked and swallowed, hoping that Defner wouldn't notice his reaction.

"Did you watch the press conference this morning? The ME said the operation was not a factor. And Pastor Roche told me the operation went well and cured his reflux symptoms. And Dr. Raven said Lange did an excellent job with his surgery."

"Lange's operation didn't kill him."

"So what did kill him?" There was no way Eddie was going to share Becca's mitochondrial explanation with Defner.

"I don't know; that's your job to find out. Whatever Lange did to me, he must have done to Pastor Roche."

"My job is to investigate murders and find evidence a prosecutor can use in court to convict." Not a denial, Eddie knew, but a deflection.

"You need to look harder. Evil lurks in that man."

This gave Eddie an opening. "You keep calling Lange evil. However, let's examine his three supposed victims. The first was probably a child molester; the second, the leader of your church, who assassinated a man who was defending the Constitution; and then there was you, a man who assaulted him after he saved a woman's life. Since you're a member of the America Salvation Church, who's to say you weren't trying to kill off Dana Peplow, pretending to get that chest tube in to finish what Roche had started?"

Vaugner started wondering if he was playing devil's advocate or defending Lange.

"That's absurd," Defner said.

"But Lange magically killing people isn't?" Eddie countered. "Why not go to the press if you feel so strongly? They love a good conspiracy theory."

"You saw what Lange did to me once. I don't want him to kill me."

Vaugner looked at Defner, who sank into sullen silence. "Anything else, Doc?"

"You're going to let him get away with this, aren't you?" Defner glared at him.

The words hung between them for a moment. Eddie stood up and opened the door to the examination room. "If you come up with any solid leads, I'd be happy to hear you out."

The doctor rose slowly, defeated. He paused in the doorway. "This isn't right. He who justifies the wicked and he who condemns the righteous are both alike an abomination to the Lord."

Eddie pictured his fist splitting Defner's nose.

"Have a nice day, Doc."

49

COVERT

Defner sat at his workstation, waiting for Lange to show up. There was a patient with a hot gallbladder, worrisome for gangrene. It needed to come out tonight, and Lange was the surgeon on call.

Since deciding to kill Lange, Defner had been carefully recalibrating his interactions with him. No more overt hostility—he'd adopted a calculated friendliness, a thin veneer of politeness and civility, though he suspected Lange could sense something off about it. No matter— Defner still enjoyed the feeling of the predator playing with its prey.

When he caught sight of Lange approaching, Defner forced a smile.

"Hey, Grayson," Defner said as he handed him the chart. Grayson gave him a funny look, which Defner ignored.

"Room 10," he said.

"I see that. It's on the clipboard."

Ignoring the rebuff, Defner continued to try to ingratiate himself further.

"I noticed you were out the last two weeks."

Without looking up from the chart, Lange said, "I was in Europe to do some Alpine skiing."

"Alps?"

"Yeah."

Defner suffered a FOMO moment. *You can't have him, Lord. He's mine.*

"Isn't March a dangerous time to ski the Alps? The snowpack is starting to get unstable, no?"

"No, it's safer in March in the Alps," Lange said dismissively. "Snowpack is more consolidated. Spring snow has better adhesion and less likelihood of sudden storms."

Fucking Lange. Always making me look incompetent or stupid.

"Well, I'm glad you were careful, man."

"I always am, Defner."

Lange held the clipboard, his back to Defner, and waved it dismissively as he headed toward Room 10.

"Cool man, well, I'm outta here. Got a hot date."

A scowl replaced Defner's fake smile.

Summer couldn't get here fast enough.

DEFNER ENTERED NORTHERN LIGHTS GUNS & Ammo to find a heavyset, full-bearded man sporting a tactical vest sitting behind a counter thumbing his phone. He packed a SIG Sauer P226-X5 on his right hip. His name tag identified him as "Randy."

Defner noticed Randy glance up at him, then put his nose back in his phone.

Fucking asshole, I should take my business elsewhere. But closing time was in less than an hour, and he wanted this done today.

"What can I do you for?" Randy said without looking up.

"I'm looking for a DesertTech SRSA2 Covert Rifle, .308 16-inch," Defner said. "I prefer black, but I'll take tungsten."

Randy clicked his phone off and looked up to greet his customer.

"What are you going to be using it for?"

"Target shooting, maybe some hunting." *Not that it's any of your fucking business.*

"For hunting, you're better off with a Remington 700 or a Winchester Model 70."

"No, I want the DesertTech. I got used to this kind of rifle in the service."

"Understandable, my man. Then, have you considered the 6.5 Creedmoor? Slightly more accuracy with an eighteen-inch barrel without sacrificing much in stopping power."

Please, just shut the fuck up and give me what I ask for. "No, I want the .308 Winchester. And actually, I'd like two barrels." Defner had chosen the .308 Winchester because it was an extremely common bullet. After shooting Lange, he'd ditch the one barrel so ballistics couldn't be used to match his weapon.

"The customer is always right. Did you have a scope in mind? I have a nice Vortex 10x32 on sale."

"I'm going with the Leupold MARK 5HD 2-10X30 M5C3 first focal plane scope. Also, the Atlas bipod and the hardware needed to mount both."

"Sweet, anything else?"

"Yeah, the Ultra gun vise, Wheeler professional reticle leveling system, and the Works All-In-One Combo Toolkit. A soft Covert carrying case."

Randy reached under the counter, pulled out Form 4473, and handed it to Defner. "Fill this out while I check our inventory," the clerk said, heading to the back of the store.

Defner took out his driver's license and began filling out the form. He provided his name, address, place of birth, height, weight, and race. He checked off "No" on all the boxes, including "Are you an unlawful user of, or addicted to, marijuana or any depressant, stimulant, narcotic drug, or any other controlled substance?"

Post hoc, ergo propter hoc—after this, therefore, because of this. As a doctor, Defner knew this reasoning led to superstitions and fallacious medical conclusions. He understood causal events must be linked by convincing evidence, and most medical advances were made based on trials involving double-blinded randomized studies to minimize observers' biases.

But this was different. This had happened to him. He had felt the satanic power disrupting the mitochondrial oxidative phosphorylation in his heart, stopping ATP and causing ischemic symptoms, rendering him powerless and fearful as Lange stood over him.

On the day Detective Vaugner dismissed his concerns, the die was cast. Since the law of man had failed, Defner would call on the law of God, and like God, show no pity.

Randy came back, trundling a cart with several boxes. "I only have the illuminated version of the Mark 5 HD you wanted. It's another five hundred dollars. I can have the non-illuminated up here in about four business days."

"I'll take the illuminated."

"Good choice. You'll see the reticle better in low light situations." Randy took the form and began entering the data into his computer for the NICS check. "This might take a few minutes," he said.

"What service were you in?"

"Navy. I was a corpsman. Now I'm an ER doc."

Randy chuckled. "With this gear, you could certainly pull in some customers."

Defner didn't laugh.

"Hey, they're quick today, and you checked out, so we're good."

From under the counter, he pulled out a small box. "You'll need these mounting rings for the scope. The A2 bipod mounts directly into the rifle, so no extra hardware is needed. What about ammo?"

"I'll go with Federal Terminal Ascent. Give me five boxes."

"You're not messing around."

"No, I'm not."

Randy pushed the cart to Defner's Corvette. "Nice wheels, man."

"Thanks. Just put everything in the shotgun seat."

Once everything was loaded and Defner climbed into the driver's seat, Randy gave the top a couple of slaps. "Happy hunting, bro!"

BACK AT HOME, Defner spread a bedspread on his dining room table and assembled the rifle with methodical precision. He liked the feel of the metal, of inserting the barrel into the chassis and snapping it into place, of the torque wrench clicking as it secured the assembly. He positioned the rifle in the gun vise and used the leveling system to level it in the longitudinal and rotational axes. Then he mounted the scope rings onto the Picatinny rail, followed by the scope itself, setting the eye relief—the critical distance between eyepiece and eye. Using the leveling system again, he ensured the horizontal and rotational axes aligned perfectly with the rifle. He tightened all screws to the correct torque specifications using the toolkit's limiters.

For the last step, he opened a drawer of his dining room credenza and took out the used .308 suppressor he'd managed to purchase on the sly after making a few discreet inquiries at a gun show. He didn't want to wait up to six months to get ATF clearance.

When he finished, he raised the rifle to firing position. It felt good in his arms, pressing against his shoulder and cheek. The eye relief through the scope was perfect—close enough for a clear view without vignetting and far enough to prevent scope bite when the rifle recoiled. His next stop would be the firing range for sighting and practice.

He set the rifle down and went to his office, retrieving a small laptop computer—a cheap 8GB model purchased with cash from Goodwill. When he was done with Lange, he would destroy it. There would be no records of searches on his phone or desktop. He pulled up Google Earth Pro and typed in Lake Campbell, Anchorage, Alaska. After the app acquired the location, he zoomed in on Lange's house and the bordering lake.

Perfect. The house sat conveniently across the water from an undeveloped lot with tree cover.

And my God will supply every need of yours according to his riches in glory in Christ Jesus.

Defner placed the ruler's crosshairs and drew a line from the house to a spot in the woods with a clear line of sight, back from the water's edge. Two hundred ninety-five yards. At that range, there would be minimal bullet drop for a .308 Winchester. He marked the GPS coordinates.

Using street view, he identified his access point. Given the housing density, he would park several blocks away in the predawn hours and approach the sniper position under the cover of darkness. But not yet —he needed a few months to let things cool down. He had just been to Vaugner with his suspicions; if anything happened to Lange now, he would be high on the list of suspects, especially with the recent purchase of the firearm. A waiting period of a few months would give him time to plan, practice at the range, and best of all, savor the anticipation of divine justice.

To everything there is a season, and a time to every purpose under heaven.

50

BREAKUP

Winter always loosened its grip reluctantly on Anchorage, putting Anchoragites through a purgatory of mud and slush from the end of March through the end of April. The transition from winter into spring was called "breakup." Dark and crusted snow melted, broke up, refroze, and melted some more.

Cars were dingy and gray, their lights dimmed with grime. Tires hydroplaned through puddles the size of small lakes, often dousing the unwary bicyclist or pedestrian. The snow receded to reveal hubcaps, cardboard, coolers, and other urban and suburban jetsam. Gravel, which had been laid down all winter to prevent ice skidding, was now propelled from the road by tires into windshields, causing dings and cracks. Rim-denting, tire-bursting, and teeth-jarring potholes lurked everywhere.

Anchoragites were joyous, however, because the mess heralded the promise of summer and long, warm days, of hiking, biking, picnics, and the explosion of green.

No breakup in Anchorage went by without someone finding a body revealed by the receding snow. Eddie got the call just after dropping Daniel off at school.

With thirteen homicides since the Peplow assassination,

Anchorage was keeping up with its rate of about thirty-six a year. Eddie had taken the lead on four of them; this would be his fifth case.

The first case was textbook: a nineteen-year-old killed over three hundred dollars' worth of meth. Suspect apprehended, now awaiting trial.

In the second case, the girlfriend had pressed a .22 against her temple while the boyfriend was breaking up with her and pulled the trigger, holding the gun at such an angle that the bullet skirted under her scalp. It exited with enough force on the other side to hit the boyfriend's heart, killing him instantly. She survived the scalp wound and got manslaughter charges. The attorney was arguing temporary insanity. Becca had told Eddie this scalp-tunneling had been reported in the forensic literature.

The third case was a liquor store clerk working the late shift at a mom-and-pop shop on Muldoon Road. The part-time employee was shot and killed for $237 and a bottle of Jack Daniel's. The security camera footage identified the perp as a six-foot-four, 320-pound Samoan gang member out on parole. In custody, with the DA building the case.

In the fourth one, a ninety-six-year-old husband with Alzheimer's stabbed his ninety-three-year-old wife, who was wheelchair-bound with severe arthritis. The daughter told the court her mother had been begging to die for months, asking her husband to "send her to heaven." After the funeral, he kept wondering when she would get home. DA declined to file charges and released him to his daughter's care. Gertie had told Eddie, "I pray I never come to that."

Despite the breakup, one thing remained frozen: Eddie's relationship with Becca. He had asked her once if Brockman had tried to contact her or intimidate her. She gave him a curt "no" and left it at that, and he didn't push it. The dinner date or get-together she'd brought up over Roche's body never came to anything. He'd brought it up once, but she begged him off with the old "I'll get back to you."

So he was now confronted with this bizarre and growing anticipation of seeing Becca at work in the morgue. *Really, Vaugner?* Even more troubling, his eagerness to see her across an autopsy table was replacing those unwanted visions of Anne on an autopsy table. It felt wrong—but wouldn't Anne have wanted him to move on? He could almost hear her chiding him, *Eddie, get over yourself and get a life.*

And he couldn't shake the feeling that he saw encouraging signs. Did a smile register more affection than just professional courtesy? Did her eyes hold his a moment longer than necessary across the steel table? No, probably not. Wishful thinking. *Maybe you need medication.*

Besides, after her relationship with Brockman, he doubted she was ready for a new one. Or maybe it was him. Who'd want a relationship with an amputee? Especially one with a kid on the spectrum, let alone with the threat of leukemia hanging over him. Talk about baggage.

Still, he just couldn't shake the feeling that there was something between them.

The latest body lay fifteen yards off the jogging trail at Goose Lake Park, nestled between the University of Alaska campus and Providence Hospital. Eddie parked beside two patrol cars. A jogger in running shorts and a hoodie, a university linguistics professor at UAA, who spotted the body during his morning run, sat in the back of one. After taking his statement, Eddie let him go.

Two patrolmen had taped off the scene and were now maintaining the perimeter. A homeless death during breakup season wasn't unusual, and unless the medical examiner found something suspicious, it wouldn't warrant CSI resources. Eddie pulled out his department phone. Basic scene documentation would suffice.

The deceased—a white, gray-bearded male preserved by winter—rested on his side beneath a makeshift shelter of scavenged lumber. His legs curled toward his chest as if seeking warmth in sleep. Plastic shopping bags stood in neat rows beside him, a Carr's shopping cart stationed nearby like a faithful companion. No signs of struggle in the snow. The only tracks leading from the path to the clearing were those left by the jogger, the EMTs, the responding officer, and now, Eddie.

A wallet perched on an overturned milk crate caught Eddie's eye. After photographing its position, he slipped on nitrile gloves and examined the contents: twenty-three dollars and a single piece of identification—a Department of Veterans Affairs card. The photo matched the deceased—*James T. Atkinson, VA HEALTHCARE ENROLLEE, SERVICE CONNECTED, PURPLE HEART*. The Army logo centered the card like a final salute.

How did a man serving his country, getting a Purple Heart, end up dying homeless and alone in the snow?

His work phone buzzed. It was Chik. He had recovered from his wounds and returned to light duty at work and was now winding things down. His last day was coming up next month. His house was up for sale, and Christina was in Copenhagen with Inuksuk looking for a place.

"Hey, Chik."

"Are you at the dead person over on Goose Lake?"

"Yes, what's up?"

"That DNA just came back on Dr. Lange. You want me to forward it to your email?"

"For Christ's sake, just tell—"

"Okay, I'll read the results. 'Results: Analysis excludes the paternal relationship between Sample A and Sample B (probability of paternity: 0%). Conclusion: Sample A is not the biological offspring of Sample B.'"

"Well, shit. I'm surprised, to be honest." And a little relieved.

"Yeah, but that's good, isn't it?"

"Yeah, Chik, it's good."

The Dracule case—*was it even a case?*—had drifted into de facto inactive status. Despite the DNA results, Eddie remained convinced Lange was at the center of everything. Familiar thoughts replayed in his head. The strange circumstances of the priest's death. The unsub on the video. The mitochondrial injuries shared with Defner. Roche's abrupt confession and death after being treated by Lange. The pieces fit too neatly around the surgeon.

Complicating matters, Eddie often returned to Inuksuk's cryptic comments about Lange's "gift." Inuksuk had meant this as a positive force, and who was to say these weren't results of such a force?

Dracule, Defner, and Roche. Were they even crimes? Murder by what means? Quantum entanglement? Assault? What was the weapon? Spooky action? And viewed on some cosmic scale, had Lange not merely meted out the justice that conventional law enforcement had failed to deliver?

He put in a call to the doctor's office and Cheryl put him through to Grayson.

"Yes, Detective?"

"Hey, Doc. Your DNA came back. No match."

"There's a surprise." Lange spoke politely. He didn't sound relieved or bitter, but Eddie caught the humiliating undertone of *you fucking idiot.* "Anything else, Detective?"

"No, that should do it."

"Okay, thanks for the call."

Eddie's email chime went off as he hung up. Chik had sent him the test results. As he looked at the numbers, he still couldn't shake the feeling that Lange was involved in the death of Dracule, father or not.

He laughed at himself. Becca might be attracted to him, and Lange could be a killer.

Maybe he shouldn't trust his feelings.

Then again, maybe he shouldn't trust his doubts.

51

A DEATH IN PROSPECT

It was a cloudless late Sunday morning in May. Gertie was working in the garden. Eddie sipped his coffee at the kitchen banquette. Daniel, next to him, was halfway through a bowl of Cap'n Crunch, reading an article on the Many Worlds Interpretation on his cell phone.

"Hey, Dad, did you know that according to the Many Worlds Interpretation, there might be infinite versions of me in parallel worlds, eating breakfast just like I'm doing now?"

"Am I there with you?"

"Yes, you could be. And so could Mom."

"Not Mom, because she'd never let you eat an infinite number of bowls of Cap'n Crunch, no matter how many universes there might be."

"Ha. Ha. Hey, actually, the snow's melted off the Tony Knowles trail. Can we get the bikes out of storage?"

"Sure. You want to do it this morning? Maybe we can go for a ride this afternoon."

"Yeah, that would be cool."

Eddie's cell went off. It was Becca. Why would she be calling him on a Sunday?

"Hi."

"Hi, Eddie, this is Becca. I'm in a bit of a jam. Can you come over?"

"Are you at the lab?"

"No, I'm home." Her voice was quivering. "Can you come?"

"Of course. What's going on?" His first thought was Brockman.

"I'll show you when you get here."

"Are you safe?"

"Yes."

"I'll be right over; give me your address."

He hung up and entered her address on his phone. She lived in Prospect Heights, an upper-middle-class neighborhood in the western foothills of the Chugach Mountains, populated by executives and professionals. "I need to go over to Dr. Raven's house. We'll have to do the bikes later."

"That's okay. Can I come?"

"No, not today. I think there's been some trouble over there."

"I hope she'll be alright. I guess we'll get the bikes some other time."

"I'm sorry."

"It's okay. I'm glad she called you for help."

She was sitting on the front steps when Eddie arrived, hunched over with her arms wrapped around her knees. Behind her Honda, he recognized Brockman's Lincoln SUV. Not seeing Brockman standing next to her, he assumed the man was either unconscious, locked in a closet, or dead, or fled the scene on foot.

Becca stood up as Eddie approached. Her face was blank. Her hair was wet, and the right side of her face was red and swollen.

"Are you okay?"

She shrugged.

"That's Brockman's car. Is he in the house?"

"Yes. Come with me. Don't bother taking off your shoes."

Reflexively, Eddie reached back for his gun. As soon as he gripped the handle, Becca said, "You don't need that."

Eddie kept his hand on his gun as Becca led him up a curved stairway, through a gallery with a seating area that overlooked the foyer, and finally into the master bedroom.

"There's Jim."

Brockman lay motionless in a way only the dead could accomplish. His body knelt at the foot of the bed, his torso bent at ninety degrees, flat on the mattress, his head turned to the left. One arm stretched along his side, and the other was pinned beneath him. He had collapsed without a reflexive response. A pistol with the familiar wave-like Walther logo with *PK380* etched in white on the slide sat on the nightstand beside the bed.

"I shot him. He's dead."

His left eye stared glassily into nothing. Just underneath it, a trickle of blood ran down from a gunshot wound onto a white duvet cover.

"You should have called 911. Also, your attorney."

"I wanted someone here I trusted. And I don't have an attorney."

For a moment, those words stirred hope in Eddie's chest. *Jesus, Vaugner, keep it real—and professional.* Besides, he realized, this more likely indicates cloudy judgment, not any deepening affection toward him.

"What happened?" he asked.

"I was in the shower, just back from a run, in the middle of washing my hair. I heard his voice say, 'Hi Rebecca' or something to that effect. He called me Rebecca when he was angry or just felt like being condescending. I was shocked to see him in the bathroom and told him to leave. I couldn't see well because of the shampoo. He had been begging for us to get back together, that we could work things out, and that he would get counseling."

As she spoke, Eddit kept surveying the scene. The bullet wound: no stippling from gunshot residue. The shot was fired at least three to five feet from the victim.

"When I told him there was no chance in hell of us ever getting back, he reached into the shower, grabbed me by my hair, and hit me in the face with his fist. I was stunned. He pulled me into the bedroom by my hair and threw me on the bed. He is—was—very strong."

The duvet cover was rumpled, and a pillow was out of place.

"He said if he couldn't have me, he was going to make sure no one else would want me. He was going to bash my face in so badly no amount of plastic surgery would make me look pretty again. And maybe even throw in a little brain damage to go along with my new looks. I scrambled backward on the bed and reached into the night-stand for my gun. I purchased it because I was afraid of this very scenario."

You fucking idiot. She's been living in fear all these months while you were fantasizing about her across autopsy tables, mooning like an adolescent, while she was going through hell with Brockman.

"I wiped the soap off my face and out of my eyes as best I could. Jim laughed and told me I didn't have the guts to use it. He said he was going to take the gun from me and—to paraphrase his words—shove the gun up my cunt and pull the trigger so no one else could ever fuck me. I mean, he was going absolutely crazy. He started to walk toward me, and I told him to stay back, but he kept coming. So I fired. Just once. The shampoo had irritated my eyes, so I aimed for his core, hoping it would stop him. Obviously, I hit high."

"What happened after you shot him?"

"He landed like that, except face down. I called out his name, and he didn't respond. I waited for what seemed like forever, holding the gun on him, waiting to see if he would try to get up. He didn't move. I got up, keeping the gun on him. I nudged him once on his butt with my foot, and he didn't respond. I was pretty sure he was dead, so I set the gun down and turned his head to check for a carotid pulse and pupillary response."

"Did you try to administer CPR?"

"No. There was no pulse or respiration; the pupils were mid-dilated and nonreactive to light. Given where the bullet entered his face and how he collapsed, I think we'll find that either the bullet or bone frag-ments went through to the brainstem. He died instantly."

To Eddie, Becca sounded like she was trying to stay clinical and detached. But a slight tremble belied the emotion underneath.

"Do you know what bullets are in the gun?"

"Winchester PDX1 Defender."

Good personal defense cartridge.

"After you determined he was dead, what did you do?"

"When he pulled me out of the shower, my hair was still full of shampoo, and my eyes were stinging. So I went into the shower and rinsed off quickly. Sorry if I washed off the gunpowder residue. I dressed, called you, and went through the house to see if he had broken in."

"Did he?"

"It appears not. After I broke up with him, I took back my keys, but he must have made copies. Call me an idiot for not changing my locks, but I didn't think an executive vice president of a major oil company would illegally enter someone's home, much less—this."

"So you were sitting on the bed when you shot him?"

"Yes, like this."

She sat on the bed and held her hands out like she was pointing a gun. "I used a two-handed, thumb-forward grip."

Off to the right, on the carpet, he saw a cartridge case. The location of the cartridge shell on the rug fit her story.

Eddie looked at the lifeless Brockman.

"I need to call this in. It will need a full crime scene investigation."

"Of course."

"You'll need to come downtown for a formal taped interview."

"Should I come down with you now?"

"Not me, Becca. I can't conduct your interview."

"Why not?"

"Because I'm—I can't be object—I'm not up on the rotation."

Becca managed a faint smile, then frowned. "It's going to be a shit show, isn't it?"

"Yes. Get yourself an attorney," he said, as he tried to figure out what was behind Becca's brief smile.

52

A DINNER, INTERRUPTED

"Okay, Daniel. Dribble twice, jump up on the retaining wall, hook shot off the backboard standing on the right leg."

"It's the only leg you got, Dad."

"Ha, ha."

It was Saturday morning. Daniel had challenged his father to a game of HORSE in the driveway. The score stood at H-O-R-S to H-O-R in Eddie's favor. Eddie dribbled twice and jumped up on the small one-foot retaining wall. His foot caught a patch of moss. He slipped backward, landing on the prosthetic leg. It made a loud snapping sound, and he fell, landing on the driveway.

"Dad!"

Eddie sat up and looked down at his prosthesis. It jutted out at an awkward angle from just below the ankle joint.

"I'm okay, but I broke my prosthesis," he said. "Can you get my crutches? There's a pair in the front hall closet."

"Sure, Dad, I'll be right back."

Daniel ran into the house. Eddie looked up at the empty blue sky.

"Fuck you. Just fuck you."

Eddie crawled over to the side of the driveway and hoisted himself up to sit on the retaining wall. He crossed the prosthesis over his good leg and inspected the damage. The hinge at the ankle was bent, and a screw had snapped. Eddie thought about removing the prosthesis, but Daniel had never seen his stump, so he left the leg on.

The boy ran out of the house, holding two crutches. "Here you go, Dad!"

Eddie stood up on his crutches, hobbled into the house, and called the prosthetics clinic's twenty-four-hour on-call number.

AN HOUR LATER, Eddie was in the prosthetics room with Kyle, who had the leg up on a workbench. Eddie sat next to the technician in a chair. His crutches leaned against the wall, and the empty lower third of his left pants leg was pinned up.

"Way to go, you fractured your rotational absorber. It'll need to be replaced."

The rotational absorber was a device between the socket and the foot that absorbed rotational movement to dampen twisting motions.

"Can you do it now?"

"No way. I don't have this in stock. I'll have to order it on Monday and ship it expedited. Plus, I've got several repairs in front of you."

"Not in stock?"

"This isn't New York City, you know."

"How long will all this take?"

"Maybe by Thursday—Friday for sure."

ON HIS WAY BACK HOME, Eddie's cell phone went off. Unknown caller. Spam probably.

"This is Vaugner."

"Hi. It's Becca."

"Becca, where are you?"

"Back in town. Got in last night."

He almost said "I missed you," but caught himself. Instead, he said, "I hope you had a relaxing time." *Oh, Jesus, what a dumb thing to say.*

"It was. Going back to work on Monday."

"So soon?"

"Yes. It will be good to be distracted by the job."

Why is she calling me?

"Is there anything I can do?"

"No, well, yes. I mean, would you like to have dinner with me?"

Becca seemed tentative.

"Uh, sure, when?"

"How about tonight? I made reservations for seven o'clock at Suite 100 on the off chance you might be available."

"Tonight?" *Without my leg on a Saturday at one of the most crowded restaurants in the city?*

"Well, if you're busy, maybe another time."

Fuck your leg. This woman is reaching out. "No, I'm not busy. Would you like me to pick you up?"

"I'll meet you there. Reservations are for 7 p.m. under the name of Rose Roberts."

"Your mother and father's names."

"You remembered. I'm impressed."

"It's the alliteration, I guess. See you at seven."

It had been three weeks since the incident with Brockman. The DA's office, working with the police, had fast-tracked the investigation, given Raven's crucial role as an assistant medical examiner with the state.

Although Becca had called Eddie to the scene, it was actually Steve Hendrik's case.

CSI, homicide, and the DA's team had worked overtime processing the information from the autopsy, ballistics, trace evidence gathered at the home, and all available eyewitness testimony. Becca's story had held up. The DA would not file charges.

Meanwhile, Brockman's story was damning. His wife had divorced him on the grounds of mental and physical cruelty. Another woman had placed a restraining order against him in Houston, Texas, for threatening violence after she had ended their relationship. The two women had portrayed Brockman as a charmer who turned out to be a controlling and jealous sociopath. He was transferred to Anchorage due to the growing stink surrounding him in Houston.

During the investigation, the medical examiner's office granted her a leave of absence, and the DA gave her permission to leave the state. She sought refuge at her parents' retirement home in St. Michaels, Maryland, to escape the press.

Meanwhile, back in Anchorage, she became a reluctant local hero of battered women who had had enough.

SUITE 100 WAS on the bottom floor of a three-story office building. Entering the restaurant, Eddie felt the glances at the one-legged man on crutches from the few people waiting for tables.

"Good evening, sir," the hostess said. "Do you have reservations?"

"Yes, under Rose Roberts?"

"Ah, yes, Ms. Roberts is already here. This way, please."

Eddie followed the woman in the black cocktail dress past the open kitchen. Cooks dressed in all black sizzled king salmon in hot pans, ladled sauces onto meats, hand-sprinkled salt, and clanked completed plates on the stainless-steel ready counter under heat lamps.

Becca, seated in a booth, wore a white ribbed turtleneck. As he approached, she gave Eddie a tentative smile.

"Hi," she said.

"Welcome back, Becca." He sat down across from her, leaning his crutches against the inside wall of the booth.

"What happened to your leg?"

"You noticed. I was going for an S."

"An S?"

As Eddie told her about the fateful HORSE event, Michael, a tall waiter with a man bun, appeared and told them about the specials, asking if they would like a "beverage from the bar." Becca ordered a martini straight up with an olive.

"Just sparkling water and lime," Eddie said.

"Then cancel my martini."

"No, go ahead."

"I don't want to be the only one drinking."

"Okay, Michael, bring the lady her martini. I'll have a Plymouth and tonic."

"What a gentleman," Michael said. He hurried away to get the drink orders in.

"Please tell me you're not a recovering alcoholic about to fall off the wagon for my sake."

"Nothing like that."

"What then?"

"The car accident that killed Anne and took my leg."

"Yes, I'm so sorry."

"One hour before the accident, I had one drink, which I had nursed through the entire meal. My blood alcohol level was below 0.02 percent, way less than the legal limit. They say this shouldn't have affected my reaction time, but even today, I ask myself, could I have reacted faster without it? Since then, I haven't felt much like drinking."

"We—I—really don't need to drink."

"No, it's okay. We should celebrate your triumphant return."

"Okay, but it's more like I slithered back in."

She was having difficulty making eye contact. She seemed distracted by inner thoughts. Her face screwed into a wry smile, and she shook her head.

Michael came with the drinks. "Are you ready to order, or would you like to enjoy your cocktails first?"

"If you could give us a few minutes and come back, that would be great," Eddie said.

Becca held up her martini as the waiter left.

"Cheers," she said, "and thanks for meeting me tonight."

Eddie clinked his glass against hers. They both took a sip—his first sip of alcohol in four years.

"How is it?" she asked.

"Good. Gin and tonic is the mystery drink. The gin and tonic tasted separately—not good to many people. Together, they're exquisite. I asked Daniel about that once. Half an hour later, he had the answer. The molecules of the botanicals—especially juniper—in gin mix with the bitter molecules of quinine. The carbonation of the tonic water helps transport these molecules up into the nose to react with receptors. It's all about the sum being greater than its parts."

She set her drink down and smiled at Eddie. "That sounds like Daniel, alright."

After an awkward pause, she said, "Have you ever shot anyone?"

"No. Less than 5 percent of law enforcement officers ever fire their weapons in the line of duty."

She sat silently, looking into her martini, then sighed.

"You remember my father didn't want me to be a cop?"

"You told Daniel that when you two first met. Yes, too dangerous for a lady, he said."

"Yes, exactly. I'm impressed you remembered."

"I'm a detective. It's a skill set."

"So my dad's a cop, my brothers are all cops, and here I am, the only one in the family who has shot and killed someone."

Eddie smiled sympathetically.

"Is that what they call ironic?"

His attempt at humor failed to elicit a smile.

"I'm sitting here wondering if you're still assessing my version of the shooting. Asking yourself if the investigation missed anything."

"Yeah, that's not surprising."

"What do you mean?"

"Killing someone is not a normal human experience. No matter the circumstance, most normal people will feel guilty about it or at least keep second-guessing themselves. Could I have avoided it? Or have done something different? Was it my fault?"

"That's me, all right, although not sure about the normal part."

"Look, Becca, we expedited things, but we did a thorough investigation—no special favors. No one is second-guessing this case. The shooting was justified, and no one involved with the case has any doubt about it."

"Well, thank you for that."

"You don't have to thank me," he replied. "And trust me, any DA would have loved to put an assistant medical examiner up on charges, believe me."

Eddie noted some commotion in the parking lot through the restaurant window. A local TV news van had pulled up in the parking lot. A cameraman was set up to catch a view of the entrance to the restaurant, and a woman in a suit and a microphone stood near the restaurant's front door.

"Does anyone know you're here?"

"Just you."

"There's a TV news van outside."

"They can't be here for me."

"Sure they can. You're still news."

"How do they even know I'm here?"

"Someone recognized you and called a news hotline."

Eddie looked around. A buzz seemed to be going through the restaurant; people were starting to look their way.

"This is no good," Becca said. "What do I do?"

Eddie put a twenty on the table to cover the cost of the drinks.

"There's an exit out the south side of the building. Head out there, and I'll pick you up."

"What about my car?"

"We'll come back for it later. Are you still hungry?"

"I could eat."

"I know just the place. Good food, very private."

53

PIEROGIES

"Gertie!" Eddie called out. "Daniel! I brought company!"

"What?" Gertie shouted from the kitchen.

He heard Daniel's door open, then slam shut.

"Hi, Dad!" Daniel yelled as he bounded down the stairs. "How did your date go with—"

He stopped halfway down.

"Wow. It's her, I mean, Dr. Raven."

"Hi, Daniel," Becca said.

Gertie came out from the kitchen, drying her hands on a dish towel.

"My word, it's Dr. Raven!"

"Please, call me Becca."

"If you call me Gertie. What are you two doing here?"

"Reporters showed up at the restaurant."

"Oh dear. Eddie, you could have called me. I look a mess."

"You look wonderful, Gertie," Becca said.

"Thank you. Welcome to our home."

"Is there anything to eat?" Eddie asked.

"You're just in luck. Come into the kitchen. I made a fresh batch of pierogies, and they were just about to go into the freezer."

As everyone followed Gertie into the kitchen, Daniel said, "Hey, Grandma, you know that in Polish, pierogi is the actual plural for pierog, don't you?"

Becca and Eddie sat at the counter. Daniel sat on the kitchen banquette and pulled out his phone to play a game. Eddie told Gertie and Daniel about their escape from reporters at the restaurant. She took an onion out, chopped it up into fine pieces, placed them in a frying pan with about a half-inch of hot peanut oil, and fried them until they were dark brown and crisp. She pulled them out with a slotted spoon, then set them onto a plate covered with paper towels, explaining, "Most people just sauté the pierogies and onions together, but I love them this way, the soft texture of the pierogies with the sweet, caramelized crunchiness of the onions. But what do I know? I'm only half Polish."

As she cooked, Gertie prevented any awkward silence with a steady stream of cheerful banter.

"Has Eddie told you about his family name?"

"No."

"When his great-grandfather came over from Germany, his name was spelled Wagner, you know, like Robert Wagner, the actor. Anyway, Wilhelm, Eddie's great-grandfather, didn't like the American pronunciation of Wagner, so he changed the spelling so people would pronounce it more like it is supposed to be."

In another pan, she melted two tablespoons of butter and sautéed about a dozen pierogi over medium heat. When the pierogi reached a nice golden brown, she put them on two plates and placed them in front of them. She brought over a sour cream container and the onions on the plate.

"Dig in, guys. Sprinkle on the onions to taste. Hands allowed for onions. Here's a spoon for the sour cream."

Becca put a dollop of sour cream on one side of the plate, cut a pierogi in half, used her knife to scoop some of the caramelized onions and sour cream, and put it in her mouth. Gertie watched her eat the pierogi as if she were a NASA engineer watching a rocket launch.

"Oh. These are so good. Comfort food."

Gertie beamed. "Thank you."

"I keep telling Grandma she should market them," Daniel said.

"I'd definitely buy them," said Becca.

As they ate, Gertie led the conversation, which covered topics such as the increased airplane noise from Ted Stevens Airport since the north-south runway was closed for repairs, the recent showing of her favorite play, *Our Town*, at the Anchorage Center for Performing Arts, how nice it was that an Alaska Native woman was playing the role of the Stage Manager, and never mind all those people grousing about DEI. After that, she went on about the melting Alaskan permafrost and all the CO_2 the scientists said would be released.

After the pierogi were finished, Gertie took Becca to the backyard for a garden tour. Daniel and his father followed. Eddie stayed on the deck to avoid walking down the steep deck stairs in his crutches. Gertie pointed out her blooming shooting stars, western columbines, irises, monkshoods, lilies (both Tiger and white), and fireweeds. Dragonflies flitted here and there. Occasionally, they would wave their hands in front of their faces to shoo away the giant mosquitoes Alaskans often called their state bird.

Daniel pointed out that he and Eddie had laid the rocks down for the border with the yard.

They all sat down on the deck. There was a bit of awkward silence when Becca asked Daniel, "So, Daniel, any further thoughts on physics versus medicine?"

Eddie was impressed that Becca remembered her conversation with Daniel, given everything that had happened.

"I was doing some research and found several med schools that have combined MD-PhD programs—like Harvard/MIT, Stanford, Johns Hopkins, University of California, and a few others."

"Sounds like you have a lot of choices, for sure," Becca said.

"Right now, I'm reading about quantum entanglement."

"What's that?" Gertie asked.

"It's about how atoms or parts of atoms can affect each other, even though they may be miles apart, or even galaxies apart."

"Why, that sounds like magic, not physics," she said. "Can you explain it to an old lady like me?"

Daniel pursed his lips for a moment. "Okay. Imagine two snowflakes falling in the sky and both spinning. Let's say one is here in Anchorage, and the other is in, say, Stockholm. And let's say the snowflake in Anchorage starts to spin right; the one in Sweden would instantly spin left. No delay. If the information traveled at the speed of light, it would take twenty-three milliseconds for one snowflake to respond to another. So, whatever information is being transferred is faster than the speed of light. They would be demonstrating quantum entanglement."

"Well, that's just weird," Gertie said.

"Physicists are working on quantum sensors," Becca continued, "that use superposition and entanglement to detect cancer long before we can now."

"Wow. How does that work?"

"I have no clue, Daniel. But physicists are going to be the major innovators in medicine in the future."

"Wow. I could be like a quantum doctor," Daniel said, perking up.

"Daniel Vaugner, QD," Eddie joked.

Becca took out her phone and started flipping through her apps.

"It's getting late. I should be going. I'll call an Uber."

"No way," Eddie said. "I'll take you."

"Can I go with you guys?" Daniel asked.

Becca smiled and put her phone back in her purse. "That would be great, if it's okay with your Dad," she said.

They all piled into the car and took the ten-minute drive back to the Suite 100 parking lot. Daniel thumbed at his phone on the way. The TV news crew was gone. Eddie pulled up next to Becca's car.

"Thanks for a great evening, Eddie. It was so normal. It's been so long since anything felt normal. I almost forgot what it was like."

You just had dinner with a one-legged homicide detective after being investigated for self-defensive lethal force, and we ran away from the press. How normal is that?

"Anytime," he replied.

"Daniel, it was nice seeing you again."

"Hey, Dad and I are going for a bike ride this Sunday, if his leg is back by then. Would you like to come?"

"Uh." Becca looked at Eddie.

"If you have other plans, that's okay."

"No plans. But my bike's in storage. I can dig it out."

"No problem," Daniel said. "Our bike carrier can take four bikes. We can make a quick stop and pick it up."

"Okay, why not," Becca said. "It'll be good to get some exercise and fresh air. I don't get out much these days."

"Okay," Eddie said, "we'll pick you up and drive over to get your bike."

"I have a new place."

"You moved?" he said, more an acknowledgment than a question.

"Yes, I'll never set foot in that house again. I rented an apartment for now. Denali Towers, you know it?"

"Yes, downtown on Denali Street."

IN THE CAR on the way home, Daniel let out a chuckle.

"What's so funny, Daniel?"

"Dr. Raven."

"What's so funny about her?"

"Not her, her name. Raven. What a great name for a forensic pathologist—like a raven pecking apart a dead carcass."

"Yuck, Daniel."

When they got back home, Daniel ran up the stairs to his room. Eddie found Gertie in the backyard, sitting in an Adirondack chair, with a glass of iced tea on the table beside her. He grabbed a glass of iced tea in the kitchen, went out to the deck, and took the chair next to hers.

"Nice night, eh, Mom?"

"Yes."

Long winters gave Alaskans an appreciation for the gift of sitting outside. Tonight, they sat silently for a few moments, soaking in the light, sights, sounds, and smells, enjoying the 11 p.m. sunlight. Eddie chuckled.

"What's tickled your funny bone, son?"

"These wall sconces on the deck. Anne and I were having a long discussion about what style the sconces should be, how much light they should give off, and all that. Then it came to her. When it's dark enough outside to need the sconces, it's too cold, and when it's warm enough to sit out here, we don't need them."

"But you got them anyway." After a few beats, Gertie followed that with, "That Dr. Raven, I mean, Becca. Terrible what she's been through. She seems like such a nice girl."

"Yes, on both counts."

"How's she coping?"

"Pretty well, but she's still questioning herself."

She took a sip of her tea.

"Having a young woman in the house again was nice. Daniel seemed to take to her quite well."

"She's going on the bike ride with us tomorrow."

"Oh, that's nice," Gertie said. She blinked a few times and smiled to herself.

"Daniel invited her."

Gertie smiled and relaxed in her chair, basking in the warmth of the late-evening sun.

They sat a few more moments in silence.

She stood up. "I'm off to bed, son."

Eddie stood up and hugged her.

"Thanks for everything, Mom. You're a great help."

"You're welcome, son. God knows I enjoy it."

After Gertie went inside, Eddie remained on the deck, her words echoing in his mind. *Having a young woman in the house again was nice.* It had been nice. For the first time in years, the house had felt complete. Becca fit naturally into their evening routine, laughing with Daniel, helping Gertie in the kitchen, asking the right questions. Anne would have liked her.

His thoughts drifted to Anne and to all the nights he'd lain awake wondering where she was, if she was. What if death itself was just another quantum state? Suppose particles could exist in multiple states simultaneously. Couldn't consciousness—couldn't Anne—exist somewhere else—like Daniel had proposed over a bowl of Cap'n Crunch—and be as real and present as the particles Daniel was describing, just beyond their ability to observe?

Spooky action.

His detective's mind flashed to the Redeemer surveillance video, Dana Peplow's out-of-body experience, Father Dracule's mysterious death, Defner's inexplicable cardiac event, and Roche's widowmaker. And Lange. There was Lange. Connected to all of it. His involvement as clear as day, but as inexplicable as, well, this quantum business itself.

Spooky action?

He finished his iced tea and headed inside.

54

TALKEETNA

Eddie's leg came in on Thursday.

As he sat in the waiting room, waiting to see Kyle, a local news correspondent was interviewing an elderly woman in a diner. The banner read "Midwife Lilly Gill Retiring After Forty Years of Practice." This caught Eddie's attention.

Lilly Gill. The name triggered something. He sat down, trying to place it. Then it hit him—she was the midwife who'd delivered Grayson Gower and signed his birth certificate.

He reached for the remote on the side table and turned up the volume.

"...for a retirement party for Lilly Gill, a certified nurse midwife who has delivered hundreds of babies at home in the Matsu Valley over the past forty years. Many of the people you see here were babies she delivered."

The audience cheered and applauded.

"Nurse Gill, what have these last forty years meant to you?"

"Bringing life into this world. And watching so many of them grow up over the years. How wonderful."

"Do you have moments or deliveries that stand out in particular?"

Gill's face froze. She gazed downward and took a breath. "Yes, there was one many years ago. A special boy. And to overcome such a tragedy to be—"

She looked up and smiled stiffly, as if catching herself before going further. "But truthfully, Matt," she continued, "each child is special. Each child is a gift."

Lilly opened her arms and gestured to the crowd around her. "You all are just so special."

To Eddie, the averted gaze and the unnecessary addition of the word "truthfully" were familiar signs of a triggered moment he had seen hundreds of times in suspects. Despite trying to caution himself not to rush to judgment, Eddie couldn't shake the feeling that the "special boy" was Lange and that the tragedy was the Gower family murder. And to overcome such a tragedy to be—what? A doctor? A surgeon? Had she kept up with Grayson Lange's life?

"Eddie?"

It was Kyle. Vaugner stood up. Kyle put him in an exam room, told him to take his pants off, and in a few minutes returned with his prosthesis.

He sat in a stool in front of Eddie and examined his stump.

"Skin looks good, Detective. Stump volume has stayed consistent. Let's get the prosthesis back on."

As he put it on, Kyle gave his usual spiel. "Keep up with your sock changes—adding or removing layers as needed during the day. You know how volume fluctuates with activity and weather."

"Yes, Kyle, you've told me many times."

"Well, I keep harping on it because you'd be surprised how many don't manage their stumps properly."

Eddie stood, testing his weight distribution.

"Gait looks good. Any rubbing or pressure points?"

"No, feels solid."

"That's what we like to hear."

THOUGHTS OF LILLY GILL nagged at him all evening. His developing theory was outlandish: the religious cult angle, his growing suspicions about Father Dracule's identity, and the seemingly super-natural elements that appeared to be the only logical explanation tying Dracule, Defner, and Roche together. The more he thought about her, the more convinced he became that the midwife knew something important about Lange's past.

Maybe he should drop it. But he couldn't. He had to know more, and he knew he would have to pursue this lead privately—off the record, on his own time and his own dime.

THE FOLLOWING DAY, Eddie searched the DMV database to find Lilly Gill's address and used that to find her phone number. He called from his personal cell phone, not his department line.

"Hello?" It was the same voice on the TV.

"Is this Lillian Gill?"

"Who is this?"

"My name is Edward Vaugner. I'm a detective with the Anchorage Police Department. I'm investigating some old cases connected to the Gower family. I saw the news segment on you yesterday and learned you were the nurse-midwife for the Gower deliveries."

"You're with the Anchorage police, you say?"

"Yes, ma'am."

"I don't know anyone in Anchorage."

"Yes, ma'am, I think you do."

There was silence. He expected her to hang up, and he heard her breathing on the phone.

"Is Grayson in trouble?"

Ah, so she had been following him. "No, ma'am. He's not in trouble."

"When would you come up?"

"How about tomorrow?"

"Tomorrow's Saturday. Could you make it around two?"

. . .

TALKEETNA, known as the Gateway to Denali, served as the staging area for summit expeditions of the highest mountain in North America. It was also rumored that Warren Harding's sudden death in San Francisco resulted from ptomaine poisoning from a crab leg he'd eaten at Talkeetna's Fairview Inn. This unfounded claim was memorialized at the Fairview Inn by the "Harding Special," a potent vodka cocktail you were advised to "drink at your own risk."

Talkeetna's unofficial motto had become "Keeping It Weird." The quirky town was ideal for starting a clandestine religious cult without judgment or interference.

Eddie left his house at 11:30 a.m., deciding to take his personal vehicle rather than his department car. This was personal business, so there were no trip reports. If something developed, he could always reinterview her in an official capacity.

The two-and-a-half-hour trip took Eddie northeast up the Glenn Highway along the Knik Arm of the Cook Inlet, then a northwest turn onto the Parks Highway, which followed the Susitna River. The drive gave him plenty of time to think about how crazy this all seemed—pursuing a theory that involved religious cults, possible supernatural elements, and a respected surgeon who might be something other than what he appeared to be.

Gill lived in a small one-bedroom clapboard cottage with a pitched roof and a picket-fenced gated front yard. A lush garden bordered the walkway up to the steps of the front porch. Attractive flower boxes adorned the windows.

Eddie parked on the street in front of her house. As he approached the gate, she opened the front door. She had short gray hair cut in a simple pixie style and was dressed in jeans and a sweater.

"Detective Vaugner?"

He raised his hand. "Yes, ma'am."

"Reach over the gate and lift the latch."

Eddie opened the gate.

"You have a lovely yard and garden. My mother is a gardener; she would really appreciate the work you have done here."

"Why, thank you, Detective."

The front door opened into a great room with a small kitchen adequate for cooking simple meals for a single person, a dining area with a table and two chairs, and a seating area, the focus of which was a single recliner facing a recent-model flat-panel television—the standard equipment for live-alones. Two doors led off the main room, one to a bedroom and one to a bathroom.

"Welcome. It's not much, but it suits me. Easy to maintain."

"It's very nice."

"I've just made some coffee. And feel free to use the bathroom."

She had set up two coffee mugs, a pint carton of half-and-half, and a box of cookies—no serving dish, just right out of the box—on the table. *Not a person who entertains much,* thought Eddie.

"Yes, coffee would be nice."

After filling the two mugs, she sat at the table. Gill avoided eye contact. Her voice was tinny, possibly a sign of stress. Eddie let her control the conversation.

He poured some half-and-half into his coffee, then took a sip.

"Nice coffee."

"It's Tarmac Black, blended and roasted right here in Talkeetna. Dead Hopper Roastery. Try a cookie. They're local as well, from the Flying Squirrel. Molasses with a hint of ginger that I find goes well with coffee."

Eddie took one from the box and popped it into his mouth.

"Oh, that's good," he said with his mouth full.

"How was the drive up?"

"Beautiful, as always. I think I'll have another cookie." *If you want to charm a hostess, eat the food she provides.*

Gill smiled, pleased with the reception of her choice of cookies.

"I notice your limp. Is that a prosthesis?"

"Yes, that's very observant of you. Most people don't seem to notice."

"Or are too polite to mention it." Gill was revealing herself to be a no-nonsense woman.

"I lost it in a car accident."

"That's too bad, I'm sorry. At least you lived."

"At least."

In the awkward silence, Eddie took another cookie. "These are too damn good."

"I can't even remember the last time I made the drive to Anchorage. I've taken the train a couple of times. But really, I have all I need out here."

Gill smiled pleasantly. Eddie was going to let her make the first move. A few seconds later, she did.

"Detective, what do you want to know about the Gowers?"

"I'm not sure. Anything you would like to share with me?"

Gill took a deep breath. "Is Grayson in some sort of trouble?"

It was the second time she'd asked that. "No, ma'am. Why would you think that?"

"You're the police, and you're here asking about his family. Maybe the brother? Grayson's uncle, Richard Gower. He disappeared just after the killings."

"No, ma'am, we have no information on him. But Grayson is not in trouble. I'm just looking for background information on the family."

After taking a sip of coffee, she took a breath and smiled at Eddie.

"I'm a midwife; I brought Grayson into the world. It feels like it was yesterday. We old people, Detective, can't remember what color socks we put on this morning, and we're happy if they match, but events that happened years ago remain crystal clear." She stood up. "I hope you don't mind if I pace a little bit."

"No, it's fine."

She walked to the window and looked out toward her garden.

"My beeper went off at around seven forty in the evening. We carried beepers back then, not cell phones. Mary Gower was in labor at home. I arrived shortly after eight. She was in bed, having regular contractions. Several people were in the bedroom—her husband, John, their first son, Tommy—I delivered him too—and Pastor Cyrus. That would be Cyrus Chase, the head of their church, the Second Advent. And his wife; I don't recall her name, but she was a mousy little thing."

Gill turned around and walked toward her chair. "It was a curious scene. John was off to the side of the room, and the pastor sat on one side of the bed, holding one of Mary's hands. She was fully dilated and crying about how much it hurt."

She sat down on the edge of the chair and leaned forward. "I told her to relax and take deep breaths. She was in the stage of labor we call the ring of fire, when the vagina and perineum become stretched. We like to hold off delivery until it passes to prevent tears as the baby passes from the body. After a few minutes, the pain stopped, and I encouraged her to push."

She stood up and headed for the kitchenette. "Would you like another cup?"

"Okay."

Gill picked up the coffee pot and poured Eddie some, then sat back in the chair at the table.

"After several pushes, the baby crowned, and it was delivered. I set him on Mary's stomach, suctioned out his mouth and nose, and divided the cord. At that point, Cyrus stood up and took the baby. John, the husband, stood up and asked, 'Is this one the child of light?' Cyrus studied the baby as if it were some sort of specimen. After a few moments, he said something like it could be of the light, but it could be of the dark. Maybe in time, he will reveal himself. Like Jesus, he must die, then rise again. Then we will know. Blah. Blah. Blah."

Interesting, thought Eddie, despite Lily's skepticism. Lange hadn't died, but he had come close in that family massacre. Close to death but saved by surgeons. Almost a resurrection, just as Cyrus had predicted. Prophecy or coincidence?

She held her hands out slightly, as if reenacting the next scene. "Holding the baby," Gill continued, "he extended his arm toward John, offering it to him. Pastor Cyrus said, 'Take him, he's yours.' After another moment of hesitation, John took the baby. But it was Cyrus who named the child; I'll never forget what he said. 'You shall name him Grayson, as he is the child between light and dark.'"

"So the pastor named the child, not the parents?"

"Yes, Cyrus named the baby. And just after that, he left. John handed Mary the baby. Tommy, the older brother, who was six, stood up and asked, 'Is he going to be my brother now?' Mary stroked the baby. 'Yes, Tommy, he is your brother.'"

"Do you have any idea about this child of light thing?" Eddie asked.

Gill smiled and shook her head. "The shtick about the Second Advent Church was how they would be the first witnesses of the second coming of Christ, the second advent, and it would be heralded by the birth of a child of light, and that the child would be born in their congregation. They quoted a passage out of Ephesians, something like, you were once darkness, and to live as children of light, but I forget the passage exactly."

She replaced her grin with a stern look.

"But I'll tell you, that whole second coming thing was a pile of bullshit, if you pardon my French."

"What do you mean?" Eddie poured some half-and-half into his cup and stirred it. He brought it to his mouth to take a sip.

"The advent, all of it. Pastor Cyrus just used it to get into the pants of the wives of the other men in his congregation. If they got pregnant, there was no problem; the families would raise them as their own. A cult thing, you know, like Manson."

Eddie put his cup down. "Wait, are you saying—"

"Yes. Cyrus was Grayson's father, not John."

The pieces clicked into place. This would explain why the DNA test showed no relation between Lange and Father Dracula and why Lange was happy to cooperate with the DNA testing.

"Are you sure?"

"Oh yes, quite sure." Gill's voice was absolute. "You could see the resemblance, especially now that Grayson has grown up." She paused, then added quietly, "The way they both carry themselves. That same intensity."

"Do you have any photographs of this Pastor Cyrus?"

"No. The whole group was weird. No cameras, and most of them didn't even have driver's licenses. A lot of them moved up here and changed their names."

"How did they make money? Get jobs? Drive cars?"

"They worked as handymen on a cash basis. Drove cars without a driver's license. Not all of them, but most of them."

"Did he ever make such claims with the others?"

"Cyrus would often claim it was his mission to bring the Child of Light into the world, but when one of his children came along, he said that the child wasn't the one. You know, like Tommy, Grayson's older brother. Grayson was the first and only one about whom Cyrus made the claim. I think he did this because people were starting to question things. You can only screw other men's wives based on a prophecy without bringing forth a prophet for so long."

"Where is the Second Advent Church located?"

"Oh, it's no longer here. That murder shocked the community. Several members left the church and started spilling out sordid details of the goings-on. No one would hire any of the members anymore. About two months after the killings, the church moved outside—all of them, without a word or forwarding addresses. It was rumored they wound up somewhere in central Oregon, but no one knew for sure. What was once their temple is now a marijuana store."

Gill reached for another cookie and snapped it in half. "I really shouldn't. I have a touch of type II diabetes, but every now and then won't hurt, especially at my age."

"And Richard Gower, the brother, went with them?"

"Oh no. Richard left immediately, within a week of the murders. We never heard from him again, either."

She put the half-cookie in her mouth.

"Did you interact with him much?"

"No."

"Did John and Richard resemble each other?"

She finished chewing the cookie and swallowed. "Actually, I remember once, at the store. I mistook Richard for John. They weren't twins, but they were certainly brothers."

"Do you know where Cyrus is today?"

"He died—I don't know—around eight or so years ago. I got a letter from a former member of the church around the time of his death. For some reason, she thought I would be interested in what happened to that creep. Well, I guess she was right—his death would be the only thing about him I'd be interested in."

So Lange hadn't lied about that either. His father really had died years ago.

"That's about all I have on the Gowers and that whole mess. I hope that helps."

"Thank you, Nurse Gill. It helps a lot."

JUST OUTSIDE OF ANCHORAGE, four F-22 Raptors in an echelon formation streaked by to the left of Eddie's vehicle. They came up silently at first. Then, even with his car windows closed, he heard the roar of the jets trailing behind them as they passed over him. As the jets dipped their left wings and veered left to head south, he found himself caught in contradictory feelings about his progress on the case.

On one hand, as a detective, he was disappointed that he would probably never find the evidence against Lange for a prosecutor to act on. On the other hand, he was oddly relieved—even glad—that he'd given it his best shot and come up short. His thoughts circled back to Lange's extreme sports. They weren't just reckless thrill-seeking, were they? Each climb, each descent, each brush with death—they were trials. Tests. Judgments. It was as if, even when the system couldn't put Lange on trial, he put himself on trial. Like those jets streaking across the sky with their stealth capabilities, Lange wielded extraordinary power and avoided detection, but not without a moral bearing, at least in *his* mind.

Maybe there was something more at work—survivor's guilt. Eddie had seen it enough in his career—the last person standing after a tragedy, haunted by the question: why me? Why did I survive when others didn't? As the sole survivor of his family's massacre, did Lange carry that burden? Did he risk his life on mountains to ask the universe, again and again, *do I deserve to live when they didn't?*

Up in the sky, the Raptors disappeared from view on their descent back to their home at Elmendorf Air Force Base beyond the Chugach Mountains.

Was Lange a monster or a messenger of some cosmic justice? Yes, there were bodies, but they were the carcasses of men who would have escaped human judgment for their monstrous acts. They acted with impunity, but Lange did not. He sought judgment, not by the laws of man, but by subjecting himself to the forces of—what higher authority? Nature? God? The quantum moral field of the universe?

Maybe I can live with that.

55

A BIKE RIDE

The next day, Eddie and Daniel picked up Becca at Denali Towers and drove to Tudor Road Storage to retrieve her bike. It was a red Trek Dual Sport, perfect for the Anchorage Trail system.

"Nice bike, Dr. Raven," Daniel said. "You may have noticed we have Specialized bikes."

"Yes. They're nice bikes, too. But why don't you call me Becca? It's much easier."

"Dad calls his mother Gertie, so I guess I can call you Becca. Is that okay, Dad?"

"Whatever the good doctor wants, Daniel."

"Okay, Becca, I'll call you Becca."

It was a short ride from the storage facility to the Goose Lake parking lot.

"Hey, Becca," Daniel said on the way, "do you like doing autopsies?"

"I like helping police detectives like your father figure out why someone died, and if they were murdered, I like doing my part to bring killers to justice."

"No, I mean the cutting-up part."

"I don't mind it. I think of an autopsy as an operation on someone who has died."

Daniel mulled over what Becca had told him for a moment. "Thank you."

"Thank me for what, Daniel?"

"My mom had an autopsy. It seemed kind of gross to me, but now I can think about it as her just having an operation."

Becca glanced at Eddie and saw a sympathetic look in Eddie's expression. He had wrestled with the same difficult image.

"Well, Daniel, you're quite welcome."

THEY UNLOADED the bikes at the Goose Lake parking lot, the same area where the dead veteran was found in the spring. Eddie used a magnetic locking pedal. The pedal had a magnet that metal pads in the sole of the bicycle shoe held onto. The pedal held the prosthesis on well, so he didn't have to think about keeping it on, and it allowed the prosthesis to change angles as he pedaled.

"Everybody ready?" Eddie asked.

From Goose Lake, they headed north, crossing a bridge over Northern Lights Boulevard, then turned west toward the coast. It was a paved trail all the way. As they headed west, they went through several urban parks: Tikishia Park, Fastchester Park, and Charles Smith Memorial Park. Pavilions were filled with family and corporate cookouts. In the surrounding grassy expanses, people tossed footballs and flung frisbees. The trails teemed with other bikers, power walkers, dog walkers, joggers, rollerbladers, and roller skiers.

The people they passed took little notice of them, taking for granted that they were a typical family out for an evening bike ride— except for the prosthesis, of course. He luxuriated in this fantasy of near-normalcy.

They went through a tunnel under C-Street and around a curve into Valley of the Moon Park, another popular gathering spot. Its main feature was a forty-foot-high rocket ship-shaped climbing tower with a spiral staircase running up the inside and two covered curved slides that descended from the second level. It was filled with kids.

"The rocket ship. I used to play on that when I was a kid."

They pedaled within a few yards of a medium-sized bush, indistinguishable from the rest of the unmowed brush that lined this part of the trail. Eddie happened to glance that way, and he noticed a pair of dried and cracked leather boots abandoned there. As one does, he fleetingly wondered how they got there, and then forgot about them, the observation never getting deeper than his temporary storage.

Four miles from Goose Lake Park, the trail ended at a T-intersection with the Tony Knowles Coastal Trail.

They stopped. "Right or left, Daniel?" Eddie asked.

"Left—we can go to Point Woronzof and then back."

"Sounds good."

They pedaled three and a half miles along the coast. There were some gentle slopes until the steep approach to Point Woronzof. Pedaling up that hill required thigh-burning effort. At the top, they all rested.

"Becca, do you know who Point Woronzof was named after?"

"No, some Russian guy?"

"Yep. Lieutenant Joseph Whidbey was an officer in the British Navy who was part of an expedition led by George Vancouver. He named this point for Count Semyon Romanovich Vorontsov, a Russian ambassador to Britain, who was a big deal in those days for keeping the peace between Russia and Britain. This marks the beginning of the Knik arm of the Cook Inlet."

A purple-tailed Fed-Ex 747 screamed just above them on its approach to runway 15 at Ted Stevens International Airport.

Following the FedEx jet, an Alaska Airlines jet roared overhead.

"Cool, huh?" Daniel said, sounding slightly winded. "We're only 1,200 feet from the end of runway 15. This is a good place to plane-watch. Our airport is the world's third busiest cargo airport."

"I didn't know that," Becca said.

"Do you notice the two different sounds coming from jets? The compressor in the front of the engine makes a high-pitched noise, and the lower roar is from wind shear as the air passes out the back of the engine. And, of course, there's the Doppler effect that alters the pitch of noises as they approach us and pass us. And see the saw-tooth pattern at the back of the engine?"

"Yes."

"They're called chevrons, and they're designed to reduce engine noise by flow-mixing. The chevrons create vortices that help mix the high-velocity exhaust with the slower ambient air. This reduces the velocity gradient that causes noise. There are other mechanisms involved, but the flow-mixing is the most important."

Eddie glanced over at Becca as she listened to Daniel's enthusiastic ramble about engines and Doppler effects. For just a moment, as she smiled and looked up at a plane passing over, the sunlight caught her hair, and the redness seemed to glow. She seemed almost unburdened, or at least lighter than she had been in months. Maybe she was having her own fantasy of normal.

"Interesting, Daniel. How do you know all this stuff?"

"I look stuff up. I hate not knowing things."

"You'll make a great doctor or researcher, Daniel, whatever you decide to go for."

"Ready to head back, guys?" Eddie asked.

His son nodded. "Sure."

Becca decided to take her bike to her apartment at Denali Towers instead of storage, so she could get back into cycling. When they got there, Daniel helped her unload it.

"Thanks for inviting me, Daniel," she said. "It was fun getting out. I needed that."

Eddie was debating whether to thank her for coming or ask if she'd like to join them again sometime, but Daniel spoke out first.

"Next time, we could ride in the other direction on the Coastal Trail. There's this really cool spot where you can sometimes see beluga whales."

"I'd like that." She smiled at both of them. "Later, guys."

They watched her wheel her bike through the building's front doors.

"She's nice, isn't she, Dad?" Daniel said as they pulled away from the curb.

"Yes, she is," Eddie said. "Very nice."

56

PAELLA

"You look very handsome, son," Gertie said. Her face was beaming.

He was wearing gray slacks and a black Tommy Bahama shirt, tails out, but Gertie inspected him with anticipatory delight as if he were a high schooler wearing his first rented tuxedo, about to pick up a prom date.

"Thanks, Mom."

The house was filled with anticipation.

"Look something up for me, will you, Daniel?"

"Sure."

"I need a wine that goes well with paella. You know how to spell it?"

"Really, Dad?"

"Oh, you're having paella. You can't find a good paella in Anchorage," Gertie said. "If it's good, get me the recipe. I'm sure it will be."

After a few clicks, Daniel said, "Here we go. This is from pair-your-wine dot com: 'Paella can be a tricky choice. Red wines, rich in tannins, can react with the oil in fish to produce a harsh metallic taste. On the other hand, against such an aromatic dish, a white wine can be overpowered. The best choice would be a rosé. It is low in tannins and has the freshness of a white to complement the weightiness of the paella, but with enough fruitiness and body of a red to stand up to it. A rosé of pinot noir or Sangiovese are excellent choices. For something more festive, a rosé cava, a Spanish sparkling wine, would also pair well.'"

"Great, text that to me."

Daniel tapped his cell phone a few times, and Eddie's phone chimed.

"Thanks. Well, I'm off."

"Let me give you a kiss," Gertie said. She was beaming.

"Jeesh, Mom, it's just dinner. Don't make such a big deal out of it."

But Eddie knew it was a big deal.

HIS FIRST STOP was the Anchorage Wine House on Minnesota Avenue, a liquor store in midtown. He headed for the "Spain" section. A fiftyish man with readers perched on his nose approached.

"I'm Mike. Can I help you find something?"

"Hey, Mike. I'm looking for a wine to go with paella. I thought a Spanish cava."

"Certainly, sir, but so you know, all cavas are from Spain."

"Oh."

"When is your dinner?"

"Tonight—I'm on my way now."

"Ah, you need one already chilled. Come with me."

Mike led Eddie to a refrigerated cabinet.

"Special occasion with a special lady?"

"You could say that."

"I'd go with the Alta Alella Mirgi Laietà. Aged thirty months. On the nose, there is grapefruit, pomegranate, and red plum, and on the tongue, softer: white cherry, watermelon, finishing with light notes of caramel and citrus. It is a bit spendy as cavas go, at thirty-six dollars, but it will stand up to the paella. I do have a cheaper one, however, almost as good."

"No, I'll take that one."

AT DENALI TOWERS, Eddie pushed the intercom button next to "506."

Since Becca's call to him three days earlier, inviting him over for dinner, his mental state oscillated between eager anticipation and panic.

This would be their second date. Were these even dates? He tried to manage expectations about both the evening's meaning and the possibilities. Amputees didn't tend to have the best body images, and now he was dealing with a forensic pathologist who saw all kinds of human deformities in her work. *Oh Jesus, why are you even going there?*

"Eddie?"

"Yes, it's me."

She buzzed him in. When he reached her apartment and rang the doorbell, he heard the peephole open and close before she opened the door.

Becca was stunning in a simple, sleeveless, cobalt-blue dress held up by spaghetti straps, with a V-front that exposed a hint of cleavage. The hem reached just below her knees, revealing slim legs that curved as gracefully as the cava bottle he held. She wore sandals with low heels, their thin straps showing off perfectly formed feet with deep red toenails. And there was Jesus, in his favorite spot, hanging from her neck.

"Wow," Eddie said. "You clean up nice."

"Thank you."

There was something different about her—the confident way she held herself, the spark back in her eyes. This was the Becca he'd first met at the Church of the Redeemer, not the shaken woman from just after the killing.

He handed her the bottle of cava.

"I couldn't show up empty-handed."

"Thank you." She inspected the bottle. "Pink champagne?"

"A rosé cava. Think of it as Spanish champagne. It has notes of white cherry, watermelon, and light caramel with citrus. Refreshing on the palate, with light acidity, enough to stand up to the saffron, chicken, and chorizo, but not so much to react with the seafood."

"My, you're quite the wine connoisseur."

Eddie chuckled. "It's either that, or Daniel googled the wine pairing, and the description is courtesy of the manager at the Wine House."

"Shall we open it now?"

"Why not?"

The apartment was small, with an L-shaped dining room and living area and an open galley kitchen separated from the dining area by a counter with three bar stools. It was nothing like her old house on the hillside. She went into the kitchen while Eddie took a seat at the counter. With a small paring knife, she cut into the foil holding the cap, untwisted the wire, and, with her thumbs, loosened the cork, twisting it off with a satisfying pop.

"It's starting to sound like a party in here," Becca said.

She took out two wine glasses. "Like most of my stuff, my champagne flutes are in storage. We'll have to settle for regular wine glasses."

"Not a problem."

She filled them halfway and handed him one. They clinked glasses and each took a sip. She put the glass to her mouth, slightly parting her lips. A small red lip print remained on her glass.

"That's nice. Good choice, Detective."

"I'm not a big wine drinker, but this is good."

"We're going to have a green salad with the paella."

She went to the refrigerator and started pulling out ingredients: romaine, arugula, plum tomatoes. She took out a jar of what appeared to be truncated thick white stalks.

"What are those?" Eddie asked.

"Hearts of palm. Take a bite."

She held one up to Eddie's mouth. He opened his mouth and bit down. The outside was firm with a slight crunch, and the inside was soft and nutty.

"These are good."

"I'll get dinner started."

"Can I help?"

"No, this is a one-woman act. Besides, most of it's already done."

She put on an apron. For the salad, she cut the hearts of palm into half-inch circles and covered the bowl with a wet paper towel before refrigerating it.

As with her dissections, every cut was confident and graceful. Like the Becca ge first met.

She retrieved covered bowls and wrapped packages from the refrigerator. A small paella pan went on the stove's large burner.

"It's not my Wolf range, but it'll do."

This apartment was a step down from the house on Stuckagain.

"Have you sold your old place?"

"Yes. And, except for my family's mementos, everything else went to the dump or the auction house. I wanted nothing in my life that Jim ever saw or touched. I rented this place furnished, except that I bought a new mattress and some of the kitchen stuff. My thinking is to give it a year and see how I feel about staying and then buy."

"A clean break. I can understand that."

"Did you know that in Alaska, you have to disclose any death occurring in a house within the past three years when you put it on the market?"

"Actually, I did. I'm a murder expert."

"It doesn't do much for the resale value of the property."

She poured olive oil into the pan and added chopped onions, garlic, and skinned and chopped tomatoes she had prepared in advance.

"I'm surprised you came back at all, frankly." *Happy, too.*

"Believe me, I thought about leaving, but I didn't want to give that shit that sort of power over me. I was hired with the prospect of taking over as chief medical examiner in a few years. I'm on track to become one of the youngest in the country. It's a tough opportunity to leave behind."

"I get it. You know, tonight—cooking, talking about your career—

you seem like the confident woman I first met, like the old Becca is back. At least what I knew of her."

"Thank you. I've decided not to be a victim anymore."

"You were never a victim."

"Just a fool, maybe."

She stirred the vegetables in the pan. "Anyway, don't you love the smell of onions and garlic sautéing in olive oil?"

Eddie was happy to let her steer the conversation toward less serious matters.

"Yes, the aroma is making me hungry."

"It's the beginning of sofrito, a Spanish base of onions, garlic, olive oil, and sometimes, as in this one, tomatoes. It's the foundation for this paella."

Once the onions were translucent, she added minced garlic and tomatoes. "It's important to skin the tomatoes and mince them finely." Then she added paprika. To finish off the sofrito, she reached for a small jar, pulled out crimson saffron threads, gently crushed them between her fingers, and sprinkled them over. "Crushing the saffron helps get the flavor out." The tiny threads began to bleed their golden color into the mixture as she stirred.

"Saffron is the most expensive spice in the world," she told him. "Did you know it takes seventy-five thousand saffron flowers to make one pound?" She laughed. "Oh my God, I sounded like Daniel!"

Becca stirred until the tomatoes were reduced to a thick sauce, the saffron scent filling the room. Next, she added some chorizo, which she had already sliced. "It's basically a seafood paella, but the chorizo gives a little bite and smokiness, as well as reinforcing the saffron color."

Opening one package, she revealed two long tubular squid bodies.

"The calamari is next. They take the longest to cook, so they go in first. So, you know how I became a forensic pathologist. How did you become a cop?"

"I was in pre-law at the University of Alaska. I had been accepted at the University of Washington Law School. During my senior year, my father went crazy, liquidated my college fund, ran off to Florida, and abandoned Gertie and me. He spent all the money, then drank himself to death."

"That sucks," Becca said.

She added Bomba rice to the sofrito and stirred just once to coat the grains with oil before spreading it evenly across the pan. Then came the saffron-infused fish stock, turning the contents a golden color.

"It looks like risotto," Eddie said.

"Ah, with one big difference. We don't stir the Bomba rice. We let it sit and cook, and it develops a crispy bottom layer—socarrat."

Eddie did his best James Cagney impression, "You dirty Socarrat."

"You don't want to char it. You want a golden brown with nutty caramelized flavor. But anyway, go ahead."

"So, lacking funds, I ditched the law school idea and became a cop. I was in the Master of Public Administration evening program at UAA, which put me in a better position to move up the ladder. Then the accident happened, and with six months to go, I suspended my studies."

"You should go back and finish that degree, don't you think?"

"That was the plan. Gertie came to live with us to help with Daniel. Then he got sick."

"What did Daniel get sick with?"

"Leukemia."

"What kind?"

"Acute lymphoblastic. Philadelphia chromosome-positive."

"I see. How long has he been in remission?"

"Three years."

"That's good. Keep the faith."

What faith? Faith hadn't done much for him or his family. *Okay, Vaugner, keep it light; she doesn't need to hear your agnostic bullshit right now.*

As they talked, Becca intermittently returned to the paella and added more fish: halibut, mussels, and shrimp. Finally, Becca picked up two lobster tails and placed them into the paella pan.

"When the shells turn red-orange and the meat turns white, it will be ready. And I'll turn up the heat a bit to get the socarrat nice and crispy."

The kitchen started to fill with an intoxicating blend of saffron, seafood, and chorizo. Becca stepped back from the stove, surveying her creation with a satisfied expression.

"I'll set the table, and the lobster should be done. Why don't you pour us some more cava?" Eddie took the cava out of the refrigerator and topped off the glasses.

He watched as she moved between the counter and the table, setting out warm plates and arranging silverware. He wondered if he would ever get tired of the way she moved, her precision, grace, and sensuality.

She turned off the heat and brought the salads to the table.

"We'll have our salads and let the paella rest."

She set the paella pan on the table and took off the lid.

"Voila! Or should I say, Listo!" The colors were magnificent—golden rice, red chorizo, pink shrimp, and the white meat of the lobster tails in their bright orange-red shells.

Using a spatula, Becca served Eddie a portion of the paella, turning the rice over, inspecting the golden brown crusty rice.

"Oh the socarrat turned out great."

"This looks fabulous," Eddie said.

"Thank you." She settled into her chair, unfolding her napkin. "Dig in."

They had a few bites.

"No, really, this is unbelievable."

"Thank you." She took a sip of cava. "Yes, your cava goes well with the paella. You could argue this isn't a true paella, as there's no chicken or rabbit. But this is my version."

"Paella a la Ravenna," Eddie suggested. "By the way, Gertie wants your recipe."

"Sure, I'd be happy to share it with her."

They finished their meal in light conversation. Eddie complimented it profusely and helped her clear the table.

"Are you ready for dessert?"

"I could be. What do you have in mind?"

She held his gaze for a moment. Her lips parted slowly. *"Brazo de Gitano con Piñones."*

She went to the kitchen, opened the refrigerator, and took out a cylindrical white cake with thick white icing covered in pine nuts.

"Brazo de Gitano is Spanish for 'gypsy arm,' and piñones are pine nuts. It's their term for pine nut cake roll."

"I sound like a broken record, but that looks delicious."

"Would you like some coffee?"

"If it's not too much trouble."

"Not at all; I have it all set to go." She pushed a button on the coffee maker.

She turned to face him, then threw her arms around his neck, pulled his face to hers, and kissed him. Eddie felt her tongue slip into his mouth. He started to get hard and pushed his pelvis into hers.

She tilted her head back to look up at him.

"The coffee needs to brew, and the cake will be better if we let it warm to room temperature."

Oh my god, is this happening?

She took Eddie's hand and led him down the corridor into the bedroom.

She sat him on the bed, stood before him, and lifted her dress off. She wasn't wearing a bra or panties. Her breasts were white silken mounds with full, pink nipples. She was fully shaved.

She pulled his head into them and, with her hand, guided a nipple into his mouth. Eddie sucked it. She moaned in response, looking down at him. She brought his hand to her vagina. It was wet.

"Are you going to get undressed?"

"I guess." He took his clothes off but left the prosthesis on and stood erect before her. She took him in her hand. "Lovely." She stroked it a few times. "Sit down."

Eddie sat down on the edge of the bed. She knelt in front of him and took him into her mouth.

"Oh wow," Eddie said.

She released him and smiled. "Let's get this off," she said, tapping his prosthesis.

"Not many people have seen this. I mean, my amputation."

"I'm a forensic pathologist. It's going to take a lot more than a BKA stump to turn me off."

Eddie reached down to remove it, but she slapped his hand.

"I'll do it. I've removed a lot of prostheses in my line of work."

She rolled down the silastic sleeve, pushed the vacuum release button on the prosthesis, and pulled it off. Then she removed the stump sock. She ran her hand down his leg, over his stump. Eddie took in a deep breath. Sensing his unease, she bent down and kissed it several times.

"Do you have much phantom pain?"

"I did at first, not so much now. They had me on Neurontin for a while, but—"

"Lie down."

Eddie lay down on the bed. She moved to straddle his stump. He could feel her wetness as she slid up and down on his skin.

"Does that feel good?"

"Yes."

Without breaking her gaze, she lifted herself and guided him inside of her. He slid in easily.

"Oh yeah," she moaned.

She rocked over him, then started moving up and down. Eddie admired her breasts bouncing and reached up to fondle them.

"Oh yeah, I love that." She ground against him until she climaxed, keeping her eyes trained on his, then collapsed onto Eddie.

"Your turn," she said, rolling over. "Do you want to fuck me?"

"Yes."

"Say it."

"I want to fuck you."

Eddie rolled on top of her. She guided him into her once more, and Eddie started pumping until he came inside her, both of them moaning together.

Afterward, sweating and glowing, she went to the kitchen.

While she was gone, he sat up and strategically arranged the sheets to make it appear that they just so happened to cover his stump.

Becca brought back two slices of the pine nut roll cake. If she noticed that he had covered his stump, she said nothing.

Since Anne died, his entire intimate life had consisted of phantoms. He had a phantom leg, a phantom wife, and a phantom love life.

But now, as they sat naked in bed, eating cake, Eddie reveled in it all—the sweetness of the dessert, her comfortable immodesty, the reality of genuine connection—and most important, the *reality* of it all.

As if reading his mind, Becca said, "You know what an acrotomophiliac is?"

"No."

"Someone sexually attracted to amputees."

"Is this about to get weird?"

Becca laughed. "No, but I wanted to assure you I'm not turned off by it."

"Thanks for that."

"I've never fucked an amputee before."

"Well, I've never fucked as an amputee before. New horizons for both of us. Thank you for being so upfront. It's a good quality you have."

They had a few more bites. "You know, I've liked you for a while, Eddie."

"Really? So I was picking up vibes, but I thought—I don't know—I was imagining it. One minute you seem, uh, interested. The next not so much. And that dinner date never seemed to materialize."

"It was Jim. I couldn't ask you to be part of that mess. Expose you, or Daniel, to that—to him."

There was an awkward silence, and then Becca laughed. "Oh my god, I just gave you a motive for murder."

"Book her, Danno!"

They finished their cake. Eddie asked for a second piece. After reveling in the flavors and small talk for another hour, Eddie said he should get home. She watched him put his leg back on and get dressed. She remained naked and walked him to the door.

"Oh, wait," she said.

She brought out a plate covered with aluminum foil. He admired her unselfconscious nudity.

"Here's some cake. It's for Gertie and Daniel. You've had enough."

She kissed him goodbye.

Eddie paused at the door. "Can I see you again?"

"Of course, since I'll need that plate back. It's part of the rental. Say hi to Gertie and Daniel for me."

57

THE SWORD OF DAMOCLES

Twenty stories up in the Captain Cook Hotel, the same building where Jack Peplow had been assassinated months earlier, Eddie and his colleagues were celebrating Chik's retirement and bon voyage. Cops were good at compartmentalizing, so the place hummed with conversation and laughter at the site of one of Anchorage's most infamous murders.

Through the floor-to-ceiling windows of the private dining space, the summer solstice sunlight painted the Chugach Mountains gold. To the south, downtown Anchorage stretched out below them, and to the west, Cook Inlet reached the horizon. The days would start to become shorter now. While Alaska was called the land of the midnight sun, in Anchorage, on the longest day of the year, the sun would set at 11:42 p.m.

"Speech!" someone called out.

Chik smiled and held up his hands. "You know I'm not one for speeches. But I do want to say thank you for this." He gestured to the premium Japanese-made golf set propped against the mahogany-paneled wall. He had been drooling over this set for months. It promised forgiveness without sacrificing performance—exactly what a retiree serious about his game required. These were actually a demo set. He would go into the dealer and get custom-fitted. "I guess someone has been talking to Christina."

"She said anything to get you out of the house." Laughter ensued.

"The best thing about surviving the gunshot is now I might live to break 90, especially with these guys," Chik said, patting his new clubs like he would a favorite child.

"Yeah, maybe from the senior tees, old man!" someone shouted. More laughter.

As the good-natured ribbing and reminiscing continued, Eddie felt his phone vibrate. He retrieved his phone from his coat pocket as he stepped away from the group. It was Gertie. Their laughter faded as he moved toward the quiet of the corridor outside the private room.

"Hi, Gertie."

"I hate to bother you at the party, but I'm so upset."

"What is it?"

"It's Daniel."

"Is he okay?"

"I don't know."

"Jesus, Mom, what is it?"

"I was just doing the laundry, and there's blood on his pillowcase. At least, it looked like blood. Then I went upstairs and saw a small drop of blood on the floor in front of the sink in his bathroom."

Shit. A bloody nose had been one of Daniel's first symptoms when the leukemia originally appeared.

"Did he tell you about it?"

"No. What should we do?"

"Don't say anything to him yet. I'll call Dr. Blake's office first thing on Monday and get him in."

"He was tired and went to bed. I just checked on him. He's sleeping."

"Okay, I'll be home soon."

He took a deep breath and forced a smile on his face. Since Daniel was asleep, he decided to stay and rejoin the party for Chik. But the fun was over. This is not something he could compartmentalize.

· · ·

WHEN HE GOT HOME from the party, he cracked Daniel's door. Daniel was already asleep.

The next morning, after a restless night, Eddie waited for Daniel to come down to breakfast. Gertie was at Mass.

"Good morning, Daniel."

"Hey, Dad."

"Can I make you something for breakfast?"

"It's okay. I'll just have cereal."

After setting himself up with a bowl of Cap'n Crunch and milk, Daniel took a seat at the counter.

Eddie sat next to him.

"Daniel, Gertie told me about your nosebleed."

"Dad, it was nothing. I was going to tell you if I had another one."

"Son, you can't ignore a nosebleed. You know that."

"I was scared."

Eddie hugged Daniel.

"Are you feeling okay?"

"Yes, I'm feeling fine."

"Well, I'm calling Dr. Blake's office tomorrow as soon as they open to see if I can get you in."

Daniel trembled in his father's arms and then began to cry. "I don't want to die, Dad."

"You're not going to die, Daniel," Eddie said, holding him tighter.

But he knew what the odds were. And so did Daniel.

MONDAY MORNING, after Eddie arrived at the office, he called Dr. Blake's office and reached his nurse. She wanted to know if Daniel had been experiencing tiredness, coughing, weight loss, or night sweats. He said no, but wondered if his son had been hiding other symptoms. She told Eddie to bring him in at twelve-thirty so they could run some tests.

After handing up, Eddie called the school to let them know he was picking up Daniel at noon. He didn't give a reason.

.   .   .

ON THE RIDE over to Dr. Blake's office, Eddie tried to make small talk. Daniel limited his responses to one-syllable words and grunts, keeping his face fixed on his phone as he played Fortnite. When they checked in, they were taken back right away. The nurse weighed Daniel and noted a three-pound weight loss since his last visit. *Not good,* Eddie thought to himself. A kid his age should have been gaining weight. They drew several vials of blood and arranged for them to return at four o'clock to discuss the results with Dr. Blake.

Walking back to the car, Eddie asked Daniel if he was hungry.

"I could eat, I guess."

They drove to the Village Inn. Daniel ordered a stack of pancakes, and Eddie had a BLT. Daniel stopped eating halfway through the pancakes.

"Are you finished?"

"Yeah."

Loss of appetite and weight loss were signs, but Eddie didn't force the issue. They would know soon enough.

THAT AFTERNOON, Eddie and Daniel were back in an exam room. Dr. Blake walked in carrying his laptop.

"What is my white count?" Daniel asked.

"Fifty-three thousand."

Eddie's stomach lurched. He remembered that a normal white blood cell count is somewhere between 6,000 and 10,000. The sword of Damocles had fallen.

"So I've relapsed," Daniel said. "Can I see my test results?"

"Sure." Blake tapped a few keys and then turned the screen to face Daniel. The boy scanned it.

"Wow." Daniel looked up at Eddie with a frightened look on his face, then back down at the report. "Too many lymphocytes and not enough platelets. That explains my nosebleed."

"What now?" Eddie asked.

"Bone marrow aspiration and biopsy," Daniel said.

"I've arranged it with general anesthesia in the operating room. Can you get to outpatient surgery tomorrow morning at seven-thirty?"

"Yes, of course," Eddie said.

Daniel sighed. "Ugh."

WHEN THEY GOT HOME, they told Gertie. She gave Daniel a big hug and promised to pray for him and light votive candles in the cathedral.

"I only have a 15 to 50 percent chance of being alive five years from now, Grandma."

"So you'll be one of them," she said. "You'll beat this. I have faith."

"Your faith didn't do much for Mom!" He turned and ran upstairs. "And me neither, while we're at it!" His door slammed.

"There you go, Edward. He's starting to sound just like you."

Eddie almost glared at his mom.

Okay, keep cool. You're not going to spiral down a crisis-of-faith monologue and bullshit ruminations. Not worth it. Not productive, and don't waste time going on about God's not this, and God doesn't do that.

"Sorry, Mom."

Later that evening, Eddie called Becca and told her about Daniel's relapse. This was not news he wanted to tell her, and probably not news she wanted to hear. She had enough baggage.

"Oh no," she said. "He'll need a bone marrow."

"Yes, tomorrow."

There was a pause. The familiar fear clawed at him, and he braced for the "this is not what I signed up for" exit speech.

Instead, she asked, "Would you like me to come with you guys? Not that I can do much, but I would be there for moral support, at least."

"I don't know. You're busy—"

"Trust me. My patients can wait."

"I'd really be grateful if you did. Let me ask Daniel."

"Okay, let me know. Anything I can do."

Eddie went up to Daniel's room. He was playing Fortnite on his computer.

"Hey Daniel, you ready for tomorrow?"

"Yeah, I guess."

"I just talked to Dr. Raven—uh, Becca. She's offered to be with us tomorrow for your bone marrow biopsy."

He put the game on pause and swiveled around to face his father.

"Really?"

"Yeah. For moral support."

Daniel glanced briefly over at the picture of him with his mother on the nightstand.

"If she would like to come, it would be fine with me. She can wait with you while I'm having the procedure done."

"Okay, I'll let her know."

"And Dad?"

"Yes?"

"Can you tell Grandma I'm sorry I yelled at her?"

58

MILK OF AMNESIA

As he entered the PAMC surgery center lobby with Daniel, Eddie spotted Becca immediately. Part of him had worried she might change her mind, but there she was. Not only did she show up, but she was there early, waiting for them. He almost teared up. "Hi, guys." A lanyard hung from her neck, indicating she was a physician with Consultant status.

"Hi, Becca," Daniel said.

At the reception desk, Eddie presented IDs and insurance cards. The receptionist put an ID band around Daniel's wrist and then handed Eddie a clipboard with a registration update form and a consent form for "Bone Marrow Aspirate and Biopsy."

As Eddie filled it out, Daniel said, "Hey, Becca, do you know the difference between an internist, a surgeon, and a pathologist?"

"Is this a joke?"

"Yeah. Internists know everything, surgeons do everything, and pathologists know everything and do everything, but it's too late."

"Good one, Daniel." She winked at Eddie as if to say, *Of course I know that joke, but who am I to steal his thunder?*

They quickly processed Daniel's registration, started an IV, and took him back to the holding area, where Blake checked in with them.

Daniel introduced Becca to Blake as "my dad's new friend, and mine too, I guess."

"Absolutely," Becca said.

Nancy Hawthorne, the anesthesiologist, came out and explained the anesthesia protocol. They would be using propofol, a white, cloudy substance.

"It goes in quickly and gets out quickly," she said.

"Milk of amnesia," Daniel said. "Crosses the blood-brain barrier very quickly because it's lipophilic—dissolves easily in fats. It's short-acting because it rapidly distributes from the central nervous system to other tissues in the body."

"Daniel—what?" Hawthorne looked at Eddie with a puzzled smile.

Eddie shrugged and smiled back. "Yeah, that's Daniel."

Two nurses came for Daniel. Eddie leaned over and kissed him on the forehead.

"See you on the other side, son."

Becca gave Daniel a thumbs-up.

ABOUT FORTY-FIVE MINUTES LATER, Blake came out to Eddie and Becca in the waiting area to let them know that everything had gone routinely.

"What about a spinal tap, Doctor Blake?" Becca asked.

"Yes. Recent literature suggests that patients do better when we hold off the spinal tap until after induction with chemotherapy. So, we'll do that later."

"Lessens the chance of inducing leukemic cells into the central nervous system?"

"Exactly."

"When will you get the biopsy results?" she asked.

"Two days," Blake said.

Shortly after, a nurse came out and led Eddie and Becca back to Daniel.

"Hey, son. How did it go?"

"Great, I don't remember a thing. Butt's a little sore, though."

"Well, guys, things look under control here, and I have to get back to the office."

"Okay," Eddie said.

"Thanks for coming," Daniel added.

"Hey, would you guys like me to be there when you discuss the results with Dr. Blake?"

Daniel lit up. "Sure, that would be great."

"Let me walk you out to your car," Eddie said.

"Can I have my phone, Dad?"

Eddie handed Daniel his phone and walked Becca through the lobby and out to the parking lot.

"Thanks for being here."

"Not a problem."

"But listen, if at any time this is too much—"

Becca held up her hand. "Eddie, shut the fuck up and get back to your son." She kissed him on the cheek, got in her car, and left.

Gertie was on them as soon as they walked through the front door.

"How did everything go?"

"He was a real trooper," Eddie said. "He's supposed to take it easy today."

"Becca was there with us."

Gertie gave her son a look. "Really? Okay, Daniel, you march right upstairs. Are you hungry?"

"I'll take a cup of ramen."

"Coming up, young man."

Eddie hugged Daniel. "I have to get to headquarters. I'll see you guys later this evening."

"No problem, I'll take care of Daniel."

59

RESULTS

Two days later, as Eddie, Becca, and Daniel sat across from Dr. Blake, he rotated his computer screen so that everyone could see it.

"This is your bone marrow, Daniel." Blake used his pen to point to an image of a sea of blue disks with a few randomly scattered, light-red, disk-like structures. "You can see a large number of lymphoblasts crowding red blood cells. These are replicating out of control and crowding out the other blood-forming cells. That's why you're anemic, and your platelets are low."

Next, Blake showed a linear array of dark, banded chromosomes in pairs, numbered 1 through 22, with two more sets separately: a long one labeled Y and the other shorter one labeled X. There were circles around the pairs labeled 9 and 22.

"This is the karyotype taken from your lymphoblasts. One strand in pair 9 is abnormally long, and one strand in pair 22 is significantly shorter."

Daniel recognized the circle pairs, named after the city in which they were discovered. "So, I have relapsed Philadelphia chromosome-positive B-cell acute lymphoblastic leukemia," Daniel said. He sighed and put his head down. "That's not good."

"What do we do now?" Eddie asked.

"It's not all bad, Daniel. You had a fairly long interval before relapsing—three years—so that improves the odds. Also, the protocol has improved. We've added a tyrosine kinase inhibitor into the mix and have better strategies than the other drugs."

"So what's the protocol?" Daniel asked.

Blake cleared his throat.

"Daniel, would you consider TBI this time around?"

"No. I'd rather be dead than deal with the long-term complications of total body irradiation. Thyroid cancer, heart, lung, and kidney damage, and having my brain fried. No thanks."

"Edward?" Blake pleaded.

"Daniel, won't you consider—"

Daniel shook his head violently. "No. No. No. NO!" Then he did one of the things he did most rarely: he began to cry.

Eddie took in a resigned breath. "Okay, Daniel. Okay." He shrugged at Blake and looked over at Becca, who nodded sympathetically but stayed out of the conversation. He reached over and patted Daniel's shoulder.

"Whatever my son wants."

"And who knows what interventions might be coming?" Daniel said, sniffing. "I'll take my chances."

"Very well then," Blake said.

From the last go-around and talking with parents of the other kids with cancer, Eddie knew this violated Blake's oncology mindset: hate the cancer, kill the cancer. And often, it seemed to many parents that cancer doctors put tumor response over the quality of life of the patient after treatment.

But Dr. Blake conceded the issue. "Okay, without TBI, here's the protocol. We'll break this into phases. First, induction. We'll use a combination of Vincristine, Doxorubicin, and PEG-asparaginase, along with high-dose dexamethasone. Plus—and this is key—we'll add Dasatinib, a newer tyrosine kinase inhibitor that specifically targets the Philadelphia chromosome. It's showing a lot of promise."

"And once I achieve remission?"

"Once we achieve remission—and I expect we will—we'll move to conditioning for transplant. Without TBI, we'll use a combination of Busulfan and Cyclophosphamide. It's intensive chemotherapy, but it's proven fairly effective, though not as effective as TBI."

Blake found it hard to let the TBI go. Daniel ignored it.

"Then the transplant?"

"Yes."

"Can we use my dad's bone marrow again?"

"Yes, I expected to."

"How long will I be in the hospital?"

"Well, Daniel, let's break it down by phases. For reinduction, you're looking at about four weeks of inpatient therapy. We might be able to do some of it on an outpatient basis if your counts stay stable and you don't experience any fevers. A lot will depend on the ANC."

"I'm sorry," Eddie said, "what's the ANC again?"

"Absolute neutrophil count. You know what the white blood cell count is, right?"

"Those are the cells in the bloodstream that fight infection?"

"Well, yes and no. The white blood cell count includes all types of white blood cells: neutrophils, lymphocytes, monocytes, eosinophils, and basophils.

"The ANC means the absolute neutrophil count. Like when you have a boil filled with pus? That's almost all neutrophils. They rise at different rates after chemotherapy than the other white blood cells, so in terms of Daniel getting an infection, we want to track those specifically. The magic ANC number is 500 because that's when he gets to go home for a couple of weeks to recover his strength and regain a decent nutritional status. Then, back in the hospital for conditioning and bone marrow transplant. We'll go over that later, but altogether," Blake continued, "you're probably looking at eight to ten weeks for the transplant admission. Total hospital time, combining both admissions, probably twelve to fourteen weeks, spread over about four months."

Daniel seemed to be calculating something in his head.

"How's the Wi-Fi in the hospital these days?"

"You know, they just upgraded. I hear they're up to gigabit speeds."

Daniel smiled. "Cool."

The doctor drummed his fingers on his desk for a moment and smiled at Eddie. "I have good news for you, Eddie. We're mostly obtaining stem cells from peripheral blood now. We'll give you a drug called Neupogen. It will increase the number of stem cells in your peripheral bloodstream. When that happens, we'll draw blood from your arm, which will flow through a machine that separates the stem cells and then return the rest of your blood to you. You won't have to go through a bone marrow harvest."

"I'd walk through hell barefoot, but okay. When do I start the Neupogen?" he asked.

"Ten days into Daniel's conditioning chemotherapy. You remember how to inject yourself?"

"Yeah, I think so."

"If not," Becca said, "I can inject him. Is it subcutaneous or intramuscular?"

"SubQ. Any other questions so far? I'll print up the treatment protocol and get it emailed to you."

"What about a port?" Daniel asked.

Oh, the port, thought Eddie, *of course.* He had forgotten (or blocked out) that part and now recalled that the "port," or Mediport, was a chamber implanted underneath the skin with a line that ran through the veins into the superior vena cava. It allowed easy access for blood draws and medication without repeated needle sticks.

"Yes, that was my next item. Dr. Briggs, the pediatric surgeon who placed Daniel's last port, is on a sabbatical. He has a locum covering for him, but that is for emergency and neonatal cases only, so I've referred you to another surgeon, Dr. Lange, for the catheter placement."

"Grayson Lange?" Eddie asked.

"Yes, you know him?"

"Yes. He's the surgeon who operated on Dana Peplow, the woman who was shot in front of the Captain Cook." He left out that Lange was also a murder suspect. "He also operated on one of my partners, Detective Uttaq, and saved his life."

"Then you know Daniel will be in good hands. I've taken the

liberty of setting it up with his office for Monday at 11 a.m. in the surgery center. Since you've been through this before and he has all your lab work, he's agreed to meet you just before the procedure to save you a trip to his office. Nothing to eat eight hours before the procedure. Be prepared to be admitted after the port is inserted. If that's inconvenient, we can reschedule, but I'd like to get cracking on this."

"No, that will be fine," Eddie said.

Dr. Lange. I'll be damned. Eddie and Becca exchanged a look. Becca smiled and shook her head.

Anchorage could be a strange small town. His *quantum* murder suspect was going to operate on his son, and he felt Daniel would be in good hands.

60

LASAGNA

"Come on in! Welcome!"

Becca greeted the Vaugner family at her door. Becca had invited them over for dinner the night before Daniel was to get his port placed.

They all came through the door bearing gifts.

Gertie held up a cake dish. "It's a German dessert, Bavarian Creme with Berries," Gertie said. "It was a favorite of Eddie's father. I thought it would complement the lasagna."

"*Bayerische Creme mit Beeren* in German," Daniel chimed in.

"Wow, that sounds delicious! Lasagna and Bavarian Creme. I love mixing traditions," Becca said with a smile. "It's so American, no?"

Eddie held up the plate he had taken the pine nut cake home on. "I finally remembered this."

Daniel held up a bottle of wine. "It's a bottle of Chianti Classico."

Eddie added, "This particular brand has a bright acidity with layers of strawberry and Morello cherry. And the tannins are beautifully integrated without— Oh, you get the idea."

"Mike from the Wine Store?"

"Yeah."

She led them all toward the kitchen. "Anyway, the lasagna is about to come out of the oven, and I'm just about to make the Caesar salad. Eddie and Daniel, would you guys like to help me with that?"

"Okay." Daniel tried to be enthusiastic, but he fell a little short.

"Okay, Eddie, first pour us some wine. Want to start with the Chianti? The glasses are up here."

"I'd love a glass as well," Gertie added.

"You got it," Eddie said, reaching for three glasses.

"What's next?" Daniel asked.

In the kitchen, Becca had set up a workspace at the counter with the precision one would expect from a forensic pathologist: a blender jar for the Caesar dressing, eggs, and garlic cloves lined up like patients awaiting attention.

Becca retrieved a mortar and pestle and a jar of anchovies from a cabinet. "Eddie, your job is to mash the garlic and anchovies, since you've got the muscle for it."

Eddie set down his wine glass and moved to the counter, accepting the tools she offered. She handed him a small tin of anchovies packed in oil

"About six filets."

"Okay, here goes," Eddie muttered as he picked filets out of the jar and began to mash the anchovies with the garlic. The pungent aroma filled his nostrils.

"Make sure to mash it into a complete paste."

"Yes, Chef."

As Eddie worked the mortar and pestle, Becca turned her attention to Daniel.

"Want to learn the proper way to coddle an egg?" Becca asked Daniel.

"Coddling an egg?"

"Oh, like when my mother used to make kogel mogel," Gertie interrupted. "Warm the eggs just enough, but never too hot or they'd scramble."

"Exactly," Becca said. "Coddling partially denatures the proteins in the egg white, and these create a more stable and lighter emulsion."

"Okay, what do I do?"

Eddie noted that Daniel seemed interested, but he wasn't his usual enthusiastic self.

Becca handed him a large spoon. "Use this spoon to drop the egg in the pot of simmering water for exactly one minute. Then, take it out and gently drop it into this bowl with the ice bath. We don't want the egg to overcook."

"Got it," Daniel said, taking out his phone.

"Well, let me do something," Gertie interjected. "I can't sit here like a bump on a log."

"Okay, Gertie." Becca handed her a salad spinner and a head of romaine lettuce. "Tear the lettuce into small pieces and put them in the spinner."

A timer chimed. Becca slipped on professional-grade oven mitts and moved to the oven. The lasagna that emerged was golden brown, with cheese bubbling at the edges.

"That looks perfect!" Gertie exclaimed, pausing from her lettuce preparation.

"Old Italian family recipe from northern Italy. We make it with a béchamel sauce instead of ricotta, like the Southern Italians," Becca said, setting the ceramic dish on a cooling rack.

"Time's up!" Daniel said, pulling the egg from the pot and transferring it to the ice bath. "What's a béchamel sauce?"

"It's made by heating butter and flour together, then gradually adding milk. It brings out the meat flavor a little more."

She went to a cabinet and took out a blender.

"Now, we're going to cheat a little bit by using a blender instead of whisking it all by hand."

"Good," Daniel said.

"How are those anchovies doing, Eddie?"

"Not good. They're totally mashed."

Becca inspected the mortar. "Oh, those look perfect." Back to Daniel, she said, "Okay, let's break the eggs into the blender."

Daniel cracked the eggs over the blender jar. They were still runny, but the whites were just slightly translucent.

"Perfect," Becca said. "Add the garlic and anchovy paste, and then the lemon juice."

"I'll just add a little salt and pepper," she said, using shakers. Then she poured out a measuring cup of olive oil and handed it to Daniel. "First-pressed extra virgin olive oil. Now, turn the blender on low speed and slowly drizzle the olive oil in."

Daniel flicked on the blender and began drizzling the olive oil as Becca added the salt and pepper.

She turned to the refrigerator and grabbed two more condiments. "And I'll just throw in a teaspoon of Dijon and two teaspoons of What's-this-here-sauce."

Daniel chuckled. "What's-this-here-sauce."

Becca looked over at Eddie, perched on the counter with his wine. They shared a glance and a smile.

We're a precarious collection of souls, Eddie thought. *Daniel, Gertie, Becca, and me. All scarred by our battles.*

In that glance, it came to him. Maybe Becca needed this—needed them. Maybe caring for someone was helping her heal.

"You got it, Daniel?"

"I got it."

"When all the olive oil is in, it should be light and airy. Well, pour it onto the salad and bring it to the table."

"Yes, Chef," Daniel joked.

"Hey, Eddie," she said softly. "Do you want to set the table?"

"Jeez! I have to do all the work around here," he teased.

"How's this look, Becca?" Daniel asked, placing the salad on the table.

"It looks perfect," Becca said, pouring the dressing from the blender onto the romaine and tossing it. "Let's eat," she declared.

They gathered around Becca's small table, the lasagna steaming enticingly and the Caesar salad glistening in a wooden bowl. A simple but elegant dinner.

With a lasagna spatula, Becca cut generous squares from the dish, serving each person.

"Not too much for me," Daniel said, shaking his head. "I'm not that hungry." Becca cut him a half portion.

"Help yourselves to the salad," she offered.

The first few bites of lasagna prompted high praise.

"This is good!" Gertie exclaimed. "I don't even miss the ricotta."

"There is a little Parmigiano-Reggiano cheese in there. Helps bind things together and adds a little nuttiness to the flavor."

The rest of the dinner was filled with small talk and laughter. Becca shared a few stories about her family. At the same time, Gertie spoke about the trials of building her apartment over the garage and the frustrations of dealing with unreliable contractors in Anchorage.

When they had finished the lasagna, everyone cleared their dishes to the kitchen. Daniel only ate half his meal.

Gertie retrieved dessert from the refrigerator, lifting the lid to reveal strawberries and blueberries atop thick Bavarian cream in small glass cups.

Daniel wandered over to the sofa and lay down.

"You okay, Daniel?" Eddie asked gently.

"Yeah, I'm just a little tired."

"You want to go home?"

"No, it's okay. I just want to lie here for a second."

Gertie and Becca brought over four plates.

"Daniel, are you having dessert?" Gertie asked, offering him a cup.

"No, I'm good," he replied listlessly.

"Maybe you should get him home, Eddie," Becca suggested.

"Yeah, we'll just finish dessert and head out."

"I'm okay; take your time, guys," Daniel said.

They started their desserts. "Oh, this is good. But I'll have to run extra laps tomorrow," Becca said.

"You're jogging now?"

"Figure of speech."

"Eat it in small bites," Gertie joked. "Not as many calories."

They finished their desserts quickly. Eddie stood up and went over to Daniel.

"Let's go, Daniel," he said softly.

"Shouldn't we help clean up?" the boy asked.

Eddie was getting the sense that Daniel seemed reluctant to leave. He knew what was waiting for him beyond the door of Becca's apartment.

"You guys will do no such thing. You need to get home. You have a big day tomorrow," Becca insisted. "Let me just pack some stuff for you," she added, moving to the kitchen to transfer the leftover lasagna into a container. Eddie followed her.

"Still okay with Lange doing his port?" Becca inquired.

"Yes. He keeps a picture of his older brother in his office, who was about the same age as Daniel when he died. Somehow that makes me feel especially good about him doing it."

"Interesting."

Eddie walked back into the living room. "Okay, Daniel, ready to go?"

"Yeah, okay," Daniel murmured, sounding more tired than ever.

Becca approached him and gave him a warm hug. "Good luck tomorrow."

She hugged Gertie and then Eddie, planting a kiss on his cheek.

"Thank you so much for a wonderful meal," Gertie said. "You're an absolute dear for having us over."

In the car, Daniel fell asleep during the ride home.

"I had a good time," Gertie said, breaking the silence. "A little bit of sunshine through the cloud hanging over us. Becca is a sweet woman. And after all she's been through."

"Yes, she seems to be coming through it," Eddie agreed.

ONCE HOME, they helped Daniel upstairs and tucked him into bed.

A few minutes later, Eddie received a text from her.

How's Daniel?

Fine. He's in bed, sleeping.

Okay. I enjoyed tonight, all things considered.

Me too.

Eddie?

Yes?

I'm very fond of you.

Me too. I mean I'm fond of you too.

I know what you meant, dumbass. What time is the procedure?

11, we have to be there at 9:30.

CU there.

61

PORT

For the second time in as many weeks, Eddie and Daniel entered the PAMC outpatient surgery center to find Becca waiting for them.

"Look, there's Becca," Daniel said.

She was sitting next to an electric fireplace, but she stood as they approached. She was carrying a plastic grocery bag.

Becca hugged Eddie and then took out a banana-like plushie with arms and legs and floppy ears.

"Here you go, Daniel—a new friend."

"Oh wow, it's Peely." Peely was one of the more popular skins in the Fortnite universe. Daniel took the figure and rubbed it against his cheek.

"Soft."

"It's a little something I thought you could decorate your room with."

"Thanks."

A Peely—not something you'd find at the spur of the moment in Anchorage at nine o'clock in the morning. This was a planned-out gift.

They were soon called back to a cubicle, where Daniel changed into a patient gown and reclined on a stretcher. He held on to his plushie. Eddie and Becca took chairs beside him.

A nurse started an IV in Daniel's left forearm. He winced slightly but remained calm.

Twenty minutes later, Lange entered the cubicle, dressed in scrubs.

"Hello, Daniel, I'm Dr. Lange. I'm here to put your port in," he said, offering an encouraging smile.

"Hi," Daniel said. "Wow. Where did you get that scar?"

Eddie and Lange exchanged glances. Lange smiled and seemed unfazed by Daniel's blunt comment on his scar.

"Childhood accident, a long time ago."

"I bet that hurt."

"A little."

"Dr. Lange, this is our friend, Rebecca Raven," Eddie said.

"As in the assistant medical examiner?"

"Yes, that one," Becca answered.

Lange smiled sympathetically. Of course, everyone in the medical community now knew who Dr. Raven was.

Lange turned his attention back toward Daniel.

"Daniel, I know you've had a port before. Do you need me to go over the procedure with you?"

"No, but do you think you can use the same incision?"

"I can certainly try. You and I will check things out with the ultrasound when you get in the OR."

Talking to the boy about the ultrasound in a familiar manner. Dr. Blake must have informed him of Daniel's intelligence, medical knowledge, and neurodivergence.

"What about you, Detective? Do you need me to go over the procedure or the risks?"

"No, I'm good."

"Infection, bleeding, puncture of the lungs, thrombosis of the veins," Daniel said.

Lange laughed. "Hey, don't scare your surgeon just before the procedure."

Daniel chuckled. "You're not scared."

"Okay, if there are no more questions, I'll see you in the OR, Daniel."

.   .   .

FIFTEEN MINUTES LATER, two attendants came for Daniel.

"Can I take Peely with me?" he asked them.

"Sure," one of the attendants said.

Eddie leaned over to give him a peck on the forehead. "See you on the other side, son. I love you."

Becca gave Daniel a fist bump. "You'll do great."

THEY ROLLED DANIEL, clutching Peely, into the operating room.

"There he is," Grayson said, who was there to greet him, standing on one side of the OR table. He helped the attendants transfer Daniel to the OR table. The room was cool and bright, filled with the sharp scent of antiseptic and the soft whir of equipment.

Frank, the anesthesiologist, in his mid-sixties, played hits from his generation at a low volume through his phone connected to speakers on his anesthesia cart. Don Henley's voice sang "Hotel California," the familiar melody oddly comforting in the sterile environment.

"Okay, Daniel, you and Peely hop on over," Grayson said.

"You know this is Peely?"

"Sure, doesn't everyone?"

Daniel slid from the gurney to the operating room table.

"Okay, Daniel, let's check out your veins."

Grayson pulled down his gown to expose the right upper chest, revealing a jagged scar where his previous port had been placed.

"We both have scars, don't we?" Daniel replied.

Grayson gave a little chuckle. "We do."

"I guess you could call us scar mates."

Grayson held up his hand. "Gimme five, Scarbro."

"Ha! Scarbros, I like that even better, Dr. Lange!"

"Hey, we're scarbros. You call me Grayson."

Daniel flashed a wide grin. "Sure, Grayson."

The doctor picked up a bottle of ultrasound gel. "Cold, Daniel."

Grayson squeezed gel on the right side of Daniel's neck and upper chest, then placed the ultrasound probe on Daniel's neck.

"Let's see what we got, Daniel."

Moving grayscale images appeared on the monitor. "There's your internal jugular vein, nice and open." He pushed down, and the vein collapsed. "Open with good compressibility."

As Grayson scanned, Daniel noticed the tattooed number on his forearm. "What do the numbers on your tattoo mean, Grayson?"

"After college, I climbed Mount Everest. That's my summit number."

"Cool."

"Okay, Daniel, I'm putting you to sleep now," Frank said.

Grayson held Daniel's hand. "Pick out a good dream. And don't worry about Peely. We'll take good care of him for you."

Once Daniel was under, Grayson took the plushie from Daniel's arm and set it on a shelf. He stood by Daniel until Frank intubated him.

Grayson went out to scrub, then returned and donned a gown, and pulled on sterile gloves. He painted Daniel's right neck and upper chest with betadine antiseptic and draped the area with sterile sheets. With the help of the circulating nurse, he placed the ultrasound probe into a sterile, clear plastic cover.

"Hotel California" faded out, and Queen's "Another One Bites the Dust" began playing through the speakers.

"'Another One Bites the Dust.' In the OR? Really, Frank?" the circulating nurse called out, laughing. "Wrong on two levels: One, dust in the OR. And two, the metaphor of biting it."

Frank chuckled, grabbed his phone, and switched to "Peaceful Easy Feeling."

"Back to the Eagles, better?"

"Much," the scrub tech said, as she organized instruments.

"How about a little T-burg, Frank?"

Grayson was referring to the Trendelenburg position, in which the patient lies supine, with the body tilted downward from the feet to the head. Frank pushed a button, and the OR table tilted slightly head down. This would help Daniel's internal jugular vein distend and make it an easier target.

Using ultrasound guidance, he located the internal jugular vein at the base of the neck, just above the collarbone. He introduced a needle attached to a syringe into the vein through the skin of the neck towards the chest at a 30-degree angle. Applying backward pressure on the plunger, he pushed the needle, which appeared bright white on the ultrasound screen, and guided it into the vessel, which appeared as a dark column running through the soft tissues of the neck. Dark red blood rushed back into the syringe, confirming successful access. "We're in," he announced, maintaining his characteristic calm.

"Take It Easy" played softly as Grayson worked with practiced efficiency. He made a small incision, passed a sheath dilator over the wire, pulled the wire and dilator out, and capped the sheath. Next, he made a transverse incision through the old scar, then fashioned a pocket beneath the skin.

"Call for the C-arm, please."

With the pocket prepared, he tunneled a catheter from it through the tiny neck incision. He measured carefully, ensuring the catheter would extend properly down the internal jugular vein into the superior vena cava, just above the right atrium of the heart. He threaded the catheter through the sheath, peeling the sheath away as he advanced it. After trimming the protruding end of the catheter, he attached it to the port chamber.

An X-ray tech arrived with the C-arm imager—perfect timing. She positioned it over Daniel's chest and pressed the pedal. The image showed the catheter tip precisely where it needed to be, just above the junction of the superior vena cava and right atrium.

"Looks good," Grayson said, thanking the X-ray tech as she wheeled the C-arm out.

He drew back on a syringe through the chamber to verify blood return, confirming proper function. Satisfied, he secured the chamber in the pocket with a stitch. Using a precise technique a plastic surgeon would approve of, he trimmed the scar edges around the incision and closed it with dissolvable sutures that would leave a fine line once healed.

Grayson applied surgical adhesive over the incision to aid healing.

"Huber needle, please," he requested. The specialized right-angled needle, with its eight-inch tubing and IV connector, appeared in his hand. He inserted it through Daniel's skin into the port chamber, secured it with a transparent dressing, and confirmed function with a final blood draw and flush.

EDDIE AND BECCA looked up to see Lange approaching them in the waiting area.

"We're all done. Daniel did great; he's in Stage Two recovery. I'll take you to him."

Eddie and Becca exchanged a surprised look. Most surgeons wouldn't take the time to escort a parent to recovery personally.

They rounded a corner to find Daniel sitting up on a stretcher holding Peely. A cup with a bent straw rested on the Mayo stand beside him.

"There's Daniel," Lange said, placing his hand on Eddie's shoulder.

"Thanks again, Doctor," he said. "Hey, son, how did it go?"

"Great. I didn't feel anything. And thanks for using the same incision, Grayson."

"Not a problem."

"So it's Grayson now?" Eddie said, smiling.

"Yeah, we're scarbros since we both have scars."

"Cool," Eddie replied, smiling at the doctor, who winked back.

Lange provided post-op wound care instructions, concluding with, "I'll be happy to remove it when the time comes."

"Yes, I want you to do it, Grayson."

"You got it." Grayson pulled out his wallet, extracted a business card, wrote down his mobile number, and handed it to Daniel. "You call me, anytime day or night, that's what a Scarbro is for. In the meantime, Dr. Blake will let me know when it's time for the port to come out." He took out another card and handed it to Eddie.

He held up his hand. "Gimme another five, Daniel."

Daniel smiled and gave an enthusiastic slap.

Eddie's eyes followed Lange as he moved through the post-op area, exchanging brief pleasantries with various hospital staff who greeted him with admiring smiles.

Lange seem to understood exactly what to say to my frightened child, Eddie thought, *perhaps because of his own childhood horrors.*

"I like him," Daniel said as Lange walked away. "He held my hand as they were putting me to sleep. He made me feel safe."

Eddie also appreciated that Lange had not mentioned the investigation and had instead focused on keeping Daniel comfortable. That was a classy move.

"Before they knocked me out, I asked about that number on his arm. He climbed Mount Everest, and everyone who reaches the top gets a summit number. That's his."

Eddie thought, given the challenges of Lange's life, that Everest seemed like the easiest summit for him to conquer.

62

PERIWINKLE

"Becca, do you know how vincristine works?"

"Yes. It disrupts the microtubules during cell division. It's like throwing a wrench into the machinery of cancer cells while they're trying to reproduce."

"That's exactly right." Daniel smiled as if Becca were his prize student. "Did you know it takes one ton of dried periwinkle leaves to produce an ounce of vincristine?"

"You'd think they'd make it synthetically these days," she said.

"They can, but it's a complicated molecule, and its precise stereochemistry makes it very expensive to produce in large amounts."

"What's stereochemistry?" Eddie asked.

They were in his room in the children's ward at PAMC following the insertion of his Mediport. Daniel sat in his bed. Peely lay next to him. Daniel held up his hands.

"Look at my hands. They look the same, but if you try to put a left-hand glove on my right hand, it wouldn't fit. That's stereochemistry, basically. Except with vincristine, imagine hands with twenty fingers.

Robin, the nurse, entered with a small 50 cc IV bag containing vincristine. Eddie felt his chest tighten at the sight of the bag of clear fluid.

On the IV pole next to Daniel, the liter bag of lactated Ringer's was empty.

"Good, the fluid is in—you should be well hydrated. Ready to get started?"

"I don't really have a choice, so yeah," Daniel said.

They had hydrated him with IV fluids to help the kidneys flush out the toxic metabolites of the vincristine.

"Last time, my BUN and creatinine stayed stable the whole time," Daniel told the nurse.

"Oh wow, you know what BUN and creatinine are?"

"Yeah, they measure kidney function."

"So you're an old pro at this."

"Yes, unfortunately."

From Daniel's prior leukemia treatment, Eddie knew chemotherapy was a double-edged sword. One blade would wreak havoc on his son's body; the other would, hopefully, save him once more.

Robin hung the IV bag on the pole, connected it to IV tubing that ran through an infusion pump, punched in a rate of 100 cc/hour, and started programming it.

"I saw this forensics show. A researcher killed his wife by injecting a fatal dose of intrathecal vincristine," Daniel said.

"Creepy, Daniel." Eddie shook his head. "What does intrathecal mean?"

"Into the spinal fluid. Drugged her drink first, injected while she was passed out."

"Horrible way to go," Becca offered.

"Really, guys?" Eddie said.

"Yes, paralysis, respiratory failure, excruciating pain, neurological deterioration, and death within forty-eight hours," Daniel said, ignoring his father.

"Of course, she received hundreds of times the dose you're getting."

"Yeah, I know."

"There are at least three reports of murder by vincristine in the literature."

"Amazing," Daniel said.

Becca nodded. "Pretty clever of the detectives to figure it out."

"Dad, I'm sure you would have figured it out, right?"

"Yes."

"With Becca's help, of course."

"I must say," the nurse said as she finished up, "this is the most, uh, interesting family conversation I've heard in a while."

It pleased Eddie that no one corrected her on the "family" part.

"My dad's a homicide detective, and Becca is a forensic pathologist, so we're used to it."

"You know the number one mistake criminals make, like this researcher did?" Eddie asked.

"What?"

"Thinking they're smarter than law enforcement. It's hard to murder someone you're connected to and get away with it."

The nurse laughed and said, "Good, I'll tell my husband that."

She waited until the fluid filled the IV tubing and was just about to emerge from the tubing connected to the Huber needle.

"Okay," she said. "We're off and running." Robin left.

"Speaking of off and running," Becca said, standing, "I have to get back to the office."

She gave Eddie a peck on the cheek and tussled Daniel's hair.

"I'll see you guys later."

After she left, Daniel asked his dad, "Are you guys in love?"

The question made him squirm. Declaring love for each other was something Eddie and Becca had not done. They expressed affection for each other and had become "a couple," but were they in love?

Eddie cleared his throat. "You know, Daniel, love is a very complicated emotion. It's like a seed you plant and nurture. And with time, that seed becomes a full plant. So I would put it this way: Becca and I have planted the seeds, and the plants seem to be growing."

"Okay, I'll take that as a maybe."

Daniel put his head back on the pillow, brought Peely up to his chest, and closed his eyes. His lips formed a slight smile.

In addition to vincristine, Daniel was treated with several other drugs with impossible names, such as asparaginase and daunorubicin, to kill cancer cells and induce remission, which means no detectable cancer cells.

Induction chemotherapy, Eddie knew, was a dance with death. It not only wiped out the cancer cells but also killed the normal blood-forming ones in the bone marrow, causing profound anemia and wiping out the patient's immune system. The protocol sent the patient and the cancer over the cliff and then snapped the patient back from the abyss, leaving the cancer to plummet into oblivion—at least if it worked.

Eddie received a text message from Polkovich: *My office today 4 p.m. Let me know if you can't make it.*

"Daniel, I need to go into the office at four today. Will you be okay with that?"

"Dad, I told you, I don't need you hanging around twenty-four seven."

AT FOUR SHARP, Eddie sat across from Polkovich's desk. Peggy Engstrom from Human Resources occupied the chair beside him, a folder resting in her lap.

"What's going on with Daniel—his treatment? How long do you expect him to be in the hospital?" Danek asked.

"He started chemo today. About four to six weeks for the initial treatment, a break at home, then back in for another few weeks. Depends on complications."

"How much time will you take off?"

"Daniel's older now. He doesn't want me hanging around too much, so it's hard to say. I'm hoping not to need a family medical leave like last time. Trying not to drain the savings account." Eddie knew he was eligible for twelve weeks of family medical leave, but it would mean going without a salary.

"Peggy? What have you got for Detective Vaugner?"

Peggy opened her folder.

"Things are different now than a few years ago when Daniel was last sick. We have a leave-sharing program where employees can donate sick leave or personal days to other employees."

"Okay," Eddie said.

"Word got out about Daniel. Your fellow detectives and the rest of the department got together and donated one day of paid personal leave each. Combined with your sick leave and personal leave, you have 90 days you can take at full pay. They've all pledged to donate more if needed."

"No, I couldn't do that. What if they need it?"

"Yeah," Polkovich said, "they knew you'd say that. That's why they did it before you could object."

"It's done, Detective," Peggy said. "All the forms are filled out. Unused leave will either stay in a pool for others or revert to the donors. But for now, it's all yours."

"I don't know what to say."

"Just say thank you," Polkovich said.

Peggy beamed. "It's nice when HR can do something positive that everyone supports."

"Do I have to take it all at once?"

"No, you can take it as you need it."

"Anything else, Peggy?"

"No, that's it."

"Thank you."

"Okay," Polkovich said, "stick around, Eddie; I have something else to discuss with you."

Peggy gathered her folder and left.

"What about the priest case?" he asked. "Dracule. Any progress?"

Eddie shook his head. "No, to be honest."

"I saw you ordered a DNA match on the priest and Dr. Lange."

"Yes."

"Why?"

Eddie gave him a recap of Defner's injuries and the parallels between Dracule and Gower.

"But DNA confirms no relation."

"So you got no motive."

"I guess not."

"And you got no means."

"Uh, no, not really."

"So Lange, in or out as a suspect?"

"Right now, uh, I'd say out."

"Okay. I'm going to clear it off the board. Still an open case, but no longer an active investigation."

"Sounds good," Eddie said. Dracule off the murder board the day Lange bonded with Daniel. Coincidental irony? Or does the universe tell you something sometimes?

ON THE THIRD HOSPITAL DAY, Eddie came into the room, accompanied by Chik. Daniel was propped up in his hospital bed playing Fortnite. Chik wore a mask and had cleared the symptoms check all visitors go through. The afternoon sun streaming through the window fell across Daniel's dark hair.

"Hi, Uncle Chik!"

"Hey, kiddo," Chik said, pulling up a chair. "How's it going?"

"Not too bad, yet."

"I brought you something." Chik reached into his jacket pocket and pulled out a small package wrapped in brown paper. He handed the package to Daniel, who carefully unwrapped it, revealing the cream-colored amulet hanging from the leather cord that Inuksuk had given Chik when he was shot.

"Whoa," Daniel said. He held the ivory piece up to the light and turned to catch the rays at different angles. "This is cool. It kinda looks like a Star Trek communicator badge—on the original series, that is."

"I think it's supposed to be a bear," Chik said. "It's carved from a walrus tusk. It's worn for protection and healing." Chik's voice carried a hint of awkwardness, caught between his modern skepticism and respect for his heritage. "My father-in-law, Inuksuk, gave it to me when I was shot, and he thought I should give it to you."

Daniel put the amulet around his neck and looked down at it. "Yeah, I like it, but it doesn't really heal people, does it?"

"It can't hurt, right? Look, here I am after getting shot."

"Yeah, but I think that was Dr. Lange. I suppose it could be both."

"Inuksuk would say it connects you to ancient wisdom and strength. At the very least, like you said, it looks pretty cool."

"It's okay with him that you're giving it to me?"

"Oh yes, he insisted on it. He would have given it to you himself, but he's back in Denmark."

How do you say 'thank you' in Inuit?" Daniel asked as he looked down at the amulet.

"*Qujannamiik*," pronounced slowly.

"Tell Inuksuk, koo-ya-na-meek, and that I'm going to wear it every day."

ONCE AGAIN, like he had four years ago, Eddie watched the chemotherapy take its expected toll on Daniel. It seemed cruel and unfair that Daniel had to endure this torture a second time. The universe had already extracted its pound of flesh; why did it demand more?

First, Daniel became profoundly anemic as he could not produce red blood cells and was transfused.

After the first week, Daniel's absolute neutrophil count dropped from its normal of 5,500 to below 500, creating a condition called neutropenia, which Daniel referred to as being "neutropunylike." He was started on antimicrobial agents, including antibiotics for bacteria, antifungals, and antivirals.

Eddie noticed his son's hair started falling out. A few strands at first, the clumps. Daniel noted that with the same clinical detachment he applied to everything else: "The chemotherapy targets rapidly dividing cells. Hair follicles divide every twenty-three to seventy-two hours, so naturally, they're collateral damage. Did you know that nose hairs serve an important filtering function? I hope they don't fall out, too."

The mucositis, a painful inflammation of his mouth and tongue, hit him harder this time—or so it seemed to Eddie—and made eating impossible.

Next, he developed hemorrhagic cystitis. Urination became painful and bloody, and a catheter was inserted into his bladder. Daniel accepted it with the same stoicism.

His platelets had fallen to zero, so he received platelet transfusions to prevent massive spontaneous bleeding.

There was also the incessant diarrhea. The same chemotherapy that wiped out his bone marrow prevented his colon from reproducing replacement cells, so his ability to reabsorb water—the colon's main function—was diminished. He continuously passed a thin, watery stool. This required extra IV hydration.

Daniel compared himself to a B-17 bomber flying a mission over Germany in World War II. "I'm getting hit by a lot of flak, but I keep flying. I'm going to complete my mission."

On day ten of Daniel's chemotherapy, his white blood cell count had fallen to zero as the four-week protocol continued. Sleep patterns, never Daniel's strong suit, were horrible. The anemia and metabolic stress made him extremely fatigued. The steroid pulses caused mood swings and insomnia. His complexion was pale and gray, his expression was glazed, he had dark circles under his eyes, and he walked with a shuffle. Daniel referred to this as his "zombie state" and joked that even Gertie could have beaten him in a face-off with a level-1 lightsword.

After four weeks, Daniel completed the protocol, and it was now a waiting game. He often referred to his neutrophil count as "flatlined," but a week later, there was a blip. His ANC was 120. As it continued to rise, his symptoms of neutropenia started improving.

The mucositis resolved, and he was able to swallow again, so the nasogastric tube was removed.

His diarrhea went down to only two or three bowel movements a day.

His urine cleared up, and the catheter was removed.

His headaches stopped.

.   .   .

"MIT HAS AN EXCELLENT MD-PHD PROGRAM," Becca said to Daniel.

They were sitting next to each other on the sofa bed in Daniel's room, and Eddie was sitting on the bed.

"What about Stanford? Closer to home," Eddie offered.

Dr. Blake entered the room.

"Good news, everyone. Daniel's ANC is at 480 this morning," he announced. "We're getting close to that magic 500."

Eddie noticed Becca taking Daniel's hand into hers. "Wonderful," she said. "Right on schedule." Her relationship with Daniel seemed to be slowly morphing into something more maternal.

"How are you feeling today, Daniel?"

"Less zombie-like," he replied.

"We need to get that count just a bit higher, but we're on the right track."

Eddie caught Becca's eye across the room. She glanced down at their joined hands, then back at him with a small, surprised smile. Progress. On all fronts. Was the universe throwing him a bone? Giving him something back? He tried not to think about it. One day at a time

63

A TIGHT GROUPING

At 10 a.m., Defner paid thirty dollars at Great North Shooting Range in Eagle River and was assigned Target 62. The range offered targets out to three hundred yards. He took an iPad out of the documents folder of his carrying case and logged on to the Longshot app. The range's Marksman camera system gave him clear views of the three-hundred-yard target. Once connected, he could toggle between close-up views of both targets to assess his shots and adjust his calculations.

From the range, Defner could see the Chugach mountains had completely greened with just a few wispy patches of snow protected by the shadows in hollows.

It was now four days past the Summer Solstice and the days were getting shorter. Ever so slightly at first, then with increasing rapidity. In a few weeks, the birch leaves would turn gold. After a brief fall, winter would come, bringing early darkness and the first snow before Halloween.

Lange wouldn't see the first leaf drop.

Defner's thoughts drifted briefly to Revus Roche, whose death had set him on this path. *Widowmaker lesion. Bah!* As sure as Satan went out from the presence of the Lord and afflicted Job with painful sores, Lange had caused the plaque that ended Pastor Roche's life.

He'd spent countless hours in prayer, seeking guidance. The Scripture spoke clearly to him: *Do not suppose that I have come to bring peace to the earth. I did not come to bring peace but a sword.*

As he set up his Desert Tech SRSA2, scope, and tripod, he reflected on his calling. The rifle wasn't just a weapon—it was an instrument of divine justice, like the sword of Gideon or the sling of David. *If you do not have a sword, sell your cloak and buy one*, Jesus had told his disciples in Luke 22:36. Defner had bought more than a sword; he'd acquired a weapon of righteous precision.

He lay in a prone position and bore-sighted the rifle by taking the bolt out of the barrel, looking from the breech down through the inside of the barrel. He positioned the gun so that the three-hundred-yard target was centered in the opening of the barrel. Next, being careful not to move the rifle, he looked through the scope. It was close. He only needed to move the scope two mils left and three mils down. He double-checked the sighting. Satisfied, he zeroed the horizontal and vertical turrets.

As he loaded .308 Winchester cartridges into the magazine, each insertion reminded him of feeding communion wafers into the mouths of the righteous. *The body of Christ.* Click. *The body of Christ.* Click.

The target had the rough shape of the torso and head of a human. As he put the crosshair in the middle of the head, he recited softly to himself, "Praise be to the Lord my Rock, who trains my hands for war, my fingers for battle," and pulled the trigger.

His first shot hit dead center of the target's head. The loud ping of the impact sent a shiver of satisfaction through him. He imagined Lange's skull shattering under the impact, ridding the world of the threat that lurked behind the facade of a compassionate surgeon. That night in the parking garage, Defner had seen the truth that others missed. It wasn't just chest pain or mitochondrial dysfunction; it was ancient evil loose in the modern world.

Four more shots followed, forming a tight group, three overlapping, the fourth barely a millimeter away. On his iPad, the cluster of holes looked like a single wound. The tightness of his grouping proved God was guiding his hands.

He thought of the Old Testament warriors, of David facing Goliath, of Ehud delivering Israel from evil. Did not the Lord go out before you? The fact that he'd encountered Lange—that he'd felt the dark power behind the surgeon's touch and survived when others had died —was his divine call to task.

As he packed up his gear, Defner's mind turned to the book of Esther, to her words about being placed in her position for such a time as this. He had been given his military service, his medical training, his shooting skills, and his ability to recognize evil—all for this purpose.

Defner put the rifle back into its case, carefully securing each component. Tomorrow, he would return to the hospital and be the emergency room doctor. In his dealings with Lange in the ER, he would continue to be polite and civil, but above all, he would be cautious. *Your adversary, the devil, prowls around like a roaring lion, seeking someone to devour.* Defner smiled with grim satisfaction.

At their final encounter, the devil would be the prey, not the hunter.

64

GOING HOME

Daniel sat on the edge of the bed, swinging his legs impatiently. Gertie was packing things up, placing items on the cart to take out to the car. They were waiting for Dr. Blake to come in and discharge him. Eddie scrolled through notes on his phone, trying to anticipate where defense counsel would try to trip him up during the upcoming cross-examination on a homicide case he'd investigated.

Daniel hadn't had a fever for a week, and he was tolerating eating by mouth. He was still vulnerable to infections, but his immune system was functional enough for him to go home.

Though still pale, he looked stronger than he had in weeks, and the alertness had returned to his eyes. The last pulse oximeter reading blinked steadily on his finger at 99 percent. The first battle in his second war against leukemia had been won.

Dr. Blake breezed in and sat in a chair. Eddie pocketed his phone.

"Well, Daniel, ANC is at 750 and hemoglobin at 8.3. The platelets are at 70,000, high enough that you won't have spontaneous bleeding, but you need to be careful about injuries. No contact sports, no rough-housing, nothing that could cause trauma."

"I guess that means no chainsaw juggling, Daniel," Eddie said.

"Not even if they're turned off?" Daniel asked, adjusting his Fortnite cap.

The boy keeping his dry sense of humor through the ordeal of chemo had been a source of comfort for Eddie.

"Not even. And with that hemoglobin," Dr. Blake said, "you'll still tire easily. Your low white count will leave you susceptible to infection, so no crowds, movies, or restaurants."

"No Village Inn? I'd love some waffles."

"I can make you waffles, Daniel, better than any restaurant," Gertie said.

"Good," the doctor said. "We don't want you getting sick and delaying your conditioning and transplant. You're essentially confined to home for now. And if anyone has even a hint of a cold—"

"I know," Daniel said. "Level 3 face masks."

"Exactly."

Gertie looked up from packing Daniel's things. "Dr. Blake, what about my garden? Should I stop like the last time?"

"For now, yes," he said. "And no bringing fresh plants or soil into the house and, Daniel, no playing around in the dirt."

"Because of the Aspergillus." Daniel nodded, the brim of his cap bobbing. "It's a fungus that lives in soil and can cause pneumonia in immunocompromised patients. You know why it's called Aspergillus?"

Dr. Blake shook his head. "I probably used to, but I don't now."

"Because under the microscope, it looks like an aspergillum, that thing priests used to sprinkle holy water."

A nurse came in with the wheelchair.

"Really? I can walk."

"Hospital policy for discharge, Daniel," the nurse said.

"They don't want a scammer falling to the floor, complaining he was too weak to walk, and then suing the hospital for back injuries," Eddie added. "Think of it as your chariot to freedom."

Daniel slid off the bed into the wheelchair, his movements still cautious. As he plopped down on the chair, his cap slipped forward, and he pushed it back with a thin hand. The NASA shirt hung loose on his frame from the weight loss during the treatment.

"A few more things," Dr. Blake added. "We'll have a nurse come by twice a week to check on you and draw blood. You'll need to continue the prophylactic antibiotics, and I want you on Acyclovir to prevent any viral infections. The pharmacy has them ready downstairs, so you can pick them up on your way out. For refills, they can transfer the prescription to your regular pharmacy if you want. And don't worry, our pharmacy is in your plan, so you'll have the same copay here."

As they wheeled Daniel toward the elevator, the staff who'd cared for him over the past weeks came out to say goodbye. Daniel had become a favorite on the floor, entertaining the nurses with random facts and corny puns.

In the elevator, Gertie adjusted Daniel's cap again—a grandmother's instinct to fuss. "Oh, I almost forgot." She reached into her purse, pulled out a gift card, and handed it to Daniel. "Here you go, Fortnite V-bucks. This should keep you occupied for a while."

"Wow. Eighty-nine dollars! Thanks, Grandma!"

The smile that spread across Daniel's face was still a bit thin and wan, but it was the most optimistic Eddie had seen in weeks.

65

A NEW MORNING RITUAL

"You cut the onions exactly right," Gertie commented, watching Becca's precise knifework.

"Becca's a forensic pathologist, Grandma," Daniel explained from the kitchen table. "She cuts up things all day for a living."

"Yeah, I bet she makes a great liver and onions! And she could get some for cheap!" Eddie quipped.

"Maybe with a nice Chianti and fava beans?" Becca laughed.

Even if Daniel didn't get the Hannibal Lecter joke, he couldn't help but laugh. "Gross, you guys!"

Daniel had come home from the hospital five days ago, and every evening Becca stopped by after work to help Gertie with dinner. Daniel spent most of his time in bed, but he made the effort to get downstairs in the evenings. As long as his energy would allow, he liked talking to Becca, even though walking up and down the stairs left him winded—more so than after his first transplant.

On a Friday night, the fifth night Daniel had been home, Becca lingered over a third—or was it a fourth?—glass of wine after Daniel had gone to bed.

"Oh, I can't drive like this. I'll take an Uber home," she said, pulling out her phone.

"Nonsense," Gertie said, gathering the dinner dishes. "The guest room is already made up. No sense in paying for a ride when we have plenty of room."

Becca's eyes found Eddie's. He smiled. "Well, you could. I mean, why not?"

Gertie showed Becca the guest room off the kitchen with its en suite bathroom. "I stayed here while they built my place over the garage. It's a nice, firm mattress, and you should be comfortable. There are towels and soap in the bathroom."

But after Gertie had gone up to bed, Becca put her arms around Eddie and gave him a deep kiss. "Tonight, I'd like to sleep where you sleep."

They looked at each other, knowing this was another step. They had slept together, but only at her apartment.

"You're in luck. I just so happen to have a spot open tonight."

He led her up to his bedroom. They quickly stripped, made love, and fell asleep. He thought of telling her that she was the first woman he'd had in his bed since Anne died, then thought better of it. Besides, she knew.

THE NEXT MORNING, like every morning at home, Eddie woke to the arpeggio playing on his phone—the same tune, the same time: 6 a.m. The sun had already been up for an hour. This morning was different, though. Eddie looked at Becca, scarcely believing she was lying in his bed. She was still sleeping, undisturbed by the alarm. A sliver of sunlight streaked across her red hair, which spread across his pillow.

He sat up carefully, not wanting to wake her. He grabbed his crutches and headed to the bathroom.

Sitting on the teak stool and showering, Eddie wondered if Becca would regret waking up in his bed. Was this an act of deeper commitment or a momentary lapse of a boundary caused by too much wine? He half expected her to be gone when he emerged from the bathroom.

Why did he keep finding it difficult to accept that Becca was in this for the long haul?

Clearly, she had done nothing but support him and his family. She seemed to love Daniel, and it was becoming clear that Becca was beginning to fill a maternal role.

It struck him.

He had lost this before. He was afraid of accepting it because he was afraid of losing it once again. A simple defense mechanism. *God, Vaugner, it's the oldest trick in the book: keep up the doubts to protect yourself.*

As he was ruminating, he caught a movement through the steamed glass of the shower. Becca had come into the bathroom. She opened the shower door and stepped in naked.

Eddie couldn't help himself. He grew hard.

"Is that a hard-on, or are you just glad to see me?"

"Yes," he said.

She came over to him, straddled his lap, pressed her breasts against his chest, and kissed him deeply. His hands found the curves of her waist. She raised herself slightly, took him in her hand, and lowered herself onto him. He slid in easily.

"God, you're wet."

"It's your fault."

She moved slowly at first, then with increasing urgency. Her fingers dug into his shoulders, her breath coming in short gasps against his ear. "Eddie," she whispered, "You're going to make me come."

The sound of her voice and her breaths in his ear pushed him over the edge, and he came inside her as she climaxed. "Oh, fuck!"

Afterward, they washed each other, laughing at nothing and everything. "Oh, you have a razor in here. Can I borrow it?"

"Sure."

As she shaved her legs, he stood up on his leg, reached around her, fondled her breasts, and gently pinched her nipples.

She giggled. "Stop it! I'm going to cut myself, and we'll have a *Psycho* shower scene!"

A feeling of warmth and joy spread through Eddie. It was hard for him to tell what excited him more: the erotic experience or the domestic intimacy.

He sat back down and admired her slick, wet body. She started shaving under her arms.

"Becca, you probably didn't want to hear this while you were shaving your pits—I love you."

"Oh, Eddie. I can't think of a more perfect time to hear it. I love you too."

They kissed once again.

HE WATCHED her dress in yesterday's clothes while he went through his morning routine: gel liner, stump sock, prosthesis. By now, Eddie removing his prosthesis and putting it back on was accepted as naturally as she accepted everything else about him and he about her.

A sudden wave of emotion hit him. Anne had stood in that same spot countless mornings, pulling on her work clothes. He had not expected this moment to affect him so strongly.

"You okay?" Becca asked.

"Yeah."

Becca turned to face him.

"You don't need to forget what Anne was to you. And from what I know about Anne, she would want you to be happy."

"Yes, she would. She really would."

She crossed to him and touched his face. "We can take it as slow as you need."

He covered her hand with his. "No, this feels right. Different, but right. But thanks."

He completed his usual routine. From the jewelry box, he selected his cufflinks, reaching past the untouched gold crucifix. Then his shoulder holster, gun, badge, and blazer

They moved quietly through the upstairs hallway, pausing at Daniel's door. Eddie opened it just enough to check on his son. Becca peered in over Eddie's shoulder. The Einstein poster looked down at them. The quote about infinity and human stupidity made Becca smile. Daniel slept peacefully. Eddie noted some stubble on his scalp. The crucifix above his bed still tilted slightly to the left.

It was the same routine. But different.

Gertie sat at the kitchen table, drinking coffee. When Eddie and Becca walked in, they felt like two teenagers who had been caught making out on the front porch. They shot each other mock guilty glances.

They poured coffee and joined Gertie at the table.

She looked at them and said, with a straight face, "I see I won't have to change the sheets in the guest room." She waited a beat. "So thank you for that."

The three of them shared a laugh. Another boundary dissolved.

66

RECON

Late in August, the light snow capped the Chugach Mountains. Anchoragites would start to argue if this was "termination dust" marking the end of summer. How deep must the snow be? How long should it last? If it melts, and then when the snow reappears, is the new snow termination dust? Is termination dust the first cap that appears or the last one that doesn't melt away?

No matter what, termination dust was the perfect sign for Defner and his task at hand.

He drove slowly past the empty lot on Lake Campbell he had picked out on Google Maps, evaluating the area with a sniper's eye. He had rented a nondescript gray Toyota Camry for this mission. The lot was nearly perfect—two acres of mature birch and spruce directly across from Lange's lakeside home. An eight-foot chain-link fence enclosed three sides down to the water. It was a mixed blessing. He would have to scale it, making him slightly more vulnerable to being spotted, but on the plus side, it would deter wanderers. Many wooded lots around Anchorage had become refuges for the homeless or places for kids to smoke pot.

He circled the block twice more, noting the distance to the nearest houses, the pattern of streetlights, and the placement of security cameras and video doorbells on neighboring properties. He then pulled over briefly to check property records on his phone. The lot belonged to a development company based in Seattle—there were no local owners to worry about.

HE RETURNED at 2 a.m. The Alaskan late-summer night was as dark as it would get, a dim sky known as nautical twilight. Dark enough to see stars but still light enough to distinguish the horizon. He'd parked his car down a side street with a clear line of sight to the lot.

He waited a few minutes. At that hour, traffic was scant. When it was clear, he moved quickly from the car, dressed in black tactical gear and carrying a black duffel bag. He crossed the street and reached the fence unseen. The bag went over first, making a soft thump in the tall grass on the other side. He took the fence in three smooth movements —jump, grab, pull—skills embedded in his military training.

He moved quickly into the woods, then squatted motionless and listened. All quiet. No dogs barking. No automatic lights turning on.

The canopy blocked out most of the dim ambient light. He reached into his duffel, took out his dual-tube night vision goggles, fitted them on his head, and turned them on. The night turned into a green dusk.

Moving through, the ground sloped gradually toward the lake. As he walked through the lot, he scrutinized the ground around him. No empty beer cans, no cigarette butts, no food wrappers or condom packets—none of the usual signs that local teenagers used the lot as a party spot. Excellent. The absence of such debris meant less chance of unexpected company during his surveillance.

Near the water's edge, he found a natural sniper's hide created by a fallen spruce. The trunk and root ball provided cover, and branches still bearing needles offered concealment. He took out his rangefinder. 298 yards to the railing of Lange's back deck. Perfect.

And my God will supply every need of yours according to his riches in glory in Christ Jesus.

Defner took off his goggles and settled into position for two hours, letting his senses attune to the environment. The lake water lapped quietly against the shore. An occasional car passed on the main road. Their headlights cast dappled light through the woods, too broken up to make out a person. He heard no voices.

From Lange's house, the only illumination was from two backyard deck lights. The house was dark, and his plane was in its slip. He imagined Lange sleeping in his bed. He'd love to sneak into his home and cut his throat, but after the incident in the garage, three hundred yards was as close as he wanted to get to him. Perhaps the surgeon wasn't home but at the hospital, carrying on his masquerade as a healer. No matter, tonight was just reconnaissance. He had Lange's surgical call schedule, so when the time came, he would know what days he would have a greater chance of being home. He was no fool; he knew it would take some providence for Lange to be at home and to be in a position where Defner could take the shot.

To everything, there is a season and a time to every purpose under heaven.

The surgeon's time would come.

Around 4 a.m., satisfied with his reconnaissance, Defner prepared to leave. He cached the duffel containing his sniper gear under the spruce trunk—water, energy bars, extra ammunition, sniper scope, the tripod, a tarp in case of rain, and camouflage netting. On his next trip, the rifle would be the only item he would have to carry over the fence. He carefully layered fallen leaves and forest debris around and over the cache, ensuring it looked undisturbed. Next time, he would settle in for the night and wait for daylight to take the shot he knew would come.

God had provided this perfect position; He would provide the perfect moment.

When He opens a door, no one can close it.

67

CROWS

Ten days after discharge, Daniel was gaining some strength, his color had continued to improve, and his blood counts had gone up. Blake said everything was on schedule for the conditioning and bone marrow transplant phase.

Morning light streamed through the kitchen windows as Daniel sat at the table, his laptop open beside an empty plate. He ate his entire breakfast of pancakes and bacon—another sign of progress. Becca sat next to him, drinking coffee and tapping on her laptop.

Eddie entered and poured himself a cup.

"Check this out, guys," Daniel said. His voice was stronger, and his eyes had started to regain their bright, curious intensity. "Scientists have discovered something amazing called quantum tunneling. Imagine you're in Fortnite, and you're trapped behind a solid metal wall. In everyday Fortnite physics, there's no way through that wall—you're stuck. But in quantum Fortnite physics, there is a slight chance that the player could suddenly appear on the other side of the wall without breaking it or going over it as if they had 'tunneled' straight through the solid barrier without disturbing it or themselves. That's like what particles do in quantum tunneling. They can pass through barriers that they shouldn't be able to."

"So you, or these particles, just, what, walk through walls?" Eddie asked.

"Not exactly walk, but yes! And here's the really mind-bending part —everything in our world, including the stuff we want to move with our minds, is made up of tiny particles that follow quantum rules. Our brains also work with tiny electrical signals and chemicals that operate at this quantum level."

"So when you think about influencing things through walls—it's not entirely impossible from a quantum perspective?" Becca said.

"If our brainwaves could somehow learn to interact with the quantum properties of matter—you know, the dual wave-particle theory—that would be like having a secret remote control that works through the quantum world!"

"Here we are at quantum doctors again," Becca joked, taking a sip of her coffee.

"You mean like telekinesis?" Eddie said. "Like that Geller guy."

"No, Dad, telekinesis is not a real thing. Quantum physics doesn't allow for the bending of spoons and that sort of fake stuff. But wave-particle interaction? That's different."

Eddie perked up. "I just thought of something, Daniel. All this quantum stuff. I wonder if this could be the god of tomorrow you were wondering about."

"Hey. Could be. Maybe God isn't in heaven. Maybe God is in the quantum world. I mean, quantum physics shows us that everything— really, everything—is connected in ways we can't see yet."

"Maybe those people who believed in animism knew more than we give them credit for," Eddie said, remembering his discussion with Daniel a few months ago.

His mind flashed to the Redeemer surveillance footage he'd watched dozens of times: the bearded man behind the panel, the priest behind the wooden door, that burst of inexplicable static across the screen. Just two men separated by a slab of wood, like particles separated by space, yet somehow connected, affecting each other, with the priest on the losing end.

Becca glanced out the window at the sunlight streaming across the yard. "It's a beautiful day. Why don't we take our coffee out to the deck? A little fresh air and sunshine might do us all good."

"Okay," Daniel said.

They gathered their mugs and moved to the back deck. Becca and Daniel stood at the deck railing, while Eddie took a seat on the chaise lounge. He admired how the oblique sunlight played on Becca's red hair.

"You cold, Daniel?" Becca asked.

"No, I'm good. It feels nice."

He looked at Becca, squinting and using a hand as a visor. "Hey, Becca, remember our conversation about quantum entanglement? Those quantum sensors?"

"Yes."

"I've been reading more about them. They've developed these quantum sensors using NV—nitrogen vacancy—in diamond crystals, where they replace two adjacent carbon atoms, one with nitrogen and the other with an empty space. Are you familiar with that?"

"Daniel, I'm just a forensic pathologist." Becca laughed. "You're talking way above my pay grade. How do they make them?"

"They fire nitrogen atoms into pure diamonds. Anyway, these are extremely sensitive magnetic field detectors. And since cancer cells have a different metabolism than normal cells, they create their own magnetic signatures. So these NV diamond center sensors can detect cancer less than a millimeter in size, or maybe individual cancer cells at some point. Much sooner than when we can see them now."

Becca paused. "Wow. I can't even imagine how they would do that."

Daniel contemplated for a moment. "Imagine using Einstein's spooky action to detect cancer early and save lives. I wonder what he would say about that?"

"I sink eets vunderbar, no metter vut de heck you are talking about!" Becca joked in her best Einstein impression, making Daniel laugh.

Two ravens lit on the fence and cawed. Daniel turned his head to look at them.

"One crow sorrow, two crows joy," Becca said.

"They're not really crows, Becca. They're ravens." Daniel chuckled. "You, of all people, should know that."

Becca laughed and looked over at Eddie. "I know, Mister Smarty-Pants, but the poem doesn't work with ravens."

"They don't migrate, you know. They hang around all winter."

One of the ravens took off, leaving one behind. The remaining one bobbed its head a few beats, cawed, and then took off.

"Hey, Becca?"

"Yes, Daniel?"

"I'm glad you're living with us. Do you think you'll stay?"

"Daniel, I'm a raven, remember? I don't migrate."

Becca turned back toward Eddie. His eyes met hers across the deck, and in that moment, without words, he allowed himself the possibility that this was really becoming something permanent. Something, well, like a family.

68

A GLINT

Roche, through his ministry, had pulled him from the pit of his cocaine and fentanyl addictions, giving him purpose through the American Salvation Church. Defner even saw his one weakness, his fondness for cocaine, as a blessing. Yes, he still snorted it occasionally for fun or energy when he needed it, but not like before, when it was a constant presence in his life. He was riding the demon; the demon was not riding him. This was a testament to his faith. And since the incident with Lange, he'd snorted it several times and had no chest pain. So it wasn't the coke; it was Lange.

Soon, he would avenge the death of Reverend Roche. Lange may have fooled everyone, but Defner knew better. *LAD lesion, bullshit.* Lange had reached through prison walls as easily as he had reached into Defner's chest that night in the parking garage. But with an important difference: *Lange killed Roche, but I survived.*

Just as the Lord saved Samson from the lion, He had saved Defner for his purpose—nothing could stop him now.

Like his recon mission, he had parked across from Lake Campbell at 2 a.m., this time in a nondescript Nissan Sentra. After making sure the coast was clear, he opened the trunk, pulled out the Desert Tech

SRSA2 with its scope in its case, strapped it to his back, crossed the street, and scaled the fence.

In the green light of his night-vision goggles, he made it to the fallen spruce and could see his lair had not been disturbed. He retrieved his cached duffel bag and then settled in for the night to await the dawn.

Joy comes in the morning.

THE SUN HAD BEEN UP since 4:30 a.m., and across Lake Campbell, two bodies stirred simultaneously beneath cotton sheets in a room darkened by blackout curtains. Jennifer and Grayson woke as they often did with their doctors' internal clocks, at around 6 a.m.

Grayson traced the curve of Jennifer's spine with his fingertips, feeling her arch into his touch. She turned to face him, her leg sliding between his, her mouth finding his. Her thigh felt his erection. Their lovemaking was unhurried and comfortable—the peaceful rhythm of bodies that knew each other well. .

"Stay in bed," Grayson said afterward, kissing her shoulder before pulling on sweatpants. "I'll make coffee."

He padded to the kitchen and ground the beans of Jennifer's favorite coffee: Kaladi Brothers Red Goat blend. While the coffee brewed, he settled at his computer for his morning ritual: the *New York Times* crossword puzzle. The smell of coffee filled the house.

Jennifer appeared in the doorway, wearing gray sweatpants and one of his T-shirts. Her dark hair was tousled from their lovemaking. She crossed to him and dropped a kiss on his temple. "The coffee smells amazing."

"Red Goat."

"Bless you."

She poured herself a cup and walked to the deck doors. "What a glorious morning," she said, sliding them open and stepping out into the crisp air.

. . .

AT FIRST LIGHT, Defner had taken out his vial of coke and snorted a few hits. He wanted to be alert and ready. Then he waited.

Finally! Movement over at the Lange house.

Through his spotter's scope, Defner watched a woman emerge onto the deck. Her thin T-shirt and sweatpants reminded him of how Lange had corrupted everything around him with unholy influence. He could make out her erect nipples. He felt himself starting to get hard.

"Then out came a woman to meet him, dressed like a prostitute and with crafty intent," Defner muttered. "Yeah, I'd tap that."

He picked up his rifle and rested it across the tree trunk. Looking through the scope, he acquired the woman's smug, smiling, beautiful face. He moved the scope to center the bulge of one her nipples in his crosshairs. "Pow." Then he panned right to center the other one. "Pow."

He ignored his stirrings, maintaining the discipline of an ascetic, hoping Grayson would soon join her.

GRAYSON GOT up from the table and went into the kitchen to pour another cup of coffee. Through the window, he admired Jennifer's shape from behind as she looked out across the lake.

Jennifer stepped back inside, heading for the coffee pot. As she poured, a smile came to her face.

"Grayson, remember when you mentioned leaving Alaska, setting up practice in the Lower 48?"

He leaned against the counter. "Yeah, I've been thinking about it more lately."

"What's holding you back?"

"Well, I've established myself here. My patients, my reputation. Starting over isn't simple." He sipped his coffee. "But then again, there are advantages. Being closer to you, obviously. New mountains to explore. The Cascades, Mount Rainier, Olympic Peninsula."

"Well, it so happens, I heard something interesting at the hospital yesterday." She poured some cream into her coffee. "I've heard rumors of a surgeon in private practice thinking about retiring sometime this year or the next and might be looking to sell his practice."

"Seattle would be nice," he said, finding himself warming to the idea. "More restaurants. No six-month winters. And"—he reached out to touch her face—"no more long-distance relationship."

Jennifer laughed. "Grayson, that's the one advantage of having you here."

"Very funny."

She walked out to the deck, then yelled out, "More seriously, you could still have a lake! Lake Washington has some lovely homes, and I know you could afford it. But hey, no pressure."

As he was admiring Jennifer's form, his eye was at the perfect angle for his averted vision to catch it—a brief flash of light from the empty lot across the lake.

His mind flashed briefly to eye physiology. The central retina, which had more cone cells, was used for colors and details. The peripheral retina had more rod cells, which were much more sensitive to light and movement but less precise. Most likely, it was an evolutionary advantage to provide warning of advancing predators. Astronomers and stargazers use this feature of the retina and use averted vision, as it was called, to detect dimmer objects in the sky.

He scanned the woods. There, again. Like sunlight reflecting off glass from inside the woods. Is someone spying on us?

Moving casually, he retrieved the binoculars from the living room shelf and went back into the kitchen. Standing away from the window, he lifted the binoculars. Set back into the woods, he could make out the dark shape of a head behind what could only be a sniper scope.

Defner. It had to be Defner. In an instant, it became clear. The smirks. The smarmy politeness. All a ruse to hide his murderous intent.

Keeping his voice light and cheery, he called out, "Hey, Jenn, can you come back in a second?"

Grayson headed to the bedroom. He heard Jennifer opening and closing the screen door. "I'm in the bedroom!"

He started changing into jeans and a T-shirt. When Jennifer came in, she had pulled her shirt off and was bare-breasted as Grayson was pulling a pair of jeans up to his waist. Next, he grabbed a long-sleeved sweatshirt.

"Oh, I thought we were— Going somewhere?"

"Listen to me carefully," Grayson said, slipping on a long-sleeved tee. "Stay in the house. Do not go outside, do not go out on the deck, and do not stand near any windows."

Jennifer laughed nervously. "What's going on?"

He went to the closet and pulled out a pair of Skechers and stepped into them.

"There may be a sniper across the lake. Maybe with a gun."

"What the fuck, Grayson—call the police."

"For now, please just do what I ask." His tone left no room for argument.

She followed him as he moved quickly to the garage and got into his Q7. He started to back out, noting Jennifer standing there, arms akimbo, still topless, with her mouth slightly agape. As the door lowered, he saw her lips tighten, and she turned to go back into the house. He hoped she would stay inside, out of view of Defner's scope.

69

A TWIG SNAPS

What the hell was Lange doing?

Sitting in his sniper's nest, his Desert Tech rifle resting on the fallen spruce, Defner was growing impatient. The morning dew had soaked through his camouflage pants, and he had been alternating between sitting and kneeling on the ground cover. Mosquitos were buzzing around him but not alighting, thanks to his repellent.

It was a beautiful morning—they should have been out on the deck.

After all, it was August, and the summer was winding down quickly.

Maybe he's screwing his whore again. I should have taken her out or at least wounded the bitch. Lange would have rushed out to her, and I could have popped him as he was kneeling over her. If she comes again, I'll do it.

Minutes crawled by.

But they who wait for the Lord shall renew their strength.

He wondered if they went out—brunch at Charlie's Bakery or Snow City Café, perhaps.

There were fifteen hours of daylight today, so—

A twig snapped.

Defner swung around, rifle rising instinctively.

Lange stood there, hands at his sides, unfazed that Defner was pointing a sniper rifle at him.

He tried to squeeze the trigger, but his finger wouldn't respond.

Fuck me.

"You know, Defner, it was so simple. Judge not, and you will not be judged; condemn not, and you will not be condemned."

Terror welled up in Defner's chest—the same paralyzing fear he'd felt that night in the parking garage. He tried to speak, but his mouth didn't work.

The last words he heard were from his nemesis. "You poor fucker. You couldn't just be a halfway decent Christian, could you?"

WITHOUT PITY OR HESITATION, Lange watched Defner's eyes widen as he slowly, against his will, began to turn the rifle on himself. He whimpered as the barrel moved toward his face. Sweat broke out across his forehead as he fought against the invisible force controlling his movements. His arms shook with resistance, but the rifle kept moving.

The barrel pressed against his lips. Defner's eyes locked with Lange's, pleading. He tried shaking his head and keeping his mouth closed. But he shoved harder, splitting a lip and breaking teeth as he forced the barrel into his mouth.

Even though there wouldn't be much back splatter, Lange moved back a few steps.

It was a stretch, but the six-foot-four Defner's right arm extended along the rifle's length, his trembling fingers barely reaching the trigger.

The last thing Defner tasted was the gun oil on the suppressor.

The last words that came to him were, *My God, my God, why have you forsaken me?*

70

SPOOKY ACTION

Grayson watched Defner pull the trigger. He knew that since the gun was in his mouth, the .308 bullet would not decelerate much and would not create much of a pressure cavity. It would maintain its spin and not yaw. For these reasons, it left a clean exit wound, his head didn't explode, and it was still supersonic when it left his skull, and made a loud crack that carried across the lake. Because of the angle of the rifle, the bullet struck the water.said

Defner's body slumped forward over his rifle and fell to the ground.

After a final twitch, he lay still. Blood started oozing from the wound in the back of his head, his mouth, and his nostrils.

Much like he stepped over Dracule's leg, Grayson walked around Defner's body to the shore of the lake and looked over to his house. He took out his cell phone. *Shit. One percent battery. Helluva night to forget to charge it.*

He dialed 911.

"Nine-one-one, what's your emergency?"

"Hello, I'm in a vacant lot on Campbell Lake. Do you have me?"

"I see you're in a lot at the southeast corner of the lake, off Victor Road."

"Yes, that's it. There's been a suicide, a self-inflicted gunshot wound. The victim is Dr. Jason Defner."

"Is the patient breathing?"

"Listen to me. This is Dr. Grayson Lange. I'm a surgeon. The patient is deceased."

"Are you safe?"

"I'm quite safe."

"Help is on the way, sir. Please stay on the line until they arrive."

"I can't. My phone's about to die. I need to make one more call."

Grayson ended the call and dialed Jennifer.

"Grayson?"

"Come out on the deck."

The whispering of the screen door opening carried across the lake, and Jennifer stepped onto the deck holding her cell phone to her ear. Grayson waved to her.

She waved back. "Thank God! Grayson! What the fuck is happening? Did I hear a gunshot?"

"Everything's fine now. You're safe. But—" His phone went dead with two beeps.

Grayson pointed to his phone and made the cut-off sign across his neck. She seemed to understand.

He gave her a thumbs-up and walked back through the woods, scaled the fence, and sat on the curb. He heard sirens, then saw two patrol cars converging on his position rapidly. Standing, he reached into his back pocket, took his wallet, then raised his hands. They shut their sirens off but kept their lights flashing. An officer emerged from each car, hands near their weapons, and approached him. He raised both hands to shoulder height, ensuring they could see he wasn't armed. Grayson read the names on their ID tags: Richardson and Trinh. Trinh had three chevrons on his collar pin—a sergeant—the higher ranking of the two.

"Sergeant Trinh, I'm Doctor Grayson Lange, a surgeon at Providence. I am not armed. I'm holding my wallet with my ID in my left hand. There's a dead body with a sniper rifle next to it about fifty yards in," he said calmly. "Self-inflicted gunshot wound."

Trinh approached Grayson, making sure Officer Richardson held back with a clear shot at Grayson if needed.

"Don't move. I'm taking your wallet," said Trinh.

"Yes, sir."

As Trinh took the wallet, Grayson could hear more sirens approaching. Trinh pulled out his Providence hospital photo ID, displaying his status as a surgeon with active privileges, then the driver's license.

"Lange," Trinh said. "Hey, are you the doc that saved Detective Uttaq?"

"That's me."

Trinh smiled. "You can put your arms down, Doc." He handed Grayson back his wallet. "I'll keep the IDs for a bit. Just routine." He then shouted out, "It's cool, Jim!"

An ambulance pulled up, and two EMTs stepped out.

Grayson called out to them, "Dr. Grayson Lange, surgeon. You've got a through-and-through GSW, high-velocity round, mouth-to-posterior skull. DOA. Just need pronouncement and ME notification."

"I know you said he's dead, but with a firearm back there, we need to clear the scene before we let anyone back there." Richardson had retrieved bolt cutters from his trunk and quickly cut a man-sized gap in the fence. Trinh and Richardson went through it with their firearms drawn. "I'll whistle twice when it's clear," Trinh said.

He and Richardson went into the woods. Grayson heard two loud whistles.

When he and the EMTs got back to Defner's body, the EMTs came forward. They quickly confirmed the obvious cause of death, called it in, and departed without a patient.

"I'll take Doc back to the car until homicide gets here," Trinh told his partner.

BY THE TIME EDDIE ARRIVED, several more patrol cars had converged on the scene. He spotted Lange sitting calmly in the back of Trinh's cruiser, talking with Trinh, who was standing next to him.

Lange waved, and Eddie signaled for him to come over.

"It's my old buddy, Detective Vaugner," Lange said.

"Okay, Doc, nice talking with you," Trinh said, leaving them to it.

"It's Defner back there," Lange said to Eddie. "Looks like he was sniping my house before he killed himself."

"Defner?" Eddie asked, recalling the man's inexplicable chest pain episode after their earlier confrontation.

"Yes, Defner."

"I'll be right back. Don't leave."

Eddie ducked through the cut fence and methodically studied the scene—the high-end sniper rifle, the blood and tissue spray pattern, the body position. Everything suggested a close-range, self-inflicted wound.

When he returned, Lange was perched on the curb. He stood as Eddie approached.

"Walk me through it," Eddie prompted.

Lange described how he saw the glint across the lake, spotted Defner with his binoculars, drove over, and clambered over the fence. "Just as I got over, I heard the crack. Then I found Defner like that." He gestured toward the sniper's nest.

"So he sets up to kill you. This was obviously well planned. Then, for some reason, he shoots himself. With a sniper rifle." Eddie said, observing Lange's demeanor.

Lange shrugged. "Yeah, that doesn't make much sense, does it? But Defner seldom did."

"Why not call 911 when you saw him from across the lake? Why drive over here and risk approaching him?"

"Good question. It seemed to make sense at the time."

Eddie stared at Lange for a minute. Of course, it didn't make sense. But what could he do? Ask Lange if he quantum-entangled Defner into shooting himself? Now he had three deaths possibly associated with Lange. And the only way to implicate Lange is to invoke some spooky action mechanism. Try taking that to the D.A.

The image of Daniel looking up at Lange, beaming at him, bonding with him, interrupted his ruminations.

Besides, with Defner, Lange was defending himself, wasn't he? It was like that line from an old western, *Some folks just need dyin'.*

When the forensics van arrived, Eddie saw one of the techs, Nia, get out, dressed in a Tyvek suit. "Hey, Nia, I need a GSR test on the doc here."

He turned to Lange. "Routine procedure, Doctor, since you were near the victim. A negative test will rule you out as having fired the weapon."

"I totally get that," Lange replied. "Like the DNA."

Eddie shrugged and looked at Lange, who smiled back at him. "Just like the DNA."

Nia pulled down the van's side panel to retrieve a colorimetric field test kit for gunshot residue. She donned nitrile gloves. She went over to Lange and asked his name and date of birth, and wrote it on the card.

"Sir, hands out, please." She tore open the kit and took out a pre-dampened swab. Carefully holding the swab by the shaft, she directed Lange, "Keep your hands steady."

As she worked, Eddie noted Lange's pristine clothing—no blood spatter. But then again, perhaps Lange didn't need proximity to affect someone. Hadn't Defner claimed Lange just stood there during his chest pain episode?

She swabbed his palms and the backs of his hands, focusing on high GSR areas, rubbing firmly for ten seconds. Once finished, she pressed the tip onto the reagent zone of the test card for five seconds. Fluid from the swab spread out onto the card.

After five seconds, she inspected the card. No color change. She held it up.

"Negative, Eddie," she said. "No gunshot residue detected."

"Thanks, Nia. And make sure you bag the victim's hands. Not that I need to tell you."

Nia smiled and said, "Roger that."

"You're off the hook, Doc," Eddie said lightly.

Becca soon arrived with the medical examiner's van and attendants during the GSR collection.

"Good morning, Detective," she said.

"Morning, Doc. Look who we have here."

"I noticed. Dr. Lange. Kind of like a reunion."

"And Dr. Defner's back there."

"Anchorage really is a small town," she remarked.

One of the attendants muttered, "Have to use the portable. Can't get the gurney through this mess."

"Oh, you poor babies," Becca teased.

"I need you downtown to make a statement."

"Now? Jennifer—Dr. Dawson is waiting for me at home. I'm sure she's very anxious. My cell phone died."

"You can use mine if you want."

"Can I just give you my statement here? I mean, you know Defner and me."

Eddie looked over at Becca. She gave him a slight smile and shrugged.

"You want to do this without an attorney?"

"I'm sure the ACLU would go nuts, but I don't think one's necessary. I want to explain what happened."

Eddie considered the options for a moment. Again, like with the DNA test, Lange seemed open and willing to cooperate.

"Okay, we'll do it in my car."

Becca gave Eddie a slight nod of approval. "Okay, I guess I'd better get down there."

IN THE CAR, Eddie pulled out his phone. "I'll record this."

As a legal safeguard, Eddie formally read Lange his rights, and the interview proceeded. The doctor recounted the events just as he had previously told Eddie, filling in some of the details but sticking to his story that he heard the gunshot just as he got over the fence.

"Had Defner threatened you at all?"

"No. In fact, he was acting weirdly friendly toward me. I see why now."

Eddie stopped the recording.

"Okay, Doc. You better go see about Dr. Dawson."

"Thanks, Detective. I really appreciate this. How's Daniel doing?" Lange asked.

"Responding well to treatment."

"Excellent. Tell him his scarbro says hi, and let me know when Dr. Blake wants the port out."

"Will do, Doc."

Lange got out and went to his car. Eddie watched Lange's Audi pull away, then joined Becca in the sniper's nest, where she knelt beside Defner's body.

The CSI photographer was finishing up.

Becca looked up at Eddie and waved him over. He knelt beside her as she opened Defner's mouth with a wooden tongue depressor and illuminated it with a penlight.

"Classic contact wound on the palate. Muzzle imprint around the entry. Stellate tearing. Powder tattooing. The weapon was pressed hard against the roof of his mouth when it discharged. Look at the suppressor. There's blood at the tip, but not spatter, which starts farther down —here. Also, relatively clean exit wound, meaning the bullet didn't decelerate, fragment, or transfer much energy. This supports the tip of the barrel being in his mouth when it fired and is consistent with a self-inflicted GSW."

"But his teeth are smashed in. Like someone forced the gun into his mouth."

Shit, thought Eddie. Like Dracule's kick through the confessional door.

Two possibilities emerged: One, Defner's inner demons decided he should kill himself instead of his intended victim after meticulously planning the assassination, or two, Lange somehow compelled Defner to turn the rifle on himself. Both sounded far-fetched, but what else was new when Lange was around?

"Could he have forced it in on himself?"

"You mean as in conflicted feelings? Trying to stop an over-whelming urge? I suppose it's possible. People do all sorts of strange things before they kill themselves."

The man had been aiming to kill Lange, so even if the second possibility held true, one could argue that it was self-defense.

The murmuring and rustling of the crime scene were interrupted by the roar of a floatplane. Eddie went down to the lake's edge and recognized the plane as a DeHavilland Beaver. *God! How do these people stand living on a floatplane lake?* He followed the plane, its floats lifting lighter and lighter from the water as its engine grew louder. The aircraft lifted off just behind Lange's house.

Becca approached him and took his arm in hers.

Eddie pointed across the lake.

"That's Lange's house. And his girlfriend, a doctor who lives in Seattle."

Dawson stood on the deck, clad in sweatpants and a T-shirt. She leaned forward toward the crime scene, supporting herself on two arms. Her posture was vulnerable, as if she were looking to the woods for an answer.

Lange appeared in the doorway behind her, pausing for a moment. She turned, startled. Obviously, she hadn't heard him coming home over the noise of the Beaver, which was now fading. Eddie could almost hear her tell Lange, *Thank God you're home!* Lange stepped out onto the deck, and Dawson ran to him, throwing herself into his arms. They held each other close, their bodies melding together in relief. After their embrace, with his arm still wrapped around her waist, they turned and walked back into the house.

"You're a good man, Charlie Brown," Becca said.

"Huh?"

"The interview in the car so he could get home."

"Oh yeah."

"I'm done here. See you at dinner."

Eddie relished the fact that "see you at dinner" had become a routine statement rather than a question.

He turned back around and looked at Lange's deck.

Whatever Lange is or whatever power he might have, he's like me—a damaged man who has found peace and comfort in another human being.

Not all spooky action occurred at a distance.

71

SCARBROS

"Dad?"

The voice filtered through Eddie's layers of sleep.

"Dad?" There it was again.

Eddie opened his eyes to darkness. Becca stirred beside him, her warmth shifting under the covers. Daniel's silhouette swayed slightly in the doorway.

"What is it, Daniel? Come in."

Daniel approachedI the side of the bed. A wet cough answered first. "I'm not feeling so good," he said, his voice thin. "And my temperature is up."

Eddie was already reaching for the bedside lamp. In its sudden light, he saw what he'd feared—the flush in Daniel's cheeks, the slight sheen of sweat on his forehead, and the way he held himself as if breathing hurt.

Becca sat up, instantly alert. Eddie was thankful she had gone to bed wearing a T-shirt. Daniel coughed again, and this time, Eddie heard the congestion beneath it, the warning rattle that meant trouble for someone without a fully functional immune system to fight back.

"How high, Daniel?" asked Becca.

"Hundred and one." He coughed. "Point two."

Eddie let Becca, with her medical authority, take charge.

"Okay, Daniel, get dressed. We're going to the hospital."

"Really?"

"Yes, you could be coming down with pneumonia. First, let me see your port site."

Daniel lifted up his pajama top.

"It's looks okay," Becca said. She pushed on the skin overlying the port.

"Does that hurt?"

"No."

"Daniel, go get dressed."

After Daniel left, Eddie let out a "Fuck," and started putting on his prosthesis.

Becca picked up her cell phone and brought up Blake's number. As a medical colleague, he had given her his number.

"Ben? This is Becca Raven. Yeah. He's coughing and has a temp of 101.2. Yes, we're getting dressed now." She hung up.

"He's going to meet us in the ER."

THEY ARRIVED at the PAMC ER at 6:20 a.m. Fortunately, Providence's ER was usually not busy at that hour. There were only two people in the waiting room.

Becca walked up to the triage station and flashed her Providence Physicians ID badge.

"Hi, I'm Dr. Raven, and I'm here with Daniel Vaugner."

"Yes, Doctor, Dr. Blake called. We're going to take Daniel right back, one sec."

She picked up a phone and punched a number. "Hey, Jill, that patient of Dr. Blake's just showed up. Okay, I'll let them know." She hung up. "Have a seat; someone will be right out."

In less than a minute, a nurse greeted them with a wheelchair and whisked them back to an isolation cubicle, where they were all instructed to put on masks. An IV was quickly started.

"Dr. Blake told us not to use the port," said one of the nurses.

After the nurse taped in the IV, she said, "Sorry, Daniel, but I have to stick you two more times to draw blood cultures."

"It's okay," Daniel said.

They clipped an oxygen saturation sensor on Daniel's index finger that connected him to a pulse oximeter. In a few seconds, the SpO2% indicator read 87. That indicated significant hypoxemia—low levels of oxygen in the blood—an indication that the lungs weren't working normally. The normal number was over 95.

A respiratory therapist slipped a nasal cannula on him, plastic tubing that circled his head with two short prongs that directed oxygen into his nose. She turned the oxygen valve on the wall, and a little ball meter shot up to the five mark, indicating five liters a minute of oxygen flow. Slowly, his O2 sat climbed up to 90.

An X-ray tech came into the cubicle. "Hi," said the tech, "I'm here to get a chest X-ray. Would you mind stepping out for a sec?"

Dr. Blake arrived just as they stepped out.

"Hi, guys," Blake said.

"Hey, Ben. They're just doing his chest X-ray," Becca said.

"How is he looking?"

"Not good. Fever, cough, chest pain, shortness of breath, low sat, 88 on room air, 90 on five liters."

"Christ."

Becca knew what that meant. "Aspergillus," she said.

"Yeah," Dr. Blake said.

"Oh God," Eddie said.

The two doctors exchanged a glance. The X-ray tech pulled out the machine. "All done, guys."

"Ben, you go in and see Daniel, I'll stay with Eddie."

"Okay."

Blake went into the cubicle, and Eddie pulled Becca aside.

"How serious?"

Becca sighed. "It carries a significant mortality rate in an immuno-compromised patient like Daniel."

"C'mon Becca, how significant? Give me a number."

"Around 90 percent."

"Fuck. Daniel will know that. He probably knows it now."

A nurse came in with some mini-IV bags. "I got some goodies for Daniel when he comes back." She hung them on an IV pole and left the room.

Blake came out. "His lungs sound pretty junky. I'm starting him on an antifungal, voriconazole, cefepime for broad bacterial coverage, and vancomycin for methicillin-resistant staph," Blake said.

"Sounds like you got the bases covered," Becca said.

They stepped back into Daniel's cubicle. Blake went to the wall-mounted computer workstation, entered his credentials, and viewed Daniel's X-ray.

"Daniel, did the tech ask you if you were wearing any jewelry?"

"No. Can I see?" Daniel asked.

"Sure, you can," the doctor said, turning the monitor so he could see it. Daniel's port was visible in the right upper chest, and the shape of the radiopaque amulet could be made out in the middle of the chest.

"Oops," Daniel said.

"It's okay, I'm interested in the lungs anyway." He took out a pen and used it as a pointer. "These white, fluffy areas infiltrate the upper lobes. It has the appearance of aspergillosis."

The X-ray tech came back with the machine.

"Sorry, have to take another X-ray; there was a piece of jewelry in the field."

"It's okay," Blake said. "I can see what I need."

"But—"

"Just make a note, doctor and patient refused second X-ray."

"Fine with me." The tech shrugged and wheeled the machine away again.

Blake went over to Daniel and said, "Let me take a look at your port, Daniel."

Looking at Daniel's chest, the doctor frowned. The skin over the area of the port chamber was swollen and red, and an angry red streak tracked up toward Daniel's neck along the catheter's path. He gently pressed the slight bulge on Daniel's upper right chest where the port chamber was. Daniel winced.

"How long has the port looked like this, Daniel?"

"It was okay when I first woke up."

"I examined it two hours ago. It looked fine," Becca said.

"It's infected. It needs to come out. Now." He reached for his phone. "I'll get the surgeon on call."

"No," Daniel interrupted. "I want Dr. Lange. He told me to let him know when it was time for the port to come out."

"But—"

"Dad, can I have his card?"

Eddie retrieved Lange's card from his wallet.

"You're going to call him?" Blake asked incredulously.

"Yes. He told me to," Daniel said defiantly.

Daniel punched in Lange's phone number and put the phone on speaker.

"This is Dr. Lange."

"Dr. Lange, I mean, Grayson, this is Daniel."

"Hey Daniel, are you okay?"

"Well, not really. I'm in the ER, and my port's infected. They say it needs to come out. I was hoping you would do it."

"Who's there with you?"

"My dad, Becca—I mean Dr. Raven—Dr. Blake, and the nurse."

"Hi, Grayson, this is Nancy," the nurse said.

"Hey, Nancy. I'm on my way in. I'll need some Betadine solution, a minor procedure tray, a quarter-inch Penrose drain, saline irrigation, a bulb syringe, five-O nylon sutures, a pack of two-by-two gauze pads, and a four-by-four Tegaderm dressing."

"You got it, Grayson," Nancy said.

"Okay, Daniel, see you in fifteen."

"Thanks."

"Wow," Nancy said. "This is the first time I've ever seen a patient call in a surgeon to the ER."

An aide came carrying some IV minibags and handed them to Nancy.

"Antibiotics are here."

"Hang the voriconazole first, please," Blake said. It was an anti-fungal drug designed to hit the Aspergillus.

Blake turned to Eddie and said, "Just to sum things up, Daniel appears to have Aspergillus pneumonia. His port is infected and conta-minating the blood, so we need to get that out."

tubing"You might as well tell him, Doctor," Daniel said. "I have about a 90 percent chance of dying of this, Dad."

Though he already knew, hearing the words from Daniel hit hard. He felt Becca rub his back.

"We have good antifungals," Blake said. "And I'll get an infectious disease consult. We'll fight the hell out of this."

LANGE APPEARED MERE MINUTES LATER, dressed in scrubs. Eddie watched Lange examine the infected port site, fingers gentle but precise. Daniel winced stoically. "Definitely needs to come out. Think you can handle a few shots, Daniel?"

"I'm pretty pain-tolerant."

"Do you want us to leave?" asked Eddie.

"No, you can stay if you don't mind a little blood and pus."

Eddie sat down in a chair and held Daniel's left hand.

Lange prepped the area with Betadine. "Okay, Daniel, here comes the barbecue sauce." The iodine-colored disinfectant stained dark brown against Daniel's pale skin.

"Here come the owies."

The lidocaine injections made small white welts against the red, inflamed area of the pocket as he infiltrated around the port and along the catheter tract. Daniel squeezed his father's hand and inhaled sharply, but didn't move or complain.

"I'm using lidocaine with epinephrine. The epi constricts the blood vessels, so there's less bleeding. You okay, Daniel?"

"Yes, Grayson."

"You shouldn't feel much of this anymore, maybe just some pressure."

Eddie admired the way Lange tried to reassure Daniel and explain everything as he went along.

Lange incised a clean line along the old scar. There was minimal blood seepage from the edges of the incision, and pus oozed out through the incision.

Using scissors, he freed the chamber from the subcutaneous tissue in the pocket. Once free, he pulled on the chamber, and the tubing attached to it came out smoothly and intact.

"Port's out."

"Already?" Daniel said, with relief in his voice.

"Done, Scarbro."

Lange filled the bulb syringe with saline and flushed out the pocket several times until the solution returned clear.

"Because of the infection, I need to leave a drain," he explained. He made a small stab incision at the pocket's lowest point. He threaded the Penrose drain, a flat, light-beige rubber tube from inside the pocket out through the stab wound. The drain would act as a wick, drawing out infected fluid that might otherwise pool beneath Daniel's skin. He fixed it in place with a suture.

Daniel looked down at the drain, and said, "You cooked the penne pasta to long, Grayson."

"*Mama mia, Daniele, scusi!,*" Lange replied. But I'm-a-ready to-a-close. Usually, I'd close this with dissolving sutures under the skin, but with the infection, simple loose nylon ones. Need to keep an eye on it."

"Okay."

Three sutures went in quickly, each knot precise and symmetrically placed. "All done. You did great, Daniel." He covered the incisions with gauze and covered everything with the Tegaderm, a cover that resembled a Saran wrap.

"Make sure they change this twice a day," Lange said, as he snapped off his gloves. "Any questions?"

"No, we got it," Daniel said.

"I'll remove the sutures in ten days."

Eddie stood up and offered Lange his hand. "Thank you, Doctor."

Lange shook his hand. Once again, he found himself grateful that his murder suspect was taking such good care of his son. It wasn't just his technical proficiency—it was the caring way in which he carried it out.

He tried to fight it, but he couldn't keep this thought from bubbling up. *Kill whatever religious scumbag you want, just help my son.*

72

TWELVE

Daniel was admitted to an isolation room on the pediatric ward. Everyone entering had to wear a gown and mask and employ strict hand sanitizing precautions. The lab work confirmed what Blake had suspected: aspergillosis was growing out of Daniel's sputum, urine, and blood.

The days in the hospital blurred together for Eddie. Each morning brought the same ritual—checking Daniel's vitals, discussing lab results with Blake, and watching his son grow weaker despite their best efforts.

On Daniel's third hospital day, Lange came by and pulled out the Penrose drain. Daniel was still alert enough to joke about his penne pasta coming out. Eddie watched the easy rapport between them, feeling that familiar mix of gratitude and unease.

"Hang in there, Daniel," Lange said as he snapped off his gloves and left the room.

When his hemoglobin levels fell to critical levels, they gave him blood. Daniel drifted in and out of sleep. He lost his appetite and just took small sips of liquids. Eddie would bring in milkshakes; he still drank those. He urinated on himself a few times, so they decided to pass a catheter into his bladder and attach it to a drainage bag. The worst thing, however, was that he seemed to lose interest in his surroundings. He stopped talking about science and playing Fortnite.

Despite aggressive treatment, Daniel continued to slip away by degrees. A week into the hospitalization, the infectious disease specialist they'd consulted had tried three different antifungal combinations, but the aspergillosis continued its relentless advance. Everyone was carefully skirting around the obvious fact: Daniel was not improving with treatment. His oxygen saturation dropped despite increasing supplemental oxygen. Each chest X-ray showed more white infiltrates than the last.

Becca had been reviewing Daniel's charts each evening, her medical expertise only confirming what they could all see—the infection was winning. When Daniel's kidney function tests came back showing early signs of failure on day thirteen, she and Blake exchanged a look that Eddie instantly recognized: Daniel was running out of treatment options.

One morning, when Daniel's oxygen saturation levels dropped to 90 despite being on a non-rebreather oxygen mask, Blake said, "We need to talk. Let's go into the family conference room."

Eddie and Becca took their seats. Blake took a deep breath. "The antifungals aren't working. His white count is actually falling, not rising. The infection is overwhelming his weakened immune system. He can't keep up his oxygen levels, even with supplemental oxygen."

"Can't we put him on a ventilator?"

"I don't think we should put him on a ventilator, and I think it's time we discuss comfort care."

"What exactly does that mean?" Eddie asked. He knew what it meant, but in his shock, it didn't register—or he didn't want it to. Maybe the doctor was talking about something different for Daniel.

"We stop aggressive treatment. Take him off the antibiotics and antifungals and focus on keeping him comfortable and managing his pain and anxiety. Let him..." His professional demeanor cracked slightly. "Let him have peace."

"No." Eddie's voice was raw. "There must be something else."

"We're doing all we can."

"What about transferring him? To Seattle Children's Hospital. They might have experimental treatments—"

"Eddie." Blake's voice was gentle but firm. "There's nothing another center would offer that we aren't already doing. Sometimes there comes a time when aggressive treatment isn't prolonging life. It's prolonging death."

Eddie slumped in his chair.

"Today's his birthday."

"Oh," Blake said.

"Daniel's turning twelve today, and we're talking about making him comfortable and letting him die? It's not the kind of birthday I had in mind for him."

"I understand." He leaned forward. "Not only is he barely maintaining his oxygen saturation, his creatinine is rising, which means his kidneys are starting to fail, and his liver enzymes are going up." As he spoke, he and Becca exchanged knowing glances.

"Becca?" Eddie pleaded, hoping she would say something to change reality.

"I'm so sorry, Eddie. It's not fair." She hugged him. "But Daniel is going into multiple organ failure. When that happens, the survival rate is basically zero, no matter what measures are taken. Putting him on a ventilator, dialyzing him when his kidneys shut down—none of that will make a difference. I wish it would, but it won't. Like Blake said, it will just prolong the inevitable."

Eddie pleaded, "Please, I know you've been through this before with other parents, but I just can't—not today."

Blake leaned forward and put his hand on Eddie's knee.

"Look, Eddie. We don't have to decide anything right now. We'll keep everything going for now and revisit this issue in a few days."

Blake and Becca exchanged glances. Becca nodded in support of the decision.

"Okay, thanks, Doc," Eddie said.

Days—my son had days. Daniel's life was collapsing in on itself like a dying star. No graduations. No career. This brilliant, beautiful boy, his little budding polymath who could explain quantum mechanics,

Greek mythology, mitochondria, and play Fortnite, wasn't going to grow up. He wasn't going to make the discoveries Eddie knew lived inside that remarkable mind, never get the chance to become that quantum doctor he'd talked about. The unfairness of it—that he was going to outlive his child—crushed him. A father shouldn't outlive his son. A mind like Daniel's shouldn't be extinguished before it had the chance to shine fully.

Eddie looked up at the crucifix on the wall. *For God so loved the world that He gave His only Son? Well, fuck that. I don't want to give up my only son, my only child. You're all-powerful, and you have to put your son through a horrible death to save people? Where's the logic in that? What kind of sick psychopath would do that?*

He broke down, his anger dissolving into tears, and collapsed into Becca's arms.

Images of Daniel and his life crowded his mind—the poster of Joni Mitchell in Daniel's bedroom. *Something's gained, and something's lost in livin' every day.* Okay, but not Daniel. Take my other leg. Take me. But not him.

Through the free association of his despondency, Becca held him. Her arms steadied him while she fought back her own tears. She didn't offer platitudes or false hope. She just held him as his world came apart.

LATER THAT EVENING, Eddie and Becca sat in silent vigil in Daniel's room. *Jeopardy!* was on the TV. One category, "Let's Get Physical," was about physics.

"I'll take Let's Get Physical for $200," one of the contestants said.

"'Nothing travels faster than this.'"

A bell chimed. "Henry," said the host.

"What is the speed of light?"

Eddie wondered how many of the Physics answers Daniel would have known.

Gertie stepped into the room, carrying a small carrot cake with a thick cream cheese icing, Daniel's favorite, with twelve LED candles aglow. "Hi, guys." Father Joseph was with her. Both wore gowns and masks.

"Hello, Edward," the father said, wearing his practiced pastoral smile. He was dressed in his clerical collar.

Gertie introduced Father Joseph to Becca, then walked over to Daniel and kissed him on the forehead. "Happy Birthday, Daniel." Daniel didn't respond.

She set the cake down on Daniel's overbed table. "They won't allow candles in here, but you can actually blow these out." Gertie smoothed Daniel's hair and sighed, "Maybe tomorrow."

Eddie watched his son's eyes flutter open briefly to Gertie's touch. He managed a weak smile before closing them again. Twelve. Just twelve years old. The unfairness of it twisted in his gut like a knife.

Gertie reached for the tethered remote and turned the TV off.

"Eddie," Gertie said softly, using his first name as only a mother could, "I brought Father Joseph. Would it be alright if he..." She glanced at Daniel's still form. "If he administered the Sacrament of the Sick and the Apostolic Blessing?"

Eddie looked at his mother. The pleading and hope in her eyes were too much to resist.

He looked over at Becca. She smiled and nodded and shrugged her shoulders slightly as if to say, *Whatever you want, I'll support you.*

"That's fine, Gertie."

Gertie smiled. "Go ahead, Father."

"Thank you, Edward."

Father Joseph opened his leather case to remove the holy oils. As he began the ritual, he said, "Through this holy anointing, may the Lord, in his love and mercy, help you with the grace of the Holy Spirit..."

When Father Joseph reached the final blessing, "...grant you a full pardon and the remission of all your sins in the name of the Father, and of the Son, and of the Holy Spirit," Eddie almost spit.

Pardon? Remission of sins? The rage churned inside his chest. Daniel had just turned twelve years old. An innocent. *What sins could he possibly need pardoning for?* Eddie's teeth ground together as he forced himself to remain silent for Gertie's sake.

When the ritual was complete, Father Joseph turned to him with what he probably thought was a compassionate expression. "Edward, perhaps this is a time to consider returning to the Church? God rewards those who follow him."

It was subtle, Eddie had to admit, but any idea that his son's suffering was in any way related to his faith or lack thereof caused him to clench a fist. For a moment, he imagined the satisfying crunch of the priest's teeth and blood spewing from his mouth as he bashed his face in.

Instead, he barely whispered the words, "Father Joseph, I let you perform your ritual. Now please take your Father, your Son, and your Holy Spirit, and get the fuck out of here."

"Eddie!" Gertie gasped, her hand flying to her throat. "Father, he's not himself—"

"Of course, of course." Father Joseph raised his hands in a placating gesture. "I understand completely." He gathered his things but paused at the doorway. "Remember, Edward—I will leave, but the Father, the Son, and the Holy Spirit abide and abound all around you."

DANIEL HUNG ON. The next day, as he was sleeping, Becca and Eddie went down to the café off the main lobby. As they sat at a table, sipping their coffee, Lange came in and got in line to place an order. When he saw them, he came straight over and sat down.

"Hi, guys."

The barista called over. "Can I make you something, Doc?"

"Just a black coffee, Marci."

"You stay right there; I'm bringing it over."

The three of them sat there awkwardly while Marci poured a cup and brought it over. "On the house."

"Thanks."

"How's Daniel doing?" Lange asked.

"Blake is talking about comfort care."

"That's tough."

"Daniel turned twelve yesterday."

Lange's eyes settled into the blackness of his coffee cup. "Twelve."

For a moment, no one spoke.

A spark went off in Eddie. He looked up at Lange. "You lost Tommy when he was twelve."

"I did."

The doctor's phone went off. "Lange... Thanks, I'll be there." He pocketed his phone.

"Well, the OR awaits," he said as he stood up. "He's a great kid. I'll come by and see him later."

"Yes, he is. Thanks for everything you've done for him."

Lange seemed to stall as if searching for something to say. "It's not over till it's over," he said, and he walked away.

What a strange bit of empty optimism, thought Eddie. But was there something about his tone? *No. I'm just grasping at straws.* It was just the doctor's vacuous attempt at consolation. He'd probably said the same thing to other families as their loved ones slipped over the precipice.

73

THE ANGAKKUQ

Daniel's life continued to slip away. Eddie had taken advantage of the sick leave donated by his fellow cops. He wasn't going to leave his son. Daniel would not die alone. He was now living at Daniel's bedside, sleeping in the recliner provided for a parent, and keeping a vigil. His only breaks were bathroom breaks, a shower, and quick meals in the cafeteria. Becca took time from work to sit with him all day and make trips to the house to bring him clean clothes.

Dr. Blake made rounds daily. Eddie realized they were more like courtesy calls at this point, but at least he didn't bring up stopping the antibiotics again. If they were helping at all, they were just keeping Daniel hanging on by a string, but it was one less decision to burden a grieving father with.

EDDIE WAS DOZING in the chair beside Daniel's bed when his phone vibrated. A text from Chik: *We're at the hospital. Coming up.*

Before he could process this unexpected message, he saw Chik enter, followed by his father-in-law Inuksuk, both gowned and masked. The elderly angakkuq moved with surprising agility despite what must have been an exhausting journey from Denmark.

"Chik? Inuksuk?" Eddie rose, careful not to disturb Daniel. "What are you guys doing here?"

Becca, who had been reviewing charts in the corner, looked up in surprise.

"Inuksuk insisted we come," Chik explained quietly. "He said he felt Daniel calling to him. Is it okay?"

"Of course. My God, you've come all this way."

Inuksuk smiled and moved directly to Daniel's bedside, placing his weathered hand on the boy's forehead. He spoke in Inuktitut, his voice deep and resonant.

"He says Daniel's *tarninga*—his soul—is beginning to wander," Chik translated. "The sickness is very strong, and he wants to perform a healing ceremony."

Eddie exchanged a glance with Becca. He'd allowed Father Joseph to perform his rituals yesterday out of respect for his mother's beliefs, though the priest's words about sin had nearly pushed him over the edge. Now here was another spiritual approach, probably just as effective as the sacrament, but Inuksuk had flown halfway around the world to offer it.

Becca smiled and nodded.

The old man's face showed concern and determination. Whatever drove him to make this journey clearly mattered deeply to him.

"Yes, we would love for him to perform his ceremony," Eddie said. "Anything to help Daniel."

Inuksuk, seeming to understand before the translation, nodded gravely and began removing items from a small leather bag: a hand-held drum, several bundles of herbs, and a carved wooden bowl. He arranged them on the overbed table, then filled the small bowl with water.

First, he began a low, rhythmic chanting, his raspy voice rising and falling in patterns that seemed to pulse with the beeping of Daniel's monitors. Chik stood nearby, translating quietly for Eddie.

"He's calling to his *tuurngait*—his helping spirits," Chik explained. "He's asking them to guide him to see what's holding Daniel's illness in place."

Inuksuk lifted his small drum and began to strike it with a thin bone beater, the gentle pulsing sound filling the small room. As he drummed, his chanting intensified, and his eyes closed in deep concentration.

"Now he's seeking to find Daniel's wandering *tarninga*," Chik whispered. "In our belief, illness can happen when part of the soul becomes separated from the body." Eddie studied Chik. Despite his claims of being a Protestant, he seemed enthralled by the ritual and proud of his father-in-law.

Inuksuk's drumming suddenly stopped. His face tensed with effort as he placed his hand on Daniel's forehead. He remained this way for several minutes, utterly still, before speaking rapidly in Inuktitut.

"He says the illness has found a path through breaks in the natural order. I'm not sure what that means, though."

Eddie shifted uncomfortably, remembering Father Joseph's words about sin.

Inuksuk dipped his fingers in the bowl of water and traced symbols on Daniel's chest around the amulet. Then he placed both hands on Daniel's sternum and continued his chant, his voice dropping to barely a whisper.

The old man's breathing changed, becoming deeper and more ragged. His body swayed slightly as he worked. Beads of sweat formed on his brow despite the cool hospital room.

Suddenly, Daniel's eyes fluttered open. He looked directly at Inuksuk. Eddie thought he saw a spark of recognition in Daniel's eyes, but he had never met Inuksuk. The boy's lips moved slightly, forming what might have been a word.

Inuksuk nodded as if understanding. He reached for a small pouch, removed a pinch of dried herbs, and sprinkled them into the water bowl. The subtle scent of something earthy and ancient filled the air. He dipped his fingers again and touched them to Daniel's lips, then to the amulet.

The ceremony continued for nearly an hour. Inuksuk alternated between drumming, chanting, and periods of deep, trance-like silence, where he seemed to be communing with unseen presences. Finally, he placed both hands on Daniel's chest and spoke a final, forceful incantation.

When he finished, the old man sat back, visibly exhausted. He turned to Eddie and spoke directly to him.

"He says he has called Daniel's spirit to return, but the sickness is very strong," Chik translated. "He cannot be certain if it will get back. He hopes *tuurngait* will help him."

Eddie nodded his thanks, remaining skeptical but moved by the old man's evident care and exhaustion.

Inuksuk said something to Chik, and Chik nodded. "He's exhausted; we're going to the hotel now. And we're flying back tomorrow. We'd stay longer, but Christina is having surgery in three days."

That they made the flight with this urgency and turnaround time just underscored the limited time Daniel had left.

"Is it serious?"

"Getting her uterus out. Fibroids, or something, so not too serious, I guess."

Eddie hugged Chik, then Inuksuk. "Thanks for this, Inuksuk."

Inuksuk smiled and patted Eddie on the back. "Much welcome," he said.

After they left, Becca said, "That was beautiful. The ritual, and that they made the journey."

"Yes, it was," Eddie replied.

He looked over at Daniel, trying to tell if he noticed a difference. He couldn't tell if it was his imagination, but he thought Daniel looked at peace.

LATER THAT EVENING, Eddie, sleep-starved, sat in the recliner beside the bed, watching his son's chest rise and fall in its irregular rhythm. No, not much had changed. Daniel's phone, resting on its charger, displayed 3:00 a.m. The room was quiet except for Daniel's raspy, labored breathing. He could hear muffled conversations from the nurses' station, punctuated by occasional laughter. It made him feel small and helpless. His only child was dying, and out there it was just another night shift. He looked at Daniel's oxygen saturation monitor. The numbers told the story: still 86. Daniel was still on the slippery slope.

74

THE TUURNGAIT

Another two days had passed. Daniel's phone read 11:38 p.m. Eddie fought against sleep. Despite Becca's urging him to rest, he resisted. He didn't want to be unconscious when Daniel passed away. But exhaustion, like a physical weight, pressed him down onto the sofa. His eyelids grew heavier with each blink. *So tired.* Eddie reached for a cushion and put it behind his head. He would just rest his eyes for a moment.

In that addled space between sleeping and waking, a soft shimmering blue and violet light lasting less than a second seemed to pierce his eyelids, reminding Eddie of the Northern Lights display.

Eddie opened his eyes and saw a figure standing at Daniel's bedside. In the dim room, lit only by monitor lights, he couldn't make out who it was at first. The figure stood there motionless at the bedside. Everything was hazy and disjointed. The form was familiar.

"Dr. Lange?"

Eddie saw the time on Daniel's phone: 2:02 a.m. Had he been asleep for hours? It seemed like he had only closed his eyes for a minute.

Lange, gowned and masked, was leaning over the bedrails, looking at Daniel. He turned around to face Eddie.

"I just came by to see Tommy. I have a flight at four this morning. I'll be out of the country for several weeks."

"Tommy?" Eddie's tired mind caught the slip.

"Did I say Tommy? I meant Daniel. I see his O2 sat is 84."

Tommy. Lange's brother. Eddie understood the slip. This had to stir feelings in the doctor.

"Yes, it's been dropping. It won't be long now."

Lange nodded but offered no comforting reply. *What was there to say?* Eddie thought.

"Where are you going?" Eddie asked.

"Down to Siula Grande to do some rock climbing."

"Siula Grande? What's that?"

"A mountain. In Peru."

"Is it dangerous?"

"It can be, but I prepare myself and go with a good team."

Eddie considered the irony. Here was his son, lying in bed with his life slipping away, and here was a man off to risk his life to prove—what? Why did he risk his life when, in this room, he could see how precious it was?

"You ever ask yourself why you do these high-risk adventures?"

"Yes, I do, many times."

"And what's your answer?"

Lange smiled. "Because it's there."

"I could have sworn there was this glow—in my eyes."

"Stress, exhaustion, and anxiety can bring on vivid dreams."

"Yes, I guess so."

"Trust me, Detective, you're holding up well." Lange looked at his watch. "I better get going."

Lange leaned over the side rails and gently tapped Daniel on his chest.

"Hey, scarbro, I'm taking off now. Hang in there until I get back, alright?"

He stood quietly for a moment, watching Daniel's labored breathing. Then he reached out and briefly touched the boy's forehead—a gesture so gentle it seemed almost paternal. Without another word or a look at Eddie, he slipped out of the room.

A few minutes later, a nurse entered the room, clipboard in hand. She was young, with dark hair pulled back in a tight ponytail.

"I'm sorry to disturb you, Mr. Vaugner. I just need to check his vitals."

Eddie nodded and watched as she moved efficiently around Daniel's bed, gentle but professional. The monitor beeped softly as she recorded the numbers. Her face revealed nothing, but Eddie had become adept at reading the subtle signs—the slight tightening around her eyes, the careful neutrality of her expression.

"Have you gotten any sleep?" she asked, adjusting Daniel's IV.

"Yeah," Eddie said. "I just conked out for a couple of hours."

"I can see why. Hmm, his temperature is up a bit, 100. We'll keep an eye on that."

The nurse left. Eddie took out his phone and googled Siula Grande. He didn't spell it correctly, but the search engine figured it out. It was an imposing-looking mountain. He came across an article entitled "The Terrifying East Face of the Siula Grande Sees First Ascent." And that was in 2022.

Because it's there. He had heard the phrase before but couldn't place it. He looked over at his son and smiled. Daniel would know. Another search. Ah—George Mallory, the British mountaineer—when he was asked why he wanted to summit Mount Everest. Of course Lange would say that.

As he watched his son sleeping, he noticed a hint of a smile on Daniel's face that hadn't been there before. It seemed so at odds with his declining numbers, the declining minutes left in his life.

Eddie leaned over the bed rails and kissed his son on the forehead, then went back to his recliner.

Looking at that smile, a thought struck Eddie. What was death to a boy who understood quantum entanglement? Who saw particles existing in multiple states simultaneously? Maybe Daniel didn't see this as an ending at all but as a transition to another quantum state.

Like those electrons he'd talked about—everywhere and nowhere at once, dancing their probability dance across dimensions.

He remembered Daniel explaining it at the kitchen table not so long ago: "When you measure them, they have to pick a spot. But before that, they're in all places at once." Perhaps that was how Daniel saw death—not as an ending, but as expanding into all possible states at once. Not ceasing to exist but becoming infinite.

The thought brought fresh tears to Eddie's eyes. Did that peaceful smile mean that even now, in his semiconscious state, his son's mind was thinking in ways he could barely grasp? While Eddie was trapped in the linear world of cause and effect, life and death, Daniel might be seeing quantum possibilities—states of existence beyond conventional understanding. *Snap out of it, Vaugner.* Here he was, doing precisely what humans had done since the beginning of consciousness—trying to pretty up death with comforting fairy tales.

Valhalla, Olympus, heaven, quantum states—just different stories people told themselves to avoid facing the truth. Death wasn't a transition to another form of existence. It was simply the end. Nothingness. His son wasn't going to become some quantum-entangled entity living in multiple dimensions. He was going to stop existing, just like Anne.

All these theories—religious, spiritual, and now even scientific— were just humanity's desperate attempt to deny the finality of death. He was a homicide detective. He knew what death was. He had seen it enough times. Bodies didn't transcend to higher planes of existence. They just stopped. The body died and decomposed, its rotting brain oblivious that it had ever had a thought or had a dream. Everything that made them who they were—consciousness, personality, that brilliant, beautiful mind of Daniel's—would switch off like a light, unaware that it ever lived and died.

Daniel started breathing heavily, and each inspiration sounded like a high-pitched gasp. *Oh God, what now?* Eddie stumbled to his feet and touched Daniel's forehead. Burning up—far hotter than he was before.

The boy's body went rigid and then began to convulse. His limbs thrashed against the bed rails, the seizure twisting his body into impossible angles.

"Help me in here!" Eddie's shout brought the night staff running. "He's having a seizure and burning up!"

"Febrile seizure," someone called out. Eddie had enough experience as a patient, parent, and homicide detective to know that hospitals had standing protocols for various emergencies so nurses could employ without having to wait to get a doctor's order. Despite the DNR order, they moved with urgent efficiency. They weren't trying to save his life—just making him comfortable.

Various members of the staff shouted.

"Lorazepam, 2 mg IV push."

"Get a cooling blanket."

"Temp's 104.8."

"Where's that Tylenol suppository?"

For several minutes, the crew scrambled. They rolled him over and inserted a Tylenol suppository. They got the cooling blanket on him.

The medications began to take hold.

To Eddie, the seizure seemed to go on forever, though it lasted only minutes. Daniel's body relaxed, his breathing evened out, still raspy.

One by one, the crew that had treated Daniel left the room, leaving him alone with his son. He was sleeping peacefully now. He looked up at the oxygen saturation monitor—84. Daniel had lost even more lung capacity. Throughout all of this, Daniel kept his smile. Had he accepted his fate? Eddie wished he could know what Daniel was thinking. Seeing. Feeling. Hopefully, the smile meant he wasn't suffering.

75

89 AND HOLDING

Pressure on his forehead pulled Eddie from a deep sleep. He opened his eyes to find Becca standing over him, her hand cool against his skin. Morning light filtered through the hospital blinds.

"Hey," she said softly. "How was the night?"

"Rough. Daniel had a febrile seizure." He told her about the crisis and the nurses' quick response. "Lange stopped by too, late last night, just before the seizures started."

"Thoughtful of him."

Becca glanced at Daniel, who was sleeping peacefully now. Her clinical eye went automatically to the monitors.

"Interesting—his O2 sat is up to 89. We haven't seen that in a while."

"Any idea what's going on?" In his exhaustion, he'd almost forgotten the numbers had been hovering at 84.

"No, but pulse oximeters have a margin of error of around 2 to 3 percentage points, so it seems it's above the margin of error."

Becca and Eddie sat in silence, their gazes alternating between Daniel and the monitor, the quiet punctuated only by the occasional beep of medical equipment. "He looks peaceful," Eddie said.

Becca squeezed his hand.

"I need to head to the office. We have a departmental meeting. I could stop at Moose's Tooth on the way back for dinner."

"A Neapolitan sounds really good right now."

She pulled down her mask briefly to kiss him on the part of his cheek not covered by his mask. "See you around five, unless I can get out earlier."

Eddie settled back on the sofa, his eyes drawn repeatedly to the oxygen monitor as if the numbers might vanish if he looked away too long. But hour after hour, it held steady at 89.

Dr. Blake came by on his hospital rounds, aware of the febrile seizure.

"We'll monitor his temperature closely. It's unusual for a patient in, uh, Daniel's condition to have a febrile seizure."

"Leave it to Daniel to go the unusual route," Eddie said.

The doctor moved over to the bed. "Hi, Daniel, how are you feeling today?" His voice carried that loud, clinical cheerfulness doctors use with sick patients.

Daniel moaned slightly but didn't respond.

He looked over at Eddie quizzically. "I wonder if he heard me?"

Blake used the stethescope kept at the bedside to listen to Daniel's chest. "Lungs sound about the same." He checked the urine bag hanging from the bed—urine was still dripping into the collection bag. "Kidneys still working." He checked Daniel's fingernails—they still had a bluish tInge.

"Seems to be holding his own. You have to hand it to him," the doctor said, making notes in the chart, "he's putting up a hell of a fight."

"His sats are up a bit," Eddie offered, gesturing toward the monitor's steady 89.

Blake nodded, but his expression remained guarded. "These numbers can fluctuate," he said, reinforcing Becca's earlier observation.

In other words, thought Eddie, *it doesn't change the overall picture.*

The rest of the day passed quietly. Becca came over with the pizza. It was half-and-half: one side was a Neapolitan for Eddie, and the other side was Thai Chicken for Becca.

Daniel slept through the day. Throughout it all, the oxygen saturation held steady at 89.

76

THE BLUE LIGHT

Four days after the seizure, Daniel's condition surprisingly seemed to hang in limbo, a pause in his decline. His temperature wavered up and down; occasional muscle jerks alarmed Eddie and worried him about his son going through another seizure. But his oxygen saturation remained stable, and he kept making urine. So, if multiple organ failure was going to take Daniel, it was taking its time.

On the fifth day, Eddie woke to find Daniel's oxygen saturation reading 91. That couldn't be right. He took the finger sensor from Daniel's index finger and put it on his. After a moment, the O2 sat monitor read 98. He put it back on Daniel's finger: 89... 90... 91. He looked at his watch; Dr. Blake would be doing rounds soon.

Eddie kept his eye on the sat monitor, which held at 91. Daniel appeared to be resting comfortably, with that curious smile still on his face.

Eddie hadn't showered in two days. Daniel seemed stable, so he decided to clean up before Dr. Blake came around. He grabbed a fresh stump stocking and sweats Becca had brought in and headed to the shower.

. . .

EDDIE SAT on the hinged seat in the shower stall. The warm water ran over Eddie's shoulders, and a thought stabbed through him—Daniel would never feel simple pleasures like these again. He would never experience the love of a woman.

The realization triggered something more profound: he was sick of death. He was sick of its constant presence in his life. The crime scenes, the victims, the perpetrators, the grieving families, Anne. Yes, like most professionals, he had built up a wall. Becca too. He and Becca could compartmentalize. But now this—watching his son slip away—death once again had broken into his personal life—you don't compartmentalize that.

It might be time for a change. Twenty years in with the department. His pension was secure. He had savings. Law school had always been in the back of his mind. Other people in their thirties and forties started new careers. He had a 3.9 college GPA. He had scored 168 on his LSAT, which put him in the top 2 percent of all takers. With his work experience, he might not have to retake it. He had enough saved to make it work. An ex-homicide detective becoming a defense attorney. Law firms might eat that up. He could make some real bucks. The Dracule case crossed his mind, and he had a brief fantasy of defending Lange, not that a DA would ever have the evidence to take it to trial.

But there was no law school in Alaska. It would mean leaving Anchorage and leaving Rebecca. Unless she would come with him? Had they reached the point where he could ask her to uproot her life and quit her job? Not when she was in line to become Chief Medical Examiner. Could their relationship survive the commute? He briefly thought of Lange and his girlfriend, the doctor who lived in Seattle. They made it work.

Why the fuck are you thinking about your future when your son is in his room, dying?

Walking back, he saw hospital staff clustered around Daniel's door. Some were commenting to a colleague; others were shaking their heads. A few turned toward Eddie with curious looks on their faces. Why was that one guy smiling?

A nurse emerged with a puzzled look on her face, hanging her stethoscope around her neck.

"Has anyone called Dr. Blake?"

Someone answered, "Yes, he's on his way."

Grief gripped Eddie's chest as his world collapsed. *Daniel died while I was taking a shower, thinking about my future.* He pushed through the group to get into the room. To get to his son.

In the room, he stopped, stunned. "Daniel?"

Daniel was sitting upright in bed, looking weak but sitting up. His head swiveled around, looking at his surroundings as if he were trying to figure out where he was. The oxygen monitor read 94 percent. Daniel's eyes found his.

"Hi, Dad," he said listlessly.

Eddie ran over to Daniel and cradled his face in his hands. He touched his son's shoulders, his chest, as if trying to assure himself that this was not an apparition.

"Daniel?"

Daniel smiled weakly. "Wow, I was kind of out of it for a while, huh?"

"Daniel. Daniel!" He drew the boy in toward him.

"Yeow. You're yanking my Foley."

Eddie let him go.

Dr. Blake arrived and was stunned to see Daniel sitting up in bed, smiling. After asking Daniel a few questions about how he felt, his face grew more incredulous as he listened to the lungs with the stethoscope. "Much clearer." He checked Daniel's fingernails. "Pink."

"What the hell is going on?" Eddie's voice shook.

Blake ignored him and addressed a nurse. "Sally, I need a CBC, metabolic panel, and a STAT portable chest X-ray."

"On it," she replied.

Why was he ordering labs? Daniel was DNR.

"What is going on with Daniel?" Eddie asked again.

"Can we step outside?"

Eddie looked back and forth between Dr. Blake and Daniel, reluctant to leave his son's side.

"Just for a second, Eddie."

Out in the hallway, Dr. Blake said, "I don't know what's going on. Something profound has happened to his immune system."

"What could it be?"

"Don't get your hopes up; I think we may be, and I repeat, may be, looking at a spontaneous remission."

"A spontaneous remission? Does that even happen?"

"Yes. It's rare, but yes, it does happen. It's like winning the pediatric oncologic lottery—you know it happens, but you never expect it to happen to one of your patients. This goes as far back as the 1890s when William Coley observed remissions in cancer after severe infections, but—I'm sorry, Eddie, I'm getting carried away here."

"How can you tell?"

"We'll see what the blood tests show. But really, we won't really know for a while—we would need sustained improvements—several bone marrows and so on. But I don't know what else this could be. I have patients waiting in my office, but I'll be back at lunch."

"Okay, thank you, Dr. Blake."

The doctor nodded, and then, as if he remembered something, he smiled and looked up at Eddie, taking each of Eddie's hands into his.

"No, Eddie, maybe it's me who should be thanking you. You kept me from stopping the antibiotics. Those few extra days—you might have saved Daniel's life. In my business, a parent's hope doesn't pay off very often, but in this case—well, let's see what the lab work shows before we start thinking miracles."

Blake took a few steps, turned and smiled, shaking his head. "This is the first time I've ever had to rescind a DNR order. "

Eddie smiled as he watched Dr. Blake triumphantly swagger down the hall, his white lab coat swinging back and forth with each step. He reached up to wipe away the tears on his cheeks that had not yet dried.

"Dad?"

"Coming." He went back into the room.

"Can I tell you about my dream? I feel like I have to say it out loud, or I'll forget it. And I want to remember it."

"Of course you can."

"I was lying here. I felt as if I was leaving. Not dying so much. Just leaving. Still, I was sad. I saw you sitting in your chair, trying to stay awake.

Then, all of a sudden, this blue light—well, I can't say that I saw it exactly, so maybe I can't say it was light. It was like a blue light, but I felt it more than I saw it. But kinda like both? Like in physics, how light acts as waves or particles. And there was this hum. Could it be a blue hum? Weird, I know, but that's what it was like."

Daniel gestured a whirling motion with his hands.

"The blue started spinning around me, like a vortex, but not scary. I was being pulled into it, but gently. In the center, there was a presence. For a moment, I thought it might be Mom, but it wasn't exactly her—more like a feeling of her. I wanted to say hi, but I couldn't speak."

He touched his chest and looked at his father quizzically.

"Was Dr. Lange here last night?"

"Yes," Eddie said, "he came by to see you. He was on his way to a trip."

"Then, it *was* Grayson standing next to me. He was kind of smiling at me, but at the same time, he looked like he was trying to figure something out. I wanted to ask him what was going on, but I still couldn't speak. But I saw Grayson as this force for good. I can't explain it. Not like a superhero, but somehow, like it was important for him to bring good into the world, like why he became a surgeon. That's when I decided I wanted to bring some good into the world by becoming a physicist and doctor. Grayson's smile changed, like my career choice made him happy, or like when you finally figure out a problem.

"Then I realized the hum, the blue hum, was somehow mixed up with the cosmic background microwave radiation. I remember I was reading about how physicists are studying connections between cosmic background radiation and entanglement.

"When he smiled, I felt this energy inside me. It seemed to start in my hip bones, then my arms and legs. Deep inside. Like in my bone marrow. This feeling stayed with me for a while; I can't say how long, really; it was hard for me to sense time. Then I felt really hot. I could feel myself shaking. It didn't hurt, but it felt like some energy, like that blue light spreading through me. I was feeling the blue now and seeing it."

Daniel closed his eyes and shivered slightly.

"The presence—whether it was Mom or something else—seemed to push me away from her. At first, I thought I was going to heaven, but as I felt myself flowing, I realized I was heading toward myself, and then I knew I wasn't going to die and that I was in what felt like a stream of life taking me back home. To you. It was kind of a tickling sensation, or maybe like being in a hot tub, but without being wet. And the humming got louder. Then there was this big flash of the blue turning into white light, almost like in the videos of nuclear explosions. Very bright, but at the same time, it didn't bother my eyes. Then everything went blank, and the next thing I knew, I woke up."

Daniel blinked a few times and smiled at Eddie.

"That was about it."

"That's quite a dream."

"You know, it seemed more than a dream. Like I was in some quantum state. What was Grayson doing when he was in the room?"

"Nothing. Just standing next to you."

"Weird, because I feel like Grayson had something to do with it. But the more I remember..." Daniel paused and touched his amulet. "There was this shaman, and he was calling back from somewhere, and then the blue light. And a drum. It's kinda mixed up."

"Yes, Inuksuk and Chik came by to see you." He'd tell Daniel about the shamanic ritual later; he didn't want to overwhelm him right now.

Eddie thought of Dana Peplow's near-death experience—another one associated with Lange. And then he remembered what Lange said about patients going through near-death experiences experiencing random visual and auditory events relevant to their own lives and to the lives of others close to them.

The detective in him couldn't help picking apart Daniel's story—the cosmic background radiation, the physics references. Of course, that was how Daniel would frame it. If he'd been into computer programming instead of physics, he probably would have seen streams of binary code reprogramming his body, or if he'd been religious, like Gertie, maybe Jesus would have appeared instead of the light.

He remembered what Blake had told him about spontaneous remissions—maybe Daniel had just won the leukemia lottery and nothing more.

But there was Lange. In the middle of it all. Three deaths. And two saved lives. The only one that really made sense was Dana Peplow. Eddie could understand a clamp across torn blood vessels and cardiac massage. But the rest?

Especially the deaths. A memory floated up—Daniel and Gertie gleefully shooting zombies on their game console, his own teasing voice decrying the vigilantism. The irony struck him now, sitting here with his prosthetic leg, remembering his own desperate choice to let them take his leg to save his life. So was Lange a cosmic vigilante? A surgeon wielding a moral knife, amputating gangrenous bits of evil to make the world a better place? Maybe Daniel was the next step. Instead of just removing evil from the universe, he was preserving good—adding something.

"Yeah, Daniel, you never know."

Holding his son's hand, he was at once the skeptical homicide detective and the joyous father who had just been granted a miracle. He was happy to let the two coexist within him and simply accept the gift he had been given.

A lab tech entered. "Excuse me. I'm here to draw some blood from Daniel. Is that okay, or should I come back later?"

"No, go ahead. And check his miracle level while you're at it."

The tech smiled. "I know, right?"

Eddie stood up from the bed. Half-formed thoughts continued to race through his mind. Miracle, dream, hallucination, spooky quantum action, fluke. Lange. Don't get your hopes up.

Oh my God, I have to call Becca. He tapped his phone, stood up, and walked out of the room as the lab tech tied a tourniquet around Daniel's arm.

"Hello, Becca?" he said breathlessly. "Hey, oh my fucking god! It's Daniel!"

EPILOGUE

Standing in the kitchen, Eddie poured four glasses of lemonade to bring back out to the porch. Neither he nor Becca had touched alcohol since the big news. It was Saturday, and like on most Saturdays now, he had the day off. He had moved up the ranks to deputy chief of operations, so work was nine to five, Monday through Friday, except during those occasional shit-hitting-the-fan periods. He was next in line for chief of police. Becca had harped on him to finish his Master of Public Administration degree, and it had paid off.

His wife, too, had risen. She was now the chief medical examiner for Alaska, the youngest ever to hold the position. They were a real Alaska law enforcement power couple.

Through the open window, he could see the top of Becca's red hair glisten as she relaxed on a chaise lounge. Gertie was in the yard, cutting flowers to put in vases in the house. Daniel followed his grandmother, carrying a basket for her to drop them in, the fear of Aspergillus in the remote past. The amulet Chik had given him dangled from his neck. He and his stepmother, whom he still called Becca, had been chatting away about his going off to the MIT Research Institute summer program for high school students about to enter their senior year. Daniel was one of eight selected out of an applicant pool of over two thousand. And though Daniel was entering his senior year in high school, he took his math and physics at the University of Alaska.

Sixteen years old, three and a half years since his recovery, and no evidence of recurrent disease. His last bone marrow biopsy a year ago had shown normal blast cells and not a Philadelphia chromosome in sight.

Yesterday, at his six-month checkup, Dr. Blake had joked, "Daniel, now that you're taller than I am, I'm going to have to fire you as a patient." But he would never fire the patient who gave him membership to a very exclusive club: pediatric oncologists following a spontaneous remission. In fact, he had decided he would keep Daniel as a patient until he turned twenty-one, three years beyond the usual age of eighteen for his patients in remission. The two were Anchorage celebrities for a while, making appearances on local news programs and talk shows. In all their appearances, the name of Grayson Lange never came up.

Eddie stepped onto the deck carrying the lemonade. "Here's the lemonade you ordered, ma'am."

"Why, thank you." She took the lemonade and sipped it. "Mmm, perfect. Not too sweet, nice and lemony."

"Good. I was going for the lemony taste in the lemonade," Eddie said.

Becca laughed. "Oh stop, you know what I mean."

She rested the glass on her belly, curved outward by her eight months of pregnancy. So far, the amnios and the ultrasounds all indicated a healthy baby boy was on the way.

Becca called out to Daniel. "Okay, Daniel, Dad's back."

"We have enough flowers, I think," Gertie said. "If you could put them on the kitchen counter."

"Sure, Grandma."

Daniel ran into the kitchen, put the flowers down, then ran back out on the deck and sat at the foot of Becca's lounge chair. Gertie pulled up a chair.

"Okay, Daniel," Becca said, "have you decided yet? Oh! He just kicked. He wants to know, too."

"Wants to know what?" Daniel asked in a teasing way.

Eddie imitated a game show host: "Okay, Daniel, are you ready to play Name! That! Baby!"

Becca wanted Daniel to feel close to his new brother, so she'd given him the "job" of naming the baby. When she told Eddie of her intention, he wasn't surprised. He remembered their first meeting when she slid the laptop in front of Daniel and gave him the job of advancing the slides.

"Yes, Ed," Daniel said, playing along. "The name I have chosen for my little brother is"—he paused for effect—"Grayson. Edward. Vaugner." He beamed proudly at his choice, with a quiver of uncertainty about how it might be received.

Eddie smiled and squeezed Becca's hand. "Grayson Vaugner," he said softly. "I love it."

"It's beautiful," Becca said.

Daniel raised both arms with fists clenched. "Yes!"

Gertie repeated the name. "Grayson Edward Vaugner. Gray means rebirth. In the church, it represents the resurrection."

"And don't forget gray as in ashes, as in rising out of the ashes," Daniel added, "like the phoenix from the Greeks."

"Grayson it is," Becca said joyously. "Everybody, say hi to Grayson!"

They all took the cue. "Hi to Grayson!" they called out in chorus and laughed.

Eddie smiled at Daniel and thought about the other Grayson. A man who had survived being put through a hell no child should endure. Worse than Daniel, maybe. Lange had turned his name, borne in scandal and perversion, into a symbol of hope, resilience, and justice.

I am proud to have a son named Grayson.

Dr. Blake talked about the inciting fever, heat shock proteins triggering cell death, natural killer cell activation, and random genetic mutations that could lead to a spontaneous remission.

Gertie, of course, knew Jesus had intervened, that Father Joseph's sacrament, and that all her novenas to St. Peregrine had paid off.

There was also the amulet and shamanic ritual performed by Inuksuk. Daniel still treasured it and never took it off.

And there was Daniel's blue light dream.

Eddie knew, in his agnostic heart, whether it was through biology, through God, through spooky action, or through a random molecular fluke, that the survivor with the scarred face and dreadful past, who, against all odds, had become a surgeon, had somehow saved Daniel.

But why had he waited till the last minute to pull Daniel from the precipice? Why not earlier, when he was putting in his Mediport, for instance? A possible explanation struck him. Daniel had been eleven when the Mediport went in and turned twelve in the hospital during his relapse, the same age as Tommy, when John Gower killed him. Did Daniel have to be the same age as Tommy? Was this some sort of quantum symmetry?

So many questions. They'd probably never be answered.

But Eddie knew this: the Universe has its own mysterious balance sheet, no matter who or what is doing the accounting. He could live with that.

The wind pushed the scent of Gertie's flowers across the yard.

Eddie's messenger app on his phone chimed. He picked it up. The ID identified it as "Chik." What time was it in Copenhagen? Just past six in the morning. He tapped his phone.

Eddie chuckled. He swiped the screen and smiled. "It's from Chik."

"What is it, Eddie?" Becca asked.

He held up the phone for her and Daniel to see. In the first photo, Chik and Inuksuk were sitting in a golf cart, beaming. There was only one set of clubs in the back, the Honmas, so Eddie assumed Inuksuk was riding along.

He swiped the phone and smiled. "I'll be damned."

He held the phone up. It was a picture of Chik's scorecard. It had yesterday's date written on it. The number 89 was circled with exclamation points next to it.

"Can you believe it? He broke ninety."

Becca smiled.

"From the men's tees, he says. Way to go, Chik." Eddie laughed—and texted back: "Wow. 89? Did Inuksuk work some shaman magic on your putting?" The moment he hit send, Chik's score struck him. 89. The first sign of remission was Daniel's oxygen saturation climbing out of the death zone to 89 after Lange's visit.

"Hi, Daniel."

A tall, thin Eurasian girl with long, straight black hair had come to the backyard. She was Daniel's classmate who had recently moved up with her family from the Midwest. This was her first summer in Alaska. She wore black leggings, Doc Martens, and a sweatshirt, with a Fortnite backpack slung over her shoulder.

"Hi, Maya," Daniel said.

"Hi, everyone." She set her backpack down. "I was just on my way back home from math club, and I thought I'd drop by."

"You just missed it," Daniel said. "We named the baby. Grayson Edward Vaugner."

"Nice name. Is that—no, wait, I'm thinking of Greystoke, the guy who became Tarzan. Where'd you get the name from?"

"A surgeon who took care of me when my leukemia relapsed. He might have even saved my life."

"Cool. I guess he'll feel honored."

Daniel exchanged a quick glance with his father, who shook his head slightly.

"Yeah," he said.

Maya and Daniel sat on the steps on the deck.

Squinting in the low sunlight, Maya said, "You know, the sunlight is nice, but sometimes I miss summer nights, sitting outside as the sun goes down and the stars. And I miss the crickets."

"You know what it's called when they rub their legs together to make the chirping sound?" Daniel asked.

"Of course," Maya replied. "Stridulation."

"You're right."

"Did you know if you count the number of chirps in thirteen seconds and add thirty-seven, you get the temperature in Fahrenheit?"

"Really? I want to check that out sometime. Next time I'm outside."

Eddie leaned over and whispered, "I think Daniel has met his nerd match."

"I think you mean found," Becca said.

He smiled. "I think you're right."

"Grayson just kicked again!" she exclaimed.

Daniel turned around and teased, "Are we going to hear that every time he kicks?"

Becca laughed. "Yeah, you just might!"

Everyone laughed. As the sound floated up, Eddie leaned back in his chaise, reached over, and took Becca's hand, gently rubbing the engagement ring and wedding band.

He would be happy living without all the answers to his questions.

A small mew gull lit on the backyard fence. It let out a high-pitched *kee-yah! key-yah!* then flew off. Eddie remembered that in shamanism, birds represented spring and the return of the sun. He thought of Inuksuk's words when he first met Lange: "He has a gift not found in many healers."

Maybe I let Lange slide. Was Daniel payback?

Although early June air in Alaska was cool, the low sun felt good on his face.

Maybe Daniel was another mountain.

He remembered Daniel saying once, "You know, Dad, the sun's rays aren't actually hot. Things only heat up when they absorb photons from the Sun and then emit the energy as infrared radiation."

He closed his eyes and basked in its warmth. And in the miracle of his family.

ACKNOWLEDGMENTS

Thanks to:

My Beta Readers: Kathy, Mardy, Jim, and Alexi

Proofreader: Kathy

Editor: Dylan Garity

And to Cheryl, who always believed in me

www.ingramcontent.com/pod-product-compliance
Lightning Source LLC
Chambersburg PA
CBHW020003120726
47903CB00004B/1121